The LADY DAUNTLESS

ELIZABETH COLE

ALSO BY ELIZABETH COLE

Honor & Roses

Choose the Sky

A Heartless Design

A Reckless Soul

A Shameless Angel

The Lady Dauntless

Beneath Sleepless Stars

A Mad and Mindless Night

Regency Rhapsody:
The Complete Collection

Love on the Run

The LADY DAUNTLESS

ELIZABETH COLE

SKYSPARK BOOKS

PHILADELPHIA, PENNSYLVANIA

SkySpark Books
Philadelphia, Pennsylvania
skysparkbooks.com
inquiry@skysparkbooks.com

Publisher's Note: This is a work of fiction. Names, characters,
places, and incidents are a product of the author's imagination.
Locales and public names are sometimes used for atmospheric
purposes. Any resemblance to actual people, living or dead, or to
businesses, companies, events, institutions, or locales is completely coincidental.

Ordering Information:
Quantity sales. Special discounts are available on quantity purchases by corporations, associations, and others. For details,
contact the "Special Sales Department" at the address above.

THE LADY DAUNTLESS / Cole, Elizabeth. – 1st ed.
ISBN-10: 1-942-31605-4
ISBN-13: 978-1-942316-05-3

Chapter 1

Scotland, Autumn 1807

TWILIGHT. IN THE GLOAMING, THE smell of the sea filled the air, though the water was hidden by hills surrounding the narrow glen. A shape burst forth from a dark grove of trees on the near side of the valley. A woman sat astride a tall roan, riding at a breakneck pace, like she was being chased by the devil himself. The woman's face was flushed with exertion, but she didn't have the look of the hunted about her. Amber hair streamed behind her like ribbons of fire, defying the falling darkness. Her creamy skin was highlighted by rosy cheeks, and a wide smile graced her face.

Gemma laughed in delight, catching her breath after the wild ride, her locks streaming down her shoulders in complete disarray. Hector was panting yet still in fine form. The tall roan was far smarter than the average horse —at least she thought so—and he often matched her mood without any need for her to give commands.

She'd been restless all day, pacing her room, wondering what had put this mood on her. With her uncle away as usual, she was almost alone in the great ruin known as Caithny castle. As a young girl, she had pretended she was a princess, lost in an enchantment, only waiting for a handsome prince to ride up and free her. As she grew older, however, she learned a bit more of the world, and that dream faded. She was now twenty years old, without a suitor or an expectation of one, and only Uncle Conall and Aunt Maura to call family.

Desperate to escape the walls of her home, Gemma had saddled up Hector and ridden into the forest. She'd left shortly after lunch, and only as nighttime approached did she turn back to the house. She didn't want to return. The crisp fall air and the dying light seemed to whisper a thousand possibilities to her. She could ride out into the night and never come back. She could ride to the seashore and hail a passing ship to take her all the way into the sunset. She might even meet her prince!

Gemma shoved such thoughts aside as she gathered her strength for a last canter through the valley before she reached the gates of Caithny. Tossing her hair free, she nudged Hector to a wild gallop, trusting the horse to carry her safely. She rode nearly fast enough to escape her life, but not quite. She led Hector to jump the last barrier, a huge fallen tree. It was like flying.

She reined the lathered horse in after the jump, letting the beast regain his breath. She glanced up at the western slope, where the sunset lingered, turning the ridge line of the forest into a screen of stark black silhouettes, without depth. She narrowed her eyes, catching a glimpse of a different shape. A man-shaped shadow on a black horse. The trees were only half bare, and the shape was not distinct. Gemma looked longer, but couldn't tell in the fading light if the form was real. Her uncle didn't like strangers on the property. She was aware of the weight of the pistol she always carried. Should she go and investigate the shape?

Hector's tired snort reminded her that the horse was not ready for another race. She shrugged, looking away from the shape. No doubt it was just the twilight playing tricks on her. She nudged Hector once, and they turned toward home.

When she reached the courtyard of the crumbling pile known as Caithny castle, Gemma earned a mild look of disapproval from Fergus, the stable "boy"—he was well over fifty.

"I thought we agreed Hector could use a day of rest," the man said, looking critically at the beautiful roan.

She offered an apologetic shrug. "I had to go out, Fergus. I was feeling cooped up." She was always feeling cooped up lately. Restless and itchy for something new.

"You'll take the beast too far one day, Gemma girl, and then it'll be too late."

"Hector hasn't begun to hit his limit," Gemma said, stroking the horse's neck. "Don't worry! No wild rides tomorrow. Just a mild one. I promised Cook I'd search out more mushrooms for dinner."

Fergus watched her. "In truth, I'd never have the heart to keep you from a ride. But you go in now. Your aunt's been asking after you."

"Asking where I am, you mean!" Gemma called back as she advanced toward the main part of the building.

The bulk of Caithny castle was impressive, even when one got closer and saw how little of it was really habitable. Massive stone towers at the corners of the place stood empty, and the tops of the walls were ragged after the mortar crumbled, allowing stones to fall. Gemma scarcely thought about whether it was odd, though. Since she was quite young, Caithny was the only home she knew.

She passed in through the heavy wooden door at one end of the courtyard, stepping into the front room her uncle insisted on calling a foyer. It was a lofty space due to the staircase that climbed around the edges, up three flights, around and around and around. She ought to go straight up those stairs to her room and change into cleaner clothes. Aunt Maura would expect her to do so. But the older woman also expected Gemma to appear without delay. Knowing that she would disappoint her aunt no matter what, Gemma walked straight ahead and down a dark hall that led to the library.

"Aunt Maura?" she asked as she opened the door. It was warm in the library, thanks to a small fire burning in the hearth. A woman sat nearby, her face shielded from direct heat by a fireplace screen.

"Come in, Gemma girl," her aunt said. The voice was cultured, thin, and little disapproving, much like Aunt Maura herself. She was full Scot, but for part of her life she lived in England, and her accent had softened considerably. It had a pleasant, gentle lilt even when she reprimanded Gemma, as she had to do all too often. "Have you been outside all day long?"

"I was riding," Gemma said, approaching the fire.

"Yes, that is plain enough. Your hair is a bird's nest of tangles, your skin so flushed and freckled...and your dress! It's more tears than fabric now. My word, girl, have you no concern for your appearance?"

"No one is around to see me," Gemma objected. That made her think of the shape in the woods. Was someone watching her? Should she be embarrassed by how wild she looked? Then she threw her shoulders back defiantly. If someone was watching her, then she was not to blame if her looks disappointed them. After all, she thought she was alone. Surely it was up to them to announce their presence. In fact, it was almost like spying....

"Well, you'd best clean up," Maura said. "You may be a wild creature all day, but you have a few hours until supper, and you will comport yourself properly while you dine at my table."

"It's not your table. It belongs to Uncle Conall." As soon as the words were out, Gemma wished she'd bitten her tongue.

Maura's face blanched, and she looked away. To a woman as proud as Miss Maura Caithny, the reminder that she was dependent on her brother's charity was especially cruel.

"I'm sorry!" Gemma said. "I didn't mean it like that. I only meant is he joining us tonight? Uncle Conall, that is?"

"He is attending to his business, I believe." Aunt Maura didn't like Conall's business—smuggling—which added insult to injury. "But you will join me at the table at half past."

Gemma turned and left. She should not have snapped at her aunt, who was endlessly kind, though strict and very proper. If only Gemma wasn't so out of sorts. She resolved to be a perfect lady at dinner. That would cheer her aunt up.

Before she could change, though, she was halted by a voice in the foyer. "Gemma girl!"

Uncle Conall stood at the door, dressed for the out-doors in boots and tough trousers and a greatcoat that concealed the rest of his outfit. He was getting older, but he was still an imposing man, built by years of hard work. When he spoke, men listened.

"Are you coming or going?" Gemma asked.

"Bit of both," he replied. Unlike Aunt Maura, his Scottish accent was undiluted. He'd lived his whole life in Caithny. "Busy times, and I'm needed down at the shore." He looked her over appraisingly, his eyes taking in her less than clean outfit. "You've been out as well, I surmise."

"I was riding."

"Meet anyone?" he asked, his eyes narrowed.

"No. I was alone the whole time."

"See you keep it that way." He grunted. "You're to stay in tonight, mind. We're to have a guest."

"Does that concern me?"

"Aye, he's here to talk business. I anticipate a run soon, for which you will be needed."

Gemma nodded. Over the past few years, she had begun to participate in what Conall termed the "family trade." As his own eyes grew weaker, he relied more and more on Gemma's sharp vision and keen senses to detect Customs agents, ships, and other threats that might ruin an evening's work. Gemma found it exciting, even though she knew it was hardly acceptable for a lady. And that again reminded her of what she saw at the very end of her ride.

"Uncle," she began. "Speaking of that, I may have seen someone during my ride after all."

He was all attention. "Go on."

"It was exactly at sunset, and the light was odd…but I was certain for a moment that I saw a man on horseback, watching me ride."

"You were certain for a moment?"

She grimaced. "I would have had to ride back around for a better look. And since I was alone I didn't think it would be wise."

"You had your pistol about you, did you not?" From his tone, it wasn't clear whether he thought she should have acted differently than she had.

"Oh, I always do," Gemma said with an easy confidence. She was an excellent shot. "But Hector was tired too, and I wasn't sure…"

Conall shrugged one shoulder. "It was probably nothing. And anyone fool enough to spy on my operations will soon regret it." He paused, looking Gemma over again. "But you be careful, girl. Don't let any stranger get close to you."

She smiled, disregarding the warning as unnecessary. "Don't worry. No man can hurt me."

Chapter 2

≈

IN POINT OF FACT, THERE *was* a shape on the ridge line. The shape was that of a man named Logan Hartley. He was extremely interested in Caithny castle, as well as anyone who lived inside—which appeared to include a pretty, redheaded woman who rode like a demon.

He'd been using a spyglass to examine the outline of Caithny, but at the sound of hooves, he swung the glass around quickly to catch sight of the newcomer.

He focused just in time to see a roan horse gather itself and jump to clear a massive tree trunk lying across the path. It was a jump he'd hesitate to take himself.

Then he saw the rider.

It was a woman, though that word seemed a weak description for the vision that appeared in the spyglass. Exhilarated after the jump, she slowed the horse down reluctantly. For a moment, Logan thought she saw him. But then she glanced up toward Caithny castle, and turned her horse toward the grounds of the very estate he came to survey.

Logan leaned back, marveling. Who was that gorgeous creature? And what business did she have with

Conall Caithny? Logan watched the place a little longer, slowly circling the grounds, committing the layout to heart, but his thoughts were hounded by the flame-haired rider.

Logan would have to plan his approach carefully. By all accounts, Conall Caithny was a ruthless, shrewd man who could sense a trick a mile off. But Logan smiled grimly as he considered his own reputation for ruthlessness. Caithny would hear him out, all right; he'd be too greedy not to. Then Logan would learn everything about the operation that was aiding the French war effort. And stop it.

Logan was a spy. He was a member of a group called the Zodiac, an organization so secret that it didn't even surface in rumors, which was exactly the way the Zodiac liked it. Logan joined the group at the invitation of a man known as Aries, the first sign of the Zodiac. Aries ran the operations of the group and supervised the assignments carried out by the members, but the assignments came from even higher up. A mysterious person called the Astronomer truly ran the Zodiac. Logan didn't know who that person was and he had no desire to.

He'd been given this assignment a few months ago, and he threw himself into it. Despite working for the Zodiac for nearly two years, he still felt like a student, a pretender. Logan wanted to carry this work out perfectly to get the appreciation of the Astronomer. Then he would be given other, more significant missions—the sort that only elite agents would be trusted with.

After seeing the beautiful rider enter Caithny castle, though, he had to admit that surprises could be pleasant too. He wouldn't mind seeing the mysterious beauty again, while he was in the wilds of the north.

When the sunlight disappeared entirely, Logan guided his horse through the trees, careful to avoid making any more noise than necessary. The fading light was deceptive, making a rider think he saw much more than was truly there. Logan could not afford to make any mistakes.

His horse, more gentle than its rough appearance suggested, picked its way through the fallen leaves, past the trees and shrubs now colored with autumn glory—although the colors were hidden now, tinted only by the silvery moonlight.

He had to return to the inn where he was staying. Although he wanted to go back to the *Mistral*, his beloved ship, Logan couldn't risk discovery by riding to where she was hidden. He'd simply have to trust his first mate to watch over the *Mistral*. Tobias would care for the ship just as well as Logan himself, for he'd helped Logan build her. He'd been at Logan's side for years.

But at the moment, Logan was on his own. He rode back to the Rose and Crown, the inn in the little town by the shore. The village was also called Caithny, taking its name from the castle that protected it once upon a time, when invasions and local wars were still real threats. Now, the castle was little more than a remnant of the past. The town, on the other hand, bustled with life and was concerned only with the present and the future.

The Rose and Crown was on the main thoroughfare, and it was not too busy that evening. Jennie, the barmaid, looked up as the door opened. Reflexively, she smiled in her friendly way, but the smile shrank a little when she saw who it was. "Oh. Evening, Mr Lockridge."

Logan offered her a thin answering smile. He knew exactly what the girl was thinking. He frightened her.

True, Logan was not a particularly intimidating man.

He'd always thought his brown hair and brown eyes were plain, though he'd been told by dozens of women that his smile was charming—beginning with his nursemaid when he was very young, and progressing over the years to other women considerably less innocent in their admiration. He was on the tall side with a lean strength from years of constantly tugging at rigging and fighting winds that sometimes seemed intent on sweeping him into the ocean. They hadn't won yet, and that was due to Logan's natural gift for balance. He always knew where to step when on board a ship. Land, however, proved to be a bit of a challenge.

But it wasn't his appearance that alarmed Jennie. It was his apparent profession—smuggler. Smugglers were known to be ruthless bastards, no matter what their outward behavior. And Lockridge was worse than most, according to the rumors.

As Lockridge, Logan was always polite and never raised his voice. He could tell that actually scared her more, but he didn't have the time to charm Jennie.

"Something to eat, sir?" Jennie asked as he sat down at the table in the corner he'd already claimed.

"No. Just ale," he replied. Jennie drew the ale and brought it to him. He looked up at her as she placed it on the table. "Any messages for me?"

She shook her head quickly, nervously. "Not today, sir."

Jennie headed back to the bar. Logan leaned back, surveying the main room.

Moments later, Tobias walked in, taking a direct path for Logan's table. "You beat me," he said.

"How's my beauty?" Logan asked, referring to his ship.

"Tucked away. She's so well hidden I have trouble spotting her, and I know where she's anchored. No one will find her. And even if they do, two men are aboard to watch things."

Logan nodded. He had every faith in Toby's assessment.

Toby got an ale from Jennie, and a much brighter smile too. Everyone liked Toby, with his light blue eyes and loud laugh. The older man appeared to be as harmless as Logan was dangerous. Not fair, Logan thought. If people knew what Toby was capable of....

Before he could think further on that, another man came into the tavern. He looked around for only a moment before he spotted Logan and Toby in the corner. He paused for a beat, then made his way directly across the room.

"You're Lockridge?" the man asked.

Logan nodded. "You have something to tell me?"

"Aye. Caithny will see you. You must come to Caithny castle at eleven o' clock this evening."

"I *must*, eh?" Logan pulled an object out of his pocket. It looked rather like a brass pocket watch, but he didn't open the lid. "Eleven?"

"Well, that's the message I was given...sir." The man looked a bit nervous, perhaps remembering that Lockridge was a name associated with some very nasty rumors.

Logan pretended to think about it for a moment, turning the brass ornament over in his hand. Then he said, "Tell him I'll be there."

The man nodded quickly. Just as he turned to leave, Logan said, "What's your name?"

"Munro."

"Thank you, Munro."

"For what?"

"For delivering the message. I'll remember your name." Logan didn't put the slightest inflection in his tone. It was impossible to tell if he was being sincere or sarcastic.

Munro certainly didn't know how to take it, so he hovered indecisively for a moment, unsure if he should be pleased, offended, or scared. He settled on pleased and bobbed his head once. "Yes, sir. Thank you, sir." He left in a hurry.

"What was that about?" Toby asked. "Why should you remember his name?"

"Lord, I don't know," Logan said with a low laugh. "I just like to see how people react. Say something a bit off from the expected and suddenly, people have to think. They can't fall back on convention because they don't know what the convention would be. So they're more revealing."

"You were such a fine young boy. But you've become rather a sneaky bastard in the last few years," Tobias noted.

"Have I? Must be the corrupting influence of the mother country."

"I know damn well to what you owe the influence. Those new friends of yours, *Lockridge*."

Toby knew that Logan was spy. He didn't know much beyond that, because the Zodiac did not like people knowing about it at all.

But Logan was feeling a little nostalgic, so he let Toby's remark pass. He looked at the object he was holding. After a moment, he pressed the button, opening the lid. "Fortune favors the bold," he said softly.

"Missing your family?" Toby asked, aware of how Logan's mood had shifted.

"I've been thinking about family lately. More than usual. I don't know why." He looked at his friend. "We haven't been back to St George's for nearly three years. Seems odd to think about it." Logan paused. "Do you miss home?"

Toby shook his head. "Home is the ship I'm on. No doubt we'll see Bermuda again."

"Spoken like a true sailor." Logan stood up and stretched, sliding the brass item back into his pocket. "Well, I waited long enough for the message to arrive. Think I'll take a walk. I need to waste a few hours before going back to the castle. See you in the morning."

"You're going to the meeting alone? I've been poking around, and I've heard of Caithny. If he catches any hint that you're not what you seem…"

"But I *am* what I seem," Logan reminded him. "A smuggler, from a long line of smugglers. I speak Caithny's language. He'll listen to me."

Toby frowned. "I don't like it."

"You can leave if you like."

"You know I'd never do that," Toby said. "But I'll leave you to your walk. Plenty of ale to keep me busy."

Logan left enough coin to cover his drink and whatever Toby would manage to put away. Leaving the smoky air of the tavern and breathing in the cool night helped his mood instantly. He'd been nervous about getting a meeting with Caithny, though he was good at hiding it. As Tobias said, Logan had become a sneaky bastard.

He didn't set out to become a spy. When Logan sailed to England on his own ship, he intended to see the country his ancestors came from, build his business, and perhaps earn a bit of respect. Almost through chance, he became a petty officer in the Royal Navy a few months after arriving in England. Though firmly of the merchant class, his family could afford the commission. And it was said that some Bermudans were more British than the British themselves. Logan's family was proud of their heritage. Of course a few generations ago, his family was dodging custom officers and naval raids. Smugglers were so misunderstood.

But now, his family was—almost—completely respectable.

However, even after Logan joined the Royal Navy as an ensign with the goal of living a perfectly law-abiding life, fate took a hand. He was more intelligent than most men—even most officers—and he was soon sent on missions requiring stealth and a sharp eye. On the continent, Bonaparte was causing all manner of worries for Britain, so Logan considered it his duty to get in the man's way. After one such mission while he served on a ship called the *Providence*, he met a gentleman who was rather more than he seemed. Logan must have made a good impression, because shortly after that, he was given an offer. If he was interested, he could join an organization called the Zodiac, a secretive group of elite agents who protected Britain against its worst enemies. Of course Logan was interested. He agreed instantly, and began his training within weeks.

Two years later, he had become an agent with a sign of his own: Aquarius. He carried out several assignments usually involving some element of smuggling, a key part of the war.

His current assignment was to identify the missing links in a supply chain that went all the way up to

Napoleon's high command. He was uniquely suited for the task, being a bit of an outsider, and a bit unpredictable. The fact that he had his own ship and crew made him even more desirable.

The Zodiac dreamed up Logan's alter ego of Lockridge. Once the story was created, other agents carefully fleshed out Lockridge's imaginary history. They slipped the name into gossip, into government reports, even among their underworld contacts. The story was simple enough. Lockridge was a young, ambitious smuggler from the New World, seeking to gain a toehold in the more established operations of Europe. He was ruthless, with no loyalty and no scruples.

Logan already knew the sort of character he had to project, but his Zodiac training gave him the tools he needed to be a good spy. He'd make use all of them when he was to return to Caithny castle tonight.

Chapter 3

≋

THE AUTUMN DAYS BROUGHT SWIFT and early sunsets. In the time between sunset and supper, Aunt Maura conducted one of her usual lessons on deportment and manners. Now presentable in her appearance, Gemma provided the correct answers for most of Maura's questions.

"An archduke would be addressed before a viscount," Gemma said in response to one, adding, "which will be *so* important at the next party we host." She put her hand to her mouth in mock horror. "Oh, no! I've forgotten that we never host anyone here…other than Conall's dubious associates, of course."

"Pertness of manner is not admirable, Gemma," her aunt said with a frown. "Nor is it useful as a display of intelligence."

"Sorry," she said, not sounding very sorry.

Maura sighed. She had several sighs, and spent a lifetime mastering each one. There was the sigh of disappointment when she found a stain or rip in Gemma's gowns. There was the sigh of resignation when Conall made a pronouncement. There was the sigh of skepticism when anyone decided something Maura did not agree with. And then there was the sigh of I-told-you-so whenever Maura's opinion was vindicated. Gemma had grown adept at translating these sighs. The latest one was a plea-to-the-angels-for-patience sigh, and it was one she heard quite a lot.

"All right, Aunt. I understand that I can't say what I'm thinking if I'm among society. Now resume."

"No, Gemma. You're misunderstanding the lesson. A true lady does not *hide* her thoughts. She takes care to only cultivate good and generous and proper thoughts in her mind. Thus no deceit is necessary."

Now Gemma sighed. "I'll do my best."

"I hope so. Now, let's shift to a different subject. Ladies are conversant in the rudiments of music, even if they have no talent for it. Tell me what you have learned about the classical masters and the sort of music created by each…"

Gemma gave another little sigh herself. She couldn't wait till they were summoned for supper.

* * * *

Conall joined Gemma and Maura for dinner in the cavernous dining hall. Their chef was competent, though no artist. He came to Caithny about two years ago at Conall's request. He'd found the man somewhere and liked his cooking, though Gemma couldn't see much that distinguished it. The chef did, however, have a strange knack for finding excellent produce that Gemma would swear was out of season. She speared a piece of aspara-gus. It was slender and bright green, just touched with a serviceable cream sauce. In spring, such a dish would be expected. But it was fall, and Gemma couldn't begin to think where Cook had gotten the vegetable. It wasn't as if Caithny castle boasted a glass house for growing.

Her hunger outweighed her curiosity, and she put the conundrum aside. Maura never commented on the meals, possibly because she rarely spoke when her brother was present. Conall talked with Gemma about news in the village of Caithny, and she answered with what she knew. Gemma often rode into the village to chat with neighbors or carry messages.

Conall seemed strangely anxious. Whoever he was meeting that evening, it must be more important than usual.

Conall noted the demure gown Gemma wore to dinner, and told her to change after the meal. "Put on the blue one you've got. Give our guest something to look at. Makes my task a bit easier if he's distracted by your pretty face."

Gemma rolled her eyes. Of course Conall would press every advantage, even to the point of using his niece as a distraction. If the visitor was looking down the front of her dress, he wouldn't be thinking clearly about the terms of the deal Conall offered. Conall didn't let *anything* get in the way of business.

Maura glared at Conall for the crude remark, but didn't say anything to oppose him. She gave a sigh of endless disappointment and excused herself from the table.

After supper, Gemma went to her room to tidy up and change into the requested dress. It was not new or fashionable. Aunt Maura, in some mysterious way, knew all about the prevailing winds of fashion in London and beyond. She said gowns worn by society ladies were shockingly modern now, with almost no corsets and barely any covering at all.

But Gemma also thought her blue dress was very pretty, so she didn't mind out-of-fashion styling. It hugged her torso with lacing across her chest, and it emphasized her narrow waist. She frowned at her reflection in the mirror, hoping the corset was effective. From years of observation and overhearing drunk smugglers, she knew men preferred women with bigger breasts. Did hers qualify? Gemma had no notion, and of course no one from whom to get an honest answer. Oh, well. The dress was pretty all the same. The blue tone of the soft wool emphasized her fair complexion and complemented her bright red hair. Annie, the maid, had already braided her hair for dinner, and Gemma saw no reason to change the style. Whoever this guest was, he'd better be impressed.

"Not that I should bother to even think of it," she muttered to herself. "What's another smuggler?" He'd be just like the rest of Conall's associates. Hardened, vicious men who looked more at home in a tavern brawl than anywhere else. One who cared for nothing but profit, or at best tweaking the British interests. Even in lowland Scotland there was still plenty of resentment against England, despite Scotland being part of the empire.

She went downstairs again. Aunt Maura was nowhere to be found, naturally. She had a gift for absenting herself whenever the slightest hint of criminal activity was afoot. In practice, that meant Conall and Maura rarely spoke or even stayed in the same room, despite the fact that they were brother and sister. It was one of the many things Gemma always thought normal, until recently.

Conall was in his parlor. He'd remain there while Gemma met their guest at the door. Conall liked to play up his position, making his guests come to him.

Gemma waited, and waited. She would not open the door to peek out. That might ruin the effect. And effect was important. How should she appear when she opened the door? Gracious? Aloof? Perhaps even queenly?

She was so lost in her thoughts that when the knock sounded, she jumped up and proceeded to answer the door just as she would if she were not expecting anything.

"Well, come in!" she burst out. "Why else come all this way if you're just going to stand—" Gemma stopped short when she got a look at the man.

He was young, perhaps only five years older than her. He had thick brown hair and warm, brown eyes that glowed in the dim light of the foyer. The tanned skin was definitely that of a sailor. But this could not possibly be a smuggler come to do business with her uncle. He was too young, and handsome, and….

And he was smiling at her. A smile that started slow and grew until her insides felt like honey.

She was lost.

"Hello," she said finally, aware that she had to say something. "You're…with Lockridge?" she asked, completely forgetting the half dozen lines she thought might serve as greetings.

He shook his head, plainly admiring her. "No."

"You're not with Lockridge?" she asked, confused, and still quite thrown by his appearance. Handsome strangers did not just wander into Caithny.

"I *am* Lockridge," he said.

"Oh." Gemma felt a weird sensation in her belly. Disappointment? Maybe. "I thought you'd be…older."

"I'm used to that. Eventually the assumption will be correct. If I live long enough."

His casual reference to death made Gemma's belly flutter again. He didn't look like the sort of man who would die.

"If you're Lockridge, you'd best come in," she said. "Conall is waiting."

Lockridge raised an eyebrow. "You're on a first name basis with him?"

"He's family, so yes."

Her answer appeared to spark even more interest. He looked at Gemma more carefully. "You're another Caithny, then."

Gemma drew herself up to her full five and a half feet. "No, I'm a Harrington. Miss Gemma Harrington. Conall Caithny is my uncle. And he doesn't like to be kept waiting."

"Well, show me in, Miss Harrington."

She did, acutely conscious of his every action. He took off his hat, then shrugged out of his great coat, flinging it carelessly onto a chair. She watched covertly. His body was thin, athletic. No doubt he spent his life on a ship.

Gemma led him down the hallway to the parlor, feeling his gaze on her as they went.

"Uncle Conall," she said as they entered the parlor, "Mr Lockridge has come to see you." She stepped aside to allow Lockridge to walk further into the room.

As she did, she was surprised to see that all the warmth she imagined in Lockridge was utterly gone. Now he stood there, his eyes dark and cold as he surveyed the room.

Conall sat in state on a large, high-backed chair by the fire, which made the walls glow a pale orange. He looked for all the world like a king in his domain. A chair stood opposite him, with no back and no embellishments. It was little more than a bench.

"Lockridge! Come in, come in." Conall gestured for

him to sit in the empty chair.

Lockridge didn't even glance at the chair, but strolled to the fireplace mantle. He bent down to the fire to warm his hands by the flame. That made his body turn away from Conall for a moment. Gemma caught a glimpse of his profile as he did so, and saw his eyes gleam as they reflected the fire. He looked devilish, if devils were handsome.

Then he stood again, and turned back to face Conall. Lockridge looked perfectly at home, just as much the master as Conall.

"Quite the old pile of stones you've got," he said to Conall, his voice just short of insulting. His accent did change how his words sounded, but that certainly wasn't the explanation for his tone.

"Been in the family for generations," said Conall. Annoyed by Lockridge's manner, he looked around the room, seeking Gemma. "Gemma girl. We'll be discussing business. Why don't you offer our guest a drink?" Conall suggested, but it held the tone of an order.

"Would you care for a drink?" Gemma asked, not feeling particularly servile.

"Anything but rum," he said, his gaze matching hers.

"You don't drink rum?" asked Conall. "I thought you were from the Indies."

"Bermuda," Lockridge clarified. "And I'll ship rum, but I won't drink it."

"We have whisky," Gemma said.

"That will do," he said.

Gemma went to the kitchen to prepare a warm, and deeply alcoholic, drink for their guest. She sighed, thinking of all the "gentlemen" her uncle had seen in his house in the past few years. "Gentlemen" was the term the villagers used to describe the smugglers keeping them supplied with rare goods. The gentlemen gave the village first pick of the goods when they arrived, in exchange for silence on the matter of where their boats lay at night, or what caves were best left unexplored by the law. Gemma had seen more of the gentlemen than most of the village, but she thought she had never seen a man as cool as the one now in her parlor. Not that he'd done anything. It was the aura of ruthlessness about him.

She returned with the drinks. When Conall saw her, he broke off whatever conversation he'd been having with Lockridge. "What were you doing with that whisky, girl? Did you grow the grain first?"

"I warmed it," she said, irritated. "It takes a few minutes for the poker to heat." They made their drinks hot in the time-tested way of heating a metal rod in the fire, then plunging it into the liquid.

"Well, bring them over. Don't dawdle. Lockridge is a man with a reputation." Conall laughed. "How many crewmen did you throw overboard on your journey here?"

"Only one," Lockridge responded. Nothing in his voice suggested it was a joke.

She walked to Lockridge to hand him the drink. She was between him and Conall as she did so, so her uncle couldn't see how Lockridge's fingers brushed hers as the drink exchanged hands. It was deliberate, and deliberately provoking. Gemma had every right to take offense and alert Conall immediately.

For some reason, she didn't. Instead, she inquired of Lockridge, "What would inspire you to throw a man overboard?"

Lockridge didn't look at her, but kept his eyes on Conall as he replied, "The man annoyed me."

"Keep the others in line," Conall said, with a nod. "That's the way to do it."

How appalling that such a handsome man should have such a cold soul. "Excuse me, I should go," Gemma said, turning to leave.

"Don't go far," Lockridge said when she reached the door. She turned at those words. Lockridge was staring directly at her, and the look in his eyes wasn't cold at all.

"Be careful what you wish for," she warned him as she left.

Chapter 4

〽️

GOOD ADVICE, LOGAN THOUGHT. HE watched the woman leave, noting how gracefully she moved. She'd surprised him when she flung the door open on his arrival. Who could be prepared for that sort of woman? The flame colored hair he remembered from the afternoon was now bound in a wide, intricate braid that fell down the center of her back. It left her face unframed, which made her strong cheekbones and bright blue eyes even more prominent. The way her skin was spotted with freckles was instantly appealing to him. Unfortunately, it wasn't this woman he came to do business with.

After Miss Harrington's departure from the parlor, he felt the better part of the evening was already over. He turned back to his host.

"So you're from Bermuda," said Caithny. "There are several versions of your history."

"Rumors do spread," Logan said. Many had been spread quite deliberately. "But it is a fact that I was born and raised in Bermuda. Been sailing ever since I could walk."

"Bermuda is part of the British Empire." Caithny said it with a certain amount of disdain.

"So is Scotland," Lockridge countered. Then he grinned. "But Bermuda is a long way from London. We have our own minds there. Just as you do here."

Caithny laughed. He liked the answer.

"Pretty thing, isn't she?" Caithny asked, with a nod toward the door Gemma had retreated through.

Logan nodded, unsure what a safe answer to that would be.

"Ah, I saw you watch her," Caithny went on. "Don't pretend you didn't notice."

"A man would have to be dead not to notice her."

Caithny leaned forward suddenly. "Aye. So let me be clear. You look at her again, you touch her, you say a sweet word to her, and you *will* be dead."

"That's very direct," Logan said smoothly. Inside, he was shaken by Conall Caithny's dramatic shift in mood. He was either playing up his role as guardian, or he truly did watch out for the young lady's virtue.

"It had better be."

"I'm here to talk business," Logan said, wanting to avoid unnecessary confrontation. "So let's get to that."

"Very well. You requested this meeting. What do you want of *me*?" Caithny asked. "I've an established operation here. What makes you think I need another man at this point?"

"I'm not offering service," Logan said grimly. "Like you, I've also got an established operation. Not as large as yours, though I hope to expand my influence. But I believe there is an opportunity for mutual profit...so long as we have a brief alliance."

"Continue."

"You lost a ship six weeks ago," Logan said. "The *Lapin*, just off the coast of Devon."

Caithny raised his eyebrow, curious at Logan's knowledge. "Aye, she sank. Bad luck."

"Luck had nothing to do with it. *I* sank her."

Caithny sat up. "And you dare come here—"

"Calm down," Logan said. "It was dark, with no moon. She came upon my ship in the lane and we fired cannon before her captain called out her colors. His mistake. We did, however, take the survivors aboard."

"And one of them spilled what he knew." Caithny sneered at the weakness of ordinary men.

"They were all grateful to be on the water and not in it. I confess I was curious, especially when one of the men lamented the loss of the cargo." Logan paused. "Thirty-six crates of rifles, destined for Napoleon's forces. Most profitable indeed."

Caithny's eyes flashed, but he then relaxed. "So he told you I was shipping rifles. Yes. It would have been profitable if the shipment went through!"

"Tough loss?" Logan asked.

"Risks are inevitable. I'll make it back."

"Would you like to make it back faster?"

Caithny looked interested. "How so?"

"You need more ships. I have one that could be put to use. I'll loan you my services for a cut of each run."

"How much of a cut?"

"Fifty percent sounds fair."

"Sounds like robbery," Caithny said. "Ten percent."

"Forty," countered Logan.

"Fifteen."

"Thirty, and the return of your loose-tongued crew member."

"Where is he?"

"Agree to thirty percent, and you'll soon know," Logan promised.

Caithny narrowed his eyes. "Why do you have spare room in your hold? What are you transporting?"

Logan gave a slight smile. "Something small but valuable."

"You ask to be cut in on a deal, but you won't reveal your angle?"

"I am offering *you* a deal," Logan said. "A fast, guaranteed delivery, at a date far earlier than you could hope to match on your own. If you could afford it, you would have got another ship by now. So you need a ship more than I need spare cargo."

"And in return you get thirty percent of the profits," Caithny said cautiously.

"*And* access to your port here in Scotland. I've got goods produced in the New World, including rum, which offer a tidy profit of their own. But I prefer not to use English ports."

"I'll consider it. You can wait in town. And don't press me. If I choose to speak to the law, they might show a keen interest in your operation, sir."

"I'll wait," said Logan, not particularly impressed by Caithny's threat. "But if I hear wind of a better offer, I'll be gone. And you'll be out a deal."

"You've come a long way to meet me. I believe you'll wait," said Caithny, sounding more confident. "But let's shake on it. Stay two nights. If you don't hear from me by then, no deal and no hard feelings."

Logan watched him narrowly, then held out his hand. "I can accept that."

Caithny reached out as well, clasping Logan's right hand in a hard grip. But then he turned Logan's hand over, surveying the skin. "You *are* a sailor," he said with cautious approval.

Logan almost laughed. Conall Caithny was no fool. A spy without the calloused hands of a sailor used to ropes and oars would have been exposed immediately. So the Zodiac had done right to send him. "I was born a sailor," he said. "I'll wait in town for your response."

"You can show yourself out." Caithny turned away, dismissing Logan for the moment.

Logan turned and left. He briefly considered exploring the inside of Caithny castle. There were a number of things he was quite curious about the location of—primarily Gemma Harrington, but also the whereabouts of Caithny's records. But he knew better than to press his luck on the first night.

He didn't see Miss Harrington as he walked to the front door and out into the courtyard. Perhaps the revelation of his so-called occupation was enough to drive her away, in which case she was an intelligent lady.

However, Logan wasn't going to leave without some snooping, and the grounds of Caithny castle begged to be surveyed. It was easy to slip into the shadows. Caithny castle was scarcely populated, and few buildings held any lights at all. When Logan looked up at the sky, he saw thick cloud cover. A good night for spying.

He moved silently, orienting himself as he explored the paths and structures. The actual castle, which was more of a manor house, was in decent repair. The windows looked to be mostly glassed in, and the stones were solid. But there were many outbuildings scattered around, the remnants of previous years, when Caithny castle probably supported the lives of several dozen people. Now, most of those buildings were crumbling, or partially dismantled. He peeked in a few storehouses, found an old cistern that appeared to be in working order, and even explored what might have been an armory long ago. More buildings stood closer to the outer wall, but Logan couldn't spend too much time wandering.

He located the stable by the unmistakable smell of straw and horse, and entered where he saw the warm glow of a lantern.

"Hello?" he called.

A short man popped out from a stall down the way. "One minute!"

"I'm in no hurry," Logan said easily. He saw his horse in one of the near stalls, and it snorted in recognition.

"You were in the house," the hostler said, coming down the aisle with a bucket in his hand. "You'll be wanting to get back to town as soon as you may," he guessed.

"Not many guests?" Logan asked.

"Up here? Never." The hostler put the bucket down and went into the stall. "Caithny isn't a man who likes others in his domain. He used to put up some of his dockworkers in one of the outbuildings, but that ended a few years ago."

"Why?"

The hostler glanced at Logan, assessing. "Did you happen to meet a young lady at the house?"

"If you mean Miss Harrington, yes."

"Well, then you know the reason. Caithny wasn't keen on men being too close to her when she grew a bit older, if you understand."

Logan understood perfectly well, and for once he fully approved of Caithny's decision making. "A man should keep his family safe," he said.

"If only he did," the hostler grunted. But he had Logan's horse out of the stall now, and was eager to have them on their way. "Here you are," the hostler said. "Gave him a bit of meal, too."

"Thank you for that," Logan said, sincerely. "What's your name?"

"Fergus, sir."

"Worked here your whole life, I'll bet."

"Not quite, but more years than I care to count. Mind how you ride in the dark. The clouds are keeping the moon at bay, and the track can be tricky."

"I'll keep that in mind, Fergus." Logan flipped a coin to the hostler as a tip, and the man caught it in midair.

Grinning, Logan mounted and rode away. His first foray was a success. Conall Caithny was interested in his offer, though he pretended indifference. He also learned that Gemma Harrington knew at least a little about the operation, because Conall didn't hide the nature of their meeting from her.

But she wasn't enough in Caithny's thrall to report Logan's flirtations immediately. Logan had to learn more about that tidbit. If Miss Harrington knew about her uncle's business, it might be a good idea to soften her up. Though she looked quite soft already, he thought, with a wry smile.

Chapter 5

≋

THE NEXT DAY, GEMMA WENT out riding again. She'd told Cook she would search out some mushrooms for supper, which she fully intended to do. And anyway, she couldn't stand to be inside walls.

The visit from Lockridge last night made a stronger impression on Gemma than she'd ever admit out loud. He was so unlike what she was expecting. Yes, he was far younger than she assumed. For him to have his own ship at his age implied that he was shrewd or ruthless or both.

But for a shrewd, ruthless criminal, Gemma couldn't stop thinking about him, with his easy grace and slow smile when he first saw her. Gemma always kept a certain distance from the sort of people her uncle employed, avoiding any familiarity. Though she was rather wild, she had a good upbringing thanks to Aunt Maura. Conall himself made it clear to his men that Gemma was under his protection. She worked with Uncle Conall because he was family, and because the exciting nature of smuggling kept her from losing her mind at the castle. But she had no intention of following in Conall's footsteps. The day she achieved her majority, she would flee Caithny castle and start living her own life…somewhere.

She rode through the woods, ecstatic to be outside.

The odor of the sea mingled with the unique scent of fallen leaves, oddly spicy with just a hint of earthiness. The day was bright and warm though, and it was pure pleasure to be riding.

When she got to where the mushrooms grew, Gemma dismounted. She tied Hector to a low-hanging branch, going on foot to find what she'd sighted the other day. She paused, sniffing the crisp air to locate the elusive odor of the mushrooms.

Just as she caught the scent, she heard a bloodcurdling yowl. She stood rooted to the spot, wondering what it could be. There was a moment of deathly silence, then the call broke out again. Gemma's blood froze, but she shook herself, casting off any thoughts of ghosts or goblins. There was a creature nearby in need of help.

She scampered to the top of the ridge, going in the direction of the sound. Once again, a yowl came from the far side of the glen below, about a hundred yards distant. Gemma almost plunged down the slope in her haste to get there.

She quickly found the source of the dreadful cries. A dog had somehow become caught in a trap, with one wounded front paw bleeding on the carpet of fallen leaves. It let out another mournful howl when it saw her approach, but Gemma spoke to it in a low, soothing voice. The dog stopped yowling and settled into a pitiful whine. She reached out a hand. The dog sniffed, and decided she was not a threat. She stroked the creature briefly, then turned to inspect the trap.

It was rusty with age, which was probably why it had not sprung closed completely. If it had, the dog's leg would have been severed. As it was, Gemma could hardly stand to look at the creature.

A few minutes tugging at the trap proved she didn't have the strength to defeat the mechanism. Worse, whenever she tilted the whole thing too far, the dog yelped and growled in pain.

"I'm trying to help you," she explained. She hated the feeling in her chest, the one she got when she saw something she could do nothing about. The dog only howled again, a heartbreaking sound carrying through the glen.

Then something responded to the howl. Gemma looked around, alarmed. What had she heard? Not a call, but definitely a sound. Looking up, she saw it on the ridge. Just like yesterday, when she thought she was seeing things in the dusk. An outline of a rider on horseback. But now it was daytime, and she knew it was real.

The rider moved down the slope toward her. She recognized the shape. *Lockridge*. Dressed in dark clothes, riding an equally dark horse, he looked just as much the devil as he had the previous evening.

Gemma watched him glance around the clearing. He twisted in his saddle. Lean, but well-muscled, like a man in constant motion.

He saw her too, of course. But he didn't smile or even greet her. He just dismounted and moved toward the dog. "Move away," he said, his voice low and unfriendly.

"No! He needs help."

"I can see that," Lockridge retorted. "But he's liable to bite you if you get too close. He could be feral. Or sick." Lockridge discarded his overcoat, revealing a form covered only by a linen shirt. "Move aside, and let me help."

"You're not going to put him down," she said in warning.

"That's not my intention. Now move. The dog's in pain. Would you have me ignore it?"

"No, of course not." Gemma shifted so Lockridge could inspect the trap. "I couldn't pull it open," she added, in a contrite tone. "I tried."

He bent down to grasp the jaws of the trap with both hands. Gemma watched as he began to pry the jaws open, the muscles in his back and arms straining with the effort. He got the trap open a precious two inches, allowing the dog to snatch its leg free. He let go the trap then, the jaws snapping closed with a sickening sound that echoed throughout the clearing.

The dog tried to run when it got free, but it was weak with hunger and pain, so it stumbled and fell almost immediately.

Gemma stepped forward instinctively, but Lockridge held up one hand to stop her. "Wait," he said.

He approached the dog, using a soft, slow voice, until it allowed him to pick it up. He carried the creature to the edge of the nearby stream and laid it down again.

Lockridge looked over to her at last. "There's a spare cloth in my saddlebag. Can you bring it here?"

Gemma nodded. She opened the saddlebag and hunted for the cloth. "Here," she said.

"Thank you." He took the cloth and started ripping it into strips. He'd done this before—and probably not for a dog.

"I'm going to touch him," she said.

Lockridge nodded absently. "He seems calm enough now. I just didn't want you to get bitten."

She put a hand on the dog's head, stroking the fur and speaking friendly nonsense. It was spotted brown and white along the body, with a head that was entirely dark brown. It had a long snout and soft ears. The dog snuffled when Gemma scratched carefully behind one ear. "Good boy," she murmured. "You're all right now."

Meanwhile, Lockridge ministered efficiently to the dog's injured foreleg, first washing it in the stream, then binding the paw. He looked around, perhaps wondering how a dog had ended up so far into the forest.

"Wandered from someone's property, perhaps?" he asked. "He's no mutt. A hunting dog, I should think."

"I can ask if anyone's lost a dog," Gemma said. "But there aren't many houses around here besides Caithny castle, and he's not ours."

The dog looked up at Logan with big liquid eyes, then licked his hand in gratitude.

"He seems to like you," Gemma said.

Lockridge shook his head once. "I've no room for a dog aboard, especially one that's never seen a ship. He'll just get underfoot. Or be washed overboard. You keep him. I'm sure you'll soon earn his devotion."

His comment reminded her of something. "Did you really throw a man overboard on the way here? Or was that something you just said to Uncle Conall?" To judge by the way he treated the dog, she found it hard to believe.

"It's true," Lockridge said, without apology. "My ship arrived with one less sailor than we started out with. And before you ask, I don't feel the least bit bad about it."

"Just because he annoyed you?"

He looked at her, his expression serious. "Do you want to know how he annoyed me?"

"I think so."

"The night before we sailed out of Portsmouth, we went for a few drinks. One of the crew went out to the alley in back. He wasn't gone very long, but I noticed that shortly after he returned, one of the barmaids came back the same way. She was crying—and those girls aren't the sort to cry easily. I had a hunch, so I had my first mate interview the girl. Toby's the sort of man people feel they can talk to."

"And had the man...hurt her?" Gemma asked, afraid to ask the obvious question.

"Yes," Lockridge said shortly. "He paid her, but she was a barmaid, not a whore, and paying for it afterward isn't the same as asking beforehand. The girl wasn't to blame for anything but not being as strong or as tough as a sailor."

Gemma didn't blink at his blunt language, because she was too busy thinking about the story.

"But you let him back on your ship. Why not simply sack him and send him on his way?"

"So he could do the same thing again?" Lockridge shook his head. "No one works for me without knowing exactly what's expected. I have rules, and he broke one. The man had his chance. He lost it."

Gemma thought for a moment, considering. "You didn't tell all this to my uncle."

"He didn't ask about the details," Lockridge said. Then he shifted. "Now, you have more immediate problems, Miss Harrington."

He picked up the dog, then stood up. "He can't be left here, and it's time for you to go. Where did you leave your horse?"

With Gemma leading the way, Logan carried the dog to where Hector was tied up.

She mounted and took the reins lightly in one hand. "Give him to me."

Lockridge lifted the dog up so it lay across the saddle. Gemma used her free hand to hold the dog close. "Good boy," she said. "It was a lucky chance we heard you today."

"Chance is a good name," Lockridge said.

Gemma smiled, liking the sound of it. "That is a good name. Do you like it, Chance?" she asked the dog. "Don't try to jump away. Good. You're very well behaved."

"He'd be mad to jump away from you," Lockridge said slyly. "I suddenly envy Chance."

"You ought to watch your words, Mr Lockridge," Gemma warned him. "Uncle Conall's punched men for less when it comes to me."

"Protective, isn't he," Lockridge said. "Not enough to keep you safe at home. But enough to threaten me last night when I admitted you were beautiful."

"What did he say?" Gemma asked. *Beautiful?*

"Oh, just that he'd kill me if I so much as touched you." But Lockridge didn't look worried. In fact, he was smiling. "So of course I wouldn't dare touch you."

Gemma noticed just then he was doing exactly that. His hand had drifted from the dog's back to her own hand. "You don't take him seriously," she said.

"Or perhaps I can't resist you."

She shrugged the easy compliment off, though she didn't shrug his hand off. "Why were you here today? Why ride by Caithny?"

"I'm curious," he said. "I like to know the lay of the land."

"What should it matter? You don't need to know anything about the land. You'll load up whatever it is Conall wants you to ship, and then you'll sail off. You need not even disembark."

"You don't know what he deals in?"

"The usual things—liquor and fabric and the like. Any

goods affected by the tariffs."

"That's all?"

"What else could there be?"

He watched her for a long moment, his eyes searching her face. Then he said, "No matter, I suppose. You get that dog back home, dryad. He ought to rest."

"And you?" she asked. "You shouldn't wander around here."

"But if I leave, how can I run into you again?"

"You shouldn't do that either." But Gemma rather did want to run into him again. "If you want to see me again, you should show me your ship."

"Not likely. She's shy," he hedged.

"Well, I'm not," said Gemma. "Please. I've never been aboard a ship," she confessed.

"What?" He was astonished by that. "You haven't? How is that even possible?"

"Uncle Conall has firm rules. I have the run of Caithny and I can ride wherever I want so long as it's not more than a day from home. But no ships. He fears I'll sail away."

"Is he right?"

"Oh, yes. I'd sail into the sunset if I could afford it… or knew how. Won't you please show me your ship? No one will know, so you need not fear Conall's wrath."

Lockridge looked as if Conall's wrath was the last thing on his mind. But then he shook his head. "Sorry, dryad. You might be telling the truth, in which case you've got my sympathy. Life stuck on land is no life at all. But you're not seeing my ship."

"You don't trust me," she accused.

He smiled. "No. And you shouldn't trust me either. Now go."

Gemma rode off, feeling even less certain about things than when she started her ride. When she returned to the house with a dog but no mushrooms, Fergus shook his head, but accepted that Chance would be joining the household.

"You should not have gone near the creature, Miss Gemma. He could have been sick or feral."

"Yes, that's just what—" She stopped herself before she mentioned Lockridge. Fergus was her friend, but she shouldn't admit that she was alone with a strange man, even for a moment. "I couldn't just leave him. Do you think he belongs to someone?"

"I don't know. He's healthy enough. A hunting breed. He might have been untrainable, though, so he was set loose."

"How horrible."

"The smarter thing would be to shoot him," Fergus said bluntly. "One doesn't risk diluted bloodlines that way."

"Fergus! How could you say that!"

"I didn't say *I'd* shoot him!" he protested. "Lord, girl, why do you think I refuse to raise dogs? A horse I'll shoot, if it comes to it. But that's to save it a painful death."

"Can we not talk about death?" she asked. "Chance needs to be cared for." And the dog was cared for, with a little nest set up in the stables and a showing of affection from Gemma.

"Be careful, miss," Fergus said. "You'll have that dog following you everywhere, and neither your aunt nor your uncle will want him in the house."

"Well, that's too bad," Gemma said. "I've little enough to my name. Why can't I have a companion?"

Chapter 6

~~~

AFTER SEEING GEMMA ON HER way, Logan didn't return to the *Mistral,* though he wanted to. Instead he went slowly back to the little town of Caithny. He didn't hurry. The countryside was too beautiful. Autumn was well advanced in the hills, turning trees to gold and honey in the mellow sunlight. He didn't have much experience of autumn, since he'd grown up near the tropics. He witnessed the season only a few times, and never in a countryside quite like this.

Fallen leaves crunched beneath his horse's hooves and the smell of damp earth mingled with the sharpness of the cool air, just tinged with the scent of saltwater. Logan could almost forget that he was here to spy on someone. He half wished he could just stay in the area for a while. He could learn a little more about Gemma Harrington.

Lord, she'd made an impression. Logan quickly turned his mind in another, less dangerous direction. The girl was not ripe for a seduction. If anything, he should make her into an ally, so he could find out what she knew. He was testing her to see if he could use her for her knowledge and her proximity to Conall Caithny.

Of course he was.

Logan laughed at himself. If his fellow agents could hear his thoughts, they'd mock him. He was here to solve a problem, not fall in love.

His steps took him to the Rose and Crown. There he found Jennie, who had a message for him.

"Munro came in, sir. He says you're to meet Caithny again tonight. Same time, at the castle."

"Thank you, Jennie."

She bobbed her head, and darted away, intent on other duties.

He found Tobias at the usual table. "So I got a message. I assume that means you spoke with Munro? He bought your story?" Logan and Toby were well aware that Caithny would try to get information out of the men working for Lockridge.

"Oh, no question," said Toby. "I had to get to my fifth ale before I could seem drunk enough to let him think he was getting answers out of me."

Logan laughed at the notion of Toby getting drunk off only five ales. "And what did you let slip?"

"Just what we agreed. He got me to admit that our cargo was rare and expensive. I then tried to cover it up, but I revealed that we transported spies and informants for a pretty penny…and all to the detriment of Britain. Munro gave Jennie the message then. He'll rush back to tell Caithny that you have no love for King George, but plenty of room in your ship."

"Good. I just need to get access to his contacts in France. Then we can shut down the whole operation."

Logan returned to Caithny castle that night. He hoped he'd see Gemma again, and in a place where he could get her alone for a moment.

He was lucky. She opened the door, looking as gorgeous as before, with those blue eyes looking boldly at him. This time though, there was no surprise in her tone. "Good evening, Mr Lockridge," she said formally. "Won't you follow me? Uncle Conall wants to speak with you."

"That's what I came for," he said.

Gemma glanced back down the hall, then said in a low tone, "Please don't tell him anything about us...meeting today."

"Wouldn't dream of it." Logan had no intention of telling Conall a thing, whether about Gemma or anything else. "Lead on, Miss Harrington."

He was shown to the same room. Conall was ensconced in his massive chair, just as before. This time, however, Logan went directly to the lesser chair opposite the man and sat down. He had wanted to provoke the man the first night. This time he aimed to appease him. Logan didn't look at Gemma again, even though she remained in the room this time. She sat down on a chair further away, looking wary.

"I've thought over your proposal, Lockridge." Conall spoke in an even tone, and his eyes bored into Logan's.

"And?"

"I find it has merit. A few short runs to negotiate the shipment of goods, and then we'll evaluate a longer partnership. I promise no more than that."

"That's more than enough," Logan said. He felt a little surge of triumph. He was in. He would complete the assignment. He knew it.

"We understand each other, then. So, to details. First you need to meet an important member of my operation."

Logan nodded expectantly. Of course a man like Caithny would have a second in command to direct things on the ground.

"Gemma," Caithny said, nodding to her.

Gemma stood up. But she did not go to fetch another man. She just walked to Caithny's side.

Logan looked at uncle and niece and back again, grasping the truth instantly. "A family business, I see." He hid his surprise, perhaps because he wasn't totally surprised. Something about Gemma's bold manner hinted at something like this.

"No objection?" Gemma asked, watching him carefully. There wasn't the slightest hint in her manner that she'd spoken with him earlier that day.

"Do you do your job well?" he returned.

"Uncle Conall wouldn't use me if I didn't."

"And what exactly does he use you for?" Logan asked.

"She's my eyes," Conall said. "She keeps lookout, sends signals, and alerts the men to the arrival of the law if they're fool enough to interfere. She also covers the men should a fight break out."

Now Logan was confused. "Covers them with what?"

"A gun, of course. She's an excellent shot," Conall said, a note of pride in his voice. "Aren't you, girl?"

"I am." She looked steadily at Logan as she said it, the blue gaze suddenly a little intimidating.

He believed her, but he didn't want to look too accepting. "I want a demonstration before I accept that assessment."

Gemma tilted her chin up defiantly. "Because I'm a woman?"

"Because I don't know you," he said evenly. But he certainly would like to. Gemma grew more intriguing every time he saw her.

"You'll take my word for it," Conall said, with iron in

his voice.

Logan shifted his attention back to the man. "No disrespect, but I won't. Everyone who works for me or with me has to be someone I can rely on, or there is no deal. I can afford to walk away from this arrangement. Can you?"

Conall's eyes flickered. "Fair enough."

"I can show you tomorrow." Gemma spoke again. "My shooting, that is."

"Why not tonight?" Logan asked.

Her expression grew even warier. "Because I'm not going to stroll out into the woods with you alone in the middle of the night, Mr Lockridge."

"I wouldn't dare suggest it, Miss Harrington. Your uncle should come along."

"We'll handle it another day," said Caithny. "Trust me, she can shoot well in the dark, but you'll appreciate it more when you can actually see what she hits."

Conall sent Gemma out of the room then, and set to discussing some of the specifics of the next run with Logan. No matter how subtly Logan plied him, Caithny was very careful to not say what he was shipping.

Logan couldn't be sure if Caithny sent Gemma away because he didn't trust her, or if he simply wanted to keep her from Logan as much as possible. Either way, Logan wanted to get Gemma alone again as soon as he could. He had plenty of questions to ask.

When he left the castle, he got his chance. Gemma was waiting near the front door to see him out.

"Meet me tomorrow," Logan said as he was about to leave. "Where we found Chance. I want to see you shoot. And without him hovering over you. If you can't work alone, you're not much use."

"I don't need a shepherd during a run," Gemma said, offended. She glanced back toward the door to Caithny's lair, then nodded once. "Eight in the morning," she said quietly.

He grinned. "I can't wait, dryad."

Chapter 7

≋

GEMMA KEPT HER WORD, THOUGH she knew it was rash to do so. She ought to tell Uncle Conall where she was going at the very least. But Conall left at dawn, and Gemma felt a thrill at the idea of doing something just because *she* wanted to. She saddled up Hector, and this time she brought Chance. After a night of rest and a belly full of food, the dog was already eager to go.

Fergus noticed the additional ammunition she carried in her saddlebag. "Expecting trouble, girl?"

Gemma laughed. "No. But I want to keep in practice."

"Another run is coming up, then," Fergus said. "And you'll be participating again." His demeanor didn't hint at whether he approved or not, but she guessed his opinion.

"Whether I join or not, the run will happen. If I can keep a few people safe, shouldn't I?"

"Poor logic, girl. It's your own safety you should be thinking of."

"And I am," she said, undaunted. "Who will hurt me if I'm armed?"

"Tell that to any dead soldier on a battlefield." He shook his head. "Go. And be careful."

She rode, though not too fast, so that Chance could

keep up. When she got to the clearing, Lockridge was waiting.

"Good morning, dryad. You didn't bring a chaperone."

"Chance's my chaperone." She reached down to pat the horse's neck. "And Hector here is not a creature to upset. I'm not worried about *you*, sir. I can take care of myself."

"So you say." He smiled, not at all offended.

She found herself smiling back. "Now that I'm here, let's get to business. I'll show you I can shoot."

"Hitting a target in the daytime isn't the same as hitting a running body in the dark of night," he warned.

"I'm well aware of that," Gemma said. "And I wouldn't claim I'm skilled at something unless I truly was."

"I'm inclined to believe you," Logan said.

He helped her dismount. Gemma pulled a paper target from her saddlebag, showing it to Lockridge to prove it unmarked by any holes. She walked a fair distance and then pinned it to the trunk of a tree.

She returned to where Lockridge stood with Hector and got her pistol out, along with the necessary ammunition. "I can fire a rifle as well," she said. "That's what I usually use for covering runs. But this will serve for a demonstration."

"Demonstrate away, Miss Harrington."

"Stand back, and keep hold of Chance, will you? Hector won't spook at a shot, but I don't know about Chance."

Gemma turned her attention to the target. She loaded quickly, readied the charge, and aimed carefully. After taking a slow breath, she fired.

"Not bad," she said critically.

"You don't even know if you hit anything," Lockridge said.

"I did." But she didn't move. She took her second pistol, loaded and primed it. She aimed and shot. She smiled. "And again."

Lockridge said nothing. Perhaps he didn't believe her. Gemma shot half a dozen times before she stopped. In all, her demonstration took a couple of minutes. "During a run, I will fire to signal the men, or to head off…ah, curiosity from the law. I've never hit anyone to kill. Wounding is usually just as effective."

Lockridge raised an eyebrow at the coolness of her attitude. "I'm not the only ruthless character around here, it seems."

She put the pistols away. "Go fetch the target," she said. "If I go, you'll accuse me of poking holes in it after the fact."

He came back bearing a paper target with five bullet holes in it, four quite near the center. One must have gone wide of the mark.

"Well?" she asked.

"I'm impressed."

She liked the way he said it. "You should be."

He waved the target meaningfully. "What made you want to learn to shoot like this?"

"I was told my father was quite the marksman. I thought…" Gemma paused.

"Yes?" Lockridge prompted.

"I thought he might be proud of me, if I was as well." She was unaccountably a little shy in confessing that to a near stranger.

But Lockridge just nodded, accepting her logic. "You're an unusual young lady, Miss Harrington."

"My aunt wouldn't agree about that last part. She despairs of making me a lady."

"If it's any consolation, I think you make for a very intriguing lady," he said. Then he looked around. "Let's walk for a while. Tell me what it was like growing up around here."

So she did. He seemed interested, asking questions, making her laugh. Gemma scarcely realized how much time was passing. They walked through the woods, seemingly without aim. Lockridge took charge of Hector, and Chance trailed at Gemma's heels. With the deceptively warm sun and quiet sounds of the forest, it was easy to forget why they were together in the first place.

Gemma realized she was talking far more than he was. "Can you tell me about growing up on Bermuda? Isn't it hundreds of miles from anywhere?"

"That's one of the best parts about it," he said. "But it's not isolated, not in the sense you mean. The trade routes pass by, and they pick up all sorts of things. Fresh water, salt, other goods. St George's is a town of thousands of people."

"Is it full of palm trees?" Gemma had only the haziest idea of the tropics.

"You're thinking too far south," he said. "There are some. But it's pines I think of. My ship's masts are made of Bermuda pine."

"I still want to see your ship," she said, hoping that he'd feel differently today.

He didn't. "I still won't let you near her."

"Why not?" Gemma asked, with an unconscious pout. "I know how to keep a secret."

"Like the ones your uncle asks you to keep?"

She frowned, not liking the question. "What do you

mean?"

"Do you have ambitions to succeed your uncle in his smuggling empire?" Lockridge asked. "You'd make a beautiful pirate, no mistake—sailing to France with your fleet of illicit goods, hobnobbing with Napoleon…"

"Why would I help our enemy?" she asked, offended. "I'm British, and so are you!"

"Caithny doesn't appear to have the same scruples."

"He wouldn't do business with the French forces," she insisted. "Just ordinary people. They need certain goods that are scarce because of the war, just as we do."

"And who do you think benefits from smuggled goods that pass through French ports?" he said. "I know that quite a lot of Caithny's are sold directly to the French army."

She opened her mouth, but didn't say anything. Why would Conall do such a thing?

"Ah, dryad," he said, more gently. "The truth is a little ugly, isn't it?"

"Assuming what you say *is* the truth."

"It is. Perhaps that's why he didn't have you stay in the room last evening. He knows you wouldn't approve of all his activities."

"Well, I wouldn't!"

He leaned a little closer to her. "But he needs your sharp eyes, doesn't he? So he doesn't tell you."

"I don't believe you," Gemma insisted. "Aiding the French would make him a traitor."

"Treachery can be profitable."

Something in the way he said it struck her. It wasn't admiring. "What do you plan to do?" she asked.

"Be reasonable. I wouldn't tell you a thing about my own plans until I knew I could trust you."

"So you don't trust me, even a little?"

"Give me a reason to," he invited her. "Tell me something."

"I'm not a fool. You're not asking me all this because of idle curiosity. You have a goal. What is it? Are you hoping to cut Conall out of a trade? You want to know what you're up against?"

"Why would I admit such a thing to you?" he asked. "You'd run right back and tell him."

Gemma shook her head. "Conall can look after himself. He always has. I'll answer your questions…but not for free."

"I'm interested," he said.

"Ha! So you're *not* just an ordinary smuggler." Gemma felt triumphant at tricking him, even a little.

But he just smiled. "I'm not an ordinary anything, dryad."

"Are you working for someone?" she asked. "Did they put you up to this?"

"Knowing that won't help you in the slightest."

"Why are you here?" Gemma asked. His probing questions and slippery answers made her frustrated, and her hands curled into fists. "You have a ship. You can go anywhere."

There was a new look on his face, as if he saw something he recognized. "True. I've always had a horizon to look at. Don't care much for these trees, even though I know the sea's just over there." He watched her carefully, then took a step toward her. "Is that the real reason you want to see my ship?"

"Yes!" Gemma said. "Won't you *please* show me?"

He laughed a little at her vehemence, but it was a kind laugh. "All right. Not today, though. I've places to be, and

I've already spent more time with you than I expected."

"Tomorrow," she said. "You promise?"

He nodded. "It's in a cove not that far away. Ride Hector down to the oak grove about an hour after noon. And you'll have to come alone, you understand," he added.

That warning brought her up short. Aboard a ship with an unknown smuggler? She ought to be wary. Logic told her to reconsider, but something in his face told her to take a chance.

She bit her lip, considering. "I do want to see your ship," she said finally. "And I'm not scared of you."

"Then come tomorrow. I'll take you to my lady."

"Lady? Why do you call it a lady?"

"All ships are women. Didn't you know?"

She shook her head. "Why?"

"Because ships and women are both temperamental, and hard to master, and beautiful."

Chapter 8

☰

THE NEXT DAY, GEMMA RODE alone to where she was to meet Lockridge. She debated all night whether to go or not. She wasn't an idiot, and there were several excellent reasons for her to avoid all danger by staying well away from Lockridge.

But she couldn't stop thinking of the ship. Ever since Gemma's parents died at sea and Conall took her in hand, she wasn't allowed near a ship. And that was despite the fact that her father made his fortune in shipping. Neither Conall nor Maura would talk about her parents, and Gemma was more curious about their silence every year. And one sure way to make Gemma want something was to tell her she couldn't have it.

So, really, it was inevitable that she would take Lockridge up on his offer.

When she rode to the meeting place, she found him waiting.

He watched her approach with a warm, pleased smile. "Good afternoon, dryad."

"Why do you call me that?" she asked, curious.

"You look like you belong to these woods," he explained.

"Well, I don't. I'm only half Scottish, you know."

"The other half dryad, I'm sure," he said.

"The other half is English," she retorted. Then she got to the more important point. "So you're taking me to your ship."

"I am. But there's a catch."

"What?" she asked.

He held up a piece of cloth. "Blindfold."

"You're joking."

"Not a bit." He nodded to the horse. "And he must stay here. I know how smart horses are. If I lead him there, he'll find it again no matter what."

"You're overly cautious. You don't have to be." But she tethered Hector to a nearby sapling, telling the horse she'd return soon.

"I'm indulging your wish to see a ship up close, because that's a daft thing to lie about, and no one should go about life without being aboard a ship," he said. "But I don't trust you entirely, you being the lovely niece of Conall Caithny and all. So you allow me to lead you there blindfolded, or you go back home."

Gemma looked at the blindfold, than at Lockridge. "This isn't some sort of trick?"

"You can trust me, dryad," he said, "though I admit you've no reason to."

"Nevertheless, I do. You can blindfold me."

He stepped up to her. "No peeking now." He tied the fabric around her head, and Gemma's world darkened.

But then he took her hands in his. "Not too tight?" he asked. His hands were rough, calloused, but warm.

"No."

"Can you see anything?" he asked.

"No."

"Are you sure? How many fingers am I holding up?"

She smiled. "None. I have your hands."

He laughed. "So you do. Let's go." He led her for-ward. Gemma wasn't sure if he chose a direct path, but she soon heard waves very close by. She came to a stop on his orders, and then the blindfold was pulled away.

She blinked. Pine trees surrounded the place, leaving only a few feet of pebbly beach around the shore. The water lapped several feet away. Anchored in the center of that narrow, hidden cove was a ship. The hull was one sleek curve of dark wood, and the masts held tightly bound sails.

"There's the *Mistral*," Logan said, pride in his voice.

"She's beautiful. But how do we get out there?"

He pointed to a rowboat. Within minutes, he got the little boat to the *Mistral*'s side, and Gemma climbed up a ladder to the deck. He followed after securing the rowboat to the side.

On deck, she looked around. "Is it safe to leave this ship unguarded?"

"I ordered the usual guards to take a break for an hour or two. I told them it was a personal matter. As you noted yesterday, it wouldn't do for anyone to know we're alone here."

Gemma pursed her lips. Certainly, she wasn't acting like a lady, not by going alone with a strange man to a place where she couldn't escape other than by jumping overboard. Aunt Maura would have a fit if she knew what Gemma had done. And she had no reason to trust Lock-ridge, other than her gut feeling.

"You think I'm being naive, don't you?" she asked. "Or stupid."

"Neither," Lockridge said. "You're correcting a gap in

your education. Not ever being on a ship is like not ever seeing the sky. What's the point of living if you don't know what it's like? Now, you wanted to meet my lady."

Starting on the deck, he told her about the ship's history, how he built it back in Bermuda, and how sharp and fast she was on the water. "No sailing today, but someday." He smiled at her. "You haven't truly met the *Mistral* until you've seen all her sails unfurled and full of wind. Until then, she's fast asleep."

Gemma was delighted at his honest pride in his ship. "You keep talking about her as if she's a person."

"She is to me. My lady."

"You love her," Gemma said suddenly, her stomach fluttering at the thought.

"I do," he said, looking around the ship. "Like she's a part of me."

Gemma looked over the side rail at the clear water. She could see the bottom, farther below than she would have expected. "It's deep here, for being so close to the shore."

"Can you swim?" he asked, moving next to her. In the surprising heat of the autumn day, he'd rolled his sleeve halfway up, and she watched his bare forearms as he leaned forward on the rail.

"Yes. Everyone expected me to be afraid of the sea, since my parents drowned. But I never was, even when I was young. And should I ever be on a ship that's sinking, I want to know how to *try* to swim ashore. I thought I owed my parents that." Gemma looked over at him. "Does that make sense?"

His eyes looked brighter on the ship, possibly because all the sunlight illuminated his face. She forgot what she was saying for a moment.

"It makes sense to me," he said finally. "How long ago did they die?"

"When I was seven, so thirteen years ago now." Gemma blinked, trying to recall their faces. "Aunt Maura has one picture of them. It was painted just after their wedding. But I don't remember much beyond that. Just a few things. My mother giving me a special cake for my seventh birthday. My father coming home in the evenings, asking me what I learned that day."

"What did he do?"

"I'm not entirely sure. Something with shipping." She shrugged. "Aunt Maura doesn't like to talk about them. And Uncle Conall never does. I don't think they got along well."

"But they made Caithny your guardian. Why not leave you with your father's people?"

"I don't know. I think he didn't have much family— my father, that is. And Mama thought London might have a corrupting influence on a young girl." Gemma suddenly burst out laughing. "And look at me now. Sneaking away from my home, and consorting with a man I hardly know."

He tipped his head toward the aft deck. "You haven't even seen the rest of the *Mistral*, dryad. Let's go before you have to ride home."

He led her through a door and into the interior of the ship. It seemed deserted, though he said the ship could accommodate a crew of up to ten. After a moment's consideration, he showed her the *Mistral*'s more esoteric features—a few secret compartments and hidden doors. Some could hide only the smallest of packages, and others could hold something as large as a person. She was impressed, and rather flattered that he showed her.

One compartment wasn't hidden nearly as well as the rest. "You can see the seam once the door is closed," Gemma said.

"You're not wrong," Lockridge said, though with pride. "No one would believe a smuggler's ship with no hiding places, so I put a couple in that exist solely to be discovered. The searchers—Customs or otherwise—feel triumphant and stop looking, and my real cargo continues safely to its destination."

"You think further than most men," Gemma said.

"Which is why I've got as far as I have." He took her hand. "Come, there's more to see, if you're daring."

He led her to the captain's quarters, his personal domain. The cabin was small, of course, in keeping with the ship's design. But it was beautifully made. The wood panels were carved with rustic but intricate patterns, and a few maps hung on the walls. The large furniture—a heavy table and a chest of drawers—was all bolted to the floor. An unlit lantern swung gently from the beam above, and a large window at the back let in light, though the glass panes were milky and bubbled, so one couldn't see much detail. This was the best location on the ship, naturally. A curtain was pulled over a place in the wall that she guessed hid a sort of bed. Everything was well-ordered and well-kept, and not made for show.

Gemma looked around. "It's beautiful, actually. I like it."

"So do I. But then, it's my home." He put one hand on a carved portion of the wall, and said in quieter, almost melancholy tone, "I know it better than my own home, now."

"Did you do these carvings?" she asked.

"Mmm. There's always a risk of the wind dying. Then

you're just killing time, with wood all round and a knife in your pocket, and nothing else to be done."

"You're not a bit like I thought you'd be," Gemma said suddenly.

He turned to her, his eyes searching. "What did you expect?"

"I don't know," she demurred.

He stepped a little closer to her. "You expected a rough, rude, greedy bastard who didn't think beyond the next haul."

"Something like that," she admitted, feeling a bit ashamed. "I'm used to that sort of man. I know how to deal with them, which is to say I avoid them."

"That's what you should do. That sort of man is dangerous, especially for a woman like you."

"Like me?"

"Beautiful. Curious. Bold. A little too eager to test the limits."

"That's what you think of me?" she asked.

"That's exactly what you've shown me. Am I wrong?"

"I...I suppose not." She stepped back, edging up against the carved cabin wall.

"Now, since we're here, tell me what you think of me?" he asked, even as he pressed her against the wall with his very presence. He didn't touch her. Not yet. "You think me dangerous?"

"I know you are," she whispered, staring into his eyes.

"You're right." He touched her neck with one finger, drawing a line from her collarbone to her jaw.

Gemma shuddered at the unexpected frisson. "Please, Mr Lockridge..."

"My given name's Logan," he said abruptly. "Call me so."

"We're not close enough acquaintances for that."

"I could tolerate a closer acquaintance, Miss Harrington," he said.

His tone made her an interesting sort of nervous, but she said, "You're too clever to muck up a deal with Conall on my account."

"So you know all about me, then?"

"You're years younger than the others I've seen work with my uncle. You have your own ship and a crew to follow you. One doesn't get that by being a fool."

"I've got where I am because I know that I have to take what I want. No one is going to just give it to me."

"Well, you can't take me," she snapped, suddenly feeling more like herself. "I'm not a thing for the taking."

Logan shook his head. "I never said you were."

"You look like you were thinking of taking something from me."

"Actually," he said. "I was thinking of giving you a kiss."

"Oh." Gemma stilled. "That I'd permit."

"I'm glad to hear it." He moved forward and kissed her. Not roughly, but the shock of the sensation was enough to make her gasp. Then Gemma leaned into the kiss, her senses awakened and eager. She'd always been curious about forbidden things, and this forbidden thing was delicious. Logan wrapped his arms around her, pulling her closer to him, bringing her into a circle of heat. After a moment he ended the kiss, and she took an unsteady breath.

"Dryad," he asked quietly. "Why did you come here today?"

"To see the ship," she said honestly. "Though now that we're here, I find I want to correct another gap in my education."

"On what subject?" he asked.

It was time to show Logan she wasn't quite as naive as he seemed to think. "Teach me to kiss. That's a subject that seems to interest you. And I'm certainly interested now."

Logan leaned back, putting his hands on her shoulders. "Why should I teach you anything?"

"Because you want to. I may not know much, but I can tell *that*," she said, meeting his gaze. "Besides, it's maddening to know there's something I don't know. Does that make sense?"

"A little," he said, as if trying not to laugh.

"Anyway, you should show me how to kiss properly."

Logan stared at her, as if considering a wholly new creature. "Properly. Maybe not the word I'd choose," he said, bringing his mouth back to hers.

Gemma felt a shiver roll over her, the sort of shiver that left her skin awake and waiting all over her body, not merely her mouth. His lips were warm on hers, and he made her want to bend toward him, erasing the gap between their bodies.

She did just that, putting her arms around his shoulders and drawing him closer. "I like what you're doing," she said simply. "What should I do?"

"To begin with, keep telling me what you like." He smiled at her in a way that made her want to melt.

He kissed her again. This time he tasted her lips with his tongue. She opened her mouth to say how much she liked it, but before she could say a word, he took the opportunity to dart inside her mouth. Gemma's fingers curled up, digging into his shoulders. "Oh, I like that," she whispered. "Do you?"

Logan nodded, then moved so he could kiss her neck. "The next lesson is that one can be kissed anywhere." Keeping one arm around her shoulder, he laid a series of light kisses down her neck, each one making her shiver a little.

"I like that too," she said. "I think I should try."

She turned her head so her lips touched the bare skin of his inner forearm. It was easy to kiss his skin up to the elbow, and she even licked him out of curiosity. "You taste like salt," she said.

"Dryad." Logan's voice had a new tone, one that made her look up to catch his gaze. She realized exactly how close they were. Her breasts were pressed against him, and his legs were pressed against hers. She shifted slightly, drawing a hiss from him.

"I think that's enough for today," he said. There was a warning in his words.

"Are you sure?" she asked. How much time had passed since they went below deck?

"Sadly, yes," he said. He kissed her once more before she could respond. "You're a little too quick a learner, and I'm feeling less civilized by the second."

Gemma was enjoying the moment too much to let it go. "What would happen if I stayed?"

"You'd be in that bed long past your bedtime."

She took a ragged breath. "Oh. I…I don't think that's a good idea."

"Sounding like a very good idea to me, which is exactly why you're leaving. Now." He stepped away with obvious reluctance. "I'd like to end this afternoon with your good opinion."

"I have a good opinion of your kiss," she said, with a laugh. It was absolutely true, and Gemma rarely saw reason to lie about things.

"You're either a natural flirt or you're looking for trouble," Logan said. But then he stood up straighter. His demeanor changed, and he looked as he had the first night, calm and cool.

Evidently over his desire to keep her on the ship, Logan led Gemma back to the deck. He sent her down the ladder and into the little boat, then rowed ashore. He didn't speak much, and his expression was unreadable.

"Did I make you angry?" Gemma asked, contrite. She never intended to end up in his arms, and certainly not so…enthusiastically. What had come over her?

"No," he said. "But I'll not do it again."

"Kiss me?"

"Be alone with you."

"You were very gallant."

"Oh, was I?" He smiled at last, though with a bitter edge. "You put yourself in fate's hands, dryad."

Gemma glanced away from him, aware that he was absolutely correct. She looked over the water instead. "We're all in fate's hands, whether we admit it or not. But I think you proved yourself to be a gentleman."

"This time," he said. The rowboat scraped against the bottom, startling them both. He got out and hauled the boat up so Gemma could step ashore without getting wet.

She did so, and then waited expectantly. "Will you blindfold me again?"

"Do you know where you are?" he asked.

She paused, then nodded. "I know this cove," she admitted. "But I promise not to tell."

He gave a rueful laugh. "Well, serves me right for thinking I could fool a native. Let's go back to your horse. It's not far."

They returned to Hector, and she mounted up.

Looking down at Logan, she said, in all seriousness, "Thank you for introducing me to your lady today. I think she's beautiful."

"It was a pleasure." He gave her a smile in return that she'd never seen before, young and open and kind. "Someday you should see her sail." His eyes seemed to burn with emotion.

"Someday," Gemma agreed. Then, before she promised Logan something terribly bold, she turned Hector around and rode away. Her heart was beating fast, and she could barely stop from singing back to the birds in the trees.

Chapter 9

≋

LOGAN TRIED NOT TO BE charmed by Gemma's last words, but he was all the same. She could have allowed him anything in the cabin, but it wouldn't have undone him like referring to the *Mistral* as his lady. He didn't know how she understood, but she did.

Every time he saw her, he liked her more. And that was dangerous. Logan had no idea what to do about Gemma. He alternately believed her and doubted her. Perhaps she was innocent, but Conall Caithny wasn't. He might well have thrown Gemma in his path to see how Logan would react. He couldn't trust anything. He didn't play fair as a spy. He should expect Caithny to be just as ruthless.

Logan walked the narrow trails of the woods for a good long while, then sat down on a stone to brood. This was growing far more complex than he imagined it could. It was not the assignment itself which had gotten complicated. It was the presence of Gemma. He wished he could discuss the developments with someone—he wanted to talk with Sophie.

Sophie would know exactly what to do about Gemma. She was also a sign of the Zodiac, and during his training, Sophie taught him several skills. She also took him aside one day, and said, "How much experience have you got with women? Talking to them, that is?"

After getting the honest answer out of him—which was that he generally thought of women as either potential wives to avoid or potential conquests to enjoy, she rolled her eyes. "You'll never get anywhere. Listen."

She gave him a few pointers on how to read and interrogate women, assuring him that it required far different techniques than those for dealing with other men. Sophie was probably responsible for half his successful assignments, considering just how often he needed to talk with —not seduce—a woman during his work. So of course he listened to every word she had to say.

And Sophie would say he should not have taken Gemma aboard the *Mistral*. He should not have kissed her and he surely should not have told her that he wanted to tumble her right into bed.

But Lord, it was nearly worth it. Her delight with the ship, her unguarded answers to his questions, and then her lovely and warm response to him in the cabin. Was she even real? A woman who lived by the sea but who'd never been on a ship?

Logan had thought he knew what he was doing—he pried a few facts and secrets out of her in the beginning. But by the time she kissed him in the cabin, he wasn't subtly drawing out information. He was losing his mind. Gemma was the most potent blend of innocence and daring that he'd ever encountered. He was already trying to think of a way to see her again.

Logan breathed deeply, and tried to calm down. Aries

would have his head if he fouled this assignment up. He had to take stock of the situation, assess his options, and proceed calmly. He couldn't talk to anyone from the Zodiac, but he had another person to trust. Tobias. Logan could rely on him for both discretion and honesty. Logan trusted Tobias with his life, and had done so for the past fifteen years.

Considering where he grew up and what his family did, it was no surprise that Logan was shipboard most of his life. He ran about the dry docks where his family built new ships, using the sturdy Bermuda pines for masts and decking and the hull. The smell of fresh cut wood was the smell of his childhood.

When he grew a little older, he joined the crew of the ship *Alliance* so he could learn the family business first hand. He was invaluable on short runs between islands, with his sharp eyes and excellent memory. He could recall where the safe coves were and where the shoals lay... even without a map. He watched and learned how the crews worked together, how the ship required constant attention to ensure she stayed seaworthy. No one paid him much mind. Logan was just like any other little boy.

But when the *Alliance* sailed on a longer journey across the Atlantic, someone did notice Logan. One of the sailors always seemed to be watching the boy. One night, he asked Logan if he'd ever got drunk. Logan hadn't, so the sailor plied the boy with rum until he was giggly, then woozy, then sick. The man took him aside, out of view of anyone else, and told him to vomit over the rail. Logan did, and passed out soon after.

He awoke much later. His pants were pulled up oddly, and he was in pain. His whole body ached and complained. His head was pounding in the aftermath of the rum, and he had a nightmare involving some violence he didn't have a name for. All he knew was that it left him with a dread he couldn't shake.

The whole next day, he stumbled through his chores, still not sure what happened. He resolved, though, to never drink a sip of rum again. The stuff was clearly bad for him.

But when he went down into the cargo hold to bring up some food for the galley, he found the same sailor waiting for him.

"Not much time today," he said. "So you'll have to do without the rum."

He grabbed Logan and clapped a hand over the boy's mouth. Logan knew his nightmare wasn't a nightmare at all. It was a memory. But now he had a much clearer picture of what happened, because it was happening again. The man was fast, but that didn't lessen the pain, or the confusion or shame. Logan cried when he was finally released. He crawled away, as if that would help.

The sailor just gave a low laugh. "Get used to it, boy. It'll be three weeks before we see land again. And as long as there's no girls on board, you'll do."

Logan tried to speak, but choked on vomit instead.

"And don't even think about saying a word to anyone, boy. I'll bleed you dry if you do. Then I'll feed you to the fish."

He left with the promise that he'd find Logan again, whenever he wanted. Logan wanted to die. He found a bottle of rum in a nearby crate, and drank it till he got sick again. It didn't take long. He shook with fear and hate the whole time.

"Logan?" a new voice called. "Where are you, lad? I sent you down for potatoes and you never…"

The galley cook, Tobias, appeared around a stack of barrels. He took in Logan's appearance and the bottle. He frowned. "Didn't think you had a taste for rum yet."

"I hate it," Logan hissed.

Toby sat down beside Logan and took the bottle out of his hand. He took a swig of what was left. "Aye, it's a demon. If you hate it, why are you down here drinking it?"

"I want to learn how to use a knife," Logan said then. He couldn't tell the cook the truth. It was too awful. But the thought of being found again by that sailor made him shake.

"To cut up potatoes?" Tobias asked.

"Potatoes. Sure."

The cook took another, more thoughtful sip. "Suppose it's never a bad thing to learn how to use a blade. You can slice a potato. Or a man, should you find yourself in a nasty situation."

"Can you teach me?"

"I could. Learn a lot from a ship's cook, you know. I've all sorts of skills, not just cooking."

"When can you teach me? When can we start?"

"We start the moment after you tell me who your first target will be."

Logan shook his head, dropping his gaze to the planking. "Can't."

"Learning to fight with a knife takes time. If you want to do it well. Otherwise, your opponent will just snatch it right out of your hand, and then where will you be? Not only will he have your weapon, he'll know you want to kill him."

"I can learn fast."

"Fast is a week or two. I could teach you for a little

while every day."

"A week? That's too long," Logan said, shuddering.

"Thought it might be. So tell me. Who do you need to fight, and why?"

Logan remembered the other man's threat. "I can't."

"I'm a bit older than you, lad. You can tell me, and I won't be surprised."

"I can't."

"You know we won't see the coast for another three weeks? And that's not even counting the leg back."

Logan buried his face in his arms, crouching into a ball until he couldn't see anything but the fabric of his sleeves, right there in front of his eyes.

"Hey now," Toby said awkwardly, putting a hand on Logan's thin shoulders. "We'll make it right. Or at least, we'll make it over. I can keep a secret. Come, lad. Tell me the name."

Logan took a few deep breaths, then whispered the name. The cook just nodded grimly, unsurprised by the revelation. "So that's how it is. Well, you lay low and avoid him till dinner tomorrow. You can hide in the galley if you like—I'll give you chores and no one will question it. But you leave him to me. I know how to deal with scum like that."

Toby wasn't lying. He kept an eye on Logan all the next day. After dinner, he muttered the plan to him. Logan obeyed Toby's instructions, and allowed the sailor to find him on the aft deck, well after the sky had gone dark. Crates of tied-down cargo and spare rope were coiled up nearby, blocking the view from the main deck.

The sailor was already half drunk when he saw Logan alone by the rail.

"Made it easy, did you," he growled.

"Stay away from me," Logan warned him.

The man grinned, showing yellowed teeth. "Or you'll do what, little boy?"

Logan shook his head. "I can't do anything."

"That's right." He loomed over young Logan, who could smell the sick scent of rum on his breath.

Before he could touch Logan, though, Toby rushed out of the spot where he was hiding. He seized the sailor and with one swift move slit his throat with a cooking knife.

Logan was astonished at the speed of the act. He just managed to jump aside as Toby pushed the dying man toward the rail and then over it. He hadn't even had time to make a sound. Toby was that fast.

The cook watched calmly as the dark waters swallowed up the sailor's body, his breathing barely faster than normal. "Now, lad. Seems to me we've both learned a bit about each other's nature. We've both got a secret to keep for the other. Way I see it, that means we're allies. Am I right?"

"Yes, sir."

"Don't sir me. I'm just a cook. Tell me, lad. What are we?"

"Allies."

Toby then pulled out his little pocket knife, and made a cut in his thumb. Logan held out his hand, knowing the ritual already. He flinched a bit when the blade bit his flesh, but when Toby pressed their thumbs together, the pain evaporated with his words. "Not just allies. Blood brothers. Yeah? We watch each other's backs."

"Yes," Logan swore. "And you'll teach me to fight with a knife."

"And you'll help me out in the galley." The cook put away the knife, an easy grin spreading across his face.

"Let's get on with it, lad."

No one paid much mind when the sailor was reported missing. These things happened. And he wasn't well-liked by the others, so few efforts were made to find out more than the obvious conclusion: he drank too much and went overboard at night.

From that moment on, Logan and Tobias were allies. Logan shadowed him on board ship. He learned everything. And as he got older and gained more responsibility, he brought Tobias up along with him, until the day he captained his own ship and needed a first mate. Who else would he trust in the role?

They were both already used to slightly shady business deals and the occasional bit of occupational spying. Tobias wouldn't blink if Logan moved into spying with a bit more seriousness. When the Zodiac came knocking, Logan told them flat out that Toby was essential to his work. Logan did agree that certain details would be secret even from Toby, including the very name of Zodiac and Logan's code name. All Toby knew was that Logan did a little spying for the right side, which was all Toby needed to know.

As far as the matter of the sailor, Logan was eventually able to put the memory away. Toby told him it wasn't his fault. If he'd been a girl in a town when the sailor happened by, the outcome would have been the same. Toby said, "Some people just don't have souls inside. They take what they want no matter who it hurts."

Logan had been unlucky, and he got taken advantage of. But he resolved to never be taken advantage of again, and he never tolerated such behavior on his ships. He kept an eye out, and if he got word of one of his crew mistreating anyone—man or woman—in that way, he dealt with it swiftly and mercilessly.

Tobias supported him in that. He was never less than honest, so Logan asked his advice on other matters. Toby was twenty years older than Logan, and he just knew more about life.

When he reached the village of Caithny, Logan found his friend in the main room of the tavern, contemplating an amber-hued drink on the table.

"What's that?" Logan asked.

Toby said, "I ordered a whisky, and Jennie brought me this."

"It looks like a whisky." Logan shrugged.

"I already had one. It's better than whisky."

Logan asked, "You're sure you only had one?"

Jennie happened to walk by just then, and Logan asked her what Toby was drinking.

"Scotch, sir. It's made here."

"In town?"

"Well, no. But not far. Caithny used to have a distillery, but it got bought a few years ago, and now it doesn't make scotch any more."

"What does it make?" Toby asked. "Seems foolish to stop making this," and he held up the glass.

Jennie just shrugged. "Don't know. Some of the men and women work there, but they don't talk about their work. And it all gets exported."

"By Conall Caithny," Logan guessed.

Jennie glanced at him. "Well, yes, sir. Almost nothing goes into or out of town unless he's involved."

Logan nodded. Everything he learned seemed to bear that out. He requested another scotch for himself, and Jennie left to fetch it.

Logan sat down across from Toby. "I have a problem."

Toby looked up alertly. "What sort?"

"It involves a lady." Since Toby never met Gemma, Logan quickly outlined her relationship to Conall, and explained her role. "Doesn't it seem odd to you? Why would the man employ his ward in his business?"

"Sounds like she's a bit of a handful," Toby said, with a shrug. "An orphaned redhead? That's asking for trouble. She probably insisted on getting involved."

"Assuming, of course, she's telling the truth," said Logan. "She might be doing exactly what Caithny tells her to do."

"Do you believe her?"

Logan paused, contemplating. "I think so."

"Do you believe her because she's a pretty face?"

"She is that," Logan said, musingly. "But something tells me she's being honest…more or less."

"Why the hesitation?"

"Well, if she's telling the truth, her uncle keeps her close. No suitors, no being around men at all. But she's seen me three times without supervision. So she's capable of tricking someone. I'm just not sure who she's tricking."

"Women are complicated." Toby took a drink.

"Truly insightful," Logan said sarcastically. "No wonder I keep you around for counsel."

"You want counsel? Here it is. That girl's got you turned around. Stay away from her if you like the life you've got."

"What does that mean?"

"Don't play ignorant." Toby leaned in. "I've known you since long before you even knew what girls were. And I've never seen you talk like this."

"Please. I'm not in love with her."

"Not yet. But she's done something to you. The longer

you stick around, the more danger you're in."

"From her?"

Toby made a sweeping circle in the air with his empty glass. "From...all this. All your business. Just watch your back, Logan."

Chapter 10

〜〜〜

GEMMA SPENT A RESTLESS NIGHT. She stayed up well past two o' clock. Her mind was racing, and to even pretend to sleep would be absurd. She kept thinking of Logan. Not just his kiss, but his expression when he showed off his ship. No one who could be so proud and loving about a wooden ship could be evil at heart. Perhaps Logan was stuck in his life, like she was stuck at Caithny.

She finally went to bed when the candle guttered out. Her memories of the day began to meld into an abstraction that was both dreamy and carnal. She imagined the *Mistral* at full sail, without a shore in sight. And only Gemma and Logan were aboard, with no one to tell them what to do. She revisited the moment when he first kissed her, and dreamed about what would've happened if she refused to leave. What had he said? *You'd be in my bed long past your bedtime.* If that had been a warning, it didn't work. The words thrilled her to her core. In the darkness of her bedroom, she touched herself until she sighed into sleep. Just one more thing she'd been told never to do…and ignored.

The next morning, she felt calmer, but still rather bemused. Gemma went down to breakfast as soon as the sun brightened the day. She was surprised to find both Uncle Conall and Aunt Maura there. The two weren't speaking. That in itself wasn't surprising, of course. Maura staunchly avoided anything related to Conall's activities, and he in turn despised what he called her sanctimonious manner. The only topic they both discussed was Gemma, since both had firm—and conflicting—opinions about her future.

This morning, Maura sat at the table, primly buttering some thick and crusty bread. Conall stood at the head of the table, drinking his coffee without sitting down. In his other hand he held a folded up letter, the seal broken. His expression was worried and distant.

Gemma looked at them both, trying to decide if they were about to argue, or if they'd just finished.

"Good morning," she said neutrally.

"Good morning, dear," her aunt said, with a smile.

Conall grunted. "What are your plans today, Gemma girl?"

She shrugged. With Logan still on her mind, she unwisely indulged a whim for honesty. "I was thinking of running off and getting married, though I don't know if I should do it before or after lunch."

Her words dropped into a shocked, cold silence. Aunt Maura stared at her with wide eyes, and then put her butter knife down with a soft clink. Conall held frozen for half a moment, then slammed his cup down on the table, breaking it and spilling the remains of his drink.

"Uncle!" Gemma yelped. "You'll burn yourself!"

"Never mind me, girl." He stuffed the letter into his jacket pocket and advanced toward her. "What the devil are you talking about?"

Aunt Maura murmured, "Your language, Conall."

He whirled around to face his sister. "She's running away, and you're berating my language, sister? Do you find her defiance amusing?"

He took one step back toward Maura, his fist tightening.

Gemma moved even faster, pulling at his arm. "Don't you dare touch her!"

Conall shifted his attention to Gemma, his gaze furious and his breath fast. "You're going to get in my way, girl," he growled.

"Every time!" Gemma snapped back. She wasn't scared for herself, but the thought of Aunt Maura being hurt sickened her. "Your very own sister! What are you thinking?"

"Your fault, girl. Talking of running off with a man!"

Gemma put her hands on her hips. "I was joking. It was a joke."

"Damn poor joke, little girl. Don't you ever say such a thing again."

"Is marriage such a dire fate that you both avoided it?"

He glanced at Maura, but only said, "I am your guardian, Gemma. I'll say if and when and whom you'll marry."

"Only until my birthday," she said.

His eyes narrowed. "You fancy being locked up until your birthday? Because I have rooms in this castle for just that purpose. I'll throw you in the old barracks. They're still in perfectly good condition."

Gemma thought of the barracks, the long, low stone building near the outer wall. She grinned. "Even if you could lock the door, I'd get out of the windows in about one minute."

"Not after I put bars on them!"

"You wouldn't dare!"

"You've not got the slightest idea what I'd dare. Now you tell me the truth this moment. Have you met a man?"

She raised her chin. "I have met a man. More than one. It tends to happen when you invite them into the house and make *me* greet them."

"So this Lockridge has eyes for you," Conall said, his voice low. "I'll fix that."

Gemma didn't like the look on his face. She said hastily, "Now you're joking, Uncle. Him? Why would I marry a smuggler?"

"He finds you pretty," Conall said, musingly. "Admitted as much to me."

"I am pretty!" she said confidently. "But I'm not a fool."

Conall stared at her. Gemma kept her chin up and refused to look away. Lying didn't come naturally to her, but she didn't want Logan to fall afoul of Conall in the middle of a run.

"He's only been here twice," Conall said finally. "You've not met him elsewhere?"

"Of course not," she said, a bald-faced lie that sounded more sincere than she expected. "Aunt Maura has taught me that ladies never consort with strange men."

"So she listened to something you said, after all," Conall said, with a look toward his sister. "Perhaps you earned your keep."

"I did my duty to our family," Maura said softly, still not looking at him. "Someone has to look out for this child."

He sneered. "And you're a mighty protector!" He looked down at himself, as if just realizing he was covered in coffee. "God, I'm going to have to change before I go out, or I'll stink of coffee beans. Gemma, you behave yourself all day, mind. And don't even mention the word marriage."

"What about wedding?" she asked, with a wicked smile.

Conall glared at her, then suddenly burst out laughing. "You're a spitfire. *I* taught you that."

"Go change, Uncle," she said. "I'll clean up here." She bent to pick up the broken china.

Conall moved away, his mood restored. "That's a good girl. I'm off. I'll have words with you tonight, Gemma."

"I'll be here," she said.

He left, and Maura let out a long, thin sigh of relief. "Sweet heaven, child. You are provoking."

"It was just a joke," she repeated. "I wouldn't have said it if I knew he'd react like that. To think he'd raise a hand to you…" Gemma felt a little stab of fear. She hated the idea that her words might cause Aunt Maura to suffer.

"Was it a joke?" her aunt asked.

Gemma looked at her more closely. "Not you too. Who would I marry out here?"

"He mentioned a name. Lockridge."

"Just the latest smuggler come to do business," Gemma said, trying to forget how he kissed her.

"You're blushing," said Maura.

"I am not."

"Is he handsome?"

Handsome? He could melt ice just by smiling. Gemma paused, then said, "Well, yes."

"Has he proposed to you?"

"Certainly not! I met him four *days* ago, Aunt." She sat at the table, ready to eat.

"Would you accept a proposal from him?"

"I have no wish to marry! I never did!"

"Don't be daft. You've always dreamed of marriage. I remember well the stories you made up in the nursery, dressing up in your mother's best gown, and telling me how you would meet your husband."

"I was a girl, playing make believe. You probably told me too many fairy tales. I'm older now. I know better."

"To think a twenty year old who has lived in seclusion half her life would tell *me* the way of the world. Marriage is the natural state for a well-born lady. And despite your wild behavior you come from good stock. Don't forget your father was the son of a baronet! You ought to embrace your future, which does include marriage, though you may not accept it now."

"How can you speak with such authority on the matter?"

Maura put the teacup down. "I was married."

"You *were*?" said Gemma. She was so surprised by the revelation that she put her crumpet down, forgetting she was ravenous. "I never knew that."

"Conall doesn't like me to talk about it. It happened before you came to live at Caithny. I was married for three years. We never had children, though my husband and I both wanted them very much."

Gemma was still stunned by the news. "You were not married! Your name is Caithny!"

"Oh, I was Mrs Edward Douglas, and very happy to be so for those brief years. I went back to my maiden name when I moved here. It seemed safer."

"Safer how? Why should it matter?"

"I didn't want to make a fuss in the aftermath of my Ned's death."

"But how did he die?"

Maura paused, then decided it was useless to hold back anything at this point. "He worked as a Customs agent. One of the deputies. He was shot by a smuggler."

"Not one of Conall's gang?" Gemma asked, aghast.

"I could never be sure," said Maura. "All I knew is that he was killed at night, while in the process of interrupting a smuggling run. He was buried in the churchyard in the village—I still visit after church sometimes. When he died, I was given a small payment out of the fund reserved for widows and orphans of the law in the town. But that didn't last very long. So I accepted Conall's invitation to live here at the castle again."

"But how could you if…. What if *he* was responsible for your husband's death?"

"What should I have done?" Maura gave a sigh Gemma never heard before. "Should I have demanded an investigation of the magistrate who is in Conall's pocket? You don't suppose it's just luck that Conall never attracts the law. He pays for the privilege."

"There must have been something to do."

"For a woman with no money and no man? No, my choices were to slowly starve or join the poorhouse, or come to live with Conall. I knew what I would do. I was living here a year when your parents came to visit us and leave you here before their voyage. After they passed, I felt I could be of some use, if I could help raise my sister's child."

"And you did!" said Gemma, smiling.

"Well, I tried. You were always a wild girl, and much more so after the death of your parents. I did my best to instill a love of God in you, and to keep you from the worst wickedness. But living in a place like this, with a man like my brother…you are surrounded by vice. It's no wonder you have joined in Conall's schemes."

"I haven't joined in them. I just…" She trailed off.

"I know what you do. You scout out the caves. You make trips into town to visit the shopkeepers and citizens, finding out what they desire for the next shipment. And you work at night! Keeping lookout while the men work on the shore. That's the most dangerous of all, Gemma. You're in peril of being hurt, or captured, or running afoul of one of the men."

"Conall would never allow that."

"It's not always a matter of what he'd allow. It only takes a moment. You let down your guard, all eyes are on the ship…"

"I keep my pistols about me for a reason, Aunt Maura."

"Now that's supposed to make me feel better!" she cried. "I despair of your ever becoming a lady."

"What need have I to be a lady? I'm stuck here. No one sees me."

"You will go to London when you achieve your majority. You will get your inheritance and you can choose a different life. But you can't go traipsing into the city dressed as a tatterdemalion and brandishing pistols! You must be civilized. You must behave according to convention."

"Well, we'll see if Conall locks me in a tower first," Gemma grumbled.

"You must not let that happen. Don't see this Lockridge again, Gemma, not for a moment. And don't mention his name to Conall. The sooner he forgets that conversation, the better."

"Yes, Aunt."

"Four days," her aunt said then.

"What?"

"You met him four days ago."

"Yes. What of it?"

"When I met my Ned, it only took two days for me to know he was the one I wanted."

"How did you know?"

Maura smiled softly, her eyes on a distant past. "Perhaps I'll tell you some day, dear."

* * * *

Later that day, Gemma passed her uncle's office door, but then her steps slowed. Conall was gone. If she wanted to peek inside, there was no better time, and Logan's hints about who Conall was shipping to haunted her. Conall kept the door locked, of course. But Gemma could get the spare key within moments. He locked it to demonstrate that it was private; he didn't expect that anyone would ever actually try to break in.

He also didn't expect Gemma to defy him. Armed with the proper key, she entered easily. It was not a tidy room, and there were not too many obvious places to look for…well, whatever she was looking for. Would it be so bad if Gemma knew exactly what she was helping to move? Why should Conall keep it hidden, if he had nothing to hide?

On the other hand, it was just as likely that he considered her a child not worth telling. She was still annoyed by their conversation that morning. Conall's flat out resistance to the idea of her getting married or even leaving Caithny was deeply irritating.

What was worse was hearing her aunt's revelation

about her marriage and widowhood. If Conall was responsible, he didn't deserve *any* loyalty. With all that in mind, Gemma decided she was entitled to a little information. Maybe she would share it with Logan, and maybe she wouldn't. But she'd find it all the same.

Conall kept few records. Part of it was mistrust, but also simply because he was a man who relied on rote memory. So there were far fewer papers about than one would expect, considering the extent of the operation Conall ran.

Gemma opened a few envelopes and carefully sorted through the papers she found, making sure to keep everything in order. Conall's handwriting was cramped and cryptic, but Gemma knew it well enough to read the contents.

Most of the papers were unenlightening. Accounts of expenses, a few lists of the men who worked for Conall, the lists of the various shopkeepers who regularly bought his contraband liquor and such. The most recent cargo appeared to be very ordinary things—hardly worth smuggling at all. She saw line items for tin, glass, produce, and some grains. How dull. Perhaps the prices of those things was higher than expected. But who smuggled apples? She'd be embarrassed to be caught with such a cargo.

It was also reassuring. Logan implied that Conall was shipping guns to the French. Gemma refused to believe it, and these ledgers proved her right. Conall was not a traitor. Of course he couldn't be! Gemma smiled to herself. She'd enjoy getting an apology from Logan when she told him.

All at once, she remembered the letter Conall had that morning. She'd seen very similar letters many times before, but it never occurred to her to wonder about them.

He had a tendency to stuff them into pockets or pouches as he went about his business. Unless he moved them to a special place, it was likely they ended up here.

With an idea of what she was looking for, she searched for letters with the same appearance. She found several, all bound together with string. She opened the pack hastily and unfolded the letters. The contents were just what she feared she'd find. The letters were from a contact in France. She squinted at the handwriting—the author was not at home in English—and read the name of a few ships, a name of what must be a small port on the coast of France, and finally the name of the sender. Lisle. Gemma repeated it under her breath. She found some scratch paper and copied all the names down. She wouldn't remember them, and it would never do to take the original letters.

Gemma stuffed the list into the pocket of her skirt, folded the letters back up, and put the bundle back. It looked almost the same as before, and Conall shouldn't notice any change.

She peeped out into the corridor again. All was quiet. Should she risk a longer look? Of course she should. Gemma was getting into the game, and after learning about the French contact, she wanted to know all of Conall's secrets.

She found a few ledger books, and added some num-bers up in her head. Conall did quite well for himself over the years. Smuggling was even more profitable that she guessed.

But when she pulled out the most recent ledger book, Gemma was surprised to see that Conall was having fi-nancial difficulties at the moment. The loss of a few ships over the past year, combined with an increase in payments to the corrupt law officials, meant Conall was running very low on funds.

Gemma flipped forward a few pages, and saw a large influx of money, but with a notation beside it. Conall had to pay it back. He was not merely broke, he was in debt.

She put the book back on the shelf, not knowing what to think. She always thought Conall was a good businessman, even if he chose a shady business. It never occurred to her that he might be in difficulty. That was not the sort of information Logan suggested he was after, and she wasn't sure she'd want to tell him.

A sound outside made her look up. If Conall caught her in the office, she'd be locked up in her room for the next three months. Gemma crept to the door, listening. Nothing.

Taking a deep breath, she eased it open.

"Gemma!" Aunt Maura was standing at the far end of the hall.

She jumped. "You startled me, Aunt!"

"What were you doing in Conall's office?"

"Um, he wanted me to file something for him. So he didn't forget. Nothing important."

Maura watched her carefully. "I thought he always kept the room locked tight."

"Yes," Gemma agreed. She held the key up. "So I should lock it right back up. Thank you for reminding me."

Maura sighed. "He trusts you with the key, does he? You're in deeper than I feared."

Gemma gave her aunt a weak smile. "Just filing a paper. Not so deep, I promise."

She was getting in deep, but not with Conall's business. She was falling for Logan, and the fact that she was willing to tell him a few names was proof. Had a few kisses turned her around so completely? No wonder she had been forbidden from men. They were more dangerous than she thought.

Chapter 11

≋

AT THE DOCKS WHERE CONALL conducted some of his slightly more legitimate business, Logan stood in a quiet spot, surveying the shore and the water. He'd already snuck into the building here over the last couple of nights, searching for the arms Conall must be storing before the run. But he found nothing, which frustrated the hell out of him. He saw dozens of crates filled with quite boring, legal items like glass jars and bolts of wool. But he couldn't find a single crate containing any sort of weapon. Conall must have a separate hiding spot, and this warehouse was just a cover.

It was very quiet, indeed, and that made Logan even more suspicious. No ships were anchored there at the moment. Not even one in for repairs. Either it was a case of bad timing and all the ships were on runs, or Conall didn't have nearly the fleet that Logan had been led to believe.

Logan ambled over to a man working at one of the docks, replacing some rotted boards. "Slow day," he commented.

"They're all slow lately," the worker said, still intent

on what he was doing. "Good for me. This needed to be done six months ago. But now I got plenty of time to do it."

"Because all the ships are on the water?"

"All two, you mean." The man hauled another board into place. "Bad year. First the *Georgette* got lost in a storm, then the new sloop never got delivered—damn crook of a builder. The Navy nearly intercepted the *Kestrel* in June, but it sank before they could board it. And the *Lapin* sank not two months ago."

"Bad luck never comes alone, does it?" Logan mused.

"No, it brings its cousins. And bad luck spreads. Less work for the village, fewer goods coming in."

"You got work here."

"For now," the man said. "But repairs don't take forever. Come winter, I'll be in need of a new job, or we'll be eating thin porridge for months."

"Isn't there a factory in town? The old distillery?"

"Aye, but there's not jobs for everyone. And it's Caithny's place too—just like here."

"He runs the town," Logan agreed. "Like a king in his castle."

The man looked up, curious at last. "Caithny doesn't usually take up with strangers. You must have talked him into something."

"You can't do business if you've no one to do business with. We both get something out of this."

"Well, here's luck to you. Caithny needs better luck. The village, I mean. Conall Caithny can make his own damn luck."

Logan nodded. "Fortune favors the bold." He bid the man good day and headed to the building nearby, where he expected to find Caithny. The place was part warehouse and part boat house. Caithny's office was at the far end, down a narrow hall.

Logan reached the doorway, but paused when he heard voices. Dropping back a step, he listened. Perhaps he'd get a scrap of information he could put to use.

The voices rose and fell. An argument, but not a fierce one. Logan tried to identify the other man in the room, but couldn't place the voice yet.

"You can't keep her forever. "

Then Conall's voice rose sharply. "Leave off, Munro! We're not going through this again. I've heard quite enough about marriage for today. You've asked and I've answered. Gemma will not be married to you. Ever."

"Thought we were friends, man. I'd treat her well."

"Friendship has nothing to do with it! And if you want to keep my friendship, you'll not ask again! I have other plans for the girl!"

Munro grumbled but apparently gave up. Logan heard footsteps and moved back around the corner. Someone, presumably Munro, left the room, but luckily went the other way from where Logan was lurking.

Logan considered the exchange with interest. Caithny let Gemma ride wild through the woods and play smuggler, but he turned all suitors away. He seemed to keep an eye on Gemma, but he didn't show the slightest inclination to protect her reputation, even if he had firm opinions about who she could marry. If he didn't want to provide for her, why wouldn't he want to see her married off? And if he did care for her, why treat her so cavalierly? Logan couldn't get his head around the conundrum. Something else was going on, and he would probably never know what it was. He would not be at Caithny long enough to get involved. *Then why do I keep thinking about it?* he wondered to himself.

Logan shook his head. Gemma was not his problem.

He stepped out and walked confidently into the office. "Caithny," he said. "Glad I caught you. There's a rumor in town that Customs is making a push on this part of the coast. Have you heard that?"

Caithny waved the news aside. "All in hand. I've an understanding with the law in these parts."

"But Customs isn't local."

"It's administered by local men. Oh, an officer from one of the districts might join them, but what's one more man? I control this coast, Lockridge. We've nothing to fear from the law."

"Aye, sir," Logan said. He smiled, thinking of what the Zodiac might say to that. Conall Caithny was so confident in his power that he was growing reckless. "If you're certain, I won't bother you any further. I've plenty of work to do before tomorrow night."

"Get to it, then. If the weather holds, tomorrow night will be clear, with a beautiful smugglers' moon rising at ten o' clock."

Logan left Caithny musing over the weather. He did in fact have work to do. His first task was to find the Customs office. Conall Caithny wasn't the only man who could cut a deal with the law.

Logan returned to town, but before he could even think about finding a Customs agent, he saw Gemma riding down the street on Hector, with Chance trotting happily alongside. She nodded coolly as she passed, and said in a voice so low only he could hear it, "Meet me behind the Rose and Crown in five minutes." Then she rode on.

He followed her instructions, and was waiting outside the back of the Rose and Crown. Several minutes later,

Gemma appeared. "I took a little longer so no one would see."

"Is that a problem? Should you be out?"

"Not with you," she said. "But...I've got some names."

He paused, a little surprised. "You do?"

"Yes. I did a little snooping and I found them."

"I thought you weren't going to betray the family business."

"It's not my family business," she said. "And besides, I think you may be right, because some of the names are French." Her voice dropped. "If you're right.... I don't want any part of it."

"Tell me. Please."

"No." She put her hand in her pocket and withdrew a slip of paper. "I won't tell you anything." She handed him the paper. "But if you just happen to come across the information, at least I can say I didn't tell you anything."

He took it and read the contents. Names of people, and possibly a location near Calais. He breathed a little sigh of relief. "That helps."

"I don't want to hear a thing about it. I have a feeling that dealing with you is going to ruin Uncle Conall."

"What makes you say that?" he asked.

"You're going to undercut him, aren't you? You say you won't deal with the French. I believe you—God knows why, but I do. But you have to sell the goods somewhere, and that means you'll take a loss, and Conall will get nothing. He'll never repay his debt then."

"He's in debt?" Logan asked, interested. "I knew he had a bad year, but he's done well for himself before."

Gemma nodded. "He took out a large loan several months ago. He must pay it back on the year, which leaves him about three months to do it. Winter is coming, which puts the smuggling business to sleep, more or less. If this run goes badly, he'll be in a very sticky spot."

"You don't sound too worried."

"By then," she said, "I'll have my majority and I'll be gone. Uncle Conall chose his fate. I'll choose mine."

"But you'll be part of the run?" he asked, feeling a new sense of urgency. He needed her for his contingency plan in case things went badly during the smuggling run.

"He needs me," Gemma said. "One last time, I'll help him. Just be careful," she said. "I have to go. Conall would likely kill us both if he caught us together."

"Then go, dryad."

But Chance barked then, causing both of them to whirl toward the entrance to the alley.

"Hey now," Toby said, raising his hands as he came toward them. "It's just me. I was looking for you...Lockridge."

"Toby," Logan said, relaxing. "You should meet Miss Harrington. She lives up at the castle with Caithny."

Toby wisely said nothing about the unconventionality of their meeting place. "How do you do, miss," he said, with a rough bob of his head. "Name's Tobias."

"Toby's my first mate," Logan said proudly. "He's kept me alive for the last couple decades."

"Sounds like quite the task," Gemma noted. Her tone was acerbic, but her blue eyes sparkled. "A pleasure to meet you, Toby. And this is Chance."

Toby bent down to greet the dog. "Fine animal," he said, with approval. "Goes with his mistress everywhere, I'd guess."

"He does indeed," Gemma replied. "And now we should both go home. Good day, gentlemen." She slipped out of the alley, leaving Toby and Logan alone.

"*Well*," Toby said after she was out of earshot. "That explains a lot."

"Don't start," Logan warned.

"You started it! A woman like that one. Don't you know red's a sign of danger?"

Logan laughed. "She appeared without warning."

"She *is* the warning. I see how you looked at her. I'll admit I like her, but that girl is going to be trouble for you."

Logan shook his head. "We're leaving here very soon. She's safe from me, and I'm safe from her."

Toby snorted. "I'd offer a wager, 'cept I don't involve ladies in a bet. You stay away from her."

"Good advice." Any promise to heed that advice would be a lie. He didn't want to avoid Gemma Harrington. He wanted to see her every chance he got. He wanted to show her the *Mistral* under full sail and convince her it was better than any castle on land.

But he returned to his room at the Rose and Crown. He had to write up what he knew for the Zodiac, in case things did not go well. Logan took a little while to compose the message, largely because he wasn't terribly comfortable with the code he had to use to write it. Some genius who Logan never met devised the code exclusively for the Zodiac to use.

The code required him to change his words into numbers and then back into other words, so none of the sentences flowed naturally. He wrote the whole thing out in plain English first, then translated it, then burned the original.

The message conveyed the newest facts he learned. Logan had every hope that he'd be able to report those facts to the Zodiac personally. But if something went wrong and he was captured or killed, he wanted there to be some clues to follow. So he reported on the names Gemma gave him, and explained about the run, and his expected outcome of detaining Caithny as soon as the run was completed.

After a moment's pause, he wrote one more letter, this one to Sophie. Logan told her about Gemma, explaining she was marginally involved in his assignment. She could use looking after if something went very wrong, if only because of her close connection to Conall Caithny. Sophie, being a female agent and also prone to striking out on her own, would be the best person to help Gemma, if it came to that. Logan also guessed that Aries wouldn't consider Gemma's role to be as important as Logan thought it was. He told himself it was a perfectly rational thing to do, and it had nothing to do with his personal feelings.

Satisfied with the messages, he sealed them and walked to the small post office on the high street.

"How long does it usually take for the post to go all the way to London?" he asked the man behind the counter.

"Few days, unless the mail coach is delayed," the man said. "Urgent news, sir?"

"Doesn't everyone think their news is urgent?" Logan answered vaguely.

"That's so," the postmaster agreed. "Gossip travels just as fast as official mail. Faster, when my wife's involved," he added with a grumble.

With the messages safely in the post, Logan left. Time was growing short. If everything went according to plan, he'd been sailing away from Caithny very soon. He'd detain Conall not long after, and then…the assignment would be over. He would have no reason to come back to Caithny. And even if he did come back, what would he say to Gemma? *Hello, beautiful. I'm a spy responsible for your uncle's arrest, thus depriving your family of its income. But don't worry, it's all for the good of king and country.*

Not a stunning beginning to a courtship. Anyway, he couldn't tell her he was a spy, which left him the option of courting her as Lockridge. Hello, beautiful. How do you feel about marrying a smuggler? Oh, and by the way, Lockridge isn't my real name, so that will be awkward during the wedding ceremony.

No, Gemma wouldn't look kindly on either approach. "Damn," Logan said to himself.

Later, Logan pulled Toby aside. "The run will happen tomorrow night. Customs may choose to do the right thing and stop the run. If so, Conall will be arrested here, and I won't risk blowing my cover."

"And if they don't?"

"Then the original plan goes into effect. All the usual rules apply. Keep the men in line, and if there's so much as a hint of conflict, turn the *Mistral* out to sea. We'll meet up again at the cove, right before the next tide. You'll be in charge of loading the *Mistral*. I'll be with Miss Harrington, wherever she is throughout the run."

"You still think that's a good idea?"

"If Caithny tries to double cross us, I want to be close to something that matters to him. And even if he's willing to let her be out at night among scoundrels with no sort of protection, I'm not. If I'm close to her, I can keep her from getting hurt."

Toby frowned. "True, I'd hate to see her hurt. But you'd use her as a hostage if Caithny turns on you? I can't picture you risking an innocent life."

"Don't tell Caithny that. He doesn't know me as well as you do."

"Let's hope it doesn't come to a hostage exchange," said Toby.

"You can hope for the best. I prefer to plan for the worst."

Chapter 12

꩜

THE NIGHT OF THE RUN came. Evening stole up softly around the day. It felt like summer more than fall, and twilight crept in so stealthily that people found themselves staring into the dark when they were sure it had been full daylight only moments before.

Gemma was one of those people. She'd been in her room, checking her pistols to make sure they were in working order. Before she knew it, the room was in near darkness, and she had to light a lantern to see what she was doing. The night would be velvety black until the moon rose later. With a clear sky, the smugglers would work with no lights at all besides the moon. No agent of the law would be able to track their movements.

It was a perfect night for smuggling. Yet Gemma still felt a sense of unease. It wasn't the usual nervousness she got before a run. This was different, and she didn't know why. But there was nothing to be done for it. She dressed as usual: in men's clothes, which would allow her to blend in with the others and also to move more easily. She had tough leather shoes, warm socks, faded trousers held up by the same belt that held her holsters, and a baggy shirt to conceal her natural shape. She pulled her hair back and tucked the tail of the braid down the back of the shirt. A wide strip of cloth covered her head and the rest of her hair. Then she put on her hat. In the dark, she'd be anonymous.

Gemma slipped downstairs and out the side door. Fergus was working in the stables, but she skirted the building, not wanting to alert him or Chance to her presence. She left the courtyard and turned right, intending to walk the path to the cove where Conall stored the goods.

Instead, she ran right into someone. She gasped, but it was covered up by a hand as the figure seized her. "Hold on, dryad," he murmured. "It's me."

"Logan?" she whispered. "What are you doing here?"

"I had a stop to make," he said, which explained nothing. "Shall we go down together?"

"I'm safe enough on my own."

"Yes, but you can protect me."

She smiled despite her nervousness. "I doubt you need my help."

He didn't respond to that, but instead looked her over in the dim light. "You're dressed quite practically."

"Oh, don't look at me. These are work clothes." Gemma rarely cared how she dressed, but she wanted Logan to be impressed. And this was a decidedly non-flattering ensemble.

"You're beautiful."

"I look like a beggar."

"I have no complaints," he said. He looked as if he was thinking about kissing her, but then he glanced away toward the shore. "We should move. You must be at your post in time."

They walked through the dark woods that concealed so much of the shoreline. Gemma led, since she knew exactly where she was going, even without a light. Logan followed, close enough that she could reach out and take his hand, which she suddenly wanted to do. She wished she was not entangled in the business of smuggling, and that he was not even more entangled in it. Logan was sharp and determined. He could make his mark anywhere. Why did he have to choose such a dangerous life?

He may have been thinking along the same lines, because when they passed through a particularly dark part of the woods, he paused and said, "Dryad?" in a voice curiously unlike his usual tone.

She stopped and turned. "What?"

He took a moment to speak again, as if he could not find the proper words. He took her hand. "Whatever happens, I'm glad to know you."

"Don't be maudlin," she said quickly, though her sense of foreboding returned. "You're not going to die on this run."

He stepped closer, put his arm around her, and drew her right up to him. "Just in case, I'm going to kiss you."

"Then do it."

He kissed her. Gemma reveled in it. She put her arms around him and held him tightly, as if she could stop him from being what he was.

After a moment he released her, taking a step away. He wore an expression she couldn't place, and it only added to her anxiety. She glanced away. "The moon is rising. We have to hurry."

Gemma moved down the path with bigger strides to make up for the time lost with the kiss. Logan kept pace with her easily, though he didn't speak again.

He melted away before they reached the shore, presumably to get to the *Mistral*. Gemma found Uncle

Conall, and listened to his last minute instructions. Ordering his men around, he looked like a grandfatherly figure directing boys at play. Conall wore a rather bright yellow coat and a red hat with a floppy brim. He smelled mainly of honey—he had beeswax rubbed into the coat's fabric to keep off the water. One would be mad to suggest such a man could possibly be a smuggler of repute. But he was, and none of the men on the beach would dare disobey him.

Gemma then headed to her post, where she could see the whole beach and much of the sloping shore, and even the promontory blocking the view to the town of Caithny beyond. It was a good spot. She could see any approaching ships and any horses that could be bearing Customs officers.

Her perch was a small natural outcropping, improved with a short wall of loose stones in a semicircle around the edge. A person could barely see the wall up close. From a distance, she would be invisible unless she lit a lantern, or fired a shot.

She checked her supplies. A lantern with the flint, and a rifle put there by Conall earlier. She had her pistols with additional shot. She was ready. She sat back, relaxing. The moon had to rise before the run could begin, or the smugglers would have to use other light, which defeated the purpose of a smuggler's moon. She scanned the woods, more out of habit than any particular sense of danger. Still, she wasn't prepared when a rustling sounded behind her.

"Charming little nest," a voice commented.

She whirled. "Logan! What are you doing here?"

"Seems like as good a place as any to watch the show."

She made a face. "All right, but why aren't you aboard your ship?"

"Toby has charge of the *Mistral*. I have another duty."

"What? Watching over me?" Gemma asked the question in a slightly tart voice, but in truth, the idea of having Logan at her side was reassuring.

"Precisely."

"Well, don't distract me."

"How might I distract you?" he asked, smiling lazily, knowing exactly what she was thinking.

Gemma blushed, glad the nighttime would hide the color in her cheeks. "Just...don't distract me at all. Or I'll shoot you."

"Touchy. Something on your mind, dryad?"

"I just don't like this," she grumbled.

"You don't like what?" he asked curiously. "My presence? The beach? Smuggling in general?"

"I'm rather glad you're here, actually. But the whole run..." She trailed off, unable to articulate her concerns. "I just have a bad feeling about tonight."

"That happen often?" he asked.

"Almost never. But I've had it all day, and I can't shake it," she confessed.

"I'll watch out for you," he said.

"Then who watches out for you?" she asked. Then she noticed a glitter in the distance. "Now keep low. See that flash? Conall just signaled. The run will begin soon."

Logan settled beside her. "Is he the only one who knows just where you are? The location of this aerie, I mean?"

"Yes. Which brings up the question of how you found it. He'd never tell you."

Logan leaned over to her, his voice low. "I was curious, dryad. Where does one hide a beautiful redheaded woman and keep her safe? So a few days ago, I looked for all the likely spots along the shore until I found this one."

She rolled her eyes, thinking of how Conall would react to the idea of Logan's reconnaissance. "Your curiosity will get you into trouble one day."

"Oh, it already has." He shifted away from her, focusing on something out on the beach. "The men are bringing the crates from the carts to the shore. They'll load the *Mistral* shortly."

Gemma leaned forward, gripping one of the pistols. "The moon's coming up. And it's one day off full. They'll have plenty of light."

"The law will too," he said grimly.

"The law almost never comes here," Gemma said. "And with no torches or lanterns on the beach, they've no reason to think something is going on."

"Isn't the full moon signal enough?" he asked. "There's a reason they call it a smugglers' moon."

"Hush," Gemma said. "We'll deal with that if it happens."

They waited for several minutes, watching the operation below, which appeared to be going smoothly. Teams of men hauled crates from hiding places all along the beach, and other men loaded the *Mistral*, which was docked at Caithny's warehouse.

A faint sound made Gemma look toward the woods. She tried to see something amid the shadows, but couldn't find anything.

"What is it?" Logan asked.

"Nothing," she said, dissatisfied. "At least, I see nothing." But her anxiety sharpened further, and she felt shaky. "Something's wrong."

Logan scanned the beach. "I don't think—"

A shot rang out, cutting off the rest of his words.

Gemma shifted to a better shooting position. "That didn't come from Conall. Someone else is here."

Logan was looking toward the trees again. "Men," he said, pointing. And not in your uncle's employ, I don't think. Customs."

She nodded. More shots rang out, and shouting rose from the beach. Gemma took a shot toward the new group. She might have doubts about Conall, but it was her duty to protect the men who worked for him.

"Did you get one?" Logan asked.

"I wasn't trying to hit anyone. That was a signal," Gemma said. "Conall will be watching me now. If he's alert, he'll see the direction I fired, and he'll know where the attack is coming from."

She tried not to sound worried. But things were quickly getting out of hand. The Customs men had come in multiple groups, sneaking into place. Soon more gunfire was being exchanged. Shots came from unexpected angles.

Gemma shot calmly, choosing to focus on what she guessed to be the main group, while Logan took over the job of reloading the pistols. She could aim to kill, but she much preferred to use her shots to force others to take cover, or to distract. A Customs agent hunched down behind a wall was an agent who couldn't attack anyone else. Her shots would give cover for the men on the beach to get away. Gemma lined up her shots carefully. It was rather like herding a flock. She used the shots to steer people where she wanted them to go, or to keep them in one place.

Logan noticed her method. "Have you even hit anyone

so far?"

"I prefer not to," she said evenly. "So does Conall. One of the reasons Customs usually doesn't bother him is that he keeps violence to a minimum."

"Something tells me that he's not completely innocent," Logan said dryly.

"If he wanted me to kill, I would never help him," Gemma snapped. "Now let me work."

Logan continued to reload the spent guns, so she could focus on her next target.

"*Mistral*'s sailing out," Logan noted after a few moments.

"What? Without all the cargo?" She didn't look, but the news surprised her.

"Those are the rules. Turn out to sea if there's an attack by land." He didn't sound concerned.

Gemma was getting very concerned. "What is going on? Someone must have alerted the magistrate. I've never seen a force of this size come to stop a run."

Her own efforts did not go unnoticed. While several of the attacking party were pinned down near some overturned rowboats, a few more on horseback circled around and made their way down the beach toward the aerie.

"They're trying to see where we are," Logan said. "So they can shoot you. Keep low, darling."

"Hard to do that if I have to take aim," she retorted.

He handed her a reloaded gun. "Be careful."

"Said the smuggler to the shooter."

He laughed. "You're doing splendidly. You've found your vocation."

Gemma sighed, but took aim. "I have no ambition to be a criminal."

"You could help me catch them, then," Logan said.

She didn't quite register what his words meant, and then it didn't matter because the moment Gemma pulled the trigger on her gun, Logan cursed and pushed her down.

"What happened?" she whispered.

"They know where we are."

"Lord, did they hit you?" Gemma asked, suddenly terrified.

He rolled away. "Either that or you did."

"Logan!" Gemma put the gun aside.

"No," he said. "You have to cover the others. Here." He handed her the last loaded pistol.

Gemma could barely sight down the barrel, she was so shaky. She found a target, and took her shot just as the smuggler crew flushed the main body of agents from their cover. After that, the tables turned and the agents were running for their lives.

No more shots came Gemma's way, and soon the worst chaos ended as the smugglers captured the attackers.

Gemma peeped cautiously over the wall. "They appear to have quit the field." She turned back to Logan, alarmed at how ashen his face was. He was holding a hand to his side, and the hand was dark with blood. "Oh, my God. I'll get you to a doctor."

"No doctor," he said. "Get me somewhere safe. You can fix me up."

"Logan, I'm not a surgeon. I can't fix a bullet wound."

"Just get me out of here."

She nodded. But where could they go? Tobias had turned the *Mistral* out to sea, so the ship was not an option. She couldn't take him to Caithny because it would be the first place an angry magistrate would look, assuming Conall did lose his grace with the law. Where did that leave her? Or maybe....

"Come," said Gemma. "It's a bit of a walk, but I have an idea."

Logan didn't ask questions. He walked next to her, leaning on her. As they went, his pace slowed markedly. "I can't go much farther," he said once.

"You don't have to," she promised. "Just up this hill."

"Aren't we going directly to Caithny castle?"

"Not exactly. Don't worry about where. Just walk. I can't drag you."

She almost did have to drag him. By the end, he was stumbling, and she gasped in relief when she pushed him past a few stone walls and into a long, low building.

Opening a wooden door in the long hall, she found what she was looking for: a furnished room. She pushed Logan inside and maneuvered him onto the rough, low bed. It wasn't much more than a mattress on a rope frame, but it was there, and Logan collapsed onto it.

Chapter 13

~~~

LOGAN SIGHED AS HE FELL onto the bed. He'd never been shot before, and he didn't like it. Every breath felt like a battle, he wanted to vomit, and little beads of sweat broke out over his skin, making him shake with cold. But he was awake, and alert, which was something.

Gemma leaned over him, her eyes huge with worry. "You're so pale."

"It's not that bad," he lied. "What's this place?" he asked, glancing around the room.

"It used to be a sort of barracks," she explained. "Years ago, some of Conall's workers didn't always have homes in town. Or they did, but they weren't welcome in them. So they stayed here. There are three rooms like this one, with a few beds in each. It's been a while since he had enough men working for him to need the place, but just in case, we've kept it up. I think Conall is hoping his business will expand and he'll hire more help again."

"Will anyone think to look here?"

"Who would think you'd run to Caithny castle?" she asked with a nervous smile. "And anyway, this building is about as far as you can get from the main house and still be within the walls. No one will notice we're here."

He shifted on the bed, wincing as a new wave of pain flared up in his side. "I don't suppose you could find me anything to drink."

She bent over him, briefly touching his face. "Just rest here for a moment. I'm going to get a few things."

"Be careful."

She left Logan, promising to return shortly. The moon had risen high, and the light coming through the east facing windows was bright enough so he could see fairly well, though all colors were muted. He chanced a look down at his shirt, seeing a large patch of darkness he knew to be blood. He kept one hand over the wound to slow the bleeding. He was scared to take it away, even though his arm ached. Well, all of him ached.

He closed his eyes and counted his breath, trying to remain calm. Getting to Caithny with Gemma's help kept him occupied. But now a thousand questions ran through his mind. Where was Toby? How was his crew? Would Conall Caithny realize that it was Logan who tipped off Customs? Was the shot an accident? The questions kept rising, and he had no answers.

Just breathe, he told himself. In. Out. In.

"Logan! Don't fall asleep!"

His eyes flew open. Gemma had returned, her arms full. A small candle lantern on a chain dangled from her hand, and the light from it made a little pool of gold to counter the moon. She placed the lantern on the small table by the bed.

"I think I found everything you might need," she said, putting things on the floor. She sorted through it all and pulled out a bottle.

"Here," she said. "It's scotch. It should help with the

pain."

He took the opened bottle and had a sip, then another. It burned down his throat, but he knew it would help dull the ache. "Thank you."

"I have some water and bandages. I can clean the wound." She sat on the edge of the bed, holding a damp cloth. "Can you take your shirt off?"

"I thought you'd never ask."

"Don't be clever, Logan. I'm not in the mood." Gemma helped him pull his shirt over his head. He bit his lip when he had to lean forward. His muscles were stiffening up in the cool air, and everything hurt. He leaned back with a sigh of relief.

Gemma surveyed his exposed body, her eyes wide.

"Impressed?" he asked wryly.

"You look terrible."

"No, then."

Shaking her head, she leaned forward, intending to clean the wound. "Take your hand off it. I need to see how bad it is."

"It's going to bleed more," he warned.

"Never mind that. Let me see."

She pulled his hand away, and hissed in sympathy when she saw the wound. "God, you must be in pain."

"It's better now I'm not moving."

She slid her hand to his back, feeling for anything else. "There's no second hole. The bullet's still inside."

He nodded. "I know. You can't just bandage it, Gemma."

"I can't?"

"No. You need to stitch it closed, or the bleeding will continue. Do you have a needle and thread?"

"I do," she said, uncertainly. "But Logan, I'm not a

surgeon."

"It's just to keep everything together until I get to a surgeon in the morning. Please, sweetheart. You have to do this."

"All right." She took a breath. "But drink more. I can't stand the thought of stabbing you with a needle while you're awake and feel everything."

"It's better than the alternative," he said.

"Which is what? Being asleep?"

"Being dead." He took another drink. "Hurry up. I'm not getting any younger."

Gemma found the needle and thread. She cleaned the wound well, but when she brought the needle next to his skin, she hesitated.

"I don't think I can do this."

"Of course you can," he said. "If you can be a crack shot, you can be a crack seamstress."

"That makes no sense. And I can't hurt you."

"You're the only one who can help me, dryad. Please."

She took a deep breath. "Get ready."

He had a final sip of the scotch. "Go."

Logan felt the needle, but the pain was nothing in comparison to getting shot. "Doing well, dryad. Keep going."

"I don't know what I'm doing," she said nervously.

"But I do," he reassured her. Though he'd never been shot himself, he'd been in plenty of bad spots, and knew how to stitch a wound. He told her how to make sure the wound would stay closed, and Gemma followed his instructions to the letter. It didn't take long, and the bleeding seemed to stop soon after. Gemma washed the wound again and then bandaged him with the cloth she'd brought.

"Sit up," she said. "I have to wrap it around you, or the bandage won't stay. Lean on me."

He did, enjoying the feel of her warm hands on him as she circled his waist with strips of the cloth. "It only took a bullet to get this close to you," he said, smiling at the absurdity of it. "I should have thought of this sooner."

"Don't you dare make light of this," she said. She pushed him back against the pillow and glared at him. "You're lucky you didn't die."

"I still may," he pointed out.

"Oh, God. If you die, I don't know what to do."

"Just haul my body to the water," he said. "I've always expected a burial at sea."

"That's not funny!"

He laid his head back. "Not joking. I really do think I'll die at sea."

"I'm not thinking about what to do with your body!"

"You're not? That's a shame." He laughed to himself. The scotch must be working. He reached out to touch her braided hair. "I wish I could see it down."

She gave him an odd look. "Would that make you feel better?"

"Certainly wouldn't make me feel worse."

"We'll see. First I want you to eat something."

"I'm not hungry."

"That's not surprising. But you lost quite a lot of blood, and if you say you're not feeling faint, you're lying," Gemma said firmly. "Food always helps for that."

He couldn't picture anything he'd want to eat. "What do you have?"

"Pears."

"What?" he asked incredulously. "It's November."

She smiled as she held up a glass jar of pear halves,

golden in the light of the candle. "Oh, there's a whole storeroom here filled with preserves and such. I always wondered where Cook gets it all. But trust me, it tastes as good as fresh."

He believed her. Just the thought of pears made him suddenly hungry. When she opened the jar and pulled out the first juicy piece, he didn't even object when she fed it to him. Having her feed him anything while he just sat there felt wildly indulgent. And *pears*.... He licked his lips, hoping to get every last drop. The fruit was packed in some sort of sweet, spiced, and possibly brandied liquid. "More, please."

Gemma smiled suddenly, and the tension left her face. "I'm so glad you can eat. You can't be dying if you want more."

He ate the next piece, just as hungry as before. Gemma's fingers were wet with the juice, and when she gave him another piece, he held her wrist and licked her fingers before he thought about it.

"Logan," she whispered. "What are you doing?"

"I didn't want to waste a drop," he said.

"If you're thirsty, have a drink."

"Whatever the doctor orders." He took a drink from the bottle of scotch, a little surprised to find it almost half gone already. But he felt much better. The shakiness was gone, and the pain dulled.

Gemma's presence was certainly helping. He smiled as he watched her, admiring how the candlelight illuminated her profile and made her hair, now coming loose from the braid, glow like a halo around her. "You're beautiful, dryad."

She laughed a little. "You must be feeling better if you can flirt again."

"I'm not flirting," he protested. "I'm stating a fact."

"Well, here's a fact. You need to rest." She put one hand on his bare shoulder, then frowned. "You're freezing."

"Loss of blood can do that. I'll live."

"I don't know about that." Gemma stood up, walking to the door of the room. She looked out at the darkness.

"Is there something out there?"

"Not that I can see. But maybe I should make certain."

The idea of her leaving sent a real shiver through him. "Please don't go," he said suddenly.

She turned back, a determined expression on her face. "You can't be rid of me that easily, Logan Lockridge."

Chapter 14

≋

SHE COULDN'T LEAVE HIM, NOT when he was only half-dressed and half-asleep...and completely intriguing. But more than that, she felt responsible for him. If Logan hadn't joined her during the smuggling run because he wanted to keep her safe, he wouldn't have got shot in the first place. She would never abandon him while he needed her.

Gemma walked back to where Logan lay. He did look better. The pallor was gone, some color returning to his skin. But his breathing was still shallow, and she knew he was cold.

She blew the candle out. "Just in case," she said. "No sense in leading people to you."

"Can you hand me that blanket you brought along?" he asked.

"I can do better." Gemma lay down next to Logan, spreading the blanket over them both. She felt bold doing it. She was literally lying down next to a man, a man she'd allow nearly any liberty. But he needed her heat, she reasoned. It was the right thing to do.

She stretched next to him, putting one hand on his chest. "Is that better?" she asked.

He made an approving sound. "Immeasurably."

Gemma tilted her head up to his. "Since we're here, why not continue the lessons you started to give me the last time we were alone? Or are you too injured to kiss me?"

"Let's find out," he said. He tipped his head and captured her mouth. He tasted like scotch and cinnamon. She felt a shock run through her bones as he kissed her. She realized how close she'd been to losing him tonight. She opened her mouth, hoping to taste more.

Logan moved slightly, and the muscles in his chest shifted under her hand. She touched him experimentally, trailing her fingers just down to where the bandage twisted around his torso.

"I'm not hurting you, am I?" she whispered.

"Pain is not what I'm feeling just now, dryad," he said, his hands slipping around her body.

"What are you feeling?" she asked.

"Anger. I'm so angry at whoever shot me. Putting me this close to you, but not able to do anything about it…"

"If you hadn't been shot, we wouldn't even be together now," she retorted.

"True enough. Kiss me again."

She did, loving the way he warmed beneath her mouth and hands. Remembering his words about how one could be kissed anywhere, she shifted so she could kiss his shoulder, then his chest. From the way his breathing changed, she guessed he enjoyed it.

"I forgot what a quick learner you are," he said.

"What else do you want to teach me?" she asked, with a wicked smile.

"Where to start," he mused. Then he reached for her hair. "I want to see it unbound."

Gemma nodded. "Hold on."

She slipped out from beneath the blanket. She stood up and reached around to loosen the braid. She shook her head as the strands came free.

"Better?" she asked.

"Beautiful."

Before he could ask her to rejoin him, Gemma pulled her shirt over her head, then slid out of the trousers. She wanted to feel as feminine as she could.

Logan inhaled when he saw her body in the dim light. "What are you doing?"

"I'm distracting you from your pain," she explained reasonably, despite the unreasonable excitement she felt.

"You're definitely distracting," he agreed.

"Good. You should focus on me." She smiled, and when she returned to the bed, she moved so she was more or less straddling him.

His eyes widened. "Sweetheart, I'm suddenly finding all sorts of reasons to recover quickly. And I don't want to take advantage of having you alone."

"Logan, you dolt, I'm the one who has the advantage."

To prove her point, she bent to kiss him again. He was already reaching for her. He moved his hands down to her thighs, then slid them back up her body.

Gemma sighed when he touched her breasts. That felt good. The sort of good that made her squirm, true, but she didn't want him to stop.

He didn't stop. His thumbs grazed her nipples. Gemma gasped, and his tongue darted into her open mouth. She felt dizzy. She laid her hands on his shoulders and focused on the kiss. But her whole body was tingling, and she couldn't stop a little moan from coming out when he squeezed both breasts lightly.

"Logan," she whispered. "Don't stop."

He moved his hands down to her stomach, then her hips, even while Gemma continued to lay kisses on him.

She murmured sweetly as he kissed her too, and gasped when he slipped one hand between her legs. He glanced up at her face. "Is that something you like, beautiful?"

"Mmm," she sighed, then whispered candidly, "Yes. That's exactly how I feel when I touch myself."

"God damn," he muttered. "Are you trying to kill me?"

"Does that bother you? I know I'm not supposed to do it," she said. "But I do anyway."

"Do it now," he said.

Gemma inhaled when she saw his expression. "You... want me to?"

His eyes were intent, passionate. He said, "I want to know what you need. Show me."

Gemma smiled. She felt shy and giddy all at once. "I think I know why people talk about having a glass of courage now."

"That explains it." He sighed. "I must be drunk to have asked that out loud."

"Why? Should you not have asked?"

"Of course not. I'm supposed to know everything and you're supposed to know nothing, remaining pure and innocent and free of desire until your wedding night."

She laughed softly. "How boring. I'd rather have you learn what I like. Watch me."

Gemma did exactly what he asked her to do, and he watched her as if she was the only woman he'd ever seen in his life. It didn't take long for him to harden beneath her, and Gemma reveled in the fact that she was responsible.

With her help, he got the rest of his clothing off, showing little attention to his wound.

"Be careful," Gemma warned.

"Don't worry about me. My turn, darling," he said. He pushed her hand aside with his, watching her face. At the touch of his fingers, she gasped and nearly buckled, putting her hands on his chest to steady herself. He moved again, drawing a low cry from her.

"You still like this?"

"Yes," she moaned. "But it's not enough." She touched him, and smiled when he closed his eyes. "Do you like that?" she asked slyly, already knowing the answer.

He continued to stroke her, wetting her, slipping one, then two fingers inside her, stretching her gently, and stoking her desire. "I want you, Gemma. It might kill me, but I want you.

Gemma bent down again, so she could lay over him. "Then don't wait, Logan. I want you, too."

Logan couldn't even think properly any more. Gemma was too overwhelming, too wildly honest. How could he resist her? He kept a firm hold on her hips, knowing how tight she would be, even as slick and fevered as she was. He slid into her, marveling at the smoothness of it. He'd never made love to a woman like this the first time.

He felt a soft obstruction, her virgin body resisting him slightly. She felt it too, and grasped his shoulders with her hands.

He wrapped his hands around her hips, thrusting into her.

She cried out, shaking. He stopped moving, only running his hands up and down her body in an effort to calm her, remind her that she was much more than the part of her that hurt.

Once she calmed, Gemma took control of their pairing, sending waves of intensity through their bodies, until they moved as one, gaining speed and certainty. She moved her hips in counterpoint to him, her breath coming faster as she approached her peak. Just when he was sure he could not hold back for a second longer, Gemma gave a little cry.

Freed by her own climax, he allowed himself to find a new rhythm, one that took every advantage of the heat and slickness of the woman over him. When he came, it took his breath away, it was so strong. Not entirely sure if he was still alive, he reached for Gemma and held her to him, their bodies spent and damp with moisture.

Gemma was grateful to be held, since she felt suddenly weak. She didn't know what to think. She wasn't sure she knew *how* to think, with the primal emotions still singing through her body.

They lay together, both aware of the other to a degree that was both pleasant and painful. Gemma was also keenly aware of how happy she was.

Logan traced patterns known only to him on her skin. "You're rare, even for a dryad," he said. "You should stay with me."

"Dryads are bound to a particular tree, are they not?" Gemma asked sleepily. "I couldn't stay with you if I were a real dryad."

"Would you come with me if I asked?" His voice was intent. "You should. We're the same."

Those words made her flush down to her toes, but despite what just happened, she hadn't lost her head entirely. "Logan, you can't *say* things like that. What should

I do? Sail around on your smuggling runs with you? Or sit at home, wondering if you'll come back alive?"

He shook his head. "What if it wasn't like that? What if I was a respectable member of society? With a position in say…government?"

"Respectable? You?" She almost laughed. "And where would you settle down? Here? Or in England? Or Bermuda?"

"Anywhere, as long as there's a harbor."

"You're a romantic. We can have mad discussions another time. Let's just get to sunrise. Don't forget that you're not entirely well."

He held her even closer. "Will you stay with me this whole night, dryad? Or is that too much to ask?"

"I'm not leaving," she said, almost offended. "What if you take a turn for the worse?"

"You're sure?"

"I am." She smiled. "I'll stay awake. But you must promise me you'll sleep."

"Kiss me first."

"Why?"

"Because we're alone and there's a full moon. And you've already accused me of being romantic."

So she kissed him, reveling in how sweet that kiss was, and how new it felt even after everything they just did to each other.

Then she tucked her head on his chest. Whatever happened tomorrow, she and Logan could see it through together. Though she kept her eyes wide at first, the sound of his breathing, and the gentle, ordinary sounds of the night lulled her into a doze. She drifted off to sleep between one breath and the next.

Chapter 15

≈

HE WAS WARM, AND VERY unwilling to move. Logan couldn't remember ever being so comfortable. He must be asleep. His mind drifted, in that grey space between dream and reality. Something tickled at his neck. Gemma's breath. Despite her assurance that she would stay awake, she was completely asleep next to him, her bright hair in glorious disarray.

He shifted under her, hoping not to wake her and break the spell. His body ached a bit. He knew that when he woke up for real, the pain would be much worse. Gemma's loveliness was doing a marvelous job of distracting him. He raised one hand and gently pulled her hair away from her face. He'd give a lot to be able to do that every morning.

There was a scratching at the door. Logan woke up completely, his body tensing. The pain from his wound surged up now. He clenched his jaw to stop a moan. *Now* he wanted whisky. Anything to dull the ache.

The scratching continued. He hadn't imagined it.

"Chance?" he said in a low tone.

An answering whine confirmed it.

The dog must have found them, and his excitement

could easily give away Logan's location. He got up as quickly as he could, trying not to disturb Gemma.

He pulled on enough clothing to not be at a disadvantage, then cracked the door. "Chance, get in here and hush…" He stopped. The dog wasn't alone.

Toby stood there. "Guess the dog's good for hunting something." Worry and anger were written all over his face. "You missed our meeting time. Did you have any intention of letting me know you lived through that little skirmish?"

Logan began to explain, "Gemma and I were on the other side, and we had to get to a place where she could fix me up."

"You got hit?" Toby asked, his concern refocusing.

"My side. I'll be all right until I can get to a doctor."

"I've heard *that* before. I remember you nearly dying of fever near Barbados."

"I just need a few days," Logan insisted.

"You don't have a few days. The next tide is about to turn, and we have to leave now."

"Now?"

"*Now,*" Toby almost snarled. "Or did you have more pressing business?"

Logan involuntarily glanced back at the bed where Gemma lay. Realizing that Toby would also have a perfect view of her, Logan pulled the door shut, though the damage was done.

"I see," was all Toby said. His voice was flat.

"We can't just leave," Logan said.

"We can't stay. The hold is full. Caithny's aboard, and if we wait for the next tide, the law will see the ship in full daylight."

"What do you mean Caithny's aboard? We only

agreed to take a few of his men along."

"He's decided to join us himself, just for the initial run. We have to go," Toby added. "We're pressing our luck already."

Logan nodded. "Give me five minutes."

"You have one, and that's generous. You're damn lucky I was able to get hold of Chance, and he was able to find his mistress. And so convenient, you being with her."

"Shut up. I'll be out in one minute."

Logan closed the door, though Chance slipped in before he did. The dog lay at the foot of the bed, evidently relieved to know where his mistress was. Logan stared at Gemma in consternation. He got his things together, all the while debating whether to break his word to Toby and spend a precious few minutes telling Gemma what was happening. But he couldn't miss the tide.

Struck by an idea, he pulled out his brass compass. He set it on the chair beside the bed. Then he leaned over and put a hand gently on Gemma's hair. "Gemma?" he said.

She murmured in her sleep.

One sharp knock sounded at the door. Logan nearly snapped at Toby, but he held it in long enough to whisper to Gemma, "Dryad, I have to leave. Are you listening?"

"Logan?" she murmured. Her eyes opened.

"Gemma, I have to go. I'm sorry. But I will come back. I promise." He kissed her and was rewarded with a sleepy smile.

"Logan," she repeated. Then her eyes closed again. "Love you."

Leaving the room was the most difficult thing he'd ever done.

They reached the ship with no time to spare. Toby hadn't been exaggerating. The sailors cursed as they fought the wind and tides, but then the *Mistral* was flying through the waters in the deceptive light just before dawn.

As Toby warned him, Conall Caithny was aboard. The older man watched Logan after the initial rush to get underway. "Where were you, then?"

"Never mind," Logan muttered.

"It's your ship," Caithny pressed. "Odd when the captain isn't there to oversee it."

"That's right, Caithny," Logan snapped, sliding back into his persona of Lockridge. "She's *my* ship. And considering you boarded her without my invitation, be glad I haven't tossed you over already."

"You wouldn't dare."

A few sailors, overhearing the exchange, slowed their work to listen in. Logan lost what little patience he had left.

"Listen, Caithny. Aboard the *Mistral*, I'm not just the captain. I'm the closest thing you'll find to God. So shut up, unless you want to spend your journey in the brig. I have one, you know."

"No need for that," Caithny said, making a show of backing off. "I was just asking."

"Well, for your edification, I was getting a gunshot wound attended to."

"You were shot?" Caithny asked, with patently false concern.

"Aye, I was. But it wasn't enough to keep me down." Of course a mere bullet wouldn't stop Lockridge. "Now everyone get back to work. I want to *fly* to France, understand?"

They understood, and moved off. The ship did almost fly, now that she was in open water with a fair wind. The run to France should only take a few days there, and a few days back, assuming the sea cooperated.

Logan tried to rest as much as he could. Luckily, his crew was experienced and needed little direction for the moment.

But all was not well. Toby's anger was cold and obvious.

"What?" Logan asked him, once he got them out of others' hearing for a moment. "What's eating you?"

"Nothing."

"Bullshit. You've barely spoken to me since we got on this ship."

"Before that, sir."

"So tell me."

Toby shook his head. "Don't know what you were thinking."

"When?"

"I know you've got an…" he paused, glancing around to make sure they weren't overheard, "…an image to maintain. But to hurt that young lady…"

"I never hurt Gemma," Logan hissed. "She chose to be at the beach. There was nothing I could do to stop her, even if I wasn't being Lockridge. But she didn't get hurt. She helped me."

"Wasn't at the beach I meant," Toby said, clearly embarrassed to be talking about it at all.

Logan paused. The bedroom. That's what Toby meant. Then he got angry again. "I never hurt her."

"You must have known the consequences, and you went ahead anyway. Or are you suggesting that I didn't see her in that bed?"

Logan's jaw clenched, and he recognized most of his anger was actually guilt. "You did."

"She's not some barmaid, you know. Regardless of

what you're pretending to be, there's a line, and you crossed it. You, of all people. That girl will pay for what you did to her."

"She will not," Logan said fiercely. "What happened last night has nothing to do with what I'm pretending to be. I intend to marry Gemma, and she knows that."

"Is that so?" Toby's expression softened into surprise.

"It is. I left her my compass." Logan laughed suddenly. "Not exactly a ring, but you did hurry me along."

"I didn't know," Toby said, chastened. "Forgive me. I was out of line."

"No, you weren't. You were keeping me in line. You were doing the right thing as you saw it."

Toby chuckled. "Compass, eh? That'll be a story to tell the grandchildren."

Logan laughed again, his temper restored. "I like the way you think, Toby. Friends?"

"To the end, Logan." Toby's answering grin made it clear that all was well between them again. Logan looked out at the horizon, watching the weather.

He thought of the compass he left her. Gemma didn't know its significance, but she'd keep it safe. He trusted her. And he didn't truly need the compass. He could read the stars, and North was in his bones. Short of a tempest, nothing could stop him from finding the right direction.

If this run went well, and he could report his success back to the Zodiac, then this assignment would be hard to top. An enemy contained, the love of his life found, and his future charted. What could be better? Now he just had to make those things happen before a storm hit.

The *Mistral* raced southward over the waters. Logan focused on his ship and his crew, while also keeping an eye on Caithny. The man's unexpected decision to join the run to France worried Logan. The older man was wily, and he certainly had something up his sleeve. Logan would have to find out what before Caithny slipped through his fingers.

Chapter 16

~~~

SHE WAS DREAMING, BUT THE dream turned dark, and Gemma woke up in an instant. "Logan," she said.

The sound moved through the room. She was alone. She knew it before she finished speaking the word. What had happened? What went wrong? She sat up in bed, looking around in the dim light. There was no trace of him. His clothes were gone. Her clothing was hung over the back of the single chair. She certainly hadn't done that last night. The deliberateness of the gesture disturbed her. Why would he do that? Why would he wake up and dress, and tidy up afterward, but not wake her?

A whining sound drew her attention to the end of the bed. Chance's head appeared, and he dared put his paws on the mattress. "Chance, how did you get here?" she asked. The dog must have nosed out her scent, and followed the trail. He wouldn't let Logan leave, would he?

She swung her legs over the side of the bed, hearing the ropes squeak softly. As her feet hit the floor, a gleam caught her attention. Logan's pocket watch lay on the seat of the chair. He hadn't forgotten it. The chain was curled up too neatly. He'd left it for her.

Gemma moved toward the chair, a strange feeling

growing in her gut. She pulled her clothes back on, then picked up the watch. Why would he leave this of all things? He didn't consider it…payment, did he?

Her hand curled around the cool metal, even as her heart began to ache. He wouldn't do that. Not after what they talked about last night, and what they'd done last night. He didn't think of her that way.

It was a beautiful object. Made of brass, and polished from long use. An H was inscribed on the front, but she couldn't think what it might stand for.

Gemma pressed the diamond set in the knob of the watch, and the lid flew open. She realized it wasn't a watch at all. It was a compass. The needle swung lazily for a few seconds, then settled. She turned so the needle lined up with a second diamond set into the north point. It sparkled softly as she tilted the compass toward her. There was a Latin phrase inscribed on the inside lid.

"Audaces fortuna iuvat," she whispered. She recognized the words well enough to guess the translation. *Fortune favors the bold.*

Logan wouldn't have left the compass if he were going to his ship, she reasoned. He would need it. No. He put it there to reassure her he'd be back very soon.

Then why not wake her and tell her so, a thin, cold, sly voice asked. The work of a moment, to wake her, tell her not to worry, and then kiss her to prove it.

Or had he? She remembered him speaking, telling her he'd be back. Was that a dream? She was too befuddled to know.

Gemma slid her shoes on, then went outside. The air was damp and still. A light mist hovered in the low places of the landscape. It would burn off later, once the sun moved higher in the sky.

No matter what, she had to get home before she was missed, though it was surely too late. She'd need to make up a story. Nearly anything would do. Tell Conall she fell from her perch, or she saw and tracked a Customs agent. Anything but the truth.

Then Gemma could send word to the tavern where Logan was staying. Or to the *Mistral* directly. He'd explain what happened. It would be all right.

Gemma rounded the wall to the castle proper, and Fergus saw her the moment she stepped into the courtyard. Chance barked a greeting.

"Gemma," Fergus hissed. "Get over here!"

She hurried over to him. "What's happening?"

"Where were you?" he asked, his eyes anxious. "You didn't come back after the run!"

"What did Uncle Conall say?"

"What do you mean? What could he say?"

"Is he angry?"

"He's not even here, girl. Did you hit your head? He's gone aboard the ship. Told us he wanted to see the run personally."

"He's aboard the *Mistral*? Lockridge's ship? Where's Lockridge?"

"On the ship!" Fergus took hold of her. "What's the matter? You look about to faint."

"I…I…don't know. Something last night…went very wrong." She couldn't put words together.

Fergus put a strong arm around her shoulders and hustled her inside through the kitchens. His concern grew when he noticed Gemma crying. He was certain she sustained some injury, and none of Gemma's protests could dissuade him.

"I'm not hurt, Fergus. Stop it."

"There's blood on your jacket!"

"It's not mine," Gemma said.

"Lord, then whose is it?"

She shook her head. "It's not important."

"You must have been injured," Fergus protested. "I'll call a doctor. You sit down here by the fire. Wait, and I'll fetch him now."

"Lord, no, Fergus! I just need to rest."

"You're hurt. You must have fallen."

She laughed, hearing the beginnings of hysterics in her voice. Oh, she had fallen. That was true enough. "Fergus. Call Annie, and help me up to my room. I need to lie down."

She was put to bed by Annie and Aunt Maura, both of whom were sure that Gemma was sick with some dire illness brought on by a night of wandering outside. She was so tired and confused, she didn't even protest.

She asked about Conall, but all she learned was he wasn't there. Fergus visited her later, and confirmed that Conall did indeed join the crew on the *Mistral*, an abrupt decision that filled Gemma with confusion and dread.

Gemma remained in bed all day. Annie sat with her for a while, then Aunt Maura was there. Gemma was never so glad to have her aunt as in that moment.

Maura put a cool hand to Gemma's forehead. "I don't believe you have a fever, but you're so flushed. I don't like it." She gave a worried smile. "I had Annie make some weak tea. You should have something."

Gemma drank the tea and ate a bit of food. It wasn't her body that suffered, though. It was her heart. After Maura left, Gemma pulled out the compass from beneath her pillow. With her finger, she traced the outline of the fancy engraved "H" on the lid of the compass—the mark of the previous owner, she presumed. Surely if Logan purchased it, there would be an "L" for Lockridge.

Gemma stared at the ceiling. He left her. He *left* her. After what she shared with him the last night, he left on his ship with no warning, and she had no idea when or if he'd ever be back. And if he did come back, would she listen to whatever he said? Would her uncle even permit her to speak to Logan? In what mad world should she hope to be with Logan? He was a criminal, and she ought to have nothing to do with him.

His absence gnawed at her. Every time she reviewed their conversations, she got more confused. He did imply he'd marry her—but only when he was half out of his mind after losing blood and then drinking too much to make up for it. In such a state a man was liable to say anything.

She'd been a fool. She followed her heart instead of her head. She trusted a thoroughly untrustworthy man, and why? Just because of the way he smiled at her. Gemma had never been so turned around. However charming and even truly caring Logan was….

Still, he should not have left her.

* * * *

A day later, she had recovered enough to appear mostly normal, and she had devised a plan while sitting in forced contemplation. She was living the wrong sort of life. There was only one remedy, which was to find a new life before anyone else made her decision for her.

She'd been waiting in the wings for far too long. She would be twenty-one in a few months. If she didn't take charge of her own life now, it would be too late. *Fortune favors the bold.*

After dressing herself, Gemma found her aunt in the small library. Maura was embroidering by the afternoon light from the window, working patiently and constantly.

"Aunt Maura?" she asked, her voice soft from lack of use.

"My dear!" her aunt said, looking up. "You are on your feet again. Does that mean you're recovered?"

"Yes." Gemma stepped up to the fire. "I've had quite a lot of time to think. I have an idea."

Maura laid her sewing aside, and watched her niece expectantly. "Go on."

"Well, you've so often spoken of my becoming a lady, of fulfilling the role my mother wanted me to have." Gemma took a deep breath. "I wish to do so."

Her aunt was curious. "Is that so? What has brought about your change of heart?"

Change of heart, indeed, thought Gemma. "I had a rude awakening, Aunt. The world is not the place I thought it was. I can't be a child any longer. I can't be wild here at Caithny. It's not my place. So let's go to London. Together. You can be my chaperone and tell me what I need to know."

Maura put a hand to her mouth. "Oh, darling child. Your uncle would never permit it."

"Then we should go *now*," Gemma said, with more heat in her voice. "Why must we always be at his beck and call? I don't want to wait for him to realize I've grown up." She knelt down and reached out to take her aunt's hands. She added beseechingly, "Let's pack and go. This week. Tomorrow. What should he care? And you shouldn't be here either. Not if he's done what you fear he did to your husband. So let's go to London. *Please*, Aunt."

Maura looked at their clasped hands. "We could," she whispered, as if convincing herself. "We could. If he's not here, he can't stop us. And if we're together…"

Gemma pressed her advantage. "Of course we can. And who better than you to help me learn about London?"

"If we get there within a few weeks, you could be presented for this Season," her aunt said. "Though you're so rough about the edges. I wonder if all can be polished in time."

"What's to learn? You've taught me over the years, and though I haven't used the lessons, I remember them. Truly. I can be cool and polite. I know how to pour tea. I can be demure and sweet."

"Perhaps you can," Maura said, with a new spark in her voice.

"Indeed! And you'll be there to help. What else is needed?"

"A wardrobe, to start. Rooms to live in. A few servants. All that costs money…" Aunt Maura stood up. "But, yes. It can be done. I'll have to see your solicitors in London to learn the exact state of your finances."

"I have solicitors?" Gemma asked in surprise.

"Your parents did. They made provision for you."

"Then that shall be our first stop." Gemma felt suddenly giddy. All she had to do was get out of Caithny. Away from Conall and Logan and the mistakes she'd made. "Oh, this will work splendidly, Aunt. A new life. A future. We need to get out of here. And there's no time to waste."

Maura looked at her speculatively. "You've not said what precisely brought this on, dear."

"A nightmare. I fancied it a dream, but I know better now. Never mind. Let's not think of it. Let's make plans!"

Chapter 17

≋

ONCE DECIDED, GEMMA LOST NO time in making her wish happen. She rushed through Caithny castle like a whirlwind, packing items she was sure she'd need, ordering the maid Annie to help her fill chests for Aunt Maura and herself, then despairing and repacking everything again.

A hitch in her plans came when she realized there was no practical way to bring Hector along with them. She agonized over the problem until she went to the stables and found Fergus. He told her he'd keep watch just as he'd always done. "If you'll stay on in London, I'll find a way to get Hector down to you eventually."

"But you can't stay here!"

"Why not? Annie and the rest of the household will. And Caithny will be back soon enough. Assuming he doesn't drop dead from pure rage when he learns you're gone, he'll still need people to keep this place going."

Gemma asked, "Do you think he'll come down to London to get me? I won't come back otherwise."

"Girl, I can't imagine what he'll do. No one's ever crossed him like this before."

"You think I'm being foolish?"

"You're being headstrong, which is just like you." Fergus smiled crookedly. "But if you want to know the truth, I'm glad you're doing it. You were never meant to stay at Caithny. When I told your mother I'd look after you, I thought it meant a few months. She wouldn't have gone, if she'd known you'd be here for years."

"I wish she hadn't," Gemma said. She stroked Hector's mane one last time. "But I'll find a way to get both you and Hector down to London soon enough." She turned to face Fergus. "That is...if you want to come?"

"Been watching out for you and your horses for so long now, what else could I do?" Fergus gave her another smile and then shooed her out of the stable. "Go. You're leaving tomorrow and you must be prepared."

The journey from Scotland down to London was horrible. The coach was jam packed with boxes and bags and crates and whatnot. Gemma and Maura were crammed inside, suffering every jolt and bump on the road. Chance lay at Gemma's feet, quietly miserable. Every night, the coach stopped at an inn, which varied in quality from pleasant to barely acceptable. Gemma almost wanted to turn back, but the thought of confronting Uncle Conall with her disobedience—and being stuck inside Caithny all winter long—was enough to keep her motivated.

They were without a maid. Annie was flatly terrified to go to London, and Gemma wouldn't dream of separating the woman from her family. Annie had a beau, too. It would be cruel to make her accompany Gemma and Maura. They'd make do until London, then hire a new maid there.

For her part, Aunt Maura never suggested retreat. She spoke mostly of the ton and the Season. She told Gemma all sorts of esoteric knowledge related to ballgowns and the role of jewelry and fans and who could be cut and who must be humored. Aunt Maura was wasted at Caithny all those years. She was an encyclopedia when it came to social niceties.

When they reached London, Gemma was amazed. She'd never seen so many people in one place. Her hazy childhood memories of London were of home life. She never recalled anything like the busy streets she saw now.

They found a hotel in the heart of the more fashionable area of the city. Gemma liked the busyness and bustle of London, but there were so many people. And so many different kinds of people. She was unsure for the first time in her life.

Though Maura told her how much fashion had changed in the past decade, Gemma didn't fully appreciate it until she saw ladies everywhere in dresses with high waists and flowing skirts so unlike her own corseted, country style. They also wore smart jackets with cutaway lines, and cunning little slippers. Gemma's shoes were meant for muddy trails and cold rains. She tried to hide her shoes under her skirts as much as possible, but she felt like everyone was looking at her when she went out.

She promised herself she would correct the problem as soon as she discovered how much credit she could get. This required contacting the solicitors, which was one of the first things Gemma and Maura did after settling into their temporary lodgings.

Maura made the appointment with the gentlemen at Pratt & Spenlow. Maura seemed even more nervous than usual. "You need not come, dear. Perhaps it would be better if I went alone, the first time…"

"But I'm curious." Gemma would not be gainsaid, and thus both ladies arrived at the office. Gemma looked

around at the heavy wood paneling and the leather upholstered furniture with a sense of delight. It felt so rich, so
modern, so London. Surely this was where she was meant
to be. If only they could ensure that it would be affordable!

An elderly gentleman emerged from a door down the
hall. He made his way toward the reception area, his gaze
locked on Gemma.

"Miss Harrington, is it?" he asked, his voice quavering
with excitement. "The daughter of Mr John Harrington?"

Gemma rose from the chair uncertainly, not sure of the
protocol. "Yes, sir."

"I am Mr Pratt. Oh, I knew it when I saw you! You are
the image of your mother, you know. Those blue eyes!
Who could forget them. Pardon me, I must sound overly
familiar, but the resemblance is striking. It was my great
privilege to know your parents before they passed."

"Ah…thank you." Gemma nodded. "This is my aunt,
Miss Maura Cait—" she began.

"I am Mrs Douglas," Maura said firmly. "How do you
do."

Gemma looked at her aunt in surprise. So she was
going back to her married name? How interesting!

"Honored, Mrs Douglas." Mr Pratt bowed, then gestured toward the hall.

They were ensconced in the office and offered tea.
Polite inquiries were made as to their plans. Gemma was
hesitant, but Mr Pratt was so delighted to meet her that he
brushed most of the formalities aside.

"Of course, of course," he said at one point. "Surely
you know you are in a quite comfortable position, financially speaking." He mentioned several figures, and
Gemma nodded quickly, hoping to appear intelligent. In

truth, she only registered half of what he said—she was preoccupied thinking that her father must have talked to this man for hours and days while Gemma scarcely remembered her father's face. It wasn't fair!

She pulled herself back to the present when Aunt Maura was speaking.

"I hope the exact nature *and* amount of my niece's inheritance will remain confidential," Maura said. "She is to have her first Season and I would prefer that she not be hounded by adventurers."

"Mrs Douglas, we respect our clients' privacy!" Mr Pratt said. "Naturally, everyone knows not to speak of private matters on the street like common gossip."

"It's just that such an amount will stir temptation."

"It is so unusual?" Gemma asked, hating to sound naive.

"Well," Pratt said, "yes. The annual income of fifteen thousand is perhaps not out of line with the wealthier citizens of London. What worries your aunt is that your principal is not entailed in any way." He paused, thinking how to explain it delicately. "Many of the aristocracy, for example, are privileged to hold vast estates. But law and custom—not to mention pride—prevent them from selling any of it off. Thus, their apparent worth comes with caveats."

"They are only land rich," Gemma said.

"Precisely. Your father's wealth comes from trade and investments, and is essentially chattel, in a legal sense." Pratt went on, "Regardless, you can be confident the money is in good hands. We've monitored the operations of the firm for years on your behalf."

"The firm?" Gemma asked, feeling silly.

"Yes. Harrington, Waite, and Talbot. Your father's

shipping concern. He owned sixty percent, while the two other partners each hold twenty. Though the directors handle most of the business. Surely you know about that?"

She glanced at Maura, who looked abashed. Gemma said only, "I know very little, sir, having lost my parents when I was so young."

"Well, you'll have considerable control upon your majority. Should you wish to, you could sell your share of the firm, or liquidate much of the other assets. You could transfer most of your wealth to cash quite readily."

"I see," Gemma said. And she did see. Some people might think of her as a walking treasure chest.

"We will not stress that aspect of your wealth," Maura said firmly. "And anyway, wealth from trade is not so revered. Perhaps no one will think of it." She didn't sound too hopeful, though.

Pratt's frown was sympathetic, but all he said was, "Well, you can learn about it at your leisure if you choose. In the meantime, you may make whatever purchases you like, my dear. Direct the bills here and think no more about it."

Mr Pratt saw them to the door of the office. "Once again, I must say it is such a pleasure to meet you. I cannot wait to tell my wife you have come to London. She knew your mother a bit, you know. Will you join us for dinner some day soon? Wonderful. We shall send an invitation. Good day, ladies. Welcome back!"

Heartened by the solicitor's confidence, Gemma and Maura breathed easier. Later that same day, they shopped a bit. Gemma had a little money with her, but by and large the shopkeepers barely seemed to expect for a lady like her to deal with cash. She was invited to buy on account, and she supplied shops with the name of her solicitors. Presumably, they would be billed and the amounts recorded.

"Doesn't it seem too easy?" Gemma asked her aunt after they purchased several pairs of gloves at a shop. "I'm not even sure how much we're spending."

"Frivolous spending is encouraged among the upper classes, and it's an excellent way to lose one's fortune." Maura glanced over at Gemma. "That is not to say today's purchases are frivolous! In London, the clothes make the man—and woman. You must fit in, which means wearing the right sort of look."

"Still, we ought to be careful. How many pairs of gloves did we buy?"

"Probably not enough," Maura said, with a laugh. "Don't underestimate the degree of difference from your old life in Scotland to your new life here. You will dress like a lady now. That means frequent changes of outfits and accessories. Your days of running around in stained and spotted items are over. "

Gemma made a face. "How dull." Surely her aunt was exaggerating. How could anyone care so much about a smudge of dirt on a glove, or a shoe left unpolished? Society had to be concerned with more important matters. Didn't it?

Chapter 18

☞

THE RUN DOWN WENT WELL. The *Mistral* had in fact been nearly full when the Customs officers began the raid on the beach. When the ship reached the small harbor on the north coast of France, Conall's four men aboard directed the unloading with confidence. Caithny's partner was there in person as well. He was a tall, broad-shouldered man who strolled out on the pier to see what was happening. Caithny hailed him in French as if the two were old friends. Logan made a mental note of the man's appearance, but then Caithny jumped to the pier and walked away with the other man, deep in a private conversation.

As Lockridge, Logan didn't have a compelling reason to intrude, so he bided his time. Overseeing the unloading was work enough. He tried to get a glimpse of the contents of the crates, but had no luck. There were more men waiting to take the crates into the new warehouse, and they looked quite serious about keeping people away.

Whatever the cargo was, it was valuable. Logan dearly wanted to know what he was shipping, but he'd just have to wait. Impatience got a man killed.

The *Mistral* was tied up at one of the docks for the night. Logan put Toby and another man on watch. The harbor seemed well hidden, but then, so did Caithny's secret harbor up in Scotland. It would be another few days before they could return. Logan knew another cargo was to be loaded when it arrived—and again, he didn't know what it was, because Lockridge's persona was a man willing to smuggle anything and ask no questions. How inconvenient.

Logan didn't sleep more than a few hours at a time, because there was plenty to do and he had to keep an eye on Caithny and his men. In addition to the short rests he could grab, Logan still felt the pain of the bullet wound he'd suffered. No one but Toby knew the extent of the injury, and unfortunately, no one could be trusted to treat the wound while they were in France.

It was a shame. After weeks of careful maneuvering, Logan would finally have the primary players in this odd smuggling scheme in one place. He wanted to get the mysterious cargo onto the *Mistral*, and then detain both Caithny and his French counterpart before they knew what was happening. Then he'd sail to London and hand everything over to the Zodiac. But it was too risky to start a fight with Caithny in his current state.

Though this should just be an ordinary run, Logan suspected something unusual would occur. Still, he was surprised by what actually happened the night the new cargo was to be loaded.

Right on time, Caithny strode up the gangplank, accompanied by another man. Logan shifted, keeping his hand close to his knife. The stranger was dressed all in black. His coat was cut close to his body, with no extra fabric to get in the way, and he wore rather tall leather boots instead of the expected shoes. His face was partially hidden by a hat—black, of course. Logan didn't like him at all. The word *assassin* came to mind immediately.

"Who's this?" he asked Caithny.

"Just what we agreed to ship," he said. "You ship cargo without questions." He indicated the man in black. "Here's your cargo—and I want no questions."

"On my ship, I ask questions if I like." Logan took a step toward the newcomer. "Cargo is one thing. I wasn't told about a passenger."

"Not a passenger. Cargo. Take the cargo back to Scotland with me, and forget about it." Caithny gave Logan a sharp look. "Is that too difficult a notion to swallow?"

"Watch your mouth on my ship. If I'd been told there was no cargo, I could have sailed with fewer crew. Your omission is costing me money."

Caithny sighed. "I'll add it to the payment you get at the end of the run. How much will this addition be?"

"You're not even going to haggle?" Logan asked, his nerves on edge. All smugglers haggled. It was in their blood. The only reason for a man not to haggle was because he had no intention of paying at all. "Doesn't sound like the Caithny I've heard about."

"I have more important things to attend to than negotiating with you." Caithny nodded to the stranger. "Find a berth below. We'll talk later."

"And watch your step, Cargo," Logan said. "It doesn't take much for me to toss unwanted ballast overboard. Ask any of my crew."

Cargo turned back. After surveying Logan for a moment, he touched his hat in a mocking salute. Then he vanished below decks.

"I'm starting to get a bit annoyed with you," Logan growled at Caithny.

"Calm down, Lockridge. We got the shipment down,

and you'll get your cut."

"Why not settle up now?"

"Once we reach Scotland again is soon enough. That was the agreement." Caithny gave him a wicked grin. "After all, I need some reason to keep you from tossing me overboard."

Chapter 19

≈

GEMMA WAS COMMITTED TO STAYING in London, but she almost regretted her decision to come. Her aunt took her to some extremely modest entertainments, and around to meet her friends—fussy matrons, the lot of them, though they were all very kind. But Gemma felt lost. She didn't have Hector to ride. She didn't have Fergus or the other household staff who she missed like family. And she didn't have any friends.

To make it worse, every time she went out for a walk or to perform some small errand, she felt as if she was being watched. The feeling only grew stronger day by day. But there were so many people! Anyone and everyone could be watching her. Gemma tried to shrug off the sensation. She simply had to adjust to the busy life of London.

One thing that could not be put off was a visit to a dressmaker. Maura said Gemma had no hope of making any sort of positive impression on society if she didn't have the proper wardrobe, since her own gowns were unsuitable for the city. They left the hotel early and were driven to a street known for having many reputable dressmakers, tailors, and modistes.

As she walked alongside Aunt Maura, Gemma's mind

was far away. She wondered where Logan was, if he even thought about her. And where was Uncle Conall? The news of him leaving Caithny was still astonishing to her, and the fact that he left on the *Mistral* with Logan filled her with a sense of foreboding. It wasn't that she thought Logan might expose her transgression—she couldn't believe that, no matter how angry she was at his abrupt departure. But those two men, together. She bit her lip in worry. Both were ambitious and both could be ruthless. It wouldn't end well....

Gemma was so lost in thought that she literally walked into a lady coming the other direction. She could have sworn no one was there, but the lady's *oof* proved otherwise.

"Oh, I am so sorry!" Gemma cried. "Do forgive me!" Would the stranger sneer at her, in her provincial clothes and northern accent?

"Goodness!" the other lady said, laughing. "That was quite a bump! Are you all right, my dear?"

"Yes, thank you," Gemma stammered. Taking a longer look at the other woman's silk shot gown, she knew this must be a fine lady indeed. She was only a little older than Gemma, but obviously sophisticated. She wore her dark hair unusually short, and had lovely dark eyes set in a narrow face. Fortunately, that face wore a smile.

"I am Sophia, Lady Forester," the woman said. She spoke with a French accent, and the *Sophia* sounded like a rare specimen. "And you are?"

"Gemma Harrington, my lady," she said, still a bit jolted. "This is my aunt, Mrs Douglas. I do apologize for my clumsiness. I was not paying attention."

Lady Forester waved the apology away. Even that simple gesture was elegant. "No need to think of it. But

perhaps you could do me a favor." She looked speculatively at Gemma. "I am on my way to the milliners, but I
am absolutely divided over which hat I want. An unbiased
opinion will help. Will you accompany me? It's just up
the street."

"Of course," Gemma said hurriedly, nudging her aunt
to nod as well. Lady Forester took Gemma's arm as if
they had been friends for years.

"You'll find my opinion untutored," Gemma confessed to her. "I have only recently come to London, and I
know nothing of the fashions here. I was going to entrust
all to the dressmaker."

Lady Forester looked horrified. "You must not do that!
They will take advantage of you quite shamelessly." Then
her eyes brightened. "I know! I will join you. Right after
this hat business is concluded. I do love looking at all the
fabrics. You don't mind, Miss Harrington?"

Something in Lady Forester's voice already wrapped
itself around Gemma's heart. What could she say? "That
would be most kind of you, my lady."

The day passed by in a whirl. Gemma felt like a
princess at the modiste's salon. Lady Forester recom-
mended Madame Lucille and apparently knew her personally, to judge by the warmth of their welcome at
Madame Lucille's discreet but well-appointed establish-
ment.

"Lady Forester!" Lucille cried. "You have brought me
a new beauty to drape, have you not?" The plump older
lady was severely dressed herself, but the number of gorgeous gowns in various states of completion proved she
knew her art.

"My *good* friend Miss Harrington is in dire need,"
Lady Forester said, with every suggestion that they'd

known each other from the cradle. "I said to her, Madame Lucille is the only artist to go to in this country."

"You are too kind," Lucille murmured. "Miss Harrington, is it? What do you need today?"

"Everything," Gemma admitted. "I have no wardrobe to speak of, and I have been told I should barely step outside until I have more appropriate garb, unless I wish to be a laughingstock among the ton."

"I doubt they shall laugh too hard," said Lady Forester. "But let us commence."

The modiste gave orders to two young women waiting nearby, who proved to be the models. They vanished and then reappeared, each wearing a new garment. "These styles are the very latest from Paris," Lucille said. "Their delicacy will highlight a young lady's figure."

Gemma wrinkled her nose a bit. "They are very pretty, but must I dress as a confection? And why are they both wearing pink?"

Assessing her new client with a professional eye, Lucille changed tactics immediately. "These are only for inspiration! Of course, you shall have fabric in your choice."

"I like that heather tweed," Gemma said, pointing at a bolt on a shelf.

"That's meant for a man's jacket," the modiste explained. "It's only here by mistake in fact."

"But I love the color. It would do for a riding habit, wouldn't it? I shall need four at minimum. I ride constantly."

"So important, to have a hobby such as that," Lady Forester said. "Let's see the habits." She made a gesture, and the two models quickly changed into riding habits.

"Oh, that's better." Gemma pointed. "I like the top of

that one, but not the flounce on the bottom. Leave that off and make it up in the heather."

"Yes, ma'am," Lucille said, a speculative light in her eye. "Indeed, there may be something in using men's fabrics for you. A lady with a certain boldness in her manner must dress the part, yes?"

Gemma nodded. "And this other one. What do you think, my lady?"

Lady Forester pursed her lips. "The lines are good. A rich brown velveteen would look smart. Add some buttons along here," she said, indicating, "Brass, I think, and keep the hood, but line it in green. That will make your hair absolutely dazzling."

Aunt Maura, still rather stunned by the sudden arrival of this Lady Forester, sat in a chair and watched it all as if it were a piece of theater.

Once Gemma got into the spirit of the day, she found herself engaged in the process. Lady Forester was invaluable, making subtle recommendations and offering what Gemma assumed to be well earned knowledge brought straight from Paris.

In general, Gemma loved more tailored looks that suited her preference for a less fussy appearance. She chose several tweeds, velvets, and thick broadcloth samples in simple, almost manly styles. Aunt Maura insisted she also order several evening gowns in a more traditional look.

As the women gazed at and argued over the merits of this or that design, Lady Forester drew out nearly all of Gemma's life story, or so it seemed. And yet she did it in such a way that Gemma never felt that she was boring her. Indeed, Lady Forester seemed quite fascinated by certain aspects of Gemma's past, and Gemma had to censor herself at a few points to avoid revealing information an aristocrat like Lady Forester would never understand or approve of. But Lady Forester was unusually sympathetic, and it was entirely too easy to want to tell her everything.

"Do you see this green silk, Miss Harrington," said Lady Forester at last. "It will make your hair glow." She then pointed to the model wearing a beautifully cut evening gown, with a low neckline, a high waist, and nothing but miles of soft folds of fabric for the skirt. "That style in the green silk will make the perfect coming out gown. One *must* make an impression that night."

"It's gorgeous. But isn't it too...daring?" she asked, secretly wondering what Logan would think if he saw her in that gown.

"Oh, no," Lucille said. "It's perfect. Just what the most fashionable ladies wear."

In the end, she acquired a nearly complete wardrobe. She even wore a new afternoon gown out of the shop. The loose fitting style was both modern and easy to wear, since it didn't have to be excessively tailored. Gemma already loved it.

"I'm famished, and no surprise. It's well past noon," Lady Forester announced when they stepped onto the street again. "Ladies, would you join me for a late luncheon?"

Gemma was flustered. "We should be an imposition."

"Nonsense. We shall be good friends, and friends cannot impose."

"I must retire to our rooms," Aunt Maura interjected, perhaps thinking Gemma should also withdraw from such august company before she made a fool of herself.

Lady Forester quashed that plan with an airy comment. "Of course, Mrs Douglas. You'll permit us to drive you to your hotel on our way to lunch, and of course I'll have my carriage bring Miss Harrington back."

While the two ladies were at lunch, several people stopped to say hello to Lady Forester, and thus were introduced to Gemma. Lady Forester took great pleasure in releasing a new and not always truthful tidbit of information every time someone appeared.

Miss Harrington lives in a charming castle in Scotland.

Miss Harrington is of course highly sought after among Scottish society.

Did you know her family is connected to the Duke of York?

She is a unparalleled horsewoman. The Prinzessin of Gutenberg once complimented her on her skill.

"You're making things up!" Gemma whispered after one gentleman left the table, convinced Gemma personally knew royalty throughout Europe.

"I do that," Lady Forester said, impishly. "It's fun. Besides, rumors are the meat and drink of society. If you start the rumors properly, you can walk in any door in London."

"But they're not *true*."

"Truth! What is that?" She waved a careless hand. "Certainly not a thing to be handed out on a whim." She leaned toward Gemma, lowering her voice. "Truth is special, a secret. Keep it close to your heart and only share it with people who deserve to know it. What is more powerful than a truth only two people know? A secret no one else shares?"

Gemma took an unsteady breath. The other woman's words made her think too much of the night she spent with Logan. Subconsciously, she reached into her reticule and curled her hand around the compass. "Sometimes, two people is too many to know a secret."

Lady Forester gave her a slow, pleased smile. "Very wise. But what are you fidgeting with, dear?"

Gemma pulled out the compass. It was as beautiful as before, and she still felt as confused as ever when she saw it.

Lady Forester looked at the compass with great interest. "What a pretty thing. May I?"

Gemma handed the piece to her with a sense of trepidation.

Lady Forester turned it around, nodding when she saw the *H*. "Is the compass an heirloom of yours?" she asked. Then she pressed the button to open the lid, revealing the spinning needle and the diamond glinting at the north point.

"No," said Gemma. "I acquired it only recently."

"So the *H* does not stand for Harrington?"

Thinking of how little she really knew of Logan Lockridge, Gemma could only give a little shrug. "I have no idea what it stands for. I keep it as a...memento, I suppose."

"What sort of memento? You don't look very happy when you discuss it," the other woman noted.

"It reminds me not everyone can be trusted."

"An important lesson, to be sure." Lady Forester closed the lid. She handed the compass back to Gemma. "Keep it safe. Perhaps one day you'll learn more about its history."

Gemma doubted it, but she slid the piece back into its pocket of the reticule. It did not occur to her until much later that Lady Forester recognized the object as a compass before she ever opened the lid.

Chapter 20

≈≈

THE RETURN FROM CALAIS DIDN'T take long. Though the winter seas were deadly cold, the few squalls that rushed overhead did nothing worse than spattering the *Mistral*'s deck with rain. Logan should be pleased, but he wasn't. The closer they got to the coast of Scotland, the more edgy he became.

Logan eked all he could out of his ship, but even so, it was past dark when they finally reached their destination. As the *Mistral* edged closer to the coast near Caithny, the wind picked up. Logan was glad he was wearing his leather overcoat. Though hardly fashionable, the leather repelled the wind and cold rain even better than the wool coats most sailors wore. He heard several of them cursing as they went about last minute business on deck. Unsurprisingly, the smuggling business, much like legitimate business, dropped off during the colder months. Cold air and rough seas made for hard sailing.

Logan watched Conall Caithny out of the corner of his eye. Caithny was still wearing his garish yellow coat and the floppy hat, both of which had to be older than Logan. Such an unthreatening figure, but Logan trusted the man less every day. Conall spoke with the few men he'd brought along every quarter hour or so, and Logan wondered what was so important.

Toby walked up to Logan. The first mate was smiling. To anyone else, it looked as if he was about to share a joke with his captain. Logan saw the look in Toby's eyes and knew differently.

"What's on your mind?" he asked, keeping his voice low and easy.

"Best part of a journey is coming into a home port," Toby said. "I always loved seeing the shore come into the view, and the outline of the trees. You made it home once more. No matter what else is happening, you can just feel all your troubles fade for a little while. A relief, it is."

"I know what you mean," Logan said.

"So why are all Conall's men not happy?" Toby went on, though he was looking out at the water. "They should be relaxed. Their jobs are done. Yet they're all nervous."

Logan surveyed the ship, noticing how Conall's men —all four of them—placed themselves on the deck, and how Conall stood up near the bow, in view of all of them. "Getting ready for a fight," he said quietly.

"And not with the law," Toby guessed. "Caithny's got something planned for you."

"That should be interesting," Logan said, keeping his tone relaxed. "Why not check on each of our men, Toby. Make sure they're ready for a signal."

"Which signal?" Toby asked.

"Depends on what happens. Keep sharp."

As Toby moved off, Logan saw another shape emerge. Cargo had just stepped on deck. Logan didn't like the man at all. He barely spoke a word since he came aboard, and he always looked as if he were planning to kill someone—not out of rage, but more out of habit. His name was still a mystery, so Logan called him Cargo, and that stuck among the crew.

On its final tack, the *Mistral* approached the pier jutting out furthest from Caithny's warehouse. Several men were standing along the pier, their attitude far too watchful for ordinary workers.

There were also too many of them. Caithny must have known there'd be no crates to be unloaded on the return. So why would he have all his men at the ready?

Logan's crew continued to work as normal, casting ropes toward the men on the pier. Several of the more athletic men even jumped aboard the *Mistral*, which didn't please Logan. No one boarded a ship without a captain's permission…unless their intentions were unfriendly. The flash of a knife blade in the hands of one those men was the last straw. Whatever was going on, Logan wanted to get the *Mistral* back out on the water, well away from the bulk of Caithny's people.

So Logan said, without looking at his first mate, "Hey Toby, remember St George's." The whole crew knew what to do when they heard the cryptic phrase.

Before anyone else could react, Toby and the rest of the *Mistral*'s crew cast off again, before the ship was fully secured. One sailer kicked the gangplank where it met the deck, and the whole works fell into the water with a splash.

"What the hell are you doing, Lockridge?" Caithny yelled.

"I could ask you the same thing," Logan returned. "Lot of men for no cargo to unload!"

A half a dozen of the men had gotten on board, but they looked around nervously when they saw things were not going as they expected.

One of them pulled out a gun, giving up the pretense of being there to unload crates. Logan was faster, and knocked it out of the man's hand. Then he seized the man and pushed him to the ground. "Someone get Caithny!" he ordered.

Scuffles broke out along the deck as men rushed towards each other, all with conflicting orders. Gunfire rang out a few times, but mostly it was grunts and hisses as a dozen or more angry men fought each other. Toby yelled for help, and Logan looked over to find him swarmed by Caithny's men. Logan hit his opponent hard in the head to knock him out, then rushed to Toby.

He pulled one smuggler off Toby, dropping him to the wooden decking.

"Stand back," he growled at the others. "Unless you want a blade in your belly."

Toby took advantage of the distraction to duck and pull down another man. He then drew out two chef's knifes—his preferred weapons. "I'll manage these, sir. Caithny's getting away." He nodded to the side of the ship, where Conall was just about to climb the rail to jump to the safety of the dock. The *Mistral* was floating free, but was barely within range for a desperate person to jump off.

"Caithny!" he shouted. "Put one foot on that rail and I'll shoot you."

"Go to hell, Lockridge!"

Logan trained his gun on Caithny. But before he could squeeze the trigger, a shot rang out. Caithny screamed and fell backward. A splash sounded just after.

Logan spun to see who fired.

Cargo lowered the gun he held, smoke wafting from

the barrel.

"You missed," Logan said. Surely he'd been the target.

Cargo gave him a thin smile, then said, "No, I didn't." Without another word, Cargo dropped the gun to the deck, turned, and launched his thin body over the rail on the seaward side, a long, dangerous dive into dark water. Logan and several others rushed to the rail. A splash proved the cargo did hit the water, but it was too dark to discern what was waves, or human, or just flotsam.

"Must be mad," one sailor muttered. "I wouldn't jump blind like that."

"Want us to go after him, captain?" another asked.

"No." Logan stared at the surface of the water. He wouldn't send anyone in against an unknown quantity like Cargo. Then he yelled, "Someone find Caithny! Him I *do* want."

A few crew were already near the place Caithny fell from. One was peering hard over the side. He pointed. "Captain! Just over there!"

Logan joined him and saw what he was pointing at. A body floated facedown in the water, already drifting farther away from the ship. It was Caithny. His distinctive yellow jacket was still visible, and the stupid hat floated nearby.

"Not moving," the sailor muttered. "Want us to haul the body up?"

Logan nodded, but then everyone heard a commotion at the pier. More men were running down the docks toward the *Mistral*, and they were well armed.

"Hell," Logan muttered. "Get underway!"

The crew scrambled to get the *Mistral* away from the dock before she could be boarded by the reinforcements, whoever they were. The men shot at the ship, but seemed disinclined to do more, especially when the *Mistral*'s crew shot back.

Logan ducked the gunfire and kept moving. He saw Munro lying flat on the deck. He turned to the nearest sailors. "You can stop firing now. Tie up Munro, along with any others left on deck." He turned to Toby. "Is anyone of ours hurt?"

"Simon blocked a blade with his arm, but other than that, it's just bruises for our men."

"Good. I want to be long gone before anyone gets the idea to send a ship after us." He muttered to Toby, "Think our cove is still a secret?"

"We can try for it," the first mate replied.

The bitter cold wind soon snapped at the canvas, and the *Mistral* sailed out into the open water as swiftly as a storm cloud moved through the night.

"Keep a sharp watch," he ordered the man about to climb the mast to the crow's nest. "We'll be moving fast. I don't want any surprises. Give a wide berth should you see anything."

"Aye, captain."

Logan's breath came harder than he liked. Since he never got the opportunity to find a surgeon he trusted, his wound wasn't healing properly. But he still had work ahead of him. Logan turned his attention to Munro, who was just coming to.

"Munro. You want to tell me who your cargo was? And why he'd shoot Caithny?"

Munro blinked and shook his head. "Don't know him. He never said a word to me."

Logan bent down to Munro's level. "But Caithny told you something, because all the men on deck and all the men on the docks were ready. Tell me what was supposed to happen."

Munro looked around, but saw absolutely no help. He was alone. "Caithny wanted your ship."

"He planned to steal the *Mistral*?" Logan asked in a low voice. "He planned to steal my ship before we even left these docks on the very first run?"

"Yes, sir. Caithny needed more ships, and he thought this would be an easy prize, if he didn't try for it until after the whole run there and back. You wouldn't suspect a thing."

"And how did that work out, Munro?" Logan stared at him.

"Please don't kill me."

"Why the hell not?"

"I…I'll tell you anything."

"Do you know anything worth knowing? Such as what Caithny was shipping?"

Munro blanched. "No one knew that. He never said, and anyone who asked more than once learned not to. Everyone is scared of Caithny."

"Nothing to be scared of now." Logan straightened up. He turned to Toby. "Take them all and cram them in the brig. Put someone on watch. If they say a single word, I want to know what it is."

The prisoners were taken away. Toby returned in a few minutes, and joined Logan as they watched the shoreline recede into the darkness.

"Well, that didn't go according to plan, did it?" Toby asked.

Logan was still furious. "He was going to steal *my* ship."

"Well, you were planning to detain him."

"So? He didn't know that."

"And what will you tell Miss Gemma about her uncle? I didn't see any blood on his shirt before he went over the rail, but he must have been shot. Combined with cold water.... Well, a man his age might not have made it to a dock even if he wasn't bleeding to death."

Logan sighed. It was the first thing he thought of, actually, when Conall dropped over the side. "I don't know how to tell her. I'll think of something."

"The truth, perhaps?"

"As much of it as I can. Caithny was a smuggler, first and foremost. She knows the risks."

"That won't make it easier to tell Miss Gemma." From the way Toby said her name, it was clear that she'd made quite an impression on him, despite their only meeting for a moment.

The ship sailed into the narrow, hidden cove. All was quiet, and Logan had to risk it. If anyone was still tailing the ship by this point, they deserved to catch them.

Once the ship was anchored, Logan told Toby he was going ashore.

"Where to?"

"Caithny castle to start. I didn't see Miss Harrington at the docks and I doubt Caithny would involve her in outright seizure of a ship. But she's got to know something."

Logan reached Caithny castle as quickly as he could. A few times, he had to pause or hide as someone ran down a path or plunged through the trees heading away from the shore.

Caithny castle was eerily quiet. A few lights shone, but it felt deserted. Logan moved into the dark courtyard. He saw a light in the stables, and another where the kitchens were. He stepped toward the kitchens, reasoning that Gemma would be in the house at this hour.

A voice stopped him.

"Can I help you, sir?"

Logan spun around, seeing Fergus about twenty steps away, near the stable doors. "Fergus."

"Yes, that's me." Fergus walked forward. "Oh. It's Lockridge, isn't it? So Caithny must be on his way home."

"I need to speak to Miss Harrington. It's important."

Fergus looked away, almost guiltily. "She's not at home, sir."

"Where is she, then?" Logan asked.

"She went to London, only a few days after Caithny left."

"*London*? Alone?"

"Oh, no. Her aunt went her. And the dog. She said she wanted to be there for the Season."

"And they left you behind?"

"Well, someone had to see to Hector."

Logan turned around, looking about the buildings. Everything was so normal, so quiet. If Caithny was dead, and Gemma was gone, there was little he could do here. Not until he learned more. What made Gemma rush to London instead of waiting for Logan to return? There was one quick way to find out.

"Listen, Fergus. I'm sailing to London when the tide turns. If you can get yourself and Hector ready in a half hour, you've got yourselves passage. Trust me, there is no reason for you to be hanging around this ruin any more."

Fergus gave him an odd look. "What's happened, sir?"

"I'll explain later. You interested?"

"Yes, sir. I'll just tell the others I'm going away, so they won't worry."

"Make it fast, Fergus. The tide doesn't wait."

Fergus was fast. He was also admirably uncurious, asking no questions about why the *Mistral* was located in a cove instead of by Caithny's docks or the wharfs of the town. He didn't ask where his employer was, either. Fergus and Hector were on board well before the tide turned.

Toby had done his duty by then, which was to haul their few prisoners out to the woods and turn them loose. They'd wander for a bit before finding the way back to their homes. Logan didn't care much about them, but he also didn't want more bodies lying around. Lockridge was ruthless, but he wasn't stupid.

So the *Mistral* sailed South again, the bow cutting though the dark water like a blade. Despite the cold, Logan stayed on deck for a while. His thoughts were too chaotic for him to retire to his quarters. All he could think about was the violence that just happened, and what he could possibly tell Gemma that might make it better.

He'd thought his assignment would be concluded tonight. Instead, his main target was dead, there was a new and deadly stranger involved, he still didn't know what Conall had been shipping, and he had only a few threads to investigate. But some of those threads were in London, where Gemma apparently was. So how could he go anywhere else?

Chapter 21

≈

LADY FORESTER CALLED ON GEMMA, breezing into the rented rooms as if she'd done it all her life. "Now, then. Your wardrobe is more or less settled, which must be a great comfort to you. But the matter of suitable housing remains to be addressed. You can't stay on here, of course."

"I never had to look for a home before," Gemma admitted.

"Ah, but I have. There are several properties that might suit you, all in respectable neighborhoods. It would not do to live somewhere unfashionable!"

Almost before she knew what was happening, Gemma had joined Lady Forester in a coach for a tour of likely homes.

The journey did not start auspiciously. Gemma hated the first house, a large stone mansion near Hyde Park. "No, it won't do at all. It's so dark and…stony." The truth was that the place reminded Gemma too strongly of Caithny, which made her uncomfortable.

The second house was too old. The third house was too large. The fourth house was too cramped, and the fifth smelled of fish guts, according to Lady Forester herself, who took one step inside and then left again.

Lady Forester showed no signs of fatigue, but Gemma

was feeling restless by that point in the search. She apologized for being so fussy.

"Nonsense," her new friend said bluntly. "One's home is one's castle. Even if it's not actually a castle," she added with a smile.

"My castle was more a crumbling pile of stones," Gemma said.

"Well, there's no reason to tell anyone that. Let them dream of you as a princess in a tower. People adore dreams." She leaned closer to Gemma. "But since I know your secret, you should call me Sophie in private. And I'll call you Gemma, which is such a pretty name."

Gemma smiled. She never truly had a female friend to call by a given name, not since she was a child. "I would like that, Sophie," she said.

The seventh place they looked at was in a quiet, tree-lined street. Not so fashionable as the other neighborhoods, perhaps, but gracious. The man who had charge of the property met them there, and explained that the neighborhood was built by wealthy tradesmen, for the most part, men who had money but not the status to live in the better neighborhoods at the time. "But time has made this street more honored, and now no one will blink at the name. A baronet lives over there," the agent said, pointing. "And here is the house for rent."

The house struck Gemma as perfect. The front hall was filled with light from the westering sun, and the rooms seemed charming and well proportioned. She smiled as she walked though the empty spaces, thinking of the furniture and wall coverings that would fit best.

"I could see this sitting room all in red and white, couldn't you? With a velvet couch by the fire."

"Lovely," said Sophie.

"Let's look upstairs," said Gemma, already on the steps. She found it as promising as the first. "This is the place I want," she declared. "What is the price?"

"The requested rent is well within your means, Miss Harrington," the agent assured her.

"Rent," she mused. "And to buy?"

Sophie raised an eyebrow. "Should you not live here for a little while before making that decision? You've only been in London for a week!"

"But I love this house."

"I will make inquiries, miss," the agent said diffidently, "and let you know if the owner wishes to sell."

* * * *

She returned to the hotel full of her old spirit. "Aunt Maura! Good news! I have rented a house."

"Gemma," her aunt said, dismayed. "Without consulting me?"

"Lady Forester was with me, and the solicitor's agent. It's a lovely place in Kingston Street. You'll see."

"Will you ever take a moment to contemplate your decisions, Gemma?"

"It was the seventh house we looked at!"

"That's not what I meant." Aunt Maura gave a thin sigh of accepting-her-cross-to-bear. "I think I may rest in my room for a while."

Sophie watched her go, but said only, "The house is rented, but there's more work to be done. You'll need servants, of course."

"Oh, yes," Gemma said. Naturally, servants did not simply appear with the house. "I've never had to hire servants, either. What is the process?"

"Just leave it to me."

"But that's far too much effort...."

"Nonsense. As it happens, I know exactly who you need. They'll be there the day you wish to move in."

And thus, within days, Gemma found herself not only with a new home but also a full staff of servants, each of whom looked as if they trained from infancy for the role.

She did not even get in the door of the new place before she met her new employees. A young man dressed as a footman *materialized* at the carriage when it stopped.

"Welcome home, Miss Harrington, Mrs Douglas," he said. "We have been expecting you. Stiles will have all the particulars."

"Stiles?" Aunt Maura asked.

"The butler, ma'am. And my name is Jem." He couldn't stop a brief grin from illuminating his face. "James Harper as I was christened, but Jem will do."

They proceeded inside, where a short man stood at attention. The butler, without a doubt. "Mr Stiles?" Gemma asked.

"Stiles," he said, with a sharp nod. He gestured to the row of people standing at one side of the hall. "Let me introduce the others to you both."

He went through the row with commendable efficiency.

Jem, of course, was already known.

Lucy Bond was the tall girl with curls in her hair, who would be the lady's maid.

Mrs Mavis, long and thin, was the housekeeper, while Mrs Rand was the reassuringly plump cook. Despite the "Mrs", Gemma later discovered neither woman was married.

A shorter young woman with black hair was Ivy, the

head housemaid.

At the end of the line, Sally Beckett was the youngest girl, not over ten, and she would be scullion, messenger, and maid of all work. "She doesn't speak, ma'am," Mrs Mavis explained. "An accident in her childhood. But she's sharp as a tack, and a good worker."

Gemma looked at Sally more carefully. The girl kept her eyes on the floor, as if afraid she'd be noticed.

"Look at me, Sally," Gemma said, keeping her voice gentle.

Big, dark blue eyes looked up at her. They were the prettiest eyes Gemma thought she'd ever seen. "I can tell already that you'll be an excellent addition to the house, Miss Sally," she said. "You must keep all these others in line, do you hear me?"

Sally's eyes grew even bigger. She took one gulping breath, then nodded firmly. No trace of a smile crossed her lips, but Gemma sensed the girl relax. This was perhaps her first position in a household.

"Now then," she said. "Who will help me to my room?"

Bond immediately took on the duty. She showed Gemma upstairs and explained she had been unpacking all the new clothes as they were delivered to the house.

The first outfits from Madame Lucille were rushed so Gemma would have a presentable wardrobe as quickly as possible. That was fortunate, because she already had a number of engagements. Meeting Lady Forester seemed to catapult her into a new social sphere she never could have attained on her own. Sophie invited her to dinners, to musical performances, to parties. Other invitations flowed in soon after. The Season had not even begun, but Gemma was already a known name.

As packages arrived, the bedroom was soon covered in tweeds, velveteens, tailored jackets, little satin top hats, and a whole collection of riding boots. Bond worked diligently to get everything sorted, and exclaimed in pleasure over the modishness and practicality of the outfits.

One thing Bond noticed immediately was that Gemma did not own much jewelry to accompany her clothing. She had a little gold cross from her mother which she wore on a chain around her neck, and a few other items, but little else of significance. When Bond saw the compass lying on Gemma's bedside table, it was her idea to add it to Gemma's jackets, just like a gentleman's pocket watch on a chain.

"But won't people think it odd?" Gemma asked.

"They'll be jealous they didn't think of it first," said Bond. "The other ladies will be beside themselves."

Gemma dressed in one of her new outfits, eager to see how it would transform her into a perfect society lady. As she stood admiring her look in front of a full length mirror, she heard a meaningful cough behind her.

Bond stood near the edge of the bed, the open case containing Gemma's pistols on the bed in front of her. "Where should these go, ma'am?"

Gemma felt a slow flush come on her. "Ah…with my other accessories, perhaps?"

Far from being shocked, the maid gave a tiny smile. "Indeed, ma'am. Do let me know which outfit you'd prefer to accessorize with these. I'll have to be sure they're polished in time."

"Not to mention deciding how to carry the ammunition," Gemma added, feeling better. Wherever Lady Forester found these servants, they were certainly up to the task.

Chapter 22

GEMMA ADJUSTED TO CITY LIFE soon enough, mostly by exploring as much of London as she could. She took Chance for walks every day, learning about her new neighborhood and the fashionable parks and lanes nearby. Even in the dark days of early winter, the city had its charms.

The dog was not a puppy, but he was still young and energetic. She enjoyed their walks, and considered Chance to be a very fine chaperone. Today, she wore one of her new walking dresses in a lovely shade of green, dark as a pine forest. Over the dress, she wore a tweed jacket that was distinctly military in style. The addition of soft brown leather walking boots, matching gloves, and a darling hat with ostrich feathers made her feel quite at home in London. Chance walked beside her, sniffing excitedly at all the new smells in the city.

She certainly caught the eyes of many people as she moved through the parks, where many of London's high society went to see and be seen. She smiled greetings to several people who were in her path. She knew better than to strike up conversations with unknown gentlemen, but her natural ebullience was on full display, and the fact that she was a pretty, slightly mysterious, and well-dressed lady made her a popular subject of gossip among those in the park.

Gemma and Chance were walking down a narrower side path when all of a sudden Chance gave one bark and bolted toward a retreating squirrel, taking Gemma by surprise.

"Chance!" she called. "Come back!"

But the dog wasn't well enough trained yet, and he disappeared among the undergrowth. Gemma called for Chance as she hurried on. She caught no sign of the dog, and grew increasingly agitated. Chance might run into a wild dog. Or run under a carriage. Or spook a horse. Or a person.

When she reached the far end of the park, where the river met the grounds, she noticed a tall, redheaded man walking toward her. And beside him was Chance, trotting along very well on his leash.

Without thinking of the proprieties, Gemma rushed toward the pair.

"Chance!" she called. The dog snapped to attention, then strained at the leash, hurrying the stranger along toward Gemma.

"Hello," he said when they reached her. "I found this dog a quarter hour ago, and thought if I walked him around, he'd sniff out his owner."

Gemma bent to hug Chance. "Oh, yes! Thank you. Chance," she added, "I can't take you out again if you run like that!"

She straightened up, focusing on the man. He was big and tall, and very well-made. He was perhaps around thirty, but something in his face suggested eternal boyishness.

He had light blue eyes, and they were looking right at her.

He handed her the leash with a smile. "Here you are."

"Thank you," she said again, somewhat embarrassed now. "Chance is usually very well behaved. I'm not sure what got into him."

"Well, whatever it is, I'm grateful," the man said. His voice confirmed what his appearance already hinted at. He was Scottish. From the highlands, to judge by the thickness of his accent. "It gives me a chance to speak to you."

Gemma knew that his behavior skirted the bounds of good manners, at least among the ton. "Do I know you, sir?" she asked, giving him a chance to explain himself.

"You don't," he said, "But I'd like to change that."

"That is very forward of you," she said, though it was hard to be offended by his words, since he delivered them in such an honest way.

"Aye, it is. I've never mastered the fine manners of the south. Lord MacLachlan, at your service, Miss Harrington."

"So you know my name."

"Every man in London knows your name," he said frankly. "I think you'll soon wish it otherwise."

"Oh, indeed?" she asked. "For all you know, I've come to London expressly for that purpose—having everyone know my name, I mean."

"Then you'll succeed." He laughed ruefully. "And here I am without anyone to make a proper introduction. Now how can I call on you later?"

So he too found the little rules of society to be rather inexplicable. She said, "Well, one way to call on me might be to come and leave your card during visiting hours. At present, I am staying in Kingston Street—the blue house on the east side."

"I'll remember that, Miss Harrington. A very good day to you." He bowed slightly.

She turned and walked away slowly, glancing back once. MacLachlan was ambling away in another direction. Chance gave her a look of confusion.

"Yes, yes, we're going home now. And you're not to run off again!" Thank goodness MacLachlan was there to catch Chance. She hoped he would call on her; hearing his voice gave her a sudden bout of homesickness. Perhaps MacLachlan might be a friend. Or more.

Without thinking about it, she slid a hand into the pocket of her riding habit, and encountered the compass. The heaviness of it broke her pleasant musings about charming gentlemen she might marry. As long as Logan haunted her heart, she couldn't be happy with another.

* * * *

Lord MacLachlan took her words seriously, and the very next day, he called on her at home. Aunt Maura was in the parlor with Gemma. In between the trickle of visitors, who were mostly neighbors, the ladies were discussing furnishings and design for the house. Only a few rooms were remotely close to finished, and Gemma had decided the house was destined to be hers forever, so she threw herself into decorating. Maura did her best to rein in Gemma's enthusiasm, in her delicate, mild way.

Lord MacLachlan was announced and Gemma told Jem to show him in.

"Who is this person?" Maura asked.

"We met in the park yesterday," Gemma said. "And I told him to call."

One elegant eyebrow went up. "Who introduced him to you?"

"Ah…" Gemma paused. "No one."

"Oh, heavens," Maura said with a sigh of long suffering. "We'll be lucky if you are invited anywhere this Season. Asking a complete stranger to call, and no one to vouch…"

"It wasn't like that! Chance got loose and Lord Mac-Lachlan found him and returned him to me!"

"I heard my name," a man's voice said.

"Lord MacLachlan!" Gemma cried out, seeing their guest enter. "I am so glad you listened to me. Please let me introduce my aunt, Mrs Douglas."

"How do you do, Mrs Douglas." MacLachlan bowed very properly to Maura, which meant he bowed quite low, since he was six feet tall, and the petite Maura was sitting. "Has your niece relayed the unconventionality of our meeting?"

"Only just, my lord," Maura admitted. But she smiled, both at MacLachlan's candor and his accent. "This time I will excuse it, since you are a countryman."

"You noticed!" he said, laughing, because of course his Scottish accent was the most noticeable thing about him. "I will not offend your sense of propriety again, ma'am. I am learning the rules of London society…slowly. And with many mistakes."

"It is like learning how to play a new game in a new language, isn't it?" Gemma asked.

"Worse. Many of the other players are doing their level best to see me fail in the most humiliating way possible." He told a story of his first day in London, in which he described so many faux pas that Gemma was sure he was making it all up. But both she and Maura were laughing at the end.

"If you don't care for city living, what brings you all the way to London this Season?" Maura asked.

He straightened up, his face a bit more serious. "The usual reason. I am in search of a wife." He looked at Gemma as he spoke.

"There are no suitable ladies in your part of Scotland?" she asked.

"The MacLachlan lands are in a rather remote area, even for the highlands," he said. "The countryside is beautiful—as are the women, naturally—but I have not found a lady to suit my needs. Thus I cast a wider net."

"And what do you offer as bait?" Gemma asked boldly.

"Besides my good looks and charm?" he returned, his smile making it clear he was making fun of himself. "I am the Baron of MacLachlan now, since my father passed three years ago. My bride gains a title, and the castle Lachlan, which is still mostly in one piece."

"More than I can say for Caithny castle, which is where I grew up! With such a prize, you must not lack for potential brides."

He sighed. "There is a catch. I am looking for a match that is financially advantageous. Lachlan's lands and people require it."

"Ah," Maura said. Her tone was understanding, though. "You need a rich woman to marry you."

"You are astute, ma'am. I have plans to reinvigorate our herds with new breeds, and to start a distillery to increase our clan's income over time. But I must find the funds to begin the work."

"And a wife does not need to be repaid, while a loan does," Gemma noted.

"Fair to say," MacLachlan agreed. "But I have no doubt I will succeed, and my wife will find herself wealthier in ten years than on the day we marry. Not to mention, she'll be Lady MacLachlan, and what's worth more than that?"

Gemma smiled. "One might accuse you of boasting, my lord. Not that *I* am accusing you, of course."

"You are far too proper and circumspect to do so, Miss Harrington."

Aunt Maura couldn't stop from laughing out loud. "Proper? Circumspect? You are describing another Miss Harrington, my lord."

MacLachlan smiled. "Then we shall have to make do with this one, Mrs Douglas, however bold she may be." He stood up then. "I must not overstay my welcome. But may I call on you again? Hearing your voices makes me think of home."

Gemma was about to answer, then looked over at Maura. She could be proper, when she tried. "Aunt?"

Maura gave MacLachlan a considering look, more for effect than any real hesitation. "We should look forward to it, my lord," she said finally.

MacLachlan gave a comic sigh of relief. "Thank the stars. Good day, ladies."

After he left, Maura sat back, shaking her head. "Incorrigible."

"I like him."

"I like him too, but you must comport yourself very carefully around such a gentleman, Gemma. He may not be at all suitable for a husband, despite his pretty story. I will make inquiries."

"I met him yesterday, Aunt! Please don't rush into assumptions."

"Why do you think he mentioned so much about his plans? He's already set his sights on you as a candidate."

"Nonsense," Gemma said, shifting uncomfortably. "I might have fifteen thousand a year, but I have no title. He's a baron, so he'd look first among the aristocracy."

"That matters less than you think." Maura frowned. "Please be most careful in the future, dear. I sensed no ill will from this Lord MacLachlan, but there will be many men in the city all too eager to trap you into marriage. Behave yourself to the utmost."

"You're exaggerating."

"Not in the least. A breath of scandal could lock you into a most distressing position. The rules are there for a reason."

A breath of scandal? A *hurricane* of scandal awaited Gemma, if Logan Lockridge ever resurfaced and told the truth about what happened between them. Which of course, he wouldn't. Not here in London.

Gemma smiled at her aunt, determined not to borrow trouble. "I will try, Aunt Maura. But he was a dear, wasn't he?"

"MacLachlan? He seemed so. Of course, he's Scottish, so that's a point in his favor."

* * * *

Gemma enjoyed her new home very much, but she felt it truly became home when Fergus arrived one day with Hector in tow.

She shouted with joy when she saw her favorite horse, and she flung her arms around Fergus so enthusiastically that the older man coughed in alarm.

"Mind my lungs, Gemma girl," he managed to say.

But his grin made it clear he was pleased.

"Oh, how wonderful!" she said. "You never even sent word that you were coming! How did you sneak out of Caithny?"

"I didn't sneak out," Fergus said, affronted. "With the master gone, who was to say no?"

"Gone? You mean Uncle Conall didn't return?" she asked, a little worry in her heart.

"I didn't see him by the time I left, and I didn't care to wait, if you understand. The rest of the staff is keeping an eye on the place till he gets back. I thought I might be of more use here."

"But how did you find us?"

"Your aunt sent me word of your doings, and the street direction was there on the letter, wasn't it?"

"Of course. You must have spent some cash on the journey. I'll repay it immediately."

"I didn't, as a matter of fact."

Gemma paused. "What do you mean?"

"That man Lockridge returned to Caithny on his own business. I told him the news—that you were here, and he said he was going to London too, and had room aboard if I wished to bring Hector to you. No charge. Said it was a shame to let a beast like Hector be wasted while his mistress was in London."

Did that mean Logan was also in London at that very moment? She wasn't sure whether to be excited or angry or scared.

"He didn't ask any fee?" she wanted to know. "Doesn't seem like very good business for a smuggler."

"Well, I didn't want to look a gift horse in the mouth, so to speak. I accepted the offer straight away, and here I am. He's more of a gentleman than most of the so-called gentlemen, for certain. Runs his ship well," Fergus added in approval.

"Hmph." Yes, it was the *Mistral* he seemed to care about most, she reminded herself.

"I'm glad you are here, however you arrived," she said. "And I'm so happy to see Hector. There's a mews behind the house. Let's go."

Gemma went with Fergus to the mews. She was not surprised to find Jem there, already readying a stall for Hector. The boy had some uncanny knack for knowing when and where he was needed. "Jem, this is Fergus. He was hostler up in Caithny, and he's brought Hector all the way down. This is Hector," she added, pointing to the horse, as if there could be any confusion. "The finest steed in the world."

"Saw the horse in the front and thought it might be yours, ma'am," Jem said. "Only be a moment before his home is ready." He nodded to Fergus. "You'll be joining the household then, sir? Mrs Mavis will see a new room is made up."

Gemma smiled. Fergus would be settled in no time. "I'll leave you both to it. Jem, please show Fergus everything. I want him to think he was born here. And let me know as soon as Hector is recovered from his journey. I can't wait to go riding with him!" Her new habit in brown velveteen, with green silk lining, was perfect, and perfectly modern. She felt sure that she'd fit into the London scene without blinking now.

Logan Lockridge wouldn't even recognize her. Not that he'd have the chance to.

Chapter 23

≈

AFTER DOCKING IN LONDON, LOGAN directed Fergus to take Hector down the gangplank. The horse was obviously pleased to reach dry land once again. Logan had no trouble learning Gemma's London address directly from Fergus, who had no reason to not share it. He would make use of that soon.

But first, he went to his own rooms. He was dead tired, and wanted sleep. The carriage he hired seemed to take years to travel the streets, but finally lurched to a halt before a nondescript house near St James. Logan entered through the front—there was no servant—and hauled himself up a flight of stairs to a door on the upper floor.

Behind that was a small suite of rooms: a sitting room, with a bedroom beyond, and a sort of study in an alcove at the other side. A fireplace occupied most of one wall in the sitting room, and there was a single armchair upholstered in worn leather nearby.

He managed to get most of his clothes off before he fell into bed. He should change the bandage, he thought, but it seemed like such a bother. Instead, he rolled himself into the blanket. The habit of doing so shipboard was ingrained by now, and he was too tired to do anything other than act on instinct.

Logan lost consciousness as soon as he closed his eyes.

He woke up when a hand grabbed his shoulder. "Logan!"

"God! What?" He opened his eyes to see a slim woman with dark hair and eyes standing over him, concern all over her face. "Sophie? What are you doing here?"

"How long ago did you return to London?" she asked, straightening up.

"I don't know," he said, blinking. "What time is it?"

"About three in the afternoon."

"The afternoon of what day?"

"Thursday!" Sophie said.

"Oh, that's not so bad. I thought you were going to say Saturday. I got here this morning. How did you know about it?" He didn't bother to ask how she got inside. Sophie held a spare key to the house, just in case. She must have been worried enough to use it, not that she'd ever been overly concerned with the legality of such actions.

"Jem passed word to me that a man called Fergus showed up at Gemma's house with a horse," Sophie explained. "He said you sailed him down."

"Yes, I did." He sat up, knowing Sophie wouldn't let him sleep any longer. Then he shook his head to clear it. "Wait. You said Jem told you that. Why are the Disreputables watching her house?"

The Disreputables were an odd group the Zodiac often made use of. They were nearly all former criminals who since became trustworthy and competent domestic servants. But because of their pasts, they had skills unusual for most lady's maids or butlers. As former pickpockets, thieves, enforcers, con artists, there was no trick a Disreputable wasn't familiar with.

"You sent me a message from Scotland," Sophie said, her concern deepening. "Don't you remember? You were worried about Gemma Harrington."

"But I didn't know she came to London until Fergus told me."

The woman smiled. "Ah, but I was lucky. I put her name among those we ask our contacts to watch for, and someone offered a tip. When she arrived in London," Sophie went on, "I took it upon myself to arrange an accidental meeting with Miss Harrington, and I've been keeping an eye on her since."

"Personally?"

"Yes. I've been playing up my socialite side. And I arranged to have the Disreputables work as her new household staff."

Logan said, "Miss Harrington won't like that when she finds out."

"Why should she find out?" asked Sophie. "Will you tell her?"

"Not if I can help it. She doesn't know anything about the Zodiac or its activities. I have other bad news to ruin her day."

"Oh?"

Logan explained what happened over the past couple of weeks. Sophie listened without interrupting, her expression intent.

He concluded with the news about the death of Conall Caithny. "I should tell her as soon as possible. I don't suppose you know a place where she'll be so I can talk to her discreetly. Considering she only knows me as Lockridge, I can't exactly call at her house in broad daylight."

Sophie said, "Wait a moment. You are in *no* condition to be seen among people. You look terrible. When was the last time you shaved?"

"Don't remember."

"You should sleep," she said.

"You woke me up."

"Because you didn't bother to send word!"

"I would have soon enough," he said. "Just wanted to get a few hours' rest. Then I should find Cutter." Logan often went to Doctor Cutter when he needed medical attention that would cause awkward questions—such as unexplained bullet wounds.

"Why see Cutter? What happened?" she asked, looking him over for injuries.

He pulled aside the sheet, revealing the bandage. "Shot."

"Idiot!" Sophie glared at him. "Get up and get dressed immediately. I'm taking you to Cutter."

"Just send word. He'll come when he can."

"We're not discussing this, Logan."

He knew better than to argue with that tone. He dressed and let Sophie drag him to the street, where she had a carriage waiting.

Once they began moving, Logan said, "So you've met Gemma. Do you like her?"

"As a matter of fact, I do," said Sophie. "Strong minded young lady, once she got her bearings. Bond told me she owns a brace of pistols. Keeps them stored by the hat boxes."

"She can use them too. Great shot." Then Logan asked, more anxiously, "How is she?"

"She's doing quite well in London—especially with Lady Forester on her side." Sophie struck a pose that could only be described as aristocratic. "I needed something to do anyway. I completed an assignment in Italy, and I've been bored. Aries hasn't given me anything new for a month."

"Bored? Is Bruce not in town?" Bruce was Lord Forester, Sophie's husband and another Zodiac agent.

"Officially, he's at his estate, attending to some family matters."

"And unofficially?"

"He's solving a little problem in Leipzig." Sophie sighed, looking out the window. "It's funny. I never used to worry about anyone but myself. Now I worry all the time."

"He's perfectly capable," Logan said, "He's not in any trouble."

"Yes, but how can I be sure until he comes back?" Sophie asked, with a sad little laugh.

"I know the feeling," Logan confessed. "I don't suppose Gemma's mentioned me at all." There was no reason why she should, he knew. But people often told Sophie more than they intended to.

"She has not," Sophie said, shooting him a glance that was either sympathetic or pitying. "But she often carries a compass with her."

"Does she?" Logan felt better hearing that.

But Sophie said only, "You'll likely want to have a talk with her when you have the chance."

"I have to tell her about Caithny. She won't like it. And this assignment seemed so simple at first." He sat back and sighed. "I'm sorry."

"For what?" Sophie asked.

"I was supposed to bring back everyone involved and put an end to the supply chain. Instead, the man I researched for three months is dead, with no way to learn more about what he knows. And another man who's obviously involved shoots my main target and disappears into the ocean. And I *still* don't know exactly what was being transported. As far as the Zodiac is concerned, I failed."

Sophie frowned at him. "It's not ideal, but don't call it a failure. Caithny is dead—that link in the supply chain *is* broken. That alone will aid our side. It was thousands of pounds of aid going to the enemy, which you reduced to zero."

"For the time being."

"The time being is the only time we have. When the French establish a new supply chain, Aries will send you or another agent to destroy that one. Or the war might be over by then. You can tell Aries all you've learned."

Logan shook his head. "I haven't learned enough. It's nothing but loose ends. I'm not going to tell Aries a thing until I understand what happened and who is involved."

She looked him over. "Very well, but not until you see Cutter."

Sophie accompanied him to Cutter's office, located in a shabby district of the city about one step away from the slums. By luck, Cutter was in. So was a dead body stretched on a long table.

"Got a moment for a patient with a heartbeat?" Logan asked.

Cutter looked up, a scalpel in hand. The doctor had a narrow face, dark eyes, and a prominent, hawk-like nose. Combined with a shock of curling black hair, he looked like a man with a strong personality—and he was. "This gentleman isn't going anywhere. Go down to the third door and wait for me. I need to clean up."

Sophie took Logan's arm and walked him down the

hallway. "At least someone understands the virtue of cleanliness," she said, sniffing.

"Hold on. I wasn't the one who insisted on dragging me here." They reached the little room Cutter directed them to, and Logan sat on the operating table, more tired than he would admit.

Cutter joined them, nodding cordially to Sophie, then looking to Logan. "What's the problem?"

"I have a bullet somewhere in my side," Logan said, pulling up his shirt to reveal the bandage.

"Hmm. And when did this happen?"

"Perhaps two weeks ago."

Cutter's expression spoke for him. He thought Logan was an idiot for waiting so long.

"I was busy," Logan defended himself.

"Well, since you're still alive, I've half a mind to leave the bullet in. Opening the wound may be worse."

"No. I need it out. I can't function with metal in my muscles."

"Very well. Let me have a look." He turned briefly to Sophie. "I assume you wish to stay? You're not frightened by blood?"

"Nor by half-dressed men," Sophie said. "Please proceed."

So Cutter did. The man wasn't an official doctor—that is, he had no license to practice. But he knew what he was doing, and he had been useful to the Zodiac before. He never asked questions. Whether it meant attending to a bullet wound, or meeting a patient who might not be exactly who they said they were, Cutter did what was needed. And he never spoke about it afterward. He believed that medicine required trust between doctor and patient.

After an initial examination, Cutter said, "All right, I

can operate. But you'll want to take something for the pain." He held up a vial of liquid.

Logan shook his head. "Just start. I don't need to avoid pain."

Cutter promptly planted a fist in Logan's jaw.

Logan was so surprised by the blow that he didn't even yell.

"Do you feel more noble now?" the doctor asked.

"Damn. Why would I?" Logan asked, rubbing his jaw.

"You wouldn't," said Cutter. "Because there's nothing noble about suffering when it's avoidable. There's nothing noble about suffering, full stop. I'll be back in a few moments to take the bullet out. Now, drink this and don't complain. And trust me, it works. In a few moments, I could saw your arm off and you wouldn't mind."

"But you're not going to, right?" Logan asked. "I mean, you haven't got so many patients you'll forget what operation to perform?"

"I'll be here to remind him," Sophie said with a faint smile. "Now, follow his instructions."

Logan dutifully drank the stuff. He waited for some great change, but noticed nothing beyond a strong desire to sleep, which was something he felt all too often lately. Cutter had disappeared, though, so Sophie turned to him and said, "There's a party at Lady Mathering's tonight. Perhaps you should go."

"I despise things like that. Besides, you already told me I look terrible and need to rest."

"Both true. But Miss Harrington will be there."

He woke up immediately.

"I thought so." Sophie smiled. "You said you wanted to speak with her, and it's a good place to meet people without drawing too much attention. I will arrange for you to be invited."

"Thank you." The news he had to tell Gemma couldn't wait.

Having even a minimal plan helped Logan relax more than the stuff he just drank down. By the time Cutter came at him with a knife, Logan was indeed beyond caring. With the faces of Sophie and Cutter wavering in front of him, he passed out.

When Logan came to, he was alone. He looked down to find a fresh bandage covering the wound. It still felt tender, but he could twist his whole torso without significant pain, so that was an improvement.

Cutter looked in a few minutes later. "Ah, you're awake. That's good—I need to operate on someone else soon."

"What time is it?" Logan asked.

"Time for you to go home and get into bed. You were lucky," Cutter said. "In most cases, this sort of sloppy stitching would have invited festering. And to wait so long before coming to me...you ought to be dead or raving with a fever."

"Sorry to disappoint."

"Just don't do it again. You need to rest. That means sleep. Go home and forget about the world for a few days. And eat food. And for God's sake, bathe."

"Yes, doctor."

"I'm not a doctor," Cutter said. "But I do have other patients."

Before Logan could ask what to pay, Cutter shook his head. "Your friend paid me before she left."

The effect of the drug lingered when he got up, giving Logan the odd sensation of floating above the floor. However, the walk to the street drained him. Cutter was right.

Sleep sounded heavenly.

But as he stepped outside into the crisp, early December night, he knew he couldn't take Cutter's advice. The assignment was far from done, and Logan wouldn't rest until he knew all the answers.

And that meant he'd have to go to a party.

Chapter 24

GEMMA WAS ETERNALLY GRATEFUL FOR the kind friendship extended by Lady Forester. The woman was unquestionably above her socially, yet welcomed her into her circle, which meant that Gemma had now met everyone in London, or so it seemed. She found herself with multiple events to attend every night. Aunt Maura did her best to keep up, but Sophie acted as Gemma's chaperone half the evenings now, and said it was a pleasure to do so.

The event at Lady Mathering's was the first full scale ball Gemma would attend after braving the ordeal at Almack's, where a terrifying council of old ladies had looked down their noses and declared her fit for dancing. Gemma never dreamed a society test could be so frightening. She half expected one lady to look into her eyes and call her impure. Maura's knuckles were white the whole time fearing Gemma would make some hideous mistake of manners.

But she didn't, and now Gemma could go nearly anywhere in London and expect proper treatment. She was a little nervous for tonight, despite the fact that Sophie had told her not to worry. She had even given Gemma an impromptu dance lesson the previous day, showing her all the latest dances, which were mysterious to Gemma, since she never even went to parties where the old-fashioned country dances were still popular. Lady Forester was an astonishingly graceful dancer, moving with total confidence through all the steps. Gemma had been quite impressed.

She hoped she would not embarrass herself by comparison. Lord MacLachlan had told her he would attend as well, and requested one dance with her. Gemma agreed instantly, even before Aunt Maura could approve it. She decided she quite liked Ian MacLachlan. He seemed as steady and comfortable as Logan was elusive and dangerous.

But as she got dressed for the party, it was Logan's reaction she was thinking of.

"Bond, is the green dress ready?"

The maid bobbed her head once. "I thought you might want that one, so I laid it out and found the matching slippers."

"Excellent." Gemma smiled at the girl.

"Oh, you do look fine in that," Bond said admiringly, after Gemma was dressed. Whenever Bond got excited, her voice slipped slightly into a thicker accent, redolent of London, but certainly not the parts of London that Gemma was permitted to visit. "Your hair simply must be put up in the silver band tonight."

"If you insist." Gemma relaxed under the girl's ministrations. Bond did have a gift for making Gemma look her best. She began to brush out Gemma's red tresses, a little song in her throat.

A short while later, Gemma stared at the wide mirror in astonishment. Bond had managed to style her hair into something sophisticated yet natural. A silver band of ribbon encircled her head several times, allowing the red locks to be bound up, a few curls slipping between the coils. Her jewelry was restrained, just little silver earrings and a silver bracelet. Her neck was left bare, and Gemma looked nervously at her décolletage. "Bond, fetch the wrap for this, will you? I may get chilly in the ballroom."

Bond shook her head even as she ran to the wardrobe to get the green silk wrap. "Don't you dare hide behind this." She brandished the wrap. "I'm guessing there will be many a gentleman to offer a warm arm should you take a chill."

Gemma frowned into the mirror. "Do you think so?" The idea was not as appealing as it ought to have been. She wondered if any gentleman would appeal to her after.... She shoved the thought away. "You're right of course, Bond. I shall dance the night away!"

"That's the spirit, ma'am."

She and Aunt Maura rode together in the coach. When they reached their destination, Gemma gave instructions for Jem to return home. A hired carriage would be easy to find for the trip back.

Soon the two ladies were swept into the glittering rooms of the party. Gemma met even more people and she struggled to keep all the names and faces in her head. She repeated the polite phrases Aunt Maura had taught her. She nodded a lot, and asked polite questions, and hoped she was not breaking some obscure rule every time she opened her mouth.

When they saw Lady Forester, Gemma caught a strange light in her eyes for a moment. Then the light was gone, and Sophie laughed. "Your dress and hair are perfect! That green! You look like a dryad, darling!"

Gemma started, remembering how Logan gave her

that name, and how she felt every time he said it. A dryad....

Before she could comment, a brace of gentlemen appeared. Gemma vaguely remembered the older one, and he quickly introduced the new gentleman as Lord Waite, adding, "But you'll recognize the name. He's one of the minor partners of Harrington, Waite, and Talbot."

Lord Waite took Gemma's hand, bowing over it. "That's true, and with apologies to your late father, you are by far the most beautiful partner now." He was exactly her height, though he carried himself so well he appeared more impressive. Perhaps all lords were taught that.

She laughed at the obvious flattery, but said, "I have a few weeks before that is true in the most legal sense."

"Nevertheless, I am pleased to make your acquaintance. May I also ask for a dance?"

She granted that, after Aunt Maura gave a cautious nod. If the man was associated with her father's business, he must be safe.

"I am a little surprised that a lord would enter into business," she said at one point.

Waite gave a rueful nod. "Still a taboo among the ton, of course. But money doesn't grow on trees. And I have an estate in Kent, so I should know! It was my own father who dared become a partner in the shipping firm, and I am glad he did so. I inherited my share about five years ago. No one wants to admit it, but the world is changing. No matter how proud I may be of my past, I will ensure my future by any means necessary—even if some others scorn my methods. And anyway, your father was also the son of the aristocracy. He understood."

"He was a third son," Gemma pointed out. "With no title for himself, and no expectations. It would have been different if he were, say, an earl."

"Perhaps." Lord Waite gave her a smile. "Enough dull talk for this evening! Tell me how you are enjoying London so far."

She chatted with him a little longer after the set. Lord Waite was very friendly, and flattering to the point of silliness. Gemma chalked it up to London manners—style was far more important than substance. But he seemed quite harmless and she told him he was welcome to call at her home. It was the polite thing to say, after all.

He returned her to Aunt Maura after a decent interval, promising to call on them soon.

Who knew so many people could fit in one space? There were candles everywhere, plus fireplaces going in each corner of the room. The air was hot and smoky and it was hard to breathe, let alone think. Gemma would have paid in gold to have a breath of cold sea air just then.

An older gentleman approached them. He wore a tentative, questioning expression. "Miss Maura Caithny?" the man asked. "Is that you?"

"Oh, my! Mr Rodney?" Aunt Maura asked, her voice suddenly girlish.

His expression turned to one of immense pleasure. "The same! Had no idea you returned to town, my dear Miss Caithny."

"In fact, it is Mrs Douglas now," Maura said gently.

His expression froze for a moment, but then he laughed ruefully. "Of course. Forgive me. Naturally a beauty like yourself would not remain unclaimed for long. Is your husband here tonight?"

"Alas, he passed away many years ago. I am in town with my niece, Miss Harrington, as it is her first Season."

"The singular Miss Harrington! I've heard the name.

So you are behind it all!"

Maura laughed. "I am only here as chaperone and guardian. My niece is original enough that no one can devise a way to make her stand out more."

"And that worries you," Mr Rodney said. "I can tell. When my own daughter had her coming out several years ago, I nearly had a heart attack every time she stepped on a dance floor. Is there anything worse than sending an innocent young lady you love out into the world?"

"It is not an experience for the faint hearted. So you too have married, if you have a daughter."

"Like you, I married and buried. I lost my wife some time ago. But I have a daughter and a son, so how can I be ungrateful for my life?"

Gemma saw the light in Maura's eyes, and said, "Perhaps you both would like to take a turn around the room? You must want to catch up."

Aunt Maura left after making Gemma swear to behave herself. Gemma did, and stood calmly at the side of the room, watching the pageantry.

Gemma brightened when she saw Lord MacLachlan coming toward her. Though she had only known him a short time, she felt very comfortable with him. Perhaps it was because both of them felt like outsiders.

Ian gave her a broad grin as he looked her over. "I'm glad I asked for a spot on your dance card early, Miss Harrington. It must have filled as soon as you stepped through the door."

"There was some interest," she noted, displaying the nearly full card as she stepped out to meet him. "But I reserved a line for you as I promised, and before supper, so you wouldn't have to fear I turned an ankle."

"You are as intelligent as you are bonn—ah, I should

say beautiful. No one down here even knows what bonny means."

"If they don't know it's a compliment, you shouldn't waste your breath on them."

Ian laughed. "Good advice. Shall we dance?"

But at that moment, Gemma's dance card was plucked out of her hand by someone from behind her. Even the satin loop slid off her wrist with only a whisper.

She whirled angrily toward whoever dared to steal it. "Exactly who do you think you—?"

The final words died in her throat. She felt as if she might lose her footing.

It was him. Logan. Just as fascinating and compelling as he'd been the very first time she saw him in the doorway of Caithny. But also not at all the way she had first seen him. His rough cut hair and stubble were gone. Now he looked as clean cut and shaven as a military officer. The clothes were different too. Instead of the rough clothes of a common sailor, he was dressed in black Hessians, buff colored breeches that fit far too perfectly, and a dark, close-fitting coat over a linen shirt. Everything was simply cut, but did nothing to hide his essential presence. The other men in the ballroom faded into insignificance beside him.

Only the eyes were the same as before. It was her Logan who was holding the dance card. But unlike the first time she met him, he wasn't smiling now.

Chapter 25

☰

LOGAN WATCHED GEMMA'S REACTION.

He had deliberately waited to make an entrance at Lady Mathering's ball. He debated the wisdom of attending at all, but one did not lightly turn down an invitation to this house, not if one wanted to avoid Lady Mathering's wrath. And Sophie, who wrangled the invitation for him, promised Gemma would be there.

The room was glittering with the crush of well-dressed, bejeweled people. White roses seemed to adorn every possible surface, and their rich fragrance warred with the ladies' perfumes. It was all quite overwhelming, and he resisted a strong urge to turn back around into the cool night air.

It only took a single scan, however, for Logan to lock his gaze on a beauty in a deep green gown. His beauty. *Gemma.* Her bright red hair was arranged on top of her head, revealing her ivory skin and utterly distracting throat. He moved down the stairs, then through the crowd. Three more steps, and he was within range of her light lavender scent. She still had not turned.

He saw the dance card when she lifted it up and laughingly showed it to the man who stood near her. Far too near her, Logan thought. He snapped the card out of her hand before he even knew what he'd do. And now he had Gemma's full attention.

"Good evening, Miss Harrington," he said. "I see you've managed to keep occupied while I was away."

Gemma stared at him open mouthed, too shocked to even respond.

The other man was willing to rush to her defense, though. "Who do you think you are?" he asked.

Logan blinked at the man's thick Scottish accent. His natural jealousy was tempered for a split second. Maybe this was a relative, in which case he ought not call the man out for daring to dance with his Gemma.

He shifted his tactics slightly, offering a breezy tone. "I'm Logan Hartley, late of His Majesty's Royal Navy. Did Miss Harrington never mention me?"

"Logan…Hartley," Gemma whispered. Her face was awash with emotions, but she was recovering from her initial shock. "Mr…Hartley, I must introduce you to Lord MacLachlan. But there's no time to chat. The next dance is his."

Logan looked down at the dance card, then glanced to the side. They were standing quite near one of the small fireplaces in the room. This one burned merrily, adding completely unnecessary heat to the party.

"Are you sure he's next?" Logan asked. "I need a bit of light to read this. Excuse me." He pushed Gemma and the Scottish lord apart, then moved to stand by the fireplace.

"Are your eyes failing?" Gemma asked in an acid voice, trailing him. She pointed to the card with a slim finger. "MacLachlan. Plain as day."

"Sorry, I don't see his name there. In fact, I don't see a

dance card at all." Carelessly, Logan flipped the card into the flames.

Gemma gasped indignantly and made a grab for the card, even though it was already burning at the edges. He gripped her arm to keep her from plunging it into the fire, but then smoothly shifted so he held her hand in his own. "And that must mean this dance is mine."

Before he could take a step away, MacLachlan put one hand on Logan's shoulder in that false hearty fashion all giant men seemed to know. "The lady will choose her partner," he said.

Turning to Gemma, MacLachlan continued, "People are beginning to notice, Miss Harrington. We can't stand here for long."

Gemma looked at both of them with fire in her eyes, then said to MacLachlan, "My lord, if you'll excuse me for a moment. I haven't seen Mr Hartley recently. A dance will do well for the *very* brief discussion we ought to have."

"That's what I thought," Logan said, though he didn't care for Gemma's tone. "Do excuse us, my lord. And get your hand off me, or it will quickly become clear that we're not all great friends."

MacLachlan did so, though only after Gemma asked him to, which set Logan's teeth on edge.

But then they were on the dance floor. Logan had Gemma's hand in his, watching as she moved through the formal steps, almost like a doll. She refused to look at him, even when the steps of the dance brought them closer together.

"Dryad," he said softly. "Please listen to me."

"I prefer you to address me as Miss Harrington."

"Do you?" He leaned closer. "We used quite a different form of address in Scotland." She shivered as he spoke, his words tickling her ear.

"Quite understandable, Mr *Hartley*, seeing as I didn't know your real name at the time." She strove to make her voice like ice, but it trembled all the same. Logan remembered Sophie's words earlier. Gemma was certainly annoyed with him, despite the fact that his leaving wasn't at all by choice.

He straightened up, whirling her in the dance, and bringing her back to his body perhaps more tightly than was necessary. "I owe you an explanation."

"I do not care to hear it." Gemma kept her voice low, as if fearing the other dancers might overhear their conversation.

"Yes you do," he said with confidence.

"Very well," Gemma snapped, causing a lady nearby to glance at her. "Do explain, Mr *Hartley*," she continued in a sweet-as-syrup tone.

"Not here." He looked around. "Come to the conservatory with me."

"That's not proper," Gemma protested, even as he walked with her toward the doors. "Besides, didn't you make enough of a scene when you burned my card?"

"An accident," he said. "I'm sure no one saw what happened."

Gemma's short laugh was the most cynical sound he'd ever heard from her. "Are you serious?" she asked. "Every move, every gesture, every word is analyzed. What will happen when people see us together?"

"It's perfectly all right. They're all too busy worrying about how *they* appear."

"I'm not going off alone with you."

"Of course you're not," he said as they passed through

the doors. "This place is practically as crowded as the ballroom." Except for the part he intended to lead her to.

The conservatory was dim and cool, with a lingering damp. Logan, his grip firm on Gemma's arm, steered her to an alcove heavily scented with lilac and pine. A stone bench sat under a pine bough, and Logan quite literally sat Gemma down on it.

She glanced around, then spoke volumes with a single raised eyebrow.

"I'm not going to compromise you here," he said, "so kindly hear me out."

"Talk quickly then."

"I didn't want to tell you like this. Gemma, believe me…"

"Believe you?" she said quietly, condemningly. "You left me rather abruptly, and now I find I don't even know your *name*. Who are you?"

"Logan Hartley. It's a long story. But you can trust everything else, Gemma."

Gemma turned away from him, and he suddenly realized how very angry she was with him. This was what Sophie warned him about.

She said, "No. I don't trust you. Today it's Hartley. Last time it was Lockridge. You're a smuggler, you're late of the Royal Navy. You're from Bermuda. You're from London—"

"I never said I was from London," he broke in. "If you let me, I can explain."

"Then do so."

He paused. The one thing he was forbidden to tell her was the truth.

She seized on his silence, assuming the worst. "I don't know a thing about you. You played a game with me, and then you left me." Her voice dropped to almost nothing. "Was that the point? Just to see how low you could drag me?"

"No." How could she possibly believe that? "No, Gemma."

She rose and took one step toward the ballroom doors, her spine straight and her demeanor icy. It was like finding Gemma's dark double. "Don't find me again. Don't speak to me again. Don't think of me again. That's all I ask."

His heart ached at that, but he couldn't let her go yet. "Wait. Before you leave, I *have* to tell you this."

She turned impatiently, her voice flat and angry. "What?"

"Your uncle is dead."

Chapter 26

❧

"WHAT?" GEMMA SAID, SHOCKED AT the words he uttered. *Dead?* All her anger at him flowed away, replaced by confusion. "What do you mean?"

Logan's eyes were troubled, almost tender. "Just what I said. I'm sorry, Gemma, but it's true."

"My Uncle Conall is dead."

"Yes. I had to tell you in person."

"And you picked this time to do it." Gemma put a hand to her forehead. "What sort of night is this? The moon must be full."

"Let me…"

"Don't." She cut him off. "Not a word. I don't want to hear anything you have to say."

She turned from him and ran back inside. It took her some time to locate someone she recognized in the crush. She saw Lady Forester dancing with some gentleman, so she would have to wait until they returned from the floor. She kept looking to the doors by the conservatory, expecting Logan to appear, but she didn't see him. Perhaps he took her words seriously.

Perhaps.

Then Lord MacLachlan found her. "Miss

Harrington?" he asked.

"My lord, I'm so glad to see you."

"What's the matter?" He looked at her in concern.

Gemma didn't want to discuss the truth, so she said, "I've come down with an awful headache, I'm afraid. I should go home. I must find my aunt and get a carriage."

"No, I'll see you both home," he said instantly. "Would you like to wait in the front hall while I locate Mrs Douglas?"

She nodded, feeling terrible about abusing Ian's good nature. "I hate to make you leave."

"It's only a party." He sent her to the front hall, saying he'd be there as soon as he could.

She waited impatiently, fully expecting Logan to appear again and make things worse. But then Ian arrived, joined by Aunt Maura.

"My dear," she said. "Whatever is the matter?"

"I don't feel well," Gemma said, not even sure it was a lie. "I want to go home."

There was a long delay as Lord MacLachlan's carriage was retrieved and brought up to the doors. MacLachlan didn't say much, other than idle comments about the party and guests. Gemma nodded and made vague replies, her mind in a whirl from seeing Logan and hearing his news. Meanwhile, Aunt Maura did her best to maintain the conversation.

The carriage ride back to the house was silent, since there was no one to perform for.

When they arrived in Kingston Street, Ian helped them out, then said to Gemma, "May I call on you tomorrow to see if you are feeling better?"

"That would be very kind," Gemma replied sincerely, briefly taking his hand. "Thank you."

She walked up the steps with Aunt Maura. Stiles, ever alert, was there to open the door.

"Ladies," he rumbled. "We were not expecting you back so soon. I'll inform the others to attend you upstairs."

Aunt Maura nodded graciously, then turned back to Gemma while Stiles helped her remove her pelisse.

"You have made a friend in Lord MacLachlan," she said. "Or is it more serious than that?"

"I couldn't say. I only just met him," said Gemma. Hadn't she said nearly the same thing about Logan, too? Why did the words feel so different? "But you're right. I feel he is a friend."

"Well, you're not suffering from a headache." Aunt Maura was no fool. "Did something upset you, then? Or someone?"

"I don't think I embarrassed myself," she said irritably.

"That's not what I meant."

"I don't wish to discuss it at the moment." How could she possibly explain Logan Hartley or Lockridge or whoever he was to others? A smuggler who appeared at society parties like he had every right to be there? Lord, someone must have issued him an invitation! Gemma was sure Aunt Maura would faint if she heard the truth about Logan.

"Tomorrow, then," Aunt Maura said, her voice firm. "I've rarely seen you run away from anything, but that's just what you did tonight."

Gemma couldn't even argue. Her aunt was all too perceptive.

She went up the stairs slowly. Gemma closed her bedroom door with a feeling of incredible relief. Her nerves had been strung tighter than harp strings, and the only wonder was that she had not snapped in half by now.

Bond arrived shortly after, and performed all the necessary duties of getting her mistress ready for bed. The ball gown was removed, a nightshift found, and then Gemma sat down to have her hair taken down and brushed.

Then she dismissed Bond, fearing to answer any of the girl's well-meaning questions about the evening. "No, I don't need anything else. I shall ring in the morning."

Bond closed the door softly behind her, bearing a cloud of green fabric in her arms.

Gemma closed her eyes for a moment, but they flew open when she heard a new sound.

"Thought she'd never leave," said a voice behind her.

Gemma turned to the French window that opened onto her little balcony. The door now stood open, and Logan slid into the room like a shadow, pulling the door shut.

"How did you…? Get out of my room at once!" she hissed at the figure advancing toward her. Before she could even think, Gemma sprang up from where she was sitting. When she reached Logan, she raised her hand and slapped him across the face. The sound was like a crack of thunder in the quiet.

He slowly turned his head back to face her, his eyes glittering in the half-light.

"You left me," Gemma gasped, torn between anger and fear. She should not have struck him, she thought wildly. She had forgotten how dangerous he could be.

"And did that make you feel better?" The voice came low and calm. Far too calm.

"Yes! No. I don't know." Without warning, tears rolled down her cheeks. Everything she'd kept inside since the morning she knew he abandoned her rushed forward in her mind. "All I know is that I woke up and I was *alone*."

"You know what happened. I told you."

"You told me nothing. You seduced me, then left me."

"Hold on a moment. *I* seduced *you*?" he asked.

"Well…" Gemma turned her head, impatiently wiping the tears away. She hated crying. "No. But you did leave me."

"I had to be on my ship to France, and the tide doesn't wait. You know that."

"Ah, of course. Your smuggling run. That certainly takes precedence over your latest conquest. Obviously, I didn't meet your expectations. My apologies."

He stepped closer, not caring that she might hit him again. "Damn it, Gemma. That's not the truth, and you know it."

"Then what is the truth?"

Logan simply wrapped her in his arms. He didn't speak, he just pulled her close to him and let her cry as the worst of her pent-up emotions poured out.

"I was so scared," she gasped out. Why did it feel so good to be held by him? She *hated* him. "You were gone, and I didn't know…"

He bent to kiss the top of her head, holding her more tightly. "God, dryad. Tell me you didn't think it was deliberate. I had no choice. You have no idea how hard it was to leave. I woke you and told you—or I tried to."

She finally remembered hazy images from that day. Him telling her something important. "I thought I had a dream," she whispered.

"I never meant to hurt you."

"But you did," she accused him through her tears. The realization she'd misunderstood something so important made her start shaking. What else had she misunderstood?

"Yes, I can see that now," Logan was saying. "I'm so sorry, sweetheart. You spoke to me. I thought you knew what I said. I didn't want to leave you then."

She took a deep, shaking breath. "Is that true?"

"I wouldn't lie about that, Gemma," he said, his voice fierce. He pulled away, looking her over. "You must have been broken, dryad. Do you want to slap me again?"

"No!" The absurdity of the suggestion almost made her laugh. Lord, she was a mess of emotions.

Then a knock came at the door. Both of them stiffened.

"Ma'am?" It was Bond's voice. "I was just passing and felt a draft. Are you all right?"

Logan looked at her, his eyes appealing.

"Yes, Bond," Gemma called out after a slight pause. "You can go to bed."

"Are you quite sure?" Bond's voice held a note of concern rather tighter than a draft would warrant.

"Yes. Don't concern yourself."

"Very well. Ring if you need...anything." Bond's footsteps padded into silence.

Gemma took a breath, wondering why she was protecting Logan when sense and propriety dictated otherwise. "What insane notion made you sneak into my room?"

"I needed to speak to you alone. About a few things, I see now, but mostly about your uncle."

Logan's more recent news returned to her brain. She'd shut it out before, too angry to really hear him. Now she did. "Uncle Conall! Good lord, what happened?"

"Where do you want me to start?"

"I want to know everything."

"You have to sit down," he said.

"It's that bad?" she asked, turning to her bed and sitting on the edge.

"Yes. And to be honest, *I* need to sit down. I haven't slept much lately." He sat beside her, slipping her hand between his own. "Where to start?" He told her the story of the run to France, the mysterious new passenger, and the return to Caithny.

"Everything fell apart," he said finally. "There were men waiting. It ended badly, and I'm afraid Caithny... didn't make it."

"Explain. Who knew you were to arrive that night? Was the local magistrate alerted somehow? Conall wouldn't have provoked them. So what happened? Did he try to bribe them, and it didn't work this time?"

Logan shook his head. "He wanted the *Mistral*. The men were his. He'd instructed them to wait for our return and try to seize the ship."

"That's stealing!" she hissed, before remembering that she was speaking to a smuggler about another smuggler. "That's also...well, it's wrong. The *Mistral*'s your livelihood. And your lady."

"And he didn't get her," Logan went on. "But there was a skirmish of sorts, and he was shot by another man, who then jumped overboard himself."

"Another man? Meaning not one of your crew?"

"No. He came back up with us on the return journey from France. I never learned his name, and Caithny made it clear it wasn't my business. I called him Cargo."

"But who was he?" she asked. "Someone working for Conall's partner? Or a rival?"

"All very good questions," said Logan. "I need to find the answers quickly."

"What's it matter to you?"

"I get extremely interested in any events that leave me full of holes."

She looked him over in alarm. "Were you hurt again?"

"Oh, now you ask after my health?"

"Yes! Were you hurt?"

"Nothing to speak of. I only had the first wound to deal with, the one you so skillfully treated. Just got the bullet out a few hours ago."

Gemma gasped. "You were carrying a bullet around in your side for weeks?"

"It possible to live with one in you for years," he said, with a shrug. "Though I am glad to have it gone." He put a hand to the place she'd stitched up for him. "I was lucky it didn't fester."

"Dear Lord." Gemma chided him, "You should have gone to a doctor as soon as you could!"

"I did," he said. "It just happened to be a couple of weeks. I was busy."

"Contending with other smugglers and Customs and the like."

"Well, yes. And the party tonight." He gave her a faint smile. "That was the worst by far."

"You behaved horribly," she said. "I can't believe you set my dance card on fire."

"I didn't like the names on it," he said, closing his eyes.

"But that doesn't give you permission to burn it!"

"Solved the problem, didn't it?" He leaned back against her pillows, his eyes still closed. "This feels like heaven."

"My bed does?" Gemma, still sitting, watched him skeptically.

"Any bed." He held out one arm. "Come here, dryad. Please."

She moved so she could lie down next to him.

He wrapped his arm tight around her. "I was wrong before. This is heaven."

Gemma thought about it, and decided it did feel very good. She tucked her head under his chin, her mind racing. "Logan. I don't know what to think about all this."

"About Caithny, you mean?"

"Yes. He was my guardian, but I can't say I thought of him as much of one. I always feared something like this would happen. He was a lucky man, but as you say, luck runs out."

"I'm sorry, Gemma," he said. "For what it's worth, I'm sorry for your loss."

"Thank you." She took a deep breath. "I shall have to tell Aunt Maura. And make an announcement, somewhere. To someone. Do I go into mourning?"

Logan shook his head. "You don't have to make a decision at the moment."

"But I do…"

"No, you don't. Conall doesn't have a funeral coming up. His body is who knows where. You need not give up your life at just this moment to play the dutiful child."

"What do you think I should do, then?"

"Just behave as before. Let me get some questions answered. There's a lot more going on than a simple smuggling run, and I don't want you to get caught in it. I'll find out, and I want the answers before Caithny's death is common knowledge. But I had to tell you. You deserve to know why your so-called guardian isn't inquiring after you."

"I did wonder that," she admitted. "Aunt Maura was

so sure he would knock down our door any day."

"You have nothing to fear on that count. Will you keep this to yourself, then? Just for a little while?"

"If you think it best," she said.

Logan held her closer. "I like it so much when you trust me, dryad."

"Yes, about that. I'm still angry at you," she warned him, though she was feeling decidedly not angry at the moment. "You have a lot to answer yourself, Logan."

"Such as?"

"Let's begin with your name. Your real name."

He nodded. "Logan Cadwalder Horatio Hartley. My mother's side is Welsh from a long time back, hence the Cadwalder. Don't tell anyone about the Horatio, though. My godfather wanted me to be the first in the family to attend Oxford and become a poet. That didn't go according to plan."

She raised her head to look at him, tried not to laugh, and failed.

"Go ahead," he said calmly, his eyes still closed. "I'm used to it."

"A poet?"

"His dream, not mine."

"Are you telling the truth?" Her eyes narrowed. "Or is this just a trick to distract me from more questions?"

"If I wanted to distract you, I'd do something more like this."

He shifted to pull her up level with him. His mouth on hers was enough to remind Gemma of everything that happened the last night they spent together. She put her hand on his chest and slid upward to touch his skin above his shirt.

Logan relaxed, happy to let her do what she wanted. "I

missed you."

"You should go," she whispered, the gentle stroking of her hand betraying her statement.

"One more kiss," he said, seeking her mouth again.

Gemma clung to him. She deepened the kiss without thinking. She wanted to devour him. He tasted her hungrily, taking everything she gave, feeling her respond to him.

He reached out to touch her thick red hair. Not breaking the kiss, he reached to pull out the ribbon that held her hair back, and it came tumbling down around them both.

"I should probably leave," he said, his voice dazed. He didn't sound like he intended to move an inch.

Gemma didn't answer, other than to tug at his jacket impatiently. "Take this off," she demanded suddenly. "And kiss me again."

He grinned. "You missed me too." He gave her a lingering kiss, his mouth teasing hers until she wanted to moan. Then he shifted enough to kiss her neck from her jaw down to her chest. Gemma squirmed, anticipating more. He'd take her clothes off at any moment, or slip his hands underneath the gown. She could tell how sharp his desire was for her, because she felt the same way.

But he seemed quite content to kiss the skin he already had access to. He moved slowly, patiently across her chest, teasing at the skin just above the line of her gown.

"Logan," she whispered. "What are you doing?"

"You did ask to be kissed, didn't you?"

"Yes, but…is that all you're going to do?"

"You want more?" he asked, his mouth still against her skin.

"Yes," she whimpered. "Yes, I do."

"I love how honest you are," he said. "You don't pretend, Gemma."

"Well, if you love it, why don't you take advantage of it?"

"Believe me, I've been dreaming of it." He moved to her shoulder, pulled the fabric on her sleeve down, and kissed the skin there. "But I'm not going to do that tonight."

"Why not?"

"Because I'm sober, and have no excuses."

"You're in my bedroom," said Gemma. "Surely the whole world would consider that a thorough compromise all on its own."

"I'm not the whole world," he said. "I know how you deserve to be treated, and that's what I'll do from here on out. You can't persuade me with scotch this time."

"So you didn't come here with the intention of seducing me?" she asked.

"Does that disappoint you?"

"A little."

He laughed, the sound making her shiver with pleasure. "That's almost enough to change my mind."

She turned her head to kiss him, and found his mouth. Another deliciously drowsy, drawn out moment of bliss. Her senses were overwhelmed and she put her arms around him. "You're going to be honorable, I can tell. But I still want to hold you."

"That's lovely, dryad," he whispered.

She held him, cradling him so he lay half on her body, his head resting on her breast. He made a sound of contentment, and she smiled, delighted she could evoke such a feeling simply by holding him.

A moment passed in silence, then another. She continued to hold him, not sure what he expected of her.

"Logan?" She looked down and saw he was asleep.

He hadn't been joking about being tired. She laughed to herself. What sort of man sneaked into a lady's room only to make use of the bed in an *almost* completely innocent way?

Sleep made his features smoother, and he looked much more peaceful. She didn't want to disturb him, so she merely pulled one blanket up around them both. She closed her eyes and listened to his breathing, slow and even.

He was right. It was lovely.

Chapter 27

≈

LOGAN AWOKE IN THE DEEPEST part of night. He was momentarily disoriented, but when he looked over and saw Gemma, he smiled. Waking up to her face was the best thing to happen to him in weeks. He shouldn't have fallen asleep, but Gemma's bed was so comfortable. Still, he hadn't intended to pass out in front of her. Cutter was right. He was pushing himself too far. He ought to rest.

And he would, just as soon as he answered the questions surrounding Conall Caithny. The man's death didn't help Logan one bit, and he feared Gemma would be drawn further into whatever was happening unless he could end it.

The appearance of Cargo disturbed him more than he let on to Gemma. The man jumped overboard, true, but something told Logan he'd see the man again. Murdering Conall Caithny might have been by accident or design, but the newcomer surely didn't intend to stop there and go home. There were too many loose threads. Too much money at stake. And with Caithny dead, Gemma might be seen as the next logical step, especially if Caithny's partners knew of her involvement in the smuggling runs. They might assume she knew names or other information.

If only he knew what was being smuggled. It was maddening. What could be so damned valuable that

Conall Caithny would sink ships to keep the secret? He'd admitted to shipping guns, but Logan now doubted that. Guns were valuable to any army. But the loss of a few loads wouldn't be the worst thing in the world. No, there was some angle he didn't understand yet. And until he could learn what it was, Gemma was at risk.

He couldn't let her know that, though. Gemma was a little too much of a gambler and would likely go chasing after a clue if she thought she could. As long as she only thought Logan's interest stemmed from him being a rival smuggler, she shouldn't get too curious. He'd solve the puzzle on his own, then he could come back for Gemma, with nothing hanging over either of them.

And his being in her room at that moment wasn't helping the cause. He shifted, intending to get up and slip away before anyone could find him there. As he told her, he would treat her the right way from here on out, and that meant avoiding any scandals.

But he wouldn't leave her with no word this time. He crossed the room to her vanity, found what he needed, and after a few minutes laid something down on the table beside the bed, just by the candlestick that now held only the burnt-down stub of a candle.

But when he straightened up, she woke, and looked at him with narrowed eyes. "I hope you're not sneaking away," she said.

He bent down to look her in the face. "I can't stay here, and you know it."

Gemma sighed and sat up, blinking in the dim light of a dying fire. She caught the edge of the compass gleaming at her bedside table, and reached out to touch it.

Logan followed the movement. "I see you kept my compass safe. I knew you would."

"Why did you leave it behind?" she asked.

He looked at her in surprise. "What else could I have left to let you know I'd return to you?"

"That was your intention?" she asked, skepticism in her tone.

"What else could it have meant?"

She said nothing, but her expression must have betrayed her line of thought.

Logan leaned toward her, putting his hand over hers. "You didn't think I would have left it as…compensation."

"The compass couldn't speak," she said tightly. "Your meaning was perhaps not as crystal clear to me as in your own head."

"God, Gemma. You thought that for weeks? You believed that?"

"I tried not to think it, but what else could I have believed?" she asked, exasperated. "You know, when I thought your name was Lockridge, I assumed this was stolen. I didn't know until last night that the H stood for Hartley."

"Did people think it stood for Harrington?" he guessed.

"I let them think so, if they asked."

Logan smiled, hoping to restore her mood. "See, darling. It was meant for you."

"I would have rather had an explanation."

"Well, now you have both. Keep it safe, though. It is an heirloom."

"You're not taking the compass back again?" she asked.

"I want you to keep it," he said. It was too soon to speak about marriage, but he would let her know exactly how significant the compass was when he did propose.

"Besides, I can hardly wear it about town, now that it's the famous accessory of the Original Miss Harrington."

"Stay with me," she said, turning toward him.

"As much as I'd love to, Gemma, you know I can't."

"I know," she said, with a pout. "But you must promise you're not leaving on the next tide."

"That's a promise. I'm not leaving London until I get to the bottom of whatever Caithny was involved in."

"You're determined to do that? Does it matter so much?"

"I'll know that when I learn what he was up to." Logan smiled at her. "You go back to sleep, beautiful."

"When will I see you again?"

"Soon. Maybe tonight."

"You can't invite yourself into my room whenever you please."

"Now who's making assumptions?" he teased her.

After giving her a reasonably chaste kiss, he slipped out the balcony doors and sidled easily down the back wall of the house. He had just touched the ground when he heard a rustle behind him.

"Well, this is awkward, sir."

Logan turned and saw Jem Harper, one of the first Disreputables. Logan had met him several times, and knew how clever the boy was. "Evening, Jem."

"Morning's more like."

"You're seeing me off the property?"

Jem nodded. "We were hired to keep Miss Harrington safe. From *all* threats."

"Including me?"

Choosing his words carefully, Jem said, "When a casual observer could get the very wrong impression that you were leaving her room at four in the morning, yes, that's a threat. Good thing you weren't here, doing just that. And good thing I didn't see anything which would compromise my employer's reputation. And good thing you won't ever do it again."

"You're giving me orders, Jem?"

The young man took a step closer to Logan, untroubled by the question. "I'm doing my duty, sir. All the Disreputables are. Just as we were asked to do. If you find fault with that, you can either take it up with Aries and the Astronomer, or you can simply fight it out with us one night. Been a while since I was in a good brawl. I sort of miss it."

"I'm not going to fight you," Logan said in disgust. "It's an absurd suggestion."

"Then just go. For her sake."

Logan did go, though Jem's words and attitude soured his mood considerably. The boy would never have spoken to one of the other signs of the Zodiac like that. Most of them were gentry or aristocracy. He knew one sign was actually a duke. But sometimes Logan felt he wasn't much further up the chain than a domestic servant, so he didn't rate as much respect.

Logan slipped out the back drive, emerging into the street only after he walked through the mews, ensuring that no one would know where he had come from, even if he was recognized. He hailed down a cab and directed it toward his home. As he rode, he reveled in the memory of sleeping in Gemma's arms, up until that damnable servant showed up as an ugly reminder of the real world. Logan sighed. He should be glad Gemma was being watched over by reliable people, however odd their backgrounds might be.

But he'd prefer to be the one who did the watching.

Chapter 28

≋

IT WAS MORNING WHEN SHE woke up again. Gemma was caught in a dreamy haze for a moment, happy without knowing why she was happy. But it only took a second for her to remember everything that had happened last night, from Logan appearing at the party to reappearing in her room.

She sighed, thinking of the hours when he did nothing more than sleep beside her. Why did it feel just as daring as what they'd done before? He promised he'd see her again. She smiled in anticipation.

She sat up and swung her legs over the edge of the bed, far too excited to go back to sleep. As she did so, she noticed a piece of her stationery on the bed stand, just under the compass. Her hand shaking slightly, she reached over and unfolded it.

Until tonight. L.

What a rogue, she thought. Leaving a note with a scandalous implication like that. What if Bond were to see it? Crumpling up the page, she got up and tossed it into the cold fireplace. Then she rang the bell next to the mantle.

Bond came in shortly after. "Morning, miss. I trust

you were not disturbed in the night?"

"Not at all. Slept like a baby," Gemma said with a smile, still thinking of Logan. She was too lost in thought to notice the odd expression that flashed across Bond's face.

"I thought perhaps you might have been disturbed," Bond said. "Jem thinks he might have seen someone on the grounds in the early morning."

Gemma came back to the present. "Well, even if that's the case, it's no one I'm concerned about. Tell Jem there's no need to worry."

"Very well. Shall I bring up your breakfast, miss?" Bond asked, her tone formal.

"Tea and toast, Bond, thank you."

"Yes, miss." Bond turned to head downstairs.

* * * *

Lord MacLachlan called on her later that day, just as he promised he would. Gemma thanked him again for escorting her home the previous night. He obviously wanted to ask if her distress had been connected to Logan Hartley, but he was far too polite to do so. Gemma stuck to her story of a headache, and reassured Ian that she felt much better this morning. Which was absolutely true, she told herself.

As they talked, Gemma thought about Ian MacLachlan. She liked him very much, but nothing in him made her dizzy or made her want to cast off all ties and go with him. But perhaps it was unfair to expect that of every man. Ian's virtues were steadiness and an obvious commitment to his family. There was nothing wrong with that. A woman would have to be daft to think him a bad choice.

And yet…she was still dreaming of Logan. A shifty, secretive smuggler.

Perhaps Gemma was just a terrible judge of character.

Ian didn't stay much longer than the commonly accepted quarter hour. He was learning the ways of London society quite well. Gemma saw him off with a smile, and hoped she knew what she was doing.

Lady Forester called on her a little while later. Gemma received her in the parlor, wearing another new afternoon dress, this one a loose fitting cream colored gown that she wore with a little cropped jacket in a heavy tweed, which did much to counter the extremely feminine lines of the skirt.

Sophie lost no time in sharing her gossip. "I have heard from several people that you were something of a hit at the party last night. Many wanted to know where you disappeared to. I gather several gentlemen thought they might get a dance…especially after your dance card accidentally fell into a fireplace?"

"I had nothing to do with it," Gemma said. "It was all Lo— that is, Mr Hartley's fault."

"Mr Hartley?" Sophie asked, her eyes widening. "Do tell."

"I have no idea what to say about him."

"Well, start with whether he's a good dancer."

"We barely danced. He told me—" Gemma broke off. Naturally, she couldn't relate Logan's actual news to Sophie. "Never mind. He's a rather complicated man."

"How interesting."

"Don't get the idea that I'm besotted. He was rude to Lord MacLachlan, and he set my card on fire just to get a dance."

"Well, the loss of the card seems to have only in-creased your cache. Still, perhaps if you see Mr Hartley again, you should guard your possessions."

"Indeed," Gemma muttered. "He'd probably steal half of London if he could."

"What was that, dear?"

"Nothing!" Gemma said, louder. "I just don't know when or where I'll see him.

"Perhaps tonight?"

"Tonight?" Gemma looked at Sophie, startled.

"At the Thornes' home! You do remember you were invited."

"Oh, I don't know…"

"You must come. Especially after leaving early last night."

"I quite agree," said Aunt Maura as she entered the room. "It would never do to disappear and then allow speculation. You must go tonight."

How could Gemma say no to both Sophie and Maura? "Very well."

* * * *

That evening, Gemma arrived at the Thornes' home at nine o' clock. Aunt Maura had another engagement with the newly rediscovered Mr Rodney, so Sophie was sworn to act as chaperone. Sophie found her immediately and led Gemma to where the Thornes stood receiving guests.

Sophie made introductions, explaining that Lord and Lady Thorne were among her closest friends.

Lady Thorne leaned toward Gemma to say, "How lovely to meet you. Sophie has told me about you!"

"Oh, she did?" Gemma asked. Lady Thorne had vivid

coloring—thick black hair and pretty green eyes—to match her jewel-toned gown. The overall effect was striking. "Good things, I hope."

"She said you just recently came to London," Lady Thorne added. "She had despaired of the Season being the slightest bit interesting until you arrived."

Sophie introduced Gemma to several other people, but then excused herself for a moment. "There's someone I must speak to," she said, the faintest hint of displeasure in her voice. "I shouldn't be long."

After Sophie left, Lord Waite appeared. "Please tell me you remember me from last evening!" He bowed, and then winked at Gemma, who smiled automatically.

"Of course, Lord Waite." She remembered him being fairly amusing, though not particularly deep.

"May I have a dance this evening as well, Miss Harrington?" he asked hopefully. "I was afraid your card would have been filled already."

"You overestimate my popularity, Lord Waite." She held out the card. "There is a line for you."

He wrote his name in, and promised he'd come claim her at the appointed time. Then he excused himself. "I signed a few dance cards this evening, though only because I assumed I'd be bereft of your company. Alas!"

She watched him leave, thinking that Lord Waite was more or less a perfect model of a London gentleman. She wasn't sure she entirely understood him.

"Imagine finding you all alone, Miss Harrington," a voice murmured behind her.

She turned, seeing Logan standing there, just as if he belonged. He took her unresisting hand in his. Only when he raised it to his lips did she say, "I'm surprised to see you here, Mr Hartley."

"Why? I did mention I would see you tonight," he replied blandly, causing a sudden flush in Gemma's cheeks.

"Yes, but I thought you meant—" Gemma stopped short, realizing she'd been about to say she hoped he would come to her room again.

"Go on," he murmured, close to her ear. "If there's somewhere else you expect me to be, I should know so I can plan accordingly."

"I don't know what you're talking about," she said quickly, stifling a laugh. "And I don't know why you're here, anyway. Or at the party last evening. Considering your vocation, I wouldn't expect you to mingle with the ton."

"You'd be surprised how often my vocation takes me into society. Or do you mean I'm not good enough for this crowd?" His gaze went flat as he said it.

Gemma wasn't sure what caused the change in mood, so all she said was, "Don't be absurd." She looked at his outfit, admitting, "You do blend in. I'll give you that."

"And you stand out," he said, surveying her in turn. "I've heard some talk, but seeing you again tonight puts the most florid praise to shame."

"What are they saying?" she asked. Logan might have heard some very different comments than the sort shared among ladies.

He smiled. "Miss Harrington is new, and unknown, and decidedly unusual. A combination of qualities to make most men take notice."

"You're jealous."

"Of course I am." He looked at her more critically. "Though I have to say I prefer you looking as you did when I first met you."

"Madame Lucille is one of the finest modistes available," Gemma protested. "This is the look London expects of a lady."

"And you care about what London expects," he said skeptically.

"I came here with the intention of joining society. It's what my parents expected of me."

"Expectations, again," he said. "How do you know what your parents would expect at this point? Wouldn't they desire your happiness over all this?" He gestured to indicate the swirl of the party.

"You're only saying that because *you* don't want it."

"You have very little idea of what I want, Gemma," he said.

"Don't say my name," she reprimanded him, even though no one could have possibly overheard it. "Lord, how did you get in here tonight?"

"Shall we ask the hostess to throw me out?" he asked, with a sudden smile. "Lady Cordelia!" he said, in a louder tone.

Cordelia was passing close by. "Why, Mr Hartley!" she said. "I thought you'd never get to London this Season."

"You *do* know him?" Gemma asked before she could stop herself.

"Miss Harrington thinks I've smuggled my way into your party," he announced to Cordelia, still laughing.

Gemma blushed. "I didn't mean it that way," she said, abashed that her speculations would be aired in front of a countess.

Cordelia didn't look offended. "I do indeed know him." Then she said to Logan, "And for as often as you travel, I count it a triumph you actually attended."

"*Travel*," Gemma muttered under her breath. What a way to describe Logan's activities.

Cordelia went on, "And if you have a moment, I have something to show you in the study."

"I always have a moment for you, my lady," he said easily. "Miss Harrington should join us. If it's what I think it is, she'll be quite interested."

"Oh?" Cordelia said. "Well, then let's slip away before I get ensnared in another conversation."

Lady Thorne led them both down a hallway to a small room at the back of the house. In the center was a large desk holding sheets of paper, covered in designs.

"A ship," Gemma said, looking it over.

"Our hostess designs them," Logan explained, "though very few people know about her hobby."

"Is it a secret?" Gemma asked.

Cordelia said, "Only in the sense that a woman in my position isn't expected to dabble in such things. But I always have, and I plan to continue." She smiled at Gemma. "I use a different name, of course. It's a very useful thing, to have a few names in your pocket."

"I expect so," Gemma said, with a glance at Logan. "But why does Mr Hartley know the truth?"

"Not obvious?" Logan said innocently. "You remember that I served in the Royal Navy for a time. And my family operates a shipbuilding operation in Bermuda. We export several ships to Britain every year."

"Mr Hartley is an invaluable resource for me," Cordelia explained. "I come up with many designs, but it takes practical experience to know if certain designs have any use. Mr Hartley always tests things himself."

Gemma blinked in surprise. Logan gave her a tiny, rather smug smile. It sounded as though Cordelia thought

him a perfectly legitimate gentleman—and a useful one.
"Well," she said. "I must get used to discovering that
rogues can be gentlemen, and countesses can be up to
something nefarious."

"Did someone just say nefarious?" Lord Waite appeared in the doorway, leaning in casually.

"Good evening, my lord," Cordelia said. "We were in
a private conversation."

"Well, I'll not keep you," Waite replied. "I'm just here
to claim my dance with Miss Harrington."

"She's busy," Logan said, his voice just this side of
combative.

"We were already finishing up," Gemma insisted. It
occurred to her that Waite was exactly the man she should
speak to if she wanted to learn about her own business.

"Good thing too. I've been searching high and low for
you!"

"How thoughtful of you, Lord Waite." Gemma smiled
and put her arm in his. She pointedly ignored the dark
look that flashed across Logan's face. Waite, pleased at
his coup, led Gemma away.

* * * *

Logan glared at the retreating figures. "What can she
want with that boring fop?"

"Perhaps she's being polite," Cordelia said.

"That has to be it. He's dull as rocks."

Sophie entered then. "Ah, here you both are. What
have I missed?"

"Just Mr Hartley's opinion of Lord Waite," said
Cordelia. "Specifically, Lord Waite taking Miss Harrington out from under his nose."

"More of a challenge than you expected, my friend?" Sophie noted dryly. "You may not have that much time to snare her. Lord Waite and Lord MacLachlan are both highly attentive, and she has not sent either of them away."

"Waite is a joke." Logan didn't like where this conversation was going.

"Perhaps not Waite. John Harrington was only the youngest son of a lord, and Waite has always been a snob."

Logan didn't know Gemma's father was connected to the aristocracy at all. Or had she said something about it? He assumed she had the same merchant class roots as he did. A little cold spot touched his spine. Fear. He shook it off.

"…but she seems to think highly of MacLachlan," Sophie was saying. "She has mentioned his name several times."

Logan's fists clenched. "Who's this Lord MacLachlan? He was hanging on her last night."

"MacLachlan is the sort of man for whom the word *dashing* was invented to describe," said Cordelia, with a laugh. "He has made an impression on the ladies this Season."

"Spare me the rapturous account of his charm. What's he after?"

"Money," Sophie said bluntly. "He has a title and lands and clan to look after, but he needs an infusion of cash to turn his fortunes around."

"So he wants her inheritance?" Logan frowned. How much could Gemma possibly be worth, considering she grew up in a crumbling wreck of a castle?

"Yes, he does. Which makes him no different than

every other man pursuing her."

"*Nearly* every other man," Logan corrected hotly.

Sophie said, "I'm only stating the facts. He's made no secret of his financial situation, or his interest in Miss Harrington."

"It sounds mercenary," Logan said.

"He argues it's an investment," said Sophie. "He expects to make it all back, and then some. Assuming he's a clever businessman, she would be unlikely to be a pauper. He certainly seems to admire her."

"She can't be interested in him."

"Why not?" Cordelia asked. "I've met him. Do you think she's repelled by his ugly face or hideous form?"

"She's too intelligent to be tricked into marrying a man out for her wealth."

"Ah," said Sophie, her eyes sparkling now.

"Don't do that," Logan warned her.

"What?" she asked, too innocently.

"The little *ah* that says I'm a complete dunderhead with no hope of understanding the situation as you do from your superior feminine vantage point."

"I've rarely heard it translated into English with such exactitude," Cordelia noted.

"At least you're both amused," he said bitterly.

Cordelia relented. "My dear Mr Hartley, have you considered explaining yourself to her? It seems a proper conversation is in order, with an emphasis on *proper*."

"What would I tell her? The truth?"

"My husband told me the truth," Cordelia said quietly, her tone now serious. "And the Zodiac endured."

"No, you guessed the truth first and he confirmed it," Logan countered, remembering the story. "Not quite the same thing."

Sophie held up a hand. "Let's all step back from the precipice, yes? Logan does not need to tell Miss Harrington his real profession. And I'm sure he'll sort out all the issues of her vast fortune when they have that discussion."

"What do you mean, *vast*?" Logan asked.

Sophie looked a bit surprised. "You don't know her expectations?"

"I haven't looked into them. I was investigating her uncle, not her."

"She'll be worth one hundred thousand at her majority, unentailed."

Logan closed his eyes. "What?"

"You heard me."

He heard her, he just didn't want to believe it. One hundred thousand. He felt sick. "That's common knowledge?"

"No. At least not yet," said Sophie. "Mrs Douglas confided it to me a few days ago. She is justifiably concerned that Miss Harrington's life could get a bit hectic should it come out. Privately, she hopes Lord MacLachlan will propose soon, and that the proposal will be accepted."

Logan nodded, not quite registering the words. Lord MacLachlan. And Lord Waite. And who knew who else. Why would Gemma even consider marrying him when she could ascend several rungs of the social ladder with a single *yes*?

"Logan?"

He blinked. Both Sophie and Cordelia were watching him. "What?"

"Is something the matter?"

"No," he said. He could barely think. One hundred thousand. "Excuse me."

He left the two ladies, walking down the hallway. He wasn't even sure what direction he was going.

Last night, he slept next to Gemma, certain it was only a matter of time before he'd be in a position to very honorably ask her to marry him. He thought they were the same. The same mind, the same goals, the same class.

One night later, and he found out she was beyond him. And if he pursued her, or if their relationship ever became known, he'd drag her down.

He couldn't see her again. Not alone.

Suddenly, he felt a hand on his arm. Sophie. "Logan, you're acting strange."

"I just got some bad news," he said.

"You mean her inheritance? Who cares? You think those men are better than you just because of a title?" she said in a low voice. "Better than either of us?"

"Aren't they? Blood matters in this world." He looked at Sophie. "Besides, what are you telling me? You were born to be a comtesse. And you *married* a lord."

Sophie protested, "But I didn't grow up knowing that. And I married for love." She flushed suddenly. Sophie was still unused to admitting that. "If you care for Gemma, you're not going to walk away from her."

"Let me make my own decisions." He shrugged her arm off. Sophie was one of his closest friends, but he didn't want her advice now.

She let go, aware of his mood. "Don't take too long, dear. And remember, fortune favors the bold."

Logan stood there while she walked away. Her words jolted him. Lord, Gemma still had his compass—a link to him no one could easily explain away. He had to get it back.

* * * *

After the dance with Waite, Gemma stood by an open window to catch her breath. She enjoyed the cool air flowing in from outside, and she also wanted to use the time to regroup after encountering Logan again. He obviously wanted to prove he was telling the truth about his name. Lady Thorne knew him perfectly well, and confirmed he was in the Royal Navy for a time. So why was he sailing up to Scotland under the name of Lockridge? Gemma shook her head. It made no sense. She was missing something important, and she didn't like it.

"Lord Waite is still on a quest to bring back punch, is he?" a woman beside her asked. "I hope you're not thirsty! He may have wandered into the smoking room."

"Lord Waite," Gemma repeated, almost forgetting who she just danced with. Then she turned to the newcomer, puzzled. "Pardon me? Have we met?"

The other lady shook her head. "No. I'm Lady Gretwood." She was a petite woman, with blonde hair and a sharp gaze. "My husband is the Viscount, you know."

Gemma did not know, nor did she particularly care. But she said politely, "Miss Gemma Harrington."

"Yes, I was dying to meet you. I thought I'd seize the moment once Waite left."

"Well, if he does not return in a little while, I can seek out a glass of punch myself."

"Very wise. Waite is not the most attentive of partners."

"I found him most solicitous."

"Oh, he's entertaining...and you're still fresh. Of course it's just dalliance on his part. Lord Waite has far too much regard for his line to dilute it, no matter how fair the face."

Gemma blinked at the backhanded comment. It took a moment, but she realized the extent of the other lady's contempt. So she was pretty but worthless? "If such ambitions are beyond me," she said, "why am I here?"

"Such a question only you can answer," the other lady said.

"No. I mean, why do I receive invitations to events such as this one?"

"Well, it's obvious, isn't it? You're just a flash in the pan. But whatever you did to catch Lady Forester's attention was clever, I'll give you that. She seems quite amused by you."

Gemma narrowed her eyes. "Amused?"

"Oh, don't act as if you didn't plan it all out. Disingenuousness doesn't sit well on you, Miss Harrington."

"You make it sound as if I chased her down. She ran into *me* on the street."

"On practically your first day in London! What a coincidence! Just happening into the path of one of London's more original personalities."

Gemma couldn't even respond. Her fury mounted. This woman thought she was lying?

"I will leave you now," she said finally.

The other woman nodded and gave a satisfied little humming sound. She clearly considered herself the winner in whatever contest of wills just occurred.

Gemma turned and began to walk away. A thought occurred to her, and she looked back. But the woman was already engaged in a conversation with two others, laughing in a way that made Gemma flush with anger and embarrassment. They were probably rehashing the conversation, discussing how opportunistic Gemma was. How funny it was Gemma thought she could buy her way into society.

She walked across the room, hoping to find a quieter place to collect herself. She didn't find it. Instead she was accosted by yet another gentleman, one she'd met but didn't remember the name of.

"Miss Harrington," he said. "How delightful to see you again."

She gave a cool nod, not wishing to admit that she scarcely knew his face.

"A dance?" he asked, fully expecting the question to be a formality.

"I have danced enough for the evening," she said, in an attempt to be polite. "But thank you."

"No more dancing? But what else are we to do?" The words were said with mock despair, but his expression became slightly lecherous. Gemma didn't want to think about what he'd like to do, but she remembered Aunt Maura's lessons. Always be polite, always be gracious. Never promise anything, and never be rude.

"Another time, perhaps." There, she thought. She'd managed a short, simple response. Gemma took a step toward the doorway.

The dandy blocked her way. It was subtle, but she had to pause or risk running into someone. She gave him a sharp look. "Did you have a question, sir?"

"It has been rumored you have some skill at shooting, Miss Harrington." The dandy looked about as he spoke, hoping for a reaction from the nearby guests. "Can it be true?"

Deny it, said the voice inside, sounding remarkably like Aunt Maura.

"I am an excellent shot," she said. Lying was not to

her taste, and her patience with this man was over. She looked around, half hoping to see Logan, though she didn't know why. He would only make the situation worse.

"How remarkable," the dandy exclaimed. "Are all the highland lasses so prepared?"

"Your command of geography is lacking, sir," Gemma returned. "Caithny is in the lowlands of Scotland…the *tamed* part of the country."

The dandy looked affronted, yet he could hardly refute her words. "If it's so tame, why do you shoot?"

"For the same reason any number of gentlemen go hunting in England. The sport amuses me. You know what would be thoroughly amusing? A demonstration. Does anyone have an apple?"

He took a step back, "I say…"

"Too scared?" Gemma sighed dramatically. "Very well then. My pastimes will have to remain the subject of idle rumor and gossip." She was growing very annoyed at just how much of her life seemed ripe for rumor and gossip. Just imagine if the ton caught wind of Uncle Conall's smuggling activities. Or her link to Logan Hartley!

Thinking of him, Gemma pulled the compass out of the jacket pocket. It sat in her hand, the brass case gleaming in the candlelight. It felt cool and heavy, the perfect counterweight the bubbly, frothy mood of the party.

"Is that a pocket watch?" someone asked curiously.

Gemma didn't open the lid. "I don't need a watch to let me know that it's time to go. Good night!"

"You can't leave," the dandy said, unwilling to let the matter rest.

As if the compass summoned him, Logan appeared at her side. "Of course she can leave," he told the other man.

"Miss Harrington is free to do whatever she likes." He offered Gemma an arm, and she took it as if reaching for a lifeline.

"I'll escort you as far as your carriage," he said, his tone formal. "Lady Thorne wouldn't want anything less."

"How much of that did you overhear?" she asked, as Logan whisked her out of the room and toward the front doors.

"Enough to want to get you away from that idiot."

"You're sweet."

"It's a matter of practicality," he said. "If you had the opportunity to show him your martial skills, I might have had to clean up the blood."

She laughed, feeling a little better already. At the door, Logan called for Gemma's carriage to be brought around.

"Just as well I'm leaving," Gemma said. "Jem waited here tonight, and he despises waiting."

A maid helped Gemma with her outer garments—the nights were definitely turning to winter. Logan also received his coat just as the footman announced the arrival of the carriage at the door.

"I'll walk you out," Logan said.

"Won't you ride home with me?" Gemma looked over at him. "Or are you truly enjoying the party?"

He shook his head. "No one will notice I'm gone. But it wouldn't be right for me to join you."

"Why not?"

He only shook his head again. "Let's not discuss it. You just go home and forget about people asking whether you shoot—not that they should care one way or the other."

They reached the carriage, and Jem looked down from the driver's seat. He didn't get down, since Logan would obviously help Gemma into the carriage.

But Gemma tilted her head up to the young man, asking, "Jem, it's perfectly acceptable for a gentleman to ride with a lady, isn't it?"

Jem looked as if he'd rather do anything but answer the question. Logan cut in, "Never mind. Whether it's acceptable or not, I have no plans to do so."

"But what if I need assistance?"

"You have a driver."

Gemma frowned at him. "Did I annoy you this evening?"

"Of course not."

"Then why are you refusing to even sit near me?"

"I'm watching out for you, Miss Harrington." Logan's voice sharpened into cold formality, and Gemma didn't have a response for that.

"Room on the driver's seat," Jem offered unexpectedly.

Logan nodded. "A compromise I can live with."

Gemma looked at him sharply, trying to decide if there was a double meaning in his words.

But Logan said nothing more. He helped her into the carriage, and then joined Jem up at the front. The carriage started to clatter down the street.

Gemma sat alone, wondering why Logan was behaving so oddly all of a sudden. Earlier in the evening, he flirted with her in full view of a hundred guests. Now he seemed to think she had to be sealed in crystal.

It wasn't at all unusual for a gentleman to ride in a carriage with a lady. Perhaps not ideal to the fussiest of matrons, but a far cry from the scandal of, say, Logan being in her bedroom, which he had little compunction about last night. She shook her head, giving up on understanding it for the moment.

The carriage rounded a turn, then lurched, one side crashing downward. Gemma shouted in alarm, but the commotion ended as quickly as it began.

"What happened?" she called out.

"No idea." It was Logan who replied. "Are you hurt?"

"My backside is feeling bruised, but that's all," she said.

Logan was at the door to help her out.

"Lord, what is going on?" Gemma asked. "Is nothing destined to go smoothly in my life?"

"Just a minor accident," he said. "We'll take care of it. Wait here for a moment."

"Good thing you accompanied me," Gemma needled him as he joined Jem by the wheel.

"Wheel broke?" Logan asked.

"That's what it *looks* like," Jem said, and frowned at the mechanism. "But there wasn't a thing wrong with it when it left the house."

Logan peered at the place where the front wheel broke off.

"Damn," Jem said.

"What?" Gemma asked anxiously.

"Pin's missing. That's why the wheel slipped off." Jem looked down the street. "It happened just after I took that left turn. There was nothing to keep the wheel on the post."

"Accident?" Logan asked, sounding as if he already knew the answer.

Jem gave him a disgusted look. "What do you think?"

"What are you suggesting?" Gemma asked. "Why would anyone disable the wheel?"

"Excellent question. In any case, you need to get

home before it gets any colder." Logan stepped away from the dark bulk of the carriage, intending to hail another driver. Gemma followed him, not willing to stand idly by.

Even though it was late, a small crowd was gathering, as always happened when an accident occurred. Gemma didn't think much about it until she saw a scuffle out of the corner of her eye. No, not a scuffle. Two boys were diving toward the street in different directions. They'd seen something one second before anyone else. A thin figure emerged from the crowd, holding a pistol.

Before Gemma could cry an alarm, a gunshot cracked through the night.

Chapter 29

〰〰〰

THE BLAST OF THE GUN was enough to scatter the small crowd. Logan ducked and moved back toward the carriage, hoping to get some cover.

His side ached sharply, and it took a second for him to realize he wasn't hit—the memory of the earlier shot was merely awakened by this one.

The shooter, who Logan recognized as the man he called Cargo, waited a moment too long to discern whether he hit or not. He saw everyone still standing and cursed incoherently. Then he turned and ran.

Logan couldn't let him get away.

"Jem, get her home safe, understand?" Logan yelled, even as he started to chase after the man.

He heard Jem's answering yell, and Gemma screaming at him to stop. But he had to catch the other man.

Cargo had a precious few seconds' lead, and he hurtled down an alley to the right. Logan followed. It might be a trap, but it didn't matter at that point. He spotted Cargo just as the man emerged into the next street. Logan saw him turn left, so he did too.

Despite the late hour, this street was crowded. Cargo was ahead, pushing past people and dodging others. Logan couldn't see a gun in his hand any longer. Maybe he'd tossed it in the alley. Which didn't mean he was unarmed. Logan had only a knife—the sort of knife any sailor would carry, good for cutting rope or fish or throats. Logan would use it tonight if he caught the man. Whether or not she was the target, he shot at Gemma, and only some extremely valuable information would delay the man's death sentence.

Logan kept running, just keeping Cargo in sight. His lungs objected. It was cold and he was still recovering. But fast as Cargo was, he couldn't quite outdistance Logan.

The chase continued through more streets, alleyways, passages between buildings. Cargo jumped over the fence into a graveyard at one point, and Logan vaulted after him. Looking over his shoulder, Cargo's foot caught a loose tombstone and he stumbled. Logan put on a burst of speed, and nearly reached him. But Cargo scrambled up and darted away.

The only thing that kept Logan going was the sound of Cargo's labored breath. The other man was tiring, too. One way or another, the chase would end soon.

Logan kept his eyes firmly on Cargo, who was tantalizingly close now, only about twenty or thirty paces ahead. Then Cargo stopped and turned, throwing something at Logan. He ducked instinctively. Something flew past him, and clattered against the stone wall of a building behind him.

Logan looked up ahead again, but Cargo was gone.

Angry at falling for the distraction, Logan moved forward again, with a little more caution. At the place where Cargo turned, he noticed a small opening between two buildings. Cargo must have gone down it. Logan followed into the dark passageway, sensing another trick ahead.

But what could he do? Cargo was his best lead now. The man must have disabled the wheel, then followed the carriage from the party, which meant he was waiting for an opportunity to attack. And that meant he had a real reason to kill either Logan or Gemma or both. What did he know? Why did he need them dead when he could simply disappear?

The passageway narrowed further, and the darkness increased. But there was a rush of air, so Logan knew he was close to the end. He was out before he knew it, stumbling into a sort of courtyard. But he had no time to look around. A force hit him from behind, and Logan tumbled to the ground.

Cargo was on top of him, something gleaming in his right hand.

Knife.

Logan shoved him off just as he swung the knife down, and Cargo went sprawling. But the bastard was also as quick as a cat, and he sprang up again instantly, still gripping his knife.

Logan reached for his too, determined to make it a fairer fight.

Cargo saw the move and actually grinned, offering a mocking little bow. Maybe he appreciated the irony of hoping for honorable warfare just then.

Logan wasn't about to ask. He jumped at Cargo, using his long-honed skills of balancing on ropes above a ship's deck to grab at Cargo without really being able to see him.

His free hand closed around some part of Cargo's clothing. Logan yanked it hard toward him, and was rewarded by a strangled sound. He must have got the jacket.

But then he was only holding a jacket. Cargo had slipped out of it and escaped Logan's grasp. A weight crashed into him again, and Logan felt a flash of heat in his right arm. Cargo's knife had made contact.

Grunting with pain, Logan swung wildly. By sheer luck, he connected with some part of Cargo's head. The other man stumbled back, unsteady on his feet.

Logan pressed forward, still swinging. He hit again, and he liked the soft crunch of some delicate bone in Cargo's face giving way.

The other man swore in guttural French, but didn't give up. He dodged the next punch, and the next. Logan finally caught him with an uppercut, snapping Cargo's jaw toward the sky.

Cargo sagged. Only the wall of the building behind him stopped him from falling back. He slid down the wall, and Logan swarmed him, pinning him down.

"I have no problem cutting your throat right here and leaving your body for the rats," Logan hissed. "As long as you keep talking, you keep breathing." He put his knife to Cargo's neck to make himself clear. "So talk."

"You won't kill me before you get answers," Cargo said, though his voice was weak.

"You're overestimating my tolerance," said Logan. "I don't like you very much."

He pressed the blade in.

Cargo's eyes widened. "I work for Lisle."

"Caithny's contact?"

"Yes." Cargo took a cautious breath. "I speak better when my throat isn't so close to getting cut."

"I expect you do. Keep talking."

"Lisle was angry at Caithny. The man owed him too much, and couldn't pay the debt."

"The debt for what?"

"The ships. Lisle fronted the money, but Caithny took too long. I was to give him until the end of the run and take what money Caithny made from it. But then everything happened at Caithny's dock. I thought he was on to me. I shot him."

"Then why shoot me tonight?"

Cargo paused, then said, "My employer doesn't like loose ends."

Logan didn't like it. "You're lying."

"No, no!" Cargo tried to move away. "Why would I lie? You can kill me right now!"

"I should," Logan said. Cargo was too shifty. Nothing he said could be trusted.

"You should," Cargo agreed, with a sudden grin. He twisted, and somehow had his knife back in his hand.

No, Logan realized, he had *two* knives. The second one had been hidden. Before Logan could dodge, Cargo sunk the tiny blade into Logan's shoulder.

But he'd been aiming for the heart, and the blade stuck in Logan's body. Cargo made a grab for it, but cursed when he realized he couldn't get it back.

Logan slashed at him once, standing up again despite the heat spreading rapidly from his shoulder to his arm and chest.

Cargo took a few steps back, evaluating his odds. Then he turned and ran.

Logan didn't have the strength to follow him. He wrenched the smaller knife out from where it had caught between bones. Blood flowed out immediately.

"I will need a whole new wardrobe," Logan hissed out loud. He managed to get the wound covered well enough so he could move around without losing more blood. He didn't want to follow Cargo out. The man would be waiting for him. So he turned around, looking for another way out of the odd space he was in.

It was like a forgotten corner of property. Buildings surrounded it, and it was as if each owner thought the courtyard belonged to someone else. Logan saw another narrow passage out of the space, and followed it. He emerged onto a new street, and looked back to see what building the space bordered.

The words were painted boldly on the front of the large structure.

"This is a joke," Logan whispered.

Harrington, Waite, and Talbot.

Cargo led him there because he knew the area. He was connected to the firm somehow, and not just because he happened to be on Caithny's smuggling run. This was getting more complicated by the minute.

Logan had to get inside the place. But he didn't dare go now.

Instead, he walked until he could find a driver who agreed to take him to the address he gave.

"Don't bleed on the seat," the driver warned. "That'll cost you extra."

Logan got out at Cutter's office, hoping to hell the good doctor would answer a knock at that hour.

Cutter did, eventually. He saw Logan's face in the feeble lamplight, and gave a sigh.

"You didn't take my advice, did you?" the doctor asked.

"It was wonderful advice, but no. Can you stitch up a couple of knife wounds?"

Chapter 30

꙱

WHEN LOGAN JUMPED OUT AFTER the retreating figure, Gemma screamed at him to stop. But it was too late. Both were gone. Gemma stared after them in shock. Did Logan turn and chase after a man who just tried to kill him?

"Are you hurt, ma'am?" Jem asked urgently. "Did you get hit?"

"No. No, I'm perfectly all right," Gemma said. Nevertheless, she started shaking a bit. "*What* just happened?"

"I'm not sure, but Mr Hartley told me to get you home safe, and that's what I'll do."

Jem would tolerate no arguments. He spied a boy who had been watching the whole fiasco, and offered to pay him to watch the crippled carriage until Jem returned. Then another carriage was hailed, and Gemma reluctantly got in, knowing that she couldn't do a thing for Logan at this point.

Jem joined the driver up top. When they arrived at the house in Kingston Street, Jem ushered her inside and said she was not to leave until they knew it was safe.

"I have to go get your carriage back, ma'am," he said, preparing to leave again.

"And that's safe?" she asked. "To return to where a man shot at us?"

"He wasn't aiming for me," the driver declared.

"Nor me!"

"You don't know that, ma'am. You and Mr Hartley were standing very near each other—either of you could have been the target. And it was your carriage he sabotaged."

Gemma stopped short. She never considered that. "Who would want to kill me?"

"I've no idea, ma'am. But I'm quite sure you'll be safer in here."

So Gemma had little to do but worry about both Logan and Jem, who were out in the streets with some armed madman.

She sat in the parlor, or rather, she tried to sit, but she could only pace the room while she wondered what was happening. Bond came in, an expectant look on her face.

"Are you not intending to go up to bed, ma'am?" she asked. "Mrs Douglas returned home and retired about half an hour ago."

Gemma looked down, remembering that she was still in her evening wear. "Oh, I can't sleep."

"What's troubling you, ma'am?"

"There was an accident on the way home. Everyone is well," she hastily assured the maid. "But Jem had to go back out to get the carriage home somehow, and I last saw Mr Hartley running toward whoever caused the whole mess, and how can I sleep when everything is up in the air?"

"I will bring you some camomile tea," Bond declared. "You can wait until Jem returns. The news of the carriage being back should help."

"Oh, Lord, the carriage can burn for all I care. It's the thought of both of them out in the night that concerns me.

If I'd had my pistols, I could have done something straight away."

"And attracted some undue attention, ma'am," Bond warned her. "You just wait here. I'll bring the tea. No doubt everything is well in hand."

Gemma drank the tea. It didn't help in the slightest. The news of Jem's return—and the retrieval of the carriage—was one burden off her back. But Logan was still who knew where, presumably following an armed attacker when he wasn't armed himself. She paced the floor, frustrated. She should have stowed one of her pistols in the carriage. Then she could have used it, or at the very least lent it to Logan. Instead, he plunged into danger, and all on her account.

Why had he done that? She finally sank onto a couch by the fire, her mind working furiously.

"Ma'am?" Bond was at the door to the parlor. "Um, you have a visitor, ma'am."

Gemma glanced at the clock. It was well after two in the morning. "What?" she asked.

"Mr Hartley is here. Came to the back entrance," she added.

"Well, show him in!"

Logan came in a moment later, looking haggard but in one piece.

Gemma rushed over to him, but checked her progress as Bond followed him in. She could hardly throw her arms around him when the other girl was watching.

"You look terrible," she said. Then she looked closer. "Doesn't that jacket belong to Fergus?"

"Mine is a bit...unwearable."

"Why?"

"Well, mostly because of the holes, and the blood."

"Did you get shot again?"

"No. He had a knife. But I'm stitched up now. Good as new." Logan looked back toward Bond. "Not your job, I know, but if a glass of brandy happened to be available…"

Bond smiled and whirled around, intent on her errand. Logan sighed and moved toward the fire. "Do you mind if I sit?"

Gemma trailed him, still terrified at the thought of him getting attacked.

"Of course I don't mind if you sit. Are you…do you need anything? I could call a doctor."

"Already been," he said. He gave her a weak smile. "Nothing to be concerned about."

"I am concerned! Logan, what happened back there? Jem thought the man might have been aiming for me."

"No. I know him. He was trying to kill me." Logan took a seat in the chair by the fire, gazing at her.

She sat back down on the couch, not trusting her ability to stand. "Why would he do such a thing?"

"I've made a few enemies," he said. "We should leave it at that."

"I will *not* leave it at that," Gemma said. "You have to tell me the truth."

"I did," he said. "A man took a dislike to me. It happens. Just be glad that nothing worse occurred."

Before Gemma could reply, Bond reappeared, bearing a tray with a single glass on it. "Do ring if you need anything else."

The maid left, leaving the door conspicuously open.

Gemma refocused on Logan. "No matter what business you're in, people don't attack their rivals without a good reason. My God, you could have been killed."

"I'm used to it," he said, taking a sip of the drink.

"Well, I'm not!"

"You hid it well. Other ladies would have fainted dead away by this point." He held up the glass in his hand in a mock toast.

"If I'm strong enough to withstand watching you near-ly get killed, then I'm strong enough to know the whole truth."

He finished the drink. "Truth. What is that? Different things to different people."

"And you'd know all about being different people," said Gemma. "When we first met, you were the image of a smuggler."

"I like to look the part," he said, his voice low.

"So it *is* a part," she said. "The role of Lockridge, that is. Lockridge isn't your real name, after all."

He blinked, then focused on her more sharply. "Go on."

"I've figured out your little secret," Gemma whis-pered. "You're not a smuggler at all."

"Of course I am. You've seen me smuggle with your own eyes."

"But have I? I put it all together. You said you were in the Royal Navy, which Lady Thorne confirmed."

"Well, that might just be a lie to impress some people I want to trick."

"No, it's not. Not only were you definitely in the Roy-al Navy, you still are! You've been playing the part of a smuggler to help the Navy catch real smugglers, especial-ly any who deal with enemies of Great Britain."

He didn't say anything for a long moment. Then he actually smiled. "You put all that together yourself, did you?"

"Who else could I discuss it with? But it fits. You claim to be a smuggler, but you're really very young to have your own ship—"

"Hold on a moment. The *Mistral* is mine," he said. "I never lied about that."

"Perhaps. But you're different from all the smugglers I ever met. You're far more of a gentleman—"

"Most of the time," he corrected.

"And you were careful that I didn't get harmed. Up in Scotland, and then again tonight, when you ran after that man. A real criminal wouldn't have let that get in the way. I've met plenty, and they care about one thing—themselves. And it explains why you were so interested in Uncle Conall's operations. You wanted that information to take back to your superiors at the Navy so you can shut the smuggling operation down."

"Very clever, Miss Harrington," he said.

"Besides, you gave me a hint in Scotland."

"What was my mistake?"

"I don't think it *was* a mistake," Gemma said. "When we were on the beach, you said *You could help me catch them*. I didn't put it together at the time. I was a bit busy. But you wanted me to know you weren't like the others."

"Oh, I'm one of a kind."

She smiled. "So I'm right, aren't I? You *are* a spy."

"I can't confirm or deny that."

"So I am right!" Gemma laughed in relief. "Oh, I knew it."

"As a matter of fact, I did do some smuggling in my life. Don't think I'm a saint."

"No one would confuse you with a saint, Logan," she said, with a wicked smile. "But I am glad to know you're on the right side. I knew there was more to you. And that means you need my help."

"Your help?" Logan stood up. "Perhaps I do need another drink."

"You don't need a drink. You need *me*. We have to investigate this whole operation together. It began with Uncle Conall, but it doesn't end there."

"Gemma, this isn't a game."

"I'm well aware of that, Logan, as the man *shooting* at us earlier tonight made clear.

You need my help. That's why you approached me in Scotland isn't it? You needed to know details of Conall's operation. So I can help now, by asking the right questions."

"I'd prefer if you weren't involved."

"A bit late for that, isn't it?" she asked. "Where should we start?"

"I lost the man's trail right near a large warehouse marked with the sign Harrington, Waite, and Talbot."

Gemma stood up too. "They're using *my* warehouse as a base?" she asked angrily.

"Maybe."

"Then we have to get inside."

"Exactly my thought."

"Excellent." She nodded. "But we won't sneak in the middle of the night. I don't want you getting shot at again."

"What do you suggest?"

"It's my business," Gemma said. "I'll demand a tour. It's time I did anyway. And who better to join me than Mr Logan Hartley, late of the Royal Navy? I'll have all sorts of ship related questions for you."

He looked as if he was about to argue, but then thought better of it. "If you promise you only go there *with* me, then yes, we'll do it. You're not to go alone under any circumstances."

Gemma smiled, triumphant. "Good. I will instruct Mr Pratt to write to the firm and set up a suitable time. And I'll make it clear I expect that time to be very soon," She was all too aware that the men in charge would likely put her off. "We'll ride together."

"You mean I'll meet you there," he said quickly. "And you will need to take along someone from the household for propriety. Perhaps Bond can accompany you."

"Oh, I hate to take her away from other duties. But Jem will drive me there, and stay just outside the building. Walking around my own place of business is hardly scandalous."

"I guess not," he agreed. "All right. Send me a message telling me when I should arrive there."

"A message?" Gemma asked. If was almost as if Logan was suddenly unwilling to be seen with her.

"Just in case," he said. As Logan was about to leave, he turned to look at her. "One more thing, Gemma. About the compass."

"I take good care of it," she said quickly. "I know it's an heirloom, but you don't have a thing to worry about."

"Perhaps I should take it back," he said, almost hesitantly.

"What did I just say? Don't you trust me?"

"It's not that I don't trust you." He sighed, and she could suddenly see how tired he was. "But you should put it away. Somewhere safe. Just until all this is over."

"Would that make you feel better?"

"Yes."

She tipped her head, then smiled. "All right. Then I will."

Chapter 31

THE MORNING AFTER THE PARTY at the Thornes' home, Gemma awoke with her head full of the revelations from last night. Logan was a spy. He was in danger because he was protecting *her,* and he was most certainly still hiding something from her.

But more quotidian troubles awaited Gemma as well. Probably through the well-informed servants, Aunt Maura heard all about the near-altercation between Gemma and whoever the dandy was from the Thorne's party. She was miserable, blaming the event on her own absence.

"Oh, this is all my fault," she said, as the two ladies were sitting at the breakfast table.

"What is?"

"Everything about your behavior."

"My behavior was perfect," Gemma said. "*He* was rude first."

"That doesn't matter! One triumphs not by sinking to another's level but by rising above it. You're just not pre-pared for this, and it's my responsibility. I should have done everything differently, and now it's too late."

"It was one evening, and it was only a simple conver-sation."

"There is no such thing among society. And it is not only that. Your clothes, your attitude. I heard about a dance card dropped into the flames the other evening. And now there's discussion of target practice! Lord, I should almost welcome my brother's arrival here, unpleasant as it may be."

"What?" Gemma felt a jolt, thinking of Conall's body being carried into their home. Did Maura intend to use a period of mourning as a shield?

But of course Maura didn't know the truth. "I'll be honest," she went on, blessedly ignorant of the facts, "I expected to hear from my brother by now. He must be furious with both of us. More so with me, I'd imagine." She gave a sigh of familial remorse. "I let him run everything about your life for so long. And now it is too late to correct course."

"We must see how things transpire," Gemma said. She thought of what Logan told her about Conall's death. He asked her to keep quiet about it, and she would, although she'd demand more details. But for now, she had to soothe Aunt Maura.

So she said, "If Uncle Conall…arrives, we'll handle that matter. Or if I'm drummed out of society circles, or if there is gossip about me…"

"Of course there is gossip. I only wonder what kind." Maura's expression was foreboding.

"Oh, You're worrying over nothing. Tell me how you enjoyed your evening out with Mr Rodney."

"Don't try to distract me, Gemma girl." But Maura blushed prettily, and it was easy enough to get her thinking of happier things.

Fortunately, Gemma's gaffe—if it was a gaffe—did not seem to have ostracized her. Or perhaps not everyone had heard what happened. In any case, she had more callers over the next two days than ever before. All of them, whether ladies or gentlemen, found reasons to invite Gemma to other events and to praise her.

Then Lady Gretwood herself came to call.

Gemma grimaced when she saw the card Ivy brought in on the tray. She showed it to Aunt Maura. "I suppose we must be at home."

Maura nodded. She said to Ivy, "Show her in."

Moments later, Lady Gretwood herself came in, all smiles.

"Good afternoon, my dear ladies!"

"I am somewhat surprised you could make the time to call, Lady Gretwood," Aunt Maura said. "You're so in demand among the ladies of the ton."

"Yes, well, it was on the way to Lady Mathering's, and I shall only be a moment."

"Don't let us detain you, if you've more important calls," Gemma said, a little tartly. She remembered the woman's harsh remark the last time they met.

But Lady Gretwood laughed as if Gemma told a great joke. "One never knows what to expect when Miss Harrington is in the room, does one?" She went on to bore Gemma with a description of a ball from the previous evening, but Gemma blinked in surprise when she realized that Lady Gretwood was finishing up by inviting her to yet another event, hosted by the lady herself. "Do say you'll come. No shortage of eligible bachelors, I promise—gentlemen worthy of your esteem."

"I thought I was but a flash in the pan," Gemma said, throwing the lady's earlier words back into her face.

Lady Gretwood didn't even blink. "Nonsense. Your intrigue seems *limitless*, Miss Harrington." Her message delivered, Lady Gretwood rose and went to the door by the foyer. She saw Jem and said, "Call my carriage, John."

"His name is Jem," Gemma corrected, though Jem had already moved to obey and was out the door.

The lady gave her an icy stare, her true personality reemerging for a moment. "As if I care in the least what his *name* is." She passed into the foyer, where Ivy would be fetching her wrap.

While the two were alone again, Aunt Maura murmured, "Leave it, dear. It's common practice among the wealthy to call all footmen John."

"You can't be serious." She looked at her aunt in disbelief.

"It makes the running of a household a bit smoother," Maura explained.

Gemma rolled her eyes. "That's the most ridiculous thing I've heard today. And I've heard quite a lot."

Lady Gretwood left the house, and a few minutes later, Jem returned, stamping his feet against the cold.

Gemma asked him, "Has anyone else called you John since you started here?"

"Not that I can recall," Jem said cheerfully. "But it's happened elsewhere, so I'm used to it. Just part of the job."

"I will not endorse the practice," she declared.

"As you say, ma'am." Jem didn't seem in the slightest bit disturbed by the occasional alteration of his name, which irked Gemma.

"How can you tolerate it?" she asked. "It's your name!"

"And my name won't change, ma'am, even if some don't call me by it." He paused. "Do you need anything else at the moment? If not, I've other duties."

"Yes, go, *Jem*," she said, waving him off. What an odd little world she was in. Where people changed the names of their servants to avoid the inconvenience of learning their real names. For the dozenth time, she asked herself why she wanted to join it.

"My mother moved in these circles," she said to Aunt Maura. "And my father was the son of a lord. Yet I feel so out of place."

"Why? After all, you grew up in a castle."

Gemma laughed out loud. "A castle! In name only."

"To those who haven't seen it, they'll think of a most grand upbringing."

"People want to believe, don't they? They make up stories to suit their dreams."

Maura smiled. "Yes, everyone does. Or nearly everyone." She looked out the window, pondering. "That was a reversal. Three days ago Lady Gretwood insulted you. And now she wants you at her own party!"

"Do you think it's a trick of some sort?" Gemma asked.

"I can't see how. But we must discover what was behind her change of heart."

"I don't believe Lady Gretwood has a heart," Gemma said.

"But she does have influence. So it behooves you to humor her."

But before they could discuss it further, Lady Forester called at the house.

"Cherie," she began, her eyes bright. "Did you know I went to six houses in the last two hours and *everyone* was talking about you?"

"Is that good?"

"It's marvelous! I could not have devised a better scene if I wrote the script myself. The young ingenue arrives, disguised as a pauper. But then she emerges as a princess in finery all her own—with a little advice from me. And for the final act? It is revealed that she is not just an heiress, but a woman of independent means!"

"Revealed?" Gemma said. "What do you mean?"

"That you alone will control your fortune! What a marvelous gift, and what appeal for a man who seeks a wife. He doesn't need to fret about crop yields or entailments, or a family controlling the strings. Gentlemen will be standing six deep at your door."

"No," Gemma said. "No. I don't want that."

"Then what do you want? You have the world at your feet." Sophie's eyes bored into hers. "What is it you want?"

Logan.

Gemma shook her head. "I don't know. But Aunt Maura and I agreed not say anything, for just this reason. I don't want to be courted by a man who just wants me so he can sell my investments! What sort of romance is there in that?"

"Is that so?" Sophie's eyes narrowed. "Well, someone talked, and now all of London knows. We must get to the truth of the matter. And that's something I happen to do rather well." Lady Forester smiled, and it was the smile of a predator.

She left, promising to share whatever news she discovered. Gemma was so upset by the revelation that she couldn't stay inside. Instead, she did what always made her feel better—she took Hector out for a ride. Though she couldn't shake Jem as groom, the lad rode far enough back that she could pretend she was alone. Or as alone as it was possible to be in the heart of London. The park with the best riding was now filled with people, most gawking at each other instead of doing any actual riding.

"Excuse me, excuse me," Gemma said pointedly, whenever someone got in her way. A few people hailed her, but she was in no mood to chat. She offered only a nod, or a brief smile. She knew better than to cut anyone, but she couldn't imagine holding a conversation with someone who might know more about her life than she did.

She suddenly wanted to know where Logan was at that moment…and if he'd magically appear and offer her passage on his ship to somewhere very far away.

Chapter 32

≋

A FEW DAYS LATER, AT four in the afternoon, the sun was rapidly dropping to the western horizon, and the height of the buildings made it nearly dark in the streets. Logan stood near the entrance to the shipping firm of Harrington, Waite, and Talbot.

He was dressed appropriately, which is to say he was dressed as a man of business. Dark colors, clean lines, and modest fabrics. He ought to look like any other gentleman on the street.

He paused when he saw a coach stop in front of the large doors. The lanky young Jem jumped down to help the occupant out.

Gemma stepped down. She was dressed in a vivid gown the color of bright blue ink. Her hat and gloves were snow-white, and the collar of her jacket was lined in white fur, making her look like exactly what she was— rare and unattainable. Her red hair gleamed in the lamp-light, and Logan's heart contracted.

But she needed his help, whether she knew it or not. Logan took a step forward, then another. Why was this such a challenge? He could run down enemy ships and capture enemy agents. But standing by Gemma was beyond his skills?

Shaking off the ridiculous notion, he got to the coach.

Gemma greeted him in a low voice, though she was beaming at him. "I haven't seen you for days," she said. "I was worried you'd sailed off."

"Not till this business is concluded, Miss Harrington."

Her face clouded momentarily. She didn't like his response, nor the formal tone in which he delivered it. But then her smile returned. "Are you ready to scout out the location?"

"Indeed. Remember, don't trust anyone you speak to in there. We don't know who's involved. If you're not sure how to respond to something, don't say anything. I'll give a suitable reply, or let you know what to say."

"Very well," Gemma said. "I trust you completely."

"Go on ahead. I'll be there in a moment."

Logan waited until Gemma was out of earshot, then turned to Jem. "I was just thinking," Logan said, as if sharing an idle comment, "that Miss Harrington might benefit from having a key to this place. Don't you think that would be helpful?"

"Aye, sir," Jem said, with a slow nod.

"Of course, I'll be with the group, as will Miss Harrington. And you'll be watching the coach the whole time."

"The whole time," Jem agreed, his smile barely hidden. "Good day, sir."

Feeling better, Logan continued on to the entrance where Gemma was waiting for him. He opened the door for her, and joined her inside.

Gemma gave her name to the nearest clerk, and soon a short man was clattering down a flight of steps to meet them.

"Good afternoon," Gemma said to him. "Mr Pratt wrote to say I would be coming. I am Miss Harrington. My father was John Harrington."

The short man bowed, then tried to offer a hand, then retracted the hand on realizing Gemma was a lady, then stepped back nervously.

"Oh, yes. Miss Harrington. I didn't expect…. That is, how do you do…. That is, my name is Dobbs." Dobbs was a pale man with thinning hair and sharp eyes. His whole manner hinted at a ratlike nervousness. This was not just a shy man behaving awkwardly around a lady. Something about Gemma in particular made Dobbs uneasy. Logan didn't like him from the first.

Gemma nodded. "How do you do, Mr Dobbs. This is Mr Hartley. He is an associate of my uncle, Conall Caithny, and I have asked him to lend his expertise to me."

"Mr Dobbs," Logan said. "How do you do."

Dobbs looked at Logan. "Expertise? What role do you play here, sir?"

"Advisor," Gemma said. "It has come to my attention that I need to learn about all aspects of my finances. That includes the firm. So I thank you for reserving an hour at the end of your day to show me the place."

"Yes," Dobbs said dubiously, still looking at Logan, as if trying to place him.

"I own a ship and have some experience with shipping, among other things," Logan said. "You might say Mr Caithny is a partner. I had occasion to meet Miss Harrington while I was at Caithny."

"My uncle placed much confidence in Mr Hartley," Gemma said.

"Still does," Logan corrected, keeping up the pretense that Caithny was still alive. "Now, let's begin the tour."

Dobbs nodded cautiously, then led them through the offices, the wharves, and the warehouse.

Logan listened carefully, and watched everything. Workers were moving around busily to get everything done by the end of the work day, which would be five for the office workers and likely not till six or seven for the other men. Dobbs spoke politely to Gemma, but Logan sensed an edge of condescension in the man's tone.

Gemma must have as well, because after a few minutes she unleashed her charm on the man. "Mr Dobbs," she said, after he gave a clipped version of operations for the last quarter. "You have done so much for the firm. I can tell that you'll be invaluable in the future. I feel so much better, knowing that you'll be handling the day-to-day work."

At that, Dobbs lost his cold demeanor and looked at the ground. "Just doing my job, miss."

"If only all gentlemen were so dedicated. I do wish my father were alive to see what good hands the firm is in." She smiled brightly at Dobbs.

The rest of his icy coating cracked. "Thank you, Miss Harrington."

From that moment, Dobbs seemed delighted to answer all of Gemma's questions. Logan hung back for a bit, admiring her cleverness.

Spurred by the man's transformation, Logan tried to be helpful himself. He asked a few questions about the firm's practices in storing goods in between shipments, and the plans for employing additional ships. He also scanned the whole building, noting where extra storerooms might be, and if anyone was paying particular attention to Gemma.

At one point, he leaned over to Gemma. "Keep him

talking for a moment," he breathed.

Gemma gave a tiny nod, then pointed to something at the other end of the warehouse.

Logan strolled over to a mass of stacked crates at one side. The pile, if it indeed went all the way back to the main wall of the warehouse, was tremendous. It would take multiple ships to carry all those crates. He walked to one end, then casually pushed at one stack, peering into the depths of the pile.

"Ah, excuse me, Mr Hartley!" Dobbs was at his elbow, staring anxiously at him. "These crates are filled with glass. We mustn't disturb them!"

"That's a lot of glass," Logan said, looking up toward the ceiling.

"Yes, well, it's a necessary commodity, isn't it? Please come away. Thank you sir."

Logan let himself be led away. Gemma was looking at him quizzically, but she said nothing.

"When will the crates be shipped?" Logan asked. "That's a huge supply. You'd need multiple vessels."

"Oh, it's all planned and accounted for, sir."

"Do you need more ships?" Gemma asked, her face bright. "Perhaps Mr Hartley would be of assistance there as well. His family runs the premier shipbuilding outfit in Bermuda, is that not true?" She looked at Logan with that innocent expression he didn't trust at all.

"Is that so?" Dobbs asked, interest in his voice.

"Indeed." Gemma replied before he could. "I have seen the ship he has in England now. You built it yourself, did you not, Mr Hartley."

"True," he said, a little shortly. He didn't want to mention the *Mistral*'s name. "I have some experience."

"Oh, don't be modest. That ship is a beauty."

"Yes, she is."

"Mr Hartley was the one who taught me why all ships are called *she*," Gemma explained sweetly to Dobbs. "Can you imagine that I, the daughter of John Harrington, didn't even know that until recently? You can see, Mr Dobbs. I am not at *all* prepared to deal with the actual business of shipping. But it is so good to see the place my father helped build!"

Dobbs walked them back to the front doors and they stepped outside into the night. A few lights gleamed near the entrance to the firm, but the street itself wasn't lit; the only other light came from a few houses with windows still uncovered. Sunset had also brought a sharp drop in temperature, and their breath steamed in the air.

"What did you see?" Gemma asked Logan as they walked toward the carriage.

"A number of things," he said. "Most significantly, I wouldn't trust Dobbs for a second. He's undoubtably working with Caithny somehow."

"What will you do?"

Logan made a frustrated noise. "I can't shadow him all day and night. I could put a Disreputable on him, I suppose."

"What's a Disreputable?" Gemma asked.

Damn. Logan realized what he'd let slip. "Ah, just a sort of person we use for odd jobs."

"'We' being the Navy?" Gemma asked skeptically. "Doesn't sound like the sort of people anyone would want to deal with."

"The name is a bit of a joke," Logan said hastily. "They're quite reliable. *I* rely on them," he added. "But it's not important. Don't worry."

"Very well," Gemma said. "What is our next step?"

"Your next step is returning home, Miss Harrington," he said, a warning in his voice. "I will follow a few leads and let you know what happens."

When they reached the carriage, Jem gave Logan a nod. Logan saw a trace of a smile on the young man's face. Evidently, he'd been successful in snagging a key.

But Logan wasn't going to alert Gemma to their extra activities. He'd get the key from Jem later. Logan opened the door.

She turned to him. "Why do I get the sense that you're freezing me out of this investigation?"

"I'm watching out for your safety," he said, hoping she'd relent and knowing she wouldn't.

"But I want to help," Gemma said.

"You did. You helped today."

"And tomorrow?" she pressed.

Logan said only, "We'll see."

"Don't you need a ride somewhere?" she asked, gesturing to the carriage. "Why not take advantage?"

"We're going different directions, Miss Harrington," he said, helping her in.

She held his hand tightly for just a moment, before letting go and sitting back in the seat. "Don't disappear on me, Mr Hartley. I will not be denied."

"That's what I'm afraid of," he said.

Chapter 33

≋

THE NEXT DAY, BOND WOKE Gemma not long after daybreak. She insisted on dressing Gemma in a morning gown and doing her hair in a simple knot. Gemma protested she had no intention of letting anyone through the door, but Bond brushed the objections away.

"No lady ever regretted looking more presentable than the occasion requires, miss. And who knows what the day may bring?"

So Gemma ate her breakfast and tried to write a few letters over the morning. She crumpled all the papers up and tossed them into the grate, displeased with her brain. "I can't put two words together," she grumbled to herself. Chance, who was lying at her feet, whined in sympathy.

Jem entered several times with cards of guests. All gentlemen, or ladies accompanied by gentlemen. Gemma looked at all of them and shook her head in disgust. So it was beginning. "Tell them I'm not at home."

Then, shortly before noon, Jem came in again. "Lord MacLachlan is here, miss. Shall I also tell him you're not at home?"

"No, Jem. Please show him in. And tell Aunt Maura he's here, should she want to join us."

Jem nodded. A moment later, MacLachlan entered. "I could feel the daggers in the gazes of all the young men on your steps. That I should be admitted while they— good Englishmen all—should be left standing in the cold."

"You were shrewd enough to pay me compliments before you heard the particulars of my fortune."

Ian stopped still. "Perhaps I should leave."

Gemma immediately regretted her words. "No! Please, I should not have said that. Forgive me. I'm in a horrible mood. Please don't leave. I...I have no one to talk to. There are so many people about, and no friends at all."

He stepped closer to her, then stooped to pet the dog's head affectionately. "I can understand. Well, not actually. I've never had a horde of ladies beating down my door— though if anyone asks, please tell them otherwise."

She smiled at the image.

"There we are," Ian said, his own smile returning. "I feared you would be undone by this fiasco."

"I may be yet. I wished to know what London society was like, and now I fear I do."

He nodded. "Not as above it all as they'd like to pretend. But better you know the truth of it now. You'll be prepared for the next battle."

"I hardly know a thing! It's all very confusing. You have not offered to take me away to the highlands with you, away from all this madness."

Ian sat down on the couch opposite. "I considered it as soon as I heard the first rumors. But if I had, you might have thought I did it precisely for that reason. When in truth it would be as much for your red hair and your nose —which next to the hair is your best feature. Let no one tell you different."

Gemma laughed. She was aware that he was trying to cheer her. She needed cheering. Ian was really a darling. Perhaps her whimsical comment was not so far off the mark. She had money. He had position. Why should she not marry him?

Because you don't love him. Not the way you love Logan.

Damn.

"My lord," she began, sobering up. "Forgive me again, for saying what I said earlier. You're a friend, and I never meant to imply that you were after my money."

Ian said bluntly, "Well, I've never pretended otherwise. I wouldn't be here in London if I didn't need to restore Castle Lachlan and its lands. But obviously I'm not just after money, or I would have marched in, proposed to any of several women who've let me know they're delighted to purchase a title, and then returned to Lachlan already."

"You'd be back home," she pointed out. "I know you prefer it there."

"When I picture my home," Ian said firmly, "the picture includes a wife who is actually happy to be there."

Then he sat back, his expression turning puzzled and thoughtful. "Let's return to the subject at hand, though. Do you know *why* these rumors are flying around? Lord knows you've never made much talk of your fortune."

Gemma groaned in frustration. "I'm in the dark. Yes, Mr Pratt told me I would control it all come my next birthday, and that I could do what I liked and spend what I liked…but the concept didn't mean much to me. I brushed it off as an excessive worry about the character of the ton." She blushed. "I must sound so green."

Ian shook his head. "It's not your fault. You didn't encourage the lot outside your door. *You* didn't say a word, after all."

She began to nod, then stopped, struck by something in Ian's words. The wild rumors raging among the ton must have a root somewhere, and Gemma thought she could guess what the root was.

"Mr Pratt," she said. "He talked to his wife, and she talked to her friends, and they shared it with their friends…it's a wonder it took this long to become common knowledge."

"What will you do?" Ian asked.

"What can I do? No one lied. I'll simply have to put up with a crowd of would-be suitors at my front door."

"Thank goodness you have a side door," Ian said.

She laughed. "Very true. And of course, I still own my pistols. So I'm not too concerned about persistent suitors." She sobered again. "But it's horrible all the same. I just want to live as I like."

"Not as others would like you to live," Ian concluded with an odd expression on his face.

* * * *

Within days, the news of Gemma's wealth—and in particular the accessibility of her fortune—seemed to spread throughout the city. More and more people called on her, or scraped acquaintance with her, and in general made a nuisance of themselves. Gemma wasn't so annoyed for herself. After all, she never hesitated to say what was on her mind. What infuriated her most were those people who ingratiated themselves with Aunt Maura, hoping to get to Gemma through her family. Aunt

Maura was far too polite to cut such people as they deserved, or perhaps she was more forgiving. In any case, the ladies of Kingston Street entertained callers every afternoon, whether Gemma wanted to or not.

But while she fumed inwardly, life went on, and she continued to attend the round of events she was invited to. The Season was well underway now, and nothing Gemma said or did put her out of the graces of the aristocrats who dictated who was who in society. Her fortune seemed to make her immune from minor faux pas, though no doubt a larger scandal—such as being compromised by Logan—would sink her just like any other woman.

Ian MacLachlan was completely absent for a while, which troubled her more than she cared to admit. But he called unexpectedly one afternoon when Gemma and Maura were entertaining a few others.

He entered diffidently, nodding politely to the guests he didn't know.

She smiled at Ian, hoping to regain the former ease she'd always felt with him. He mostly sat quietly, chatting with the others, but offering little on his own. The young Miss Fletcher, who was definitely marriage-minded, paid him quite a bit of attention. But her mother took her out of the room ten minutes later, saying they had other calls to make.

On the edge of her hearing, Gemma heard Miss Fletcher whisper, "But he's a baron, Mama."

The older woman harrumphed. "I'll not send my only daughter to live at the ends of the earth, no matter what the title."

At first, Gemma was amused that the terribly plain Miss Fletcher thought she might catch Ian's attention. But then she glanced at Ian, and felt a keen sense of remorse.

It was shallow of her to think Ian would disdain Miss Fletcher simply because she wasn't a beauty. London was getting to her.

A few moments later, the others left as well, leaving Ian as the only guest. Maura excused herself to fetch a few letters from her room. She wanted to give Gemma a moment with Ian.

Gemma seized the opportunity. "What kept you away these past few days?"

He looked pensive. "I made light of my reasons for coming to London this Season," he said. "But it is true that I am looking for a wife of means. Yet hearing one hundred thousand made me reconsider."

She tipped her head, puzzled. "It is too *much*?"

"In a way…yes. I never set out to be a fortune hunter, merely careful in my choice of a bride. But can you trust any suitor now?"

"I trust you," she said bluntly. "Indeed, you've been nothing but honest since we met."

"Have I?" he asked, more to himself than to her.

"My lord," Gemma said, "I enjoy your company. I forbid you from…ruminating on this matter. And please don't stop calling on me. Who should I have to defend me from the real fortune hunters who—as you noted—are lining up outside my door?"

"I will be your champion, Miss Harrington," he said, giving her a sudden smile. "Against whatever threats come your way."

"Thank you, my lord." Gemma thought of something. "You know, I am to have a birthday in a few weeks."

"I have one of those every year," Ian said.

"Pertness of manner is not admired among the ton, sir," Gemma said, mimicking her aunt. "My point is that I intend to have a party. I will send out invitations, of course, but you must come."

"Is there anything particular about this party I should know?"

"Well, I haven't started planning it much," Gemma said, thoughtfully. "But it's my twenty first birthday. I want to make it grand."

Ian stood, preparing to leave. "I have no doubt at all that you will make it an event to remember."

Gemma found out only later how prophetic his words would prove.

Chapter 34

∿

LOGAN KNEW WHAT IT WAS like to be becalmed—when the wind died, and a ship simply had to drift, waiting for a fresh breeze to fill the sails again. The same feeling was descending on him now. He could see the shore in the distance, but he couldn't reach it. He was tantalizingly close to a revelation, but he had to wait for information to come to him. It was maddening.

Worse, every time he saw Gemma, he wanted her more. Not just in that moment, but to keep. And that was the one thing he'd never be allowed to do. But even if he couldn't keep her, he could keep her safe. He just had to find the root of Caithny's operation.

He'd already asked for assistance, and he was confident he'd get answers. Logan reached his destination, the Whitby Club, where nearly all of the Zodiac agents were members. Sophie was a notable exception, as the club was naturally closed to women...although that only kept Sophie out some of the time. Otherwise, it provided a good place to meet without attracting attention.

Inside, he was greeted by the staff, who seemed to know everyone and, to Logan's secret relief, never appeared to mind that Logan wasn't an aristocrat, like most of the other members. "Evening, Mr Hartley. Sir Nathan is awaiting you in the Tabard Room."

Logan nodded and went up the stairs. The Tabard Room was small, and the walls were predictably decorated with tabards, lending a distinctly medieval air to the place.

Sir Nathan Bancroft was indeed waiting. "Good evening," he said. Bancroft was once a sign of the Zodiac. He'd left the group rather abruptly—Logan didn't know details, but heard it was a bad situation. After a while, Bancroft resumed some limited activities, such as gathering information for active agents. The blond man was very good at it.

"Sorry if I'm late," Logan apologized.

Bancroft merely shook his head. "I was enjoying a moment of calm."

"Wish I could say the same."

"I did what you asked," Bancroft said, after Logan closed the door. "Looked up Conall Caithny's finances and creditors. It was tougher than I expected. He had long list of creditors, and most of them don't exactly have offices."

"What did you find?" Logan asked.

"As you already learned up in Scotland, Caithny borrowed very heavily. Normally, the creditors would have been down his neck, but he somehow assured them all the debt will be paid off by the end of January. So they're holding back—for now." Bancroft paused. "News of his death would change things considerably, of course."

"He said it would be paid off by the end of January?" Logan frowned. Why did that disturb him?

"Yes. He claimed he had a very valuable shipment that would come in by then."

"But that doesn't make sense," Logan pointed out. "He had no ships left to carry *any* shipment. He even tried to steal the *Mistral* from me."

Bancroft raised one eyebrow. "I imagine that didn't go well for him."

"I wasn't the one who shot him," Logan said. "Though I certainly wanted to when I found out his plan."

"Your point is a good one, though," said Bancroft. "Unless it's carrying diamonds, no ship's hold could carry a cargo valuable enough to pay off his debts. And the security of a single ship? Even if it's insured, what money-lender would risk it?"

"I wouldn't," Logan said flatly.

Bancroft rubbed his jaw thoughtfully. "And the creditors who hold Caithny's notes are hardly the most reputable."

"Are you sure he said it was a shipment that would come in?"

"Actually, one of the men I managed to track down phrased it differently." Bancroft repeated it to Logan right down to the inflection in the voice: "I have quite a valuable commodity to be disposed of by the end of January."

Logan felt a chill run down his spine. "I don't like that at all. Caithny must have been planning something unusual. No wonder he was nervous. I wish he hadn't died during the run. He was the only one who could answer these questions."

"Not necessarily," Bancroft said. "I learned one other thing. Caithny had a partner in his operation."

"Dobbs," said Logan. "I met him when I was poking around the shipping firm one day."

"No, not Dobbs." Bancroft waved that name away as unimportant. "I heard about him—he was only a subordinate. There was someone else, a silent partner who is powerful enough to make creditors think twice. That's probably the real reason Caithny was able to delay the repayment as much as he did."

"Who?"

"That is the question."

Logan stood up. The room was too small to pace, but he tried anyway. "You said Dobbs was a subordinate. But I think he was in Caithny's confidence, if he was the contact in London. Maybe Dobbs also knows who this other man is, or he knows how to find him. Who would give Conall so much backing? And why?"

Bancroft smiled. "It's moments like these which make me so happy to no longer be an agent. You're a sign. It's up to you to find out."

Chapter 35

DESPITE THE CHILL AIR, GEMMA had her daily ride as usual. Chance, who enjoyed running alongside the horse, accompanied them. She rode alone, except for Jem riding as groom discreetly behind her, since she was rather pre-occupied and didn't care for human company. Instead, she turned the matter of Logan over in her mind.

A few days had passed since Gemma saw Logan. His attitude toward her had changed from what it had been in Scotland. At first, she attributed it to the scenery—London was enough to alter anyone's mood. But it didn't actually make sense, because the first few times she saw Logan in the city, he was just as engaging and even flirta-tious as he was before. Something happened the night of the party at the Thornes' home. By the time Logan saw her out the door, after the dandy taunted her, he acted as if he hardly knew her. She'd scarcely seen him since then, other than the times he was risking his life for her. Gem-ma wished she could talk to him, but he conspicuously avoided being alone with her, which made things difficult.

Still, life was continuing on. Sophie was helping her plan her birthday party. The task delighted her new friend, who had a flair for the dramatic. Gemma was happy to leave the details to Sophie.

When the frigid winter cold finally got to her, she turned back and walked Hector to the mews.

"Want me to brush him down, ma'am?" Jem asked when he followed her in with the other horse.

"No, I like to do it," she said.

Jem nodded and moved off to tend to his mount.

She sang under her breath as she brushed Hector down and saw to his feed.

Logan's voice came out of nowhere. "What are you singing?"

Chance danced right up to Logan, begging for attention. Logan reached down to scratch the dog's ears, probably cementing a lifetime of loyalty.

Gemma looked on, wishing she could have such a simple interaction with Logan. "I was wondering if I'd ever see you again."

"I said I would let you know when I discovered something," he said. He glanced at Jem, who continued to work as if nothing was going on. Gemma could tell the young man also wasn't going to offer them any privacy— he was chaperoning quite well considering how oblivious he seemed.

"So? What do you have to tell me?"

Logan said, "I'm going to sneak into your shipping firm's warehouse tonight to find some evidence against Dobbs, who I'm sure has a role to play in all this. I just need to retrieve a key from Jem."

He said the last part loud enough that Jem couldn't ignore it.

"Jem? Why would he have a key?"

"I told him to steal it while we were on the tour of the

firm."

"You told him to..." Gemma trailed off. "Logan, you can't order my household staff to act as thieves!"

"Oh, never mind about me, ma'am," Jem said. "It was too easy to count as theft."

"Jem, you shouldn't do that again," she warned. "Listen to Mr Hartley, that is."

"Yes, ma'am."

She turned back to Logan. "And you can't possibly think I'd let you break into my own business without me!"

Logan shook his head before she could say more. "No. Absolutely not. A daytime tour with an escort is one thing. Sneaking in at night is quite another."

"I'm going to order Jem to give me the key," Gemma said. "You have no choice."

"True, sir," Jem chimed in. "I've been ordered not to listen to you any more." He barely concealed his amusement.

"I could break in without a key," Logan said

"But you'll leave evidence that you did so," she countered quickly. "You want to get in and out without raising suspicion."

He looked at her with narrowed eyes. "Are you sure you only learned how to shoot in Scotland? Not how to negotiate?"

Gemma smiled. "So I'm right. You need to be subtle."

"Yes. I hope to learn what I need in one night, but it might take longer."

"Then you could use an extra person to make the work go faster," Gemma said. "I volunteer."

Logan looked away. "That's not.... No. I can't even begin to explain how wrong.... Just no."

"The key is with my employee," Gemma reminded him, pointing to Jem. "And he's giving it to me. I'll be right here at midnight. You can take me with you, or not go at all. Do we have a deal?"

He stared at her for a long moment, then said, "Deal. Wear something warm and practical, just as if it's a smuggling run. And bring your pistols."

"You think I'll need to use them?"

"If you're hurt, or caught, or compromised in any way, I'd like you to shoot me, because it will be my fault for agreeing to this."

"I could never shoot you. See you at midnight."

* * * *

Later that evening, she pleaded a headache and went up to her room at eleven. There, she stripped out of the bright gown she wore to dinner. In the very back of the wardrobe, she found her old shirt and trousers folded up neatly. She never dreamed she'd use them again, but some part of her mind must have held out hope for the old wild Gemma to return.

And tonight, she did. Gemma dressed quickly, then strapped her gun belt at her waist. She didn't have a man's coat anymore, but her dark brown wool cloak should work just as well. She pulled her hair back and tied it at the nape of her neck. Finally, she opened the case that held her pistols.

That was when Bond walked in.

The maid was carrying a tray, and when she got a look at Gemma in her absurd outfit, Gemma fully expected her to drop it with a crash and a scream.

But Bond just stood there. Finally she said, "I hoped

Jem was joking about what he overheard this afternoon, but it seems not. Will you be needing extra ammunition, ma'am?"

Gemma carefully put the pistol on the bedspread. "I hope not, Bond. If I may say, you're taking this remarkably well."

"I have seen worse." Bond put the tray down on a side table. "I don't suppose I might enquire as to what you're doing?"

"I'm going out," Gemma said.

"So I made the camomile tea for nothing, then."

"Of course not. I have time for a cup."

"Oh, good." Bond proceeded to pour, and then crossed the room to hand the cup to Gemma. "Mind you, it's a bit hot."

"You're not going to tell me I'm mad?"

"Not my place to say, ma'am."

"You're not going to run to Aunt Maura and tell her I'm running off into the night?"

"Would that help at all?" Bond asked. "I think it wouldn't. What would help is you telling *me* what you've got planned. Do you have any idea what would have happened if I came up here and found you gone? Are you forgetting that someone shot at you only a few nights ago?"

"I haven't forgotten, Bond. That's why I'm dressed like this. I'll blend in."

"Not with that hair, ma'am. Come, sit down. It ought to be braided and you need a hat."

Gemma sat as directed, and Bond was soon working to weave Gemma's hair into a complicated looking plait.

As she worked, Bond said, "I don't suppose you'll tell me where you're going."

"My father's shipping firm. I have reason to believe there is evidence that will help me discover the facts of a smuggling scheme that includes war profiteering. Possibly even who took that shot the other night."

"Are you going alone?" Bond asked pointedly.

Gemma considered lying, but then discarded the notion. Bond was proving amazingly capable so far. Perhaps telling her a bit of truth would help.

"I'm not going alone, Bond. I won't tell you who I am going with, but it's someone I trust."

Bond nodded cautiously. "Yes, ma'am. And when do you expect to return?"

"Within a few hours. Perhaps three in the morning. It should be relatively quick, and safe."

"That's why you're taking the guns? Because of how safe it will be?"

"Don't try to stop me, Bond."

"I shan't. But what you're doing is foolhardy and quite dangerous."

"I did worse up in Caithny," Gemma said, putting the pistols in their holsters. "You wouldn't have recognized me."

"I hope no one recognizes you tonight, ma'am. What you may have got away with up in Scotland will be harder to explain away in London."

"That's my problem," Gemma said. "Now, if you please, find me that hat. I wouldn't want to be late."

"Heavens, no," Bond muttered, but turned to the wardrobe. She returned with a hat of dark, heavy felt. It hid most of Gemma's hair and part of her face.

"Be careful."

"Thank you, Bond. I shall be."

At midnight, Gemma slipped out the side door. She

had to bribe Chance to stay in the kitchen, and she was helped by Sally, who had woken and gone to the kitchen for a late snack. The young girl put her arms around the dog and gave Gemma a solemn nod. "Thank you, dear," Gemma whispered.

She headed toward the mews, where Logan waited close by Hector.

He surveyed her with approval. "You look perfect," he said. "Ready for adventure?"

"Whenever you are. And I have the key."

Logan led her toward the street. In the nighttime, and dressed at they were, Gemma felt a wonderful sense of anonymity. After weeks of being the Original Miss Harrington, dressed in fancy gowns and shoes and hats, now she could just be Gemma, the girl who rode and shot and got into trouble without a care for how it would affect her reputation. It felt like slipping into old shoes.

They hired a cab, Logan calling out the street corner and Gemma swinging into the cab itself.

Inside, she laughed silently, suddenly delighted with the evening. "This should be fun," she said.

"I'm glad you're enjoying yourself," Logan said. "There is a risk, Gemma. If we're found out, things could get unpleasant."

Gemma pulled aside the cloak to reveal one pistol. "I'm quite ready. Don't forget that I've been in the middle of smuggling runs before."

"This is different," he said. "If I tell you to do something, or run somewhere, or leave me, you have to do it. Understand?"

"I'm not going to leave you," she retorted.

"If you don't promise, Gemma, I'll take you right back home. This isn't a game."

She saw the look in his eye. "Very well. I promise."

"Good." He relaxed. "Granted, we'll probably be alone the whole time. The firm doesn't even hire a watchman."

Gemma sat back, considering. Alone with Logan. This could be a whole different kind of dangerous.

Logan saw her smile. "What?" he asked, curiously.

"Nothing," she said. "Thank you for inviting me along."

"I could tell no argument would stop you."

They reached the shipping offices and left the cab, making the last part of the journey on foot. Logan led her to a shadowed alley. There, they walked to a small side door that Gemma hadn't noticed on the first, official visit. "Key," he said.

She pulled it out of her shirt, where she wore it on a long ribbon.

Logan opened the door easily with the stolen key. "Wait here." He slipped inside, and Gemma waited, watching the alley for any sign of movement. There was nothing, and soon Logan extended an arm and drew her into the darkness of the warehouse.

She could see nothing, but she felt Logan standing close enough to touch. "How did you know about that door?" she asked in a whisper, which sounded too loud in the echoing dark.

He leaned in and spoke quietly into her ear. "You didn't think that I came along solely to answer questions about shipping, did you?"

His breath tickled her ear, and led her mind down several dangerous paths. "So what did you do? Memorize the floor plan of the warehouse?"

"I make a habit of remembering how to get in and out

of places. You never know when it might come in handy."

His lips brushed her ear, and she shivered pleasantly. "Are you here to flirt with me, or to get information?" she asked, trying to tamp down the desire he'd summoned.

"I wanted to work alone," he reminded her.

By then, her eyes adjusted to the very dim light in the warehouse, and she saw his expression, which was not that of a man wishing to be alone.

"Time to go to work, agent," she said, a little breathlessly.

"Offices first." He took her hand, and they stepped silently around the stacks of crates and boxes stored in the warehouse.

It was easy enough to find Dobbs' desk. Logan told Gemma to light the lamp while he searched through the papers.

"Keep the light shielded. And listen carefully," he added. "If you hear anything larger than a mouse, we'll need to hide."

"What are you looking for?" she asked, holding the lit lamp toward him.

"No one knew what Caithny was shipping, but whatever it was, it was valuable. I need to know if I'm to understand what's really happening."

He searched through Dobbs' materials, working quickly but without any evidence of sloppiness. Gemma peeked out into the hallway every once in a while.

"I thought you learned what was on the manifest up in Scotland," she said. "Or did I sneak into Uncle Conall's office for nothing?"

"You found the legal items," he agreed. Then he held up a ledger. "Same items here. Tin. Glass. Grains. Some produce. It's listed here because an empty manifest looks suspicious."

"Or you're determined to make something out of nothing."

"Those crates were not carrying those items," he swore. "Those would be packed completely differently. Tin isn't crated the way produce is. And how could fresh fruit or vegetables be stored for—" he glanced at the ledger, "six months, which is what this says here."

"Who says it was fresh?" Gemma asked.

"What else could it be?"

"Preserved. Cook served us such food all the time at Caithny. You had some yourself up there. Remember the pears?"

Logan put down the ledger book and stared at her.

"What?" Gemma asked nervously.

"Tin. Glass. Produce. Oh, my god."

"What's so odd about that?"

"Shipped *together*," he said, as if to himself. "Bring the light. Come on."

He grabbed her hand and led her from the office and back to the warehouse itself. They walked to the huge pile of crates that Dobbs was so keen to get Logan away from.

"You think all these crates are full of contraband?" she asked.

"I don't think there are that many crates after all. That's what I was looking at the other day. We're meant to think these stacks go all the way to the far wall. But they don't. They're only two deep. Dobbs is using them to conceal something else."

Shoving aside a stack of boxes, he revealed a door. "See?"

"A separate room," Gemma whispered.

Together, they got the door open, and in the dark space

beyond, they found more crates. But this time, Logan smiled.

"This was the shipment I was supposed to take over to France next," he muttered. "Dobbs never found a replacement ship, so they're just sitting here."

"What's inside?"

"Let's find out."

Logan quickly pried open a crate and yanked out a quantity of packing straw. He pulled a tin can from the crate, then read the label.

"Peas." He said it the way one might expect to say *gold*.

"This is what we came for? That's what he was hiding?" Gemma asked skeptically. "A tin of peas?"

"Doesn't look like much, does it?"

"I don't understand. You said Conall was shipping guns to the French."

"Because I couldn't think of anything else that would command such a price. But as it happens, he stumbled on something more valuable."

"But one can purchase food anywhere."

"Not in the middle of a battlefield. And not on the high seas." Logan held up the can. "Trust me, there were times when I would have paid anything for just this amount. And when produced by the ton, able to feed thousands of men...it changes everything."

Logan ticked off the items Gemma mentioned after she searched Conall's books. "Tin. Glass. Produce. Grains. Not too exciting, are they? The manifest was technically the truth—I'll bet Caithny found that amusing. Several boring, ordinary items. Unless you put them together."

"I don't know what you mean."

"I know a bit about life at sea, and at war. Food is precious. Governments have been searching for ways to get healthy food to their armies for decades." He paused. "Caithny found one. Or rather, he found someone else who did, and discovered a more profitable way to sell the product."

"Cook!" Gemma said. "The man he brought to Caithny a while ago. He must have found a better way to store the preserves. He tested his methods for *our* dinners. That's why I was eating asparagus in October!"

"And that's why Caithny preferred to sink his ships rather than let them be captured. That's why no one knew what he was shipping."

"Fool. The British government would have paid just as well, with no risk of betrayal."

"Maybe," said Logan. "But Caithny knew the real value of the cargo was the secret of its creation. Selling above board to the British would likely mean giving up the details of the secret too. Conall Caithny didn't just want to make money off a few holds of cargo. He wanted to control the supply."

"So he accepted a deal with the French." Gemma said, disgusted.

"Napoleon is determined to win this war at any cost, so he'd pay well. Whoever bought the shipment on behalf of the army probably took great care that the source of the shipments never reached his superiors. He merely told them the product was expensive but reliable. Chances are that the operation couldn't have gone on for more than several months. The items would be noticed, and the truth would have got out and the French would have sent one of their men to discover the process. They would have stolen either the maker or the recipe…or both."

"So you were still right. He wasn't simply shipping food. He was shipping war supplies. Wait a moment. He was in debt," Gemma said, remembering. Was that a flaw in the explanation?

Logan nodded. "Yes. Expensive commodities are sometimes more trouble than they're worth. He was unlucky. He had to sink a few ships within too short a span of time. It was the only way to hide the truth—discovery of his cargo would be far worse than losing it. But he needed funds to get more ships for future runs. He was forced to ask for the money from his contact in France."

"And that made him beholden. He couldn't get out, not even when it grew more dangerous."

"He was trapped—" A sound made him stop. "Did you hear that?"

Chapter 36

≋

"FOOTSTEPS," GEMMA SAID, HEARING THE same thing. "I thought you said the firm doesn't hire a watchman."

"Someone's here. Let's go."

She blew out the light, and they got away from the secret storage area by the time the footsteps reached it. But someone definitely knew they were there.

Logan pulled Gemma along as they searched for an escape, or at least a better hiding place. All were too open. In the dark they seemed shadowy and safe, but as soon as a lantern arrived, two people would be obvious.

They passed door after door. Gemma opened one and looked in. The quality of the sound in there was completely different from the other places in the warehouse. It was close, muffled.

"Fabric," she murmured, noticing there was no echo. "All bolts of linen and silk." She looked over. "Logan! In here."

Logan pressed against her, pushing her back into the open doorway. "Hush," he muttered. "They're coming down the hall."

He got them both though the door, then pushed it shut just as a faint light glimmered in the hallway.

"They'll see us if they open the door," Gemma said in a low urgent voice. "We have to hide, fast."

She thought she remembered the room from the tour. "Come. There's enough fabric that we can hide among the loose bolts. I'll put my cloak over us. It's practically new. It'll look like just another bolt."

"Excellent," Logan breathed.

They moved as quickly as they could in the utter dark. Gemma relied on her memory, pulling Logan along to where she was sure there was a sort of tower of stacked wool and muslin. On the side opposite the door, her feet got tangled in loose bolts, all piled on the floor. She stifled a gasp and grabbed Logan's arm, pulling him close to her. "Careful where you step," she warned.

He moved to cover her body with his, then Gemma whirled her cloak over them both. Pressed against the other bolts, they were in a close, warm cocoon.

They waited for what felt like an hour, but had to be only minutes. The door opened, and a pool of light washed through the room, just visible where the edge of the cloak met the floor. Gemma gripped her pistol hard, praying she wouldn't have to use it.

"Anything?" a voice asked. Footsteps moved into the room, almost to their feet. Surely whoever was after them was gazing right at their hiding spot.

An agonizing pause. "Not in here," said someone else.

"Let's move on. Someone was here. Find out where they went." The door snapped shut again, and the room plunged into darkness once more.

Logan put a finger over her lips for silence, and they both held their breath while the footsteps faded outside. Gemma finally lowered her pistol, exhaling soundlessly. Then she leaned to Logan's ear and asked in the softest voice possible, "Are we safe?"

"Do you even know what that word means?" he breathed back.

"I know I'm safe with you."

"That isn't true," he said. He shifted, pulling away from her.

Gemma leaned forward to stop him, wishing she could see his face. "Don't do that."

"What?"

"That thing you've been doing since you got to London. You're avoiding me. Why?"

"I'm with you right now," he said.

"Because I forced you to bring me along."

"And now that we're done, I'm taking you directly back."

"And then what?" she demanded, keeping her voice low. "Unless you need me for some detail of your investigation, you have no intention of seeing me again, do you?"

"You've got quite enough of a social life, Gemma. All your lords calling on you. You don't need me."

"Yes, I *do* need you," she said fiercely. "Or do you really think I'm so changeable? I love you."

"You shouldn't say that. You can have whoever you want, dryad. You've got a fortune. A real one. And you're beautiful, and free."

"My fortune is a deterrent?" she hissed. "Then I'll throw it into the sea."

"Don't do that. Just…make your choice based on sense, not sentiment." Logan sounded defeated.

"I think it makes perfect sense to marry the one man I love." She stopped, struck by a terrible thought. "What aren't you telling me? Do you not love me?"

"I love you like no one else on earth," he said, the words bursting out as if he couldn't contain them any longer. "Gemma, of course I love you. Which is why I won't drag you down."

Gemma glowed at the first words, but could barely understand the last part. "I'll tell. I'll say you slept with me. Then you'll *have* to marry me. You're too honorable to do anything else."

"You wouldn't. Besides, who would believe you? There's nothing to be gained."

"I'd gain you," Gemma said. "And they would believe me. I've got your compass." Her eyes widened. "That's why you wanted it back!"

"No, I wanted to protect you. Once I knew how it could trap you, it was dangerous to let you keep it."

"I want to be trapped."

"Gemma, you could do far better than me."

"I'll decide that, thank you!" She moved to stand in front of him. "You're really going to walk away from me? Even though I'm begging for you?"

"You don't know how to beg," he said.

"I'll learn, if that's what it takes." She reached out and found his hand in the dark. "Meeting you was the single best thing to happen in my life. I felt like you woke me up. I don't want to live without you. Please don't abandon me now that I'm not useful to you."

"It was never about you being useful," he said, his voice hot. "You think I'd sleep with you out of convenience? Or that I'd keep risking my ship and my name and my life to keep you safe if I didn't love you?"

He kissed her, as if he hadn't been with her for years. Gemma wrapped her arms around him, just in case he thought he could get away from her.

But he didn't want to get away, to judge by how close he pressed himself to her. It was pitch black, and their pursuers could return at any moment. But she was in the dark with the one she loved, and suddenly that was all that mattered.

Clothing was pulled aside, tangled and lost in bolts of soft, silencing fabric. They found each other in the darkness and their breathing was the only sound, and it was absorbed by the linen and cotton and silk all around. When he pulled her to the floor, she couldn't have asked for a finer bed, or anyone else to share it with.

They could barely see each other, but they used their hands. Gemma relearned Logan's body by touch, and let him relearn hers.

He didn't just use his hands. Pushing her gently down, he knelt over her. He kissed her, starting at her lips, but moving rapidly lower, to her breasts, and then her stomach, then lower.

Gemma gasped in surprise. "What are you doing?" she whispered when his intent became clear.

"Oh, now you want to play it safe?" he asked. "Trust me."

She trusted him, and once she got past her shock, Gemma decided she quite liked it when Logan did scandalous things to her.

Her whole body seemed to catch fire, thanks to his tongue, but she whispered, "Enough. I want *you* now."

Logan shifted to settle himself between her legs. Gemma reached up and ran her hands over his shoulders to his back, sighing as he entered her.

"I never thought I'd get this close to you again," he said, his voice raw.

"You're the only one who will get this close to me,"

she promised.

She nearly cried out toward the end, but Logan found her mouth in time, and muffled her cry with a kiss.

Afterward, they lay tangled together, their breathing slowly returning to normal. Gemma shivered as her skin cooled, but she had no idea where her clothes were.

She reached out to find them, but touched the little lantern first. "Logan," she said. "Do you think it's safe to make a light?"

"If we shield it as much as we can."

Gemma found the flint and struck it. The candle was soon glowing again, and she tucked the lantern by a shelf, so that most of the light was hidden, and none reached the door.

She turned back to see that Logan had pulled a few yards of silk free from a nearby bolt. He wrapped her up in it. "Warmer now?"

"Mmmm, yes. Thank you."

He held her close. "I missed you."

"Of course you did. You were suffering nobly for no reason."

"I had a reason. When I thought we were the same class, it was easy. You should have told me that you were born gentry, and that you were worth so much. I wouldn't have dared get close to you."

"We are the same class," Gemma countered. "We're the class that has no patience for class."

He laughed, the sound immediately absorbed by the dulling wool of their bed. "Oh, you're telling me you don't enjoy being the darling of the ton."

"Not especially. It's interesting, and I've met people I wouldn't otherwise. But I don't like the gossip or the cats or mercenaries who only see my fortune. Society isn't at all what I thought it would be. It's just another game, with fancier clothes and stranger rules."

"You've just described espionage," he noted, surveying her. He tucked a piece of hair back behind her ear, his touch lingering on her cheek.

"Yes, but I'm reasonably sure the parties are less deadly," she said. "Don't pretend that it's not incredibly dangerous to be a spy."

"It is," he agreed. "But would you ask me to stop?"

"No," she said firmly. "That would be like asking you to sink the *Mistral*, or to stop breathing. I won't start a marriage by asking you to stop being who you are."

He kissed her again, pulling her tight against him. "Then you wouldn't regret it?"

"If you'd be willing to step aside because you had some notion that it would be better for me just proves you are exactly who I want." She beamed at him, then pushed one finger into his chest. "However, the ideal solution would have been you telling me your concerns immediately, instead of keeping it all inside."

"Lesson learned," he said. "When you keep secrets for a living, it can be difficult to talk. But I'll do my best."

"All the same," she confessed, "I don't know how I'll stand it. Being on the margins while you're in danger. Just waiting."

He shifted so he could look her in the eyes. "What if you didn't have to?"

"What?"

"Just a little idea I had. Join me. As an agent."

"That's absurd. I'm a woman. How could I be a spy for the Royal Navy?"

"Well, you were only half right when you guessed. That's not who I work for."

"Then who?"

"It's a group called the Zodiac. I *was* in the Royal Navy, which is how an agent from the Zodiac noticed me. I've been able to slip through quite a few rules and regulations because I'm now a sign. But unlike the more military branches of the government, the Zodiac recognizes the value of women's contributions."

"Is that true?"

He smiled. "You can ride. You can shoot. You've worked with smugglers and you dance with lords. You handled yourself wonderfully tonight. You would be perfect."

She shook her head, but her eyes were bright. "That's daft."

"No, it's brilliant. We could work together. You would be with me the whole time. Assignments to France, to Scotland, wherever. Maybe America or the West Indies. With us together on the *Mistral*, who could stop us?"

"You're serious."

"Yes." He found her hand and twined it with his own.

"You want to marry me and then have us both work as spies."

"At least until the war is over. Then we do whatever we choose…together."

Gemma's heart was beating fast with the possibilities. With Logan, on the *Mistral*, and the world in front of them. "I'm not giving back the compass until you're officially mine," she said.

He nodded. "I can live with that. Now, let's find our clothes. Technically, we're still in enemy territory."

* * * *

Logan returned her to her home while the night sky was still dark. She loved the new way he looked at her, how comfortable it felt to hold his hand in the dark of an anonymous coach. Everything that was wrong was now right. There were plans to be made, and many things to decide. But everything would happen in the proper time.

"I have to speak to a few people, dryad," he told her, while they traveled home. "Explain how dauntless you are, and how perfect you'll be as an agent."

"What if they say no?"

"They won't." He smiled smugly.

"Even though I'm a woman?"

"Especially because of that. You'll see."

He leaned over to kiss her, and Gemma reveled in the touch of his lips on hers. It was just as exciting as the very first time he kissed her, when he agreed to teach her a lesson.

She laughed softly.

"What?" he asked, smiling.

"Nothing," she said. "I was just thinking that you probably had no idea what you were bound for when you first met me."

"If someone told me," Logan said, "I wouldn't have believed them. But I admit that I was enchanted from the first sight of you."

"When you showed up at my doorway," she confessed, "I couldn't believe a man with such a warm smile could be that nefarious."

"What do you think now?"

"You're far more nefarious than you let on."

He gave her another kiss, then said, "You'll soon learn all about it."

"I'll have to rearrange my life, won't I?" she asked.

"If I join your group, I can't exactly live in a London house full of servants while I'm skulking about spying with you."

His expression was mischievous. "It'll change less than you think. Trust me."

"I do trust you."

"Good." He kissed her again, lightly, before leaving her at her door.

Neither of them saw the shadow move behind them.

Chapter 37

≋

NOW CONFIDENT THAT HE HAD the largest question answered, Logan went to the headquarters of the Zodiac. Because the Zodiac was an organization of spies, naturally the headquarters were not labeled as such, nor were they anywhere near the usual government buildings. Instead, the Zodiac operated out of a handsome looking, but ordinary, red brick building at the corner of Powell and Gate Streets.

Once a person actually entered the building, it was easy to get lost in the unexpectedly confusing corridors. Logan privately thought the whole structure was inspired by the Gordian Knot. One had to negotiate twisting hallways, duck through odd side doors, and pass dark corridors before finding a door—unmarked and unremarkable—on the fifth floor.

Logan knocked. Though it was late, he heard quick footsteps on the other side. A blonde woman opened the door.

"Hullo, Miss Chattan," Logan said.

"You'd better come in," she replied, with no trace of surprise.

"I'll let him know you're here. We wondered how you

were faring." Her tone made it clear that Logan should have come in sooner.

"I sent reports," he pointed out.

"Reports are not the same thing as seeing an agent back safe." Chattan gave him a little smile before she opened an inner door. "Sir? Aquarius is back."

"Excellent." That one word drew Logan inside the office. Chattan followed silently, notebook in hand.

The man who spoke was Julian Neville, and if most people were asked to describe a spy, they'd describe someone who looked nothing like Julian. This was one of the reasons he was such a good spy. He was of perfectly average height. He wasn't especially good-looking or especially ugly. His sandy colored hair was halfway between light and dark, and his expression could be perfectly bland when he wanted it to be.

It wasn't bland now. He offered Logan a smile of greeting and told him to sit down. "How do things stand?"

"Conall Caithny was tied up with a network of smuggling, all designed to avoid tariffs and benefit the French cause. We suspected that, but I've now got the names and faces of those who are directly involved."

Julian nodded. "Good. The sooner we cut off the supply of arms, the better."

"About that," Logan began. "He's not smuggling guns."

"He's not?" Chattan broke in, her hand poised above the notebook. "But the amount of money exchanged…"

"I know," Logan said. "Arms were the natural guess. But that's not what he was running."

"So what is it?"

Logan produced the tin of peas. "Food. Specifically, preserved food that will last for months in storage, able to feed soldiers who would otherwise not have access to enough high quality food to survive."

Julian picked up the tin. "The French government has been offering a prize to anyone who is able to create a fast and affordable way to preserve food. The equivalent of over ten thousand pounds, I think."

"That's not high enough, to judge by the money Caithny was getting paid. He must have found someone who knew how to manufacture preserved food on a large scale. Caithny used him to make the product, then he sold it to the French for a massive profit. He was a clever man."

"You keep saying *was*. Where's Caithny now?" Julian asked.

"Dead." Logan gave a brief version of the events leading to Caithny's shooting. "I thought the trail was cold until Miss Harrington arranged to let me get inside her father's shipping firm. That's when I came across Mr Dobbs. He was the man in London who hid most of the cargo until the right time to ship for France."

"We'll need to track down the French contacts," said Julian. "And we'll need to find out where this was being manufactured. Our side needs this technology."

"There's an old distillery in the town of Caithny," said Logan. "Conall Caithny took it over not long ago. That's where some of it is being made. Oh, and the cook who worked up at Caithny castle seems to be the one who really knows the process."

Julian nodded. "Then I'll send an agent there very soon. Not you," he added, before Logan could offer. "You need a rest."

"Well, with twelve agents available," Logan said, "you'll find the answers soon enough."

"But I don't have twelve agents," Julian said, rather too casually.

"Eleven, then. Though you'll never convince me that as Aries, you don't handle the odd assignment on your own."

"Got you there," Chattan noted.

"Can I ask how many you do have?" Logan remembered his offer to Gemma. She absolutely could work among the Zodiac. And perhaps she was needed even more than he thought.

"Not enough," Julian said grimly. "Our Capricorn died last year. Sagittarius is training potential agents, so he's not in the field. And Pisces has yet to be replaced after his untimely death."

"Bad luck to take the sign of a traitor," Chattan added.

"Then there's the matter of Cancer."

"Injured," Chattan explained to Logan. "Still performing assignments, but of a very specialized kind. And of course...Leo," she added, almost to herself.

"What happened to him?" Logan asked.

Chattan glanced at Julian, who just growled, "Tell him."

"We don't know," Chattan said, her eyes downcast, as if she blamed herself. "He went missing during an assignment, and there's been no word at all. Our inquiries went nowhere."

"You're down *four* agents?"

Julian nodded. "Roughly. I need more people, but finding those with the right qualities and who are trustworthy is easier said than done."

No wonder Julian and Chattan never seemed to sleep.

"Well," said Logan. "I might be able to help you there."

Chapter 38

※

IN THE MORNING, GEMMA AWOKE smiling. Now that she was assured Logan would remain in her life, all the details that confused her so much fell away. She laughed at how much she thought she needed society to accept her, or a fancy house in town, or a wardrobe others would admire. No, that was not the person she had grown up to be. Gemma was comfortable in shadows, and she was driven to protect the ones she loved. When had she ever stayed safe at home when there was something to be done that no one else could do? She knew now who she was supposed to be.

That did not mean everything was made easy. She dreaded the conversation she would have with Ian Mac-Lachlan. She had come to care about him very much, and she didn't want to hurt him. But a letter would be too cold and cruel. She had to speak to him directly.

She wrote to Ian inviting him to call on her one morning. She dressed with care, looking at all her outfits and trying to find one that would look mature and sober.

Bond asked her over and over exactly what she wanted, but Gemma couldn't explain herself well, so she just got frustrated.

"If the brown taffeta is too brown," Bond said, showing admirable patience, "perhaps you'd like to wear the pearl grey silk?"

Gemma wrinkled her nose in thought. "Yes, try that."

Soon she stood in front of the mirror again, debating. "Do I look sincere, Bond?"

"Always, ma'am."

"But for speaking to a gentleman?"

Bond paused, then said, "Depends on what you wish to say to the gentleman. And who the gentleman is."

"Lord MacLachlan. Oh, what if he thinks I'm shallow?"

"The gentleman seems to think quite highly of you. He would never call you shallow."

"But if I tell him he ought not to court me any longer…"

The maid raised an eyebrow. "Is that what you'll tell him?"

"Yes. I can't lead him on. But I can't think how to begin."

"I'm not an expert in matters of courtship. But if I may be so bold, I would say that speaking from the heart is the only way to ensure the truth. What the gentleman does with your words after is his affair."

"Oh, Bond, that's true. Has Jem proposed to you yet?"

The normally composed lady's maid colored and smiled, looking down at her feet. "Not as such. But we… have an understanding. When we're able, we will marry and settle down together. But our circumstances don't permit it just yet."

"How long must you wait?"

"Only a few years, I hope."

"Years! Bond, how can you stand it?"

"We are lucky to often find employment in the same house. That helps, because he isn't so far. And we both want to help—" She checked herself, looking caught out. "Excuse me, ma'am. Prattling on about my own life when you must be made ready! Come sit at the vanity."

Bond did all the finishing touches to Gemma's appearance, then sent her downstairs, where she awaited Ian's arrived with trepidation.

"Good morning, my lord," Gemma said, when he entered. "Thank you for coming."

"Anything to please you, Miss Harrington."

"That is something I'd like to address."

"Oh?"

"Please sit down. I've poured some tea for us."

"Why do I feel as if I'll need to follow it with a stiffer drink?" he asked lightly.

She now recognized the tactic he was using—he was preparing to deflect the seriousness of the conversation away, to make whatever it was he sensed coming at him hurt less. How had she missed that part of his personality for so long? Perhaps she was close enough to him now that she could see the true Ian. Which was a shame, really, considering what she had to tell him.

"Lord MacLachlan," she began. "Though you have never asked me anything in particular, you've pursued me with commendable zeal, because you've convinced yourself that I'm the ideal woman for you. Rich, pretty, and Scottish enough to satisfy. But I'm not your ideal."

"You sound very certain. If I may ask, why not?"

"We don't wish for the same things, my lord. You love your land and your family. You'd never leave your home unless you had to. I've heard you talk about it, and it sounds gorgeous. But when I think about staying in one place for the rest of my life, it just sounds like a prison, no matter how pretty the view."

He leaned forward earnestly. "You would learn to love it."

"I might," she admitted. "But not for years and years. And until then, I'd be miserable. I need to *see* things. I need to *go* places. I want to sail somewhere. I want to *fly.*"

"That I couldn't offer," Ian confessed.

"And even if all that wasn't the case, there's another reason I could never marry you. I love another." She paused. "I don't say that lightly, or to hurt you. You speak of a marriage being a business arrangement, but I've seen a few examples of your tenderness, and your temper. Would you ever be content, knowing your wife wasn't yours entirely? Even if you married a real princess and had a mountain of gold, you'd never forgive her if you didn't have her whole heart."

He took a long breath, all the teasing gone. "Correct, Miss Harrington."

"So I'm afraid your search must continue, for your sake. Your princess is in another castle."

He smiled, a bit sadly. "I hope the gentleman who claims your heart is worthy of it, Miss Harrington. Who is it, if I may ask?"

"Well, do you remember the gentleman who set my dance card on fire?"

"I'm not likely to forget that. So Mr Hartley is the one?"

"He is. I should add that his behavior that evening was unusual."

"I should hope so." Ian thought about it for a moment, then laughed sadly. "Well, that's an end to it. My courtship, that is." He stood up, though he didn't move toward the door.

"Please don't be angry at me." Gemma stood too, worried she had insulted him.

But he shook his head. "It's not you I'm angry at, Miss Harrington. I came to London seeking a rich bride who would solve all my problems. But such an arrangement would never be ideal, and I'd be solving one problem but gaining another."

"You must not give up—your plan is perfectly reasonable in theory. There must be many women who would be proud to marry you."

"I've met some," he noted, without bitterness. "But none suited, and now I understand why. My situation is far more complicated than simply getting access to more funds. I came here for the wrong reasons entirely. I must go back home and find a solution on my own."

"You'll leave London? Don't be too hasty, please. I should hate to think I drove you away. I should have told you sooner, but I simply didn't know my own heart, and…"

"Miss Harrington." Ian looked at her, with a new expression on his face. One more serious and resolute than she'd seen before. "Don't blame yourself for anything, please. You're right. I pursued you because I wanted you to be my ideal. You have saved us both from a serious mistake."

"It should feel like a relief then," she said, "and it doesn't."

"Not yet," he said. "But once we both realize the truth, we'll both feel better." He bent and took her hand, kissing it very lightly. "I'm glad to know you, Miss Gemma." He straightened up. "I'll see myself out."

Gemma let him go, too overwhelmed to think if it was wrong to let him walk out like that.

The very next day, she got a note from Ian.

"My dear Miss Harrington,

I have thought about our talk yesterday. Indeed, I have thought of little else. Know that if you ever need anything, I am willing to do whatever you may ask. IMcL"

She read the note over and over, feeling simultaneously happy and sad. Ian was a good man. He deserved a woman who truly loved him heart and soul. Gemma folded the note up carefully, then she placed it in the pocket of her writing desk, thinking that her time in London was proving far more educational than she ever dreamed.

Chapter 39

GEMMA WAS IN A STATE of waiting. Logan promised to tell her whenever his superior approved the idea of Gemma working as a spy. Until then, she could do little but maintain her life as an ordinary lady of society. Ian MacLachlan didn't call on her, of course. Gemma expected that, though she hoped he would feel welcome at her birthday party, which was coming up very soon. Lord Waite still pursued her, though even he seemed to sense that his efforts were in vain.

What she hoped most was that she could persuade Logan to announce an engagement during her birthday party. A public announcement would solve several problems. It would destroy the plans of fortune hunters who still hung on her. It would make it clear that Gemma considered Logan Hartley to be a worthy suitor, despite his lingering misgivings about their respective classes. And it would allow Logan to see her with much more freedom, because once they were engaged, he wouldn't be bound by the more stringent rules governing how most unmarried men and women were permitted to interact.

"Please," she said to Logan, when they had a moment to discuss it. "You need to let go of your notion that you won't be accepted as a suitor. And anyway, my opinion is the one that really matters. Everyone else will fall into line then. Aunt Maura may seem proper, but she's a dear. You'll see."

"Just wait until I can arrange for you to meet my superior. Once that's resolved, I'll feel much better about making plans for the future."

So she waited. Meanwhile, Gemma's birthday was approaching, and invitations to her party were highly sought after. Sophie had suggested a masquerade—I *adore* a masquerade, she said—and Gemma was intrigued by the idea. Just in time, she thought of a costume and Madame Lucille agreed to make it.

She told Madame Lucille her idea in the strictest confidence. "I want everyone to be surprised at the unmasking!"

Madame Lucille nodded vigorously. "I shall not breathe a word! You will dazzle them in this creation, Miss Harrington! Have faith in Madame!"

Gemma was confident that the lady would deliver, and indeed, the costume was sent on the morning of the party.

Bond pulled the costume from its box. She exclaimed appreciatively at the workmanship of the gown and the mask. "Ma'am, you will *slay* gentlemen in this."

"Oh, I hope it doesn't come to that," Gemma said, with a laugh. "But Madame Lucille outdid herself, don't you think?"

"It's…amazing. You must put it on!"

Gemma did, with Bond's help. When she stood before the mirror, it wasn't a woman who looked back. It was a dryad.

The gown was made of layers of silk, from an earthy brown to a dark forest green to a lighter golden color. The effect was like sunlight through trees. Adding to the effect were the hundreds of little cut leaves sewn to the outer layer in such a way that they shivered whenever Gemma took a step.

"Oh, ma'am. You need emeralds. There's no other option."

"Do I have emeralds?"

"Oh yes. The new necklace with the oval cut stones. And I'll do your hair up with the silver circlet. That won't interfere with the mask."

Gemma held the mask up to her face and couldn't stop a giggle of pure delight. The mask was also covered in layers of leaves, the greens in a dozen shades. "Too much?"

"No. It's perfect."

The evening of the party arrived. Sophie came early, in order to help Gemma perform the duties of greeting guests and all the other last minute things associated with hosting a party for London's elite. Her costume was as impressive as Gemma's, though in a different way. She was dressed as a swan, and the elaborate feathered mask, complete with a beak, concealed her face very well. Her gown was white, and she wore feathered wings at her back. She was naturally slender, so the effect was that of a willowy, white feathered beauty.

"You look astonishing," Gemma said, admiring the costume. "No wonder you insisted on a masquerade."

The crowd filled out quickly. Aunt Maura was dressed as an extremely elegant fairy, and unsurprisingly, Mr Rodney—now a brown bear—stuck close by her side. Gemma saw Logan for a moment, and she stayed hidden so she could get a better look at him. The appeal of a mask was undeniable. Gemma felt that she could do any number of things she couldn't do while people were looking at her...such as ogle a gentleman from a safe distance with no repercussions.

Logan was dressed as a pirate. Of course. He wore the longer style coat of the previous century. It was velveteen and adorned with rows of brass buttons, looking very martial in style. His shirt was white, and featured the fancier neckties of the age. She thought the look suited him well. He looked equally comfortable with the saber attached to his waist. She feared it was completely real, though of course the blade itself was concealed by the scabbard. He wore only a domino mask, which did little to conceal his identity—not that many people knew who Logan Hartley was. It didn't appear to matter. Ladies turned their heads whenever he passed. The masquerade certainly freed people of constraint!

Gemma's eyes narrowed when a blonde in a stunning gown and a peacock mask tried to get Logan to dance with her. He bowed politely, perfectly in character, but evidently refused. The lady looked stunned, and Gemma smiled. Logan belonged to her.

Later, she stood at the edge of the crowd of people, watching the festivities. Gemma was enjoying her anonymity immensely. Since it was a masque, she didn't have the same hostess duties as would normally be expected, and she refused to tell anyone who she was. It was all a great deal of fun. Then a pirate accosted her.

"I've been looking for you," he said, his voice warm.

"How do you know who I am?" Gemma replied delightedly.

He took her by the hand, leading her away from the

crowd. "Because you're the most beautiful dryad here."

"Do you like it?" she asked.

Logan paused to survey her, looking very much like a pirate considering a prize. But then his smile emerged. It was the same slow smile that melted her on the first night she met him. "You wore this for me."

"Yes," she admitted, her heart beating faster.

"We can leave now," he said, his tone serious. "I have a ship, you know. We could sail anywhere."

Her breath caught in her throat, and it took a moment before she could give a little laugh. "I can't do that, silly. Not until the unmasking. And there's a birthday cake."

"After that."

"There's no need to steal me," she whispered. "We've already agreed to marry."

"But no one knows," he said. "What if someone steals you first, dryad?"

"They won't." She put her arm through his. "Now walk me over to that window. I need air."

He did, and then said he had to leave her. "Even at a masquerade, there are a few conventions. I can't monopolize you the whole evening."

"Come back and find me before the unmasking."

"I promise." He kissed her hand, then disappeared into the crush, leaving Gemma in a pleasant haze.

While she remained there, another person approached her, a woman all in black.

"Good evening," said the lady. She wore a black velvet half mask with cat ears at the top, and long almond shaped eye holes. There were even whiskers. Combined with the long, black, and rather clinging fabric, the feline effect was strong. "May I join you?"

Gemma nodded.

"Crowded tonight," the lady commented.

"You're enjoying the masquerade?" Gemma tried to see who she was. She had issued nearly all the invitations, so she should be able to guess.

"Oh, I love a masquerade," the cat replied. "So many people, and so many opportunities to let their true person-alities out. It's funny, isn't it? As soon as people think their name is unknown, they behave just as they like. One can find out so much more about a person when they're pretending to be someone else."

"What sort of things?"

"It depends on the person." The cat pointed at a lady dressed like a Greek goddess. "She's married, but having an affair."

"How can you possibly know that?"

"Her lover passed her a letter during a dance."

"You're guessing. You can't have read it."

The cat gave a soft laugh. "What other sort of letter is passed on a dance floor?"

"Well, even so, how do you know...never mind. You saw her wearing a wedding band."

"Very good. You see, it's one thing to have eyes, but so much depends on understanding what you see. You say I'm guessing, but intuition is just a way to explain the way people think of a hundred tiny things and then make a conclusion based on facts."

Gemma was intrigued by the cat's conversation. "What else is happening around us?" she asked.

"You tell me," the cat invited.

Gemma looked around the crowd, but it was difficult to concentrate on the scene in front of her. She kept re-turning to the case she and Logan were trying so hard to understand.

"How do you know what's important?" she mused out loud. "Out of all this," she said, waving her hand over the crowd, "maybe only one or two things matter. The rest is distraction."

"True," the cat agreed.

"Furthermore," Gemma said, still thinking of things outside the party, "there are still missing pieces. I don't know everything yet."

"That's why you persevere, Miss Harrington."

"Did I tell you my name?"

"Everyone knows your name. Would you wish it otherwise? If so, you'll need another name soon." The enigmatic cat rose in an elegant cloud of black silk and velvet. She wished Gemma good evening and left, her message evidently delivered.

Gemma sat alone for a few more moments. So many people seemed to know her, and all of them had advice.

She stood up, determined to find Logan. Though it was some time till the unmasking, she hoped to join him for a dance.

It took a while for her to make her way through the gathering, but she at last reached the doorway to the parlor, where she thought she detected Logan's voice. His subtle but distinctive accent couldn't be disguised even with a costume.

She intended to go right in, but an odd phrase made her halt, and she waited. Perhaps her intuition told her that something was off.

Logan was speaking again, "…I will find out. One of the Disreputables will infiltrate that place within the next day. Best thing the Zodiac ever did, hiring them."

"You want to send someone from this house? Or is there another Disreputable to spare?" That was Sophie,

Gemma was shocked to realize. Why would Sophie be speaking to Logan about matters related to the secret group he called the Zodiac?

"Ivy can do it," Logan responded. "No one will recognize her, and there are plenty of Disreputables left here to see to Gemma."

Gemma pressed herself against the wall. *Disreputables. See to Gemma.* The conversation would have made no sense, except that Logan mentioned the word Disreputable once before. And now Sophie used it. Which meant that she too must be a spy like Logan. One of the Zodiac, the group he claimed was working for the good of the nation and the empire.

Suddenly, everything fit. The feeling of being watched when she arrived in London. Her "chance" meeting with Lady Sophie, who knew Logan's precious compass was a compass even though she neglected to mention she knew Logan so well. The ease with which all the servants appeared in her home. Logan's ability to get into and out of the house with no alarm given.

Everyone was working together to manipulate everything Gemma did. For her money? Just because she was linked to Conall Caithny? Whatever the reason, they all assumed that she was too stupid to ever notice. Worse, if not for a few slips, she never would have noticed. Anger rose up in her. She hated the notion that she was being moved about by others' whims. Was that why Logan professed to love her? She took a deep breath, and her temperature shot up, a sure sign she wanted to scream in frustration.

Logan left the room, intent on whatever errand his spying demanded. The hall was dark enough that he didn't see her, pressed against the wall as she was. She watched him go, her eyes narrowed in sudden suspicion. She didn't even know what she wanted to say to him. But Gemma was too furious to allow both spies to get away.

She stormed toward the door, and found Sophie alone. She held the swan mask in her hands, and looked over curiously.

Seeing Gemma, she smiled. "Your party has been quite the success so far."

"To think I nearly missed the unmasking," Gemma said. Her voice was low, but she knew it wouldn't remain that way for long.

"Is it time?" Sophie asked, instinctively looking at the clock on the mantle. "No, we have hours."

"Not that unmasking," Gemma hissed. "I meant the Disreputables."

Sophie's expression shifted from warm to carefully neutral. "The Disreputables?" she echoed, as if repeating a foreign word. "Can you explain?"

"Perhaps *you* can explain. You brought them to my house. The house you helped me find. You've hovered over me since the day we met. I thought it was an accident, but it wasn't. You arranged to bump into me. You knew what you were doing from the first. Because *he* wanted you to."

Sophie took a step toward her, still watching. "He?"

"Logan. He couldn't watch me—not with all his smuggling runs and digging up dirt. So he put you on it. You're part of it too—his little group."

"His group of friends, you mean," Sophie said, offering the option of escape.

Gemma didn't take it. "I know what you are. You and him. Signs of the *Zodiac*. And now I know about the servants. Everyone's watching me, but not because they care about me. Just this case."

"That is not true, Gemma. We don't want to see you hurt."

"But you don't care about much beyond that. Stop trying to convince me otherwise. You *planned this*!" Gemma burst out at Sophie. "All of you, didn't you?"

"It's true Logan wrote to me, he asked me to look out for you—"

Gemma laughed, a despairing sound. "I've never been in control of my own life, have I? Not once. Always there was someone, finding some way to make me do what he wanted, to get me to move to the next square. Conall ordered me around in Scotland. You're no different here."

"Friends watch out for each other, Gemma."

"Don't call me your friend! I was your...project. Everything you did, you did for Logan."

Sophie tried to calm her. "You're distraught. You only know part of the picture. Let me order tea for you, cherie."

"No!" Gemma cried, then put her hands to her face. All at once, she stopped pacing. "I mean, yes. Please. I am not myself."

Sophie went to the bell pull. Mavis appeared within seconds. Sophie gave her the order for tea, and she left.

"Lady Forester," Gemma said formally. "May I ask for a few moments of privacy. I need to compose myself."

"I'll wait in the dining room until Mavis brings tea." Sophie silently withdrew.

As soon as the door closed, Gemma took her hands away from her face. She knew what she had to do. She had only a few minutes until the damnably efficient Mavis returned. Blessedly, someone had left a pelisse flung over the edge of the couch. She grabbed it, not caring who it belonged to. Moving as quietly as she could, Gemma hurried to the French doors at the far side of the room, the ones that opened to the garden. The latch turned easily, and Gemma slipped out into the night.

The cold air felt as fresh as snow on her face. She made her way toward the mews, moving along the narrow pathway between the walls of the house and the evergreen hedge. She'd slip through the mews to the street beyond, then hire a carriage. It would take her...well, anywhere. Anywhere that was far from London, from society, from false lovers and false friends.

But before she reached the street, something moved in the corner of her vision. She stopped dead when she saw a ghost standing very near the entrance to the mews.

"Gemma," the ghost said.

Gemma stared at the figure, gaping. "Uncle Conall?"

"Who else, my girl?"

She felt cold, and not because of the air outside. "He said you were dead!"

"Can't get rid of me that easy, Gemma girl." Conall coughed, but otherwise looked as alive as she was. "Is my sister around?" He looked anxiously toward the house.

"Aunt Maura's inside. Shall I send for her?"

"No!" Conall said quickly, waving a hand. "No. No sense in startling her. I've been keeping a low profile, and no one knows I'm in the city."

"What are you doing here? In London?" She walked toward him. "Why didn't you send word? Why aren't you back at Caithny?"

"I came to fetch you, Gemma girl." Conall gave her a weak smile. "I didn't send word because there are those who want me dead—I fooled them, but I can't keep on without help. I know I've not been a model guardian. But we're family, are we not? Come back with me. Or are you so happy here?"

Gemma paused. She didn't know how to answer that question. Sometimes she was happy, such as when she was alone with Logan. And other times she was furious at people who thought they were better than her. And sometimes she was just confused. So all she said was, "You want me to come back to Caithny with you?"

He nodded eagerly. "Aye. We've got an empire to build, girl. Ships sailing to every port in Europe. Legally. You'll see."

"You plan to use my inheritance to fund the business?" she asked. "Just as you did my whole life. That's what happened, isn't it? You kept a huge part of my allowance. You spent it."

"I spent it on our family business!" Conall protested. "So you didn't get a slew of pretty dresses when you were a girl. You would have got them all dirty in a day anyway. It was all for the best. You grew up into quite a creature, Gemma. You should thank me."

She wanted so badly to believe him. Conall's decisions were harsh, but he sounded as if he thought he was doing right. But still, she held back. "I have a life in London, Uncle. I...don't want to go back to Caithny. Not yet. It's too lonely there."

His mouth tightened. "You're ignoring my wishes?"

"Yes, and you shouldn't be surprised." She looked back at the house, wondering if her absence was noticed yet. "I waited long enough to make my own choices. You saw to that."

"I know what's best, girl." Then he sighed in a way that would make Maura envious. "Oh, if you're set on your fate, then who am I to keep you from it? I'll learn to live alone at Caithny. No family at all. But if you're happy here…"

"Don't say that, Uncle!" Her words came out tartly, but she was stabbed by the thought of leaving Conall alone. "I didn't say I'd never come back. Just not immediately."

"But now is when you're needed, girl. This wound has half taken my life. Who can I trust but my blood?"

"Are you in pain?" she asked worriedly. It occurred to her that Conall didn't look healthy. He leaned to one side, as if in pain. Her natural sympathy pushed other thoughts aside.

"Oh, aye. But what would you know of pain?" he added morosely. "You're young and full of life."

"You must stay here until you're healed," she said, reaching for him.

Conall shook his head. "Can't. I can't be seen. Not by anyone." He looked around, as if expecting spies to leap out at any moment. Then he leaned over to her ear and whispered, "It's now or never, girl. Fate led you outside tonight. You're meant to come away from here."

Her mind was in a whirl of emotions. Logan was a spy who put spies on her. He couldn't be trusted. At least she knew what Conall wanted in life. And he was asking for her help. How could she say no to family?

"All right," she said impulsively. "Let's go. And go quickly. They'll find me gone any moment now."

Conall let out a sigh of relief. "That's my girl. Come. Follow me. Ah, Fortune's smiling tonight!"

She let Conall take her by the hand, and followed silently, thinking of the inscription on the compass. Was that what it meant? Was she being bold? Or was she just running away?

Neither of them noticed a small shape hiding in the darkness of the dead garden. Sally Beckett hunched down in the shadows, even more silent than usual, her large blue eyes taking in everything that happened just outside the house.

* * * *

Conall and Gemma traveled quickly in order to put some distance between them and the house. She hoped the Disreputables wouldn't dream that she left the house completely. With luck they would search the rooms first, and the truth would only dawn on them when it was too late to do anything.

Gemma thought about going back to saddle Hector, but she instantly decided not to risk it. She didn't want be seen through the windows.

So they walked, with Gemma holding tight to Conall's hand. She was worried he couldn't walk well on his own. The cold wind cut through her pelisse and her gown and her slippers soon enough. Her anger kept her warm only so long. Her pace slowed, but Conall said they couldn't stop, as if he was also afraid Logan or Sophie or one of those damn disreputable servants would magically catch up.

The late hour and the foul weather kept the streets mostly clear, but she looked very out of place, and she was desperate to get inside. The neighborhoods grew shabbier, dingier, and more dangerous.

"Need a bed, missy?" a voice called from a darkened doorway. A dirty face leaned out, and Gemma jumped back, startled.

She hurried on, hearing the coarse, hacking laugh of

the beggar behind her. At last, they stood before their destination, a modest town home in a poor neighborhood.

Conall dug out a key in his pocket.

"Hurry, Uncle Conall!" Gemma said.

The door popped open abruptly. "Got it. We're home."

This was home? Gemma wanted to cry. "Oh, Uncle, I never should have come to London."

He reached out and took her by the wrist, pulling her inside. "Don't do that. Get in here, girl. It's freezing out and you're dressed as if you just escaped Bedlam. Are you wearing *leaves*?"

She looked down at the skirt of the dress left exposed. "It's a costume." She held up the oak leaf mask. "For my party. A masquerade to celebrate my birthday tomorrow."

"Yes, your birthday. We mustn't forget that." Conall grinned. "Well, well. I'm glad you came, Gemma girl. Come upstairs where it's warm. You must be tired."

He led her up a flight of steps to his rented rooms. Soon, she was seated next to a small but cheerful blaze in the grate, and Conall put a drink into her hands. "Have a bit of this, girl. Warm you right up."

It was brandy. Gemma sipped it, finding it sweeter than usual. But it did warm her up and, at Conall's urging, she drank the whole glass, which was not something she'd usually do.

"You look sleepy, girl." Her uncle turned down the bedsheets to the only bed. "Come, lie down and close your eyes. I'll lie by the fire. No need to worry about anything now. I'll take care of everything."

She nodded. A wave of fatigue swept over her, and she wavered a bit as she stood and made her way to the bed. "I'll just take a nap."

"A long nap, Gemma girl," he said. "And tomorrow

everything will be different."

She lay back, and was dreaming almost before her head hit the pillow. Just before she lost consciousness completely, she thought she heard Logan calling her name. Then she slid into darkness.

Chapter 40

≋

"SHE'S GONE?" LOGAN ASKED.

"That's what I said." Sophie paced angrily up and down the room. "Where the hell could she have gone?"

Logan didn't answer. He was too busy being stunned at the news. What could have driven Gemma to leave her own party to rush out into the winter night without any warning?

"She just left?" he asked Sophie. "Had something upset her?"

"Yes!" Sophie snapped. "She realized she was surrounded by us, and that upset her! You didn't tell her about the Disreputables?"

"Of course not. Well, once, by accident. But don't blame me. You hired them," he protested.

"At *your* request!"

He shook his head. "We can fight about that later. Now what matters is locating her."

Bond entered, slipping in the door and pulling it tightly shut behind her. "My lady?" she asked Sophie. "I think there's something both of you will want to see."

She held out a folded note. "This came for Miss Gemma a few days ago. She kept it in her writing desk."

"You read it?" Sophie asked.

"Of course, my lady," Bond said without a trace of shame. "That's my job. I didn't say anything because it didn't appear to matter. Until now."

Sophie unfolded the note and read it through quickly. Then she handed it to Logan, saying, "Keep your temper. Remember that we're surrounded by people."

Logan read it, and fought to follow Sophie's advice. "That..." He couldn't think of a nasty enough word for MacLachlan. Sophie supplied him with a few in French, though her cool tone made it clear she didn't agree with any of the terms.

"He's still after her," Logan said. "For a lord, he's quite the thief."

Bond coughed delicately. Logan sent her a dark look, and the maid—who used to be a jewel thief—blinked innocently at him. "For what it's worth, sir, thieves rarely advertise their intentions. Lord MacLachlan has always been quite open about his."

"Such as his intention to snatch Gemma away under everyone's nose?"

Sophie took the note back. "Keep calm. If she kept this note, perhaps she did go to MacLachlan's home. He isn't here at the ball, you'll note."

"Everyone's wearing masks."

"Yes, but none of our masked guests are six feet tall and speaking in a highland brogue."

"He told the mistress he would decline the invitation after she told him not to court her any longer," Bond added helpfully.

"Which means he may be at home this evening, which means it's possible Gemma went there to seek help."

"I'll go," Logan said grimly.

Sophie asked, "Is that wise, considering your mood?"

"My mood will not improve until I see Gemma again." Logan turned to the door. "With luck, she's there and she'll come back without too much of a fuss. Just keep the guests occupied until we return."

"If you don't find her there, bring MacLachlan here."

"Why?"

"I may need him. The unmasking is scheduled for one o' clock," Sophie warned.

"I'll do what I can," said Logan. "If we're not back... improvise."

Sophie gave him a smile. "That's what I do best."

Logan flung his coat on and rushed into the night. Within half an hour, he was pounding at the door of the town house where Lord MacLachlan was staying.

He pushed past a startled valet. "Bring MacLachlan down here immediately. Don't ask questions, just go."

MacLachlan appeared moments later, clearly annoyed. "What the hell is the meaning of this?"

Logan cut him off. "Where's Gemma?"

"You refer, I assume, to Miss Harrington," said Ian in a cold tone.

"Yes, of course. Where is she?"

"Why are you asking me? According to her own words, *you're* the one she chose." Ian added the last part in an incredulous tone.

Logan thrust the letter toward Ian. "This was found at her residence."

Ian opened the note and read it over. "Aye. I sent this. What of it?"

"Then you admit that you all but invited her to elope with you."

"Grow up. It says nothing of the kind," said Ian. "You

make it sound as if I'm a rover out to kidnap her."

"Aren't you? You wanted her money."

"Marriages are made for such reasons," Ian snapped. "You're worldly enough to know that. Back home, I've got a family to care for. Lands to maintain. A clan to provide for and watch over. That's what it means to have a title. It's not a prize, Hartley. It's a responsibility. I'm willing to make an alliance to bring my fortunes back to where they should be. My whole family relies on me. I've never lied to Miss Harrington about my plans. And I'm not bamboozling her. *If* she marries me, she'll become a MacLachlan. I'll care for her till my dying breath. Can you say so much? You act like you want to duel over her. I outgrew such brainless romanticism by the time I was fifteen. Perhaps you should too."

"You don't have the slightest hint of how fast I grew up. But that's not the point. All I want to know is if you're intent on pursuing Gem—Miss Harrington." Gemma wasn't exactly an innocent now, but the thought of some witless, boorish dandy pressing attentions on *his* lover made his hands curl into fists.

"I wouldn't oppose the notion, but my offer was purely out of friendship. I may not have any claim on her heart, but I'll be damned if I stood by when I could help at all. So I wrote to let her know that if she needed assistance, she should consider me."

"That's all?"

"That's all." Ian blinked, finally realizing the implications of Logan's initial question. "Wait, are you saying that she's not to be found?"

"That's exactly what I'm saying. Her maid found your letter in Miss Harrington's room. But the lady has fled her home with no word as to where she's gone."

"When did this happen?"

"This evening. Perhaps two hours ago now. Their initial search uncovered nothing. Then we found your letter, and thought...."

"Of course, of course. God damn." Ian frowned. "She never came here, or tried to contact me. I swear that."

"I believe you," Logan said, with a sigh. "But if she didn't come to you for help, where could she have gone?"

"I don't know, but I'll help you search." He made a move as if to get ready to leave the house.

"No, wait!" Logan shook his head. "We first have to return to the party."

"Hardly the time for levity."

"You're needed there. Don't ask me how, just know that it might help her. And we both want that."

"Yes, sir," Ian said with a wry grin. "You are used to giving orders, aren't you?"

"Just as you are, I suspect. But in this, can we be allies?"

"For her sake, yes."

They headed out into the cold night.

Chapter 41

LOGAN RETURNED TO GEMMA'S HOUSE, his mood grimmer than before. He was so certain that she'd fled to MacLachlan's. But Ian's distress was all too real. Gemma wasn't with him, and he had no idea where she had gone. So that meant Logan was without a lead again.

Sophie was still at the house when he returned. "No word?" he asked, already knowing the answer. The servants all wore distracted, upset looks. Even the unflappable Stiles looked perturbed.

"No," she said. "I knew Gemma was upset, but I miscalculated. I never expected her to dash off into the snow."

"Well, she did. And what are we to do now? People will ask questions if she doesn't appear at the unmasking of her own party!"

"I'll handle that." She took MacLachlan's arm. "And I'll need his lordship to help the deception."

"Me?" said Ian.

"Yes. You have been seen to court her, you're a plausible escort, and no one knows she discouraged you. Do they?"

"You do," Ian noted, "and I doubt you learned it from

Miss Harrington."

"I know a lot of things," Sophie said. "Now come with me. For Gemma's sake."

"Yes, my lady."

The unmasking came and went. Through the grace of all Sophie's performance skills, the addition of a red wig from her personal collection—which Ivy had been sent to fetch—and Ian MacLachlan to aid the illusion, she carried off an impersonation of Gemma to perfection.

Only Maura Douglas wasn't fooled, but she held her tongue until a safer moment, when Sophie pulled her into the little room where Logan waited, and Sophie quickly explained the problem. Maura's face slowly blanched to a worryingly pale tone.

Ian also entered, but only long enough to put his greatcoat on. He looked a little stunned every time he glanced at Sophie. But he kept his composure. "I'll leave now," he said. "It's still possible Miss Harrington will try to contact me at my home."

"Thank you for your help, my lord," Sophie said.

He only shook his head. "I've no notion who you people are. But I know when I'm out of my depth. I'll send word if I learn anything. I expect the same courtesy."

Logan nodded. "At the earliest possible moment. I give you my word."

Ian accepted that. "I'll leave out the windows then. Seems to be the fashion."

Sophie watched him go through the French doors. "I like him."

"Most women do," Logan muttered.

"He helped us tonight."

"He bought us a few hours," Logan agreed. "But we still have no idea where Gemma has got to."

"Mr Hartley?" Mrs Rand came in, with Sally Beckett next to her. "The lass has something to tell you."

"Sally!" Bond said. "What are you doing out here when guests are present?"

"She knows something," Mrs Rand said. "She heard us talking about Miss Gemma's disappearance in the kitchen. She tried to tell me straight away but I admit I called her a pest. But she's a persistent thing."

"Well?" Logan asked, trying to his keep his voice gentle despite his impatience. The young girl stared at him with gigantic blue eyes. "I'm not really a pirate," he explained, guessing at the problem. "It's a costume for the party."

"She knows that, sir. It's just that Sally doesn't speak."

"Then how can you tell us anything?"

Sally looked at the side table shyly. At Mrs Rand's urging, she walked over to where an inkwell and a small stack of papers sat. She picked up the pen as if it were Excalibur, then dipped it in the ink and started to write. Slowly, and with careful, untutored precision.

"That's right, lass," Mrs Rand said. "You're doing well."

Logan and the others waited in agony until Sally finished her work. She walked the paper toward them. Sophie smiled and pointed her to Logan, who took the paper, the ink still wet and dripping. Sally's writing was rough block letters, and her spelling was inventive. But Logan read it out: UNCLUE ALIV SAW HIM.

"Uncle? You mean Miss Harrington's Uncle Conall? You saw him?"

Sally nodded.

"He was here? Tonight?"

She nodded again, vigorously.

"How did you know who he was?"

Sally returned to the desk and wrote an addendum.

Logan read, "MISTRIS SED NAME. LEF W HIM. Thank you, Sally. So Conall is alive after all. He must have been watching, and when Gemma left, he seized the opportunity and took her somewhere."

"I thought she was happy to get away from him," said Sophie. "Would she go with him?"

"My brother has always been a persuasive man," Maura noted, "Even when good people know better than to trust him. And the shock of seeing him alive—perhaps he pretended he needs her help. Gemma would never turn away from that."

"But Gemma didn't particularly enjoy assisting him in smuggling. Is she so crucial to his plans?" Logan guessed.

"Gemma's wealth has been keeping his business afloat these past few years," Maura said, "because he forced *me* to hand over the interest payments. Understand that the will is quite clear about who has access to the principal. Only Gemma will be able to touch the inheritance, and then not until her majority."

"Her birthday. This birthday," Logan said.

"Yes. Once she's twenty-one, she is the sole person able to use the money."

"But she doesn't have a will herself," Logan guessed. "So the law would very likely award the inheritance to her living guardian. And that's Conall Caithny."

Maura's eyes went wide. "But after her birthday, the terms change. Conall would no longer be her guardian. And she hasn't made a will, so her shares in the firm might be split among the other partners. Conall would have to fight much harder for a share." She looked at the clock. "It's after one in the morning now, so it *is* her birthday. He'll act today or not at all. You have until this coming midnight," she said, her words barely audible. "Please find her."

Logan looked at his costume. "I have to wear something normal. And I wish I had my gun instead of a damned antique sword."

"I can fetch the mistress' pistols, sir," Bond offered, as if she were offering the use of a handkerchief.

Maura put her hand to her face. "That girl!" Then she looked at Bond. "Yes, Bond. Bring Gemma's pistols down. If they can possibly assist in her rescue, I can't think of a better use for them."

She turned to Logan. "But please don't let it come to violence."

He shook his head. "That lies with your brother, I'm afraid."

Chapter 42

~~~

GEMMA AWOKE, GROGGY AND DISORIENTED. She sat up in the strange bed, momentarily forgetting what brought her there. She was still wearing her green ballgown, now wrinkled and stained. A few silk leaves had pulled loose and lay on the sheets and on the floor, as if they had blown loose in a gale. She looked over at the ladder back chair. The mask dangled from it, the empty eyes staring at her from behind a leafy screen.

"Hello?" she asked out loud. The room was quiet. There was a window, but it was shuttered from the outside. She leaned forward to peer out of the crack between the shutters. The light was murky. Was it later the same night? Or had she lost an entire day? The sudden growl in her stomach suggested the latter.

The events of the previous night filtered back to her. Logan's words to Sophie, and the whole farce of the servants "protecting" her, when all anyone really wanted was to spy on her.

She turned onto her side, remembering Logan's expression when he saw her costume. That smile nearly turned her heart inside out. He knew she chose the costume just for him. And he loved her for it.

Gemma squeezed her eyes shut, trying to get Logan's smile and words out of her head. But she couldn't. He didn't speak like a man out to trick her. He saved her life more than once, he protected her from threats she didn't even see coming, and he did it all because he loved her.

He loved her. Gemma opened her eyes again. She *knew* that was true. Whatever he'd done—including the use of those particular servants—he'd done to keep her safe. And how could Gemma complain about Jem or Bond or Stiles or any of the others. Even Fergus said they were among the best people he'd ever worked with.

Aunt Maura would be so disappointed! Gemma winced when she imagined the older woman's expression on hearing Gemma had fled the house.

She sighed. She behaved like an absolute child last night. She allowed her anger to get the better of her and now who knew what would happen? She should not have left. Logan was probably furious. No, she corrected. He was probably frantic. He'd be furious later, once she found him and showed him she was perfectly safe. And Lord, how embarrassing it would be to apologize to him —and to Sophie, who had become one of Gemma's closest friends in her life, despite the fact that she might not be who she claimed to be at all. Her actions were what mattered. Sophie helped her at every turn. It would be utterly hypocritical to pretend otherwise.

Logan even asked Gemma to join him. How would she convince whoever was in charge of the Zodiac that she could be trusted if she ran away during a tantrum? She took a deep breath. She would go back and apologize to Logan. She could do it.

Her plan of running away back to Caithny sounded

completely daft now. What had she been thinking? Her future was with Logan, and Logan was here in London—for now. She had to find him before he left.

Motivated to set her life back on pace, she got up and went to the door. She turned the knob, but the door remained firmly in place. She tugged irritably, her mind still a bit foggy. Why did the stupid door not work as it should? After a few moments of rattling, it dawned on her that the door was locked.

She could not get out.

She sat down on the edge of the bed, confused. Why should the door be locked? Was she a prisoner?

Gemma shook her head. No, of course not. She came here willingly. She must have been exhausted to sleep so heavily. And Conall must have gone out. But why lock the door? She got up again and paced. Her stomach growled again. If she didn't eat, she'd be weak and cranky soon. Nervousness fluttered up inside, when she realized she had no idea when Conall was coming back.

She looked around the room. There was little of interest. Conall's clothing was carefully packed in a small case. A few books, but nothing readable. One was a volume of English law—how dull, and the other was a bible printed in German—incomprehensible. "Must have been in the room when Uncle Conall rented it," she muttered.

She waited for an hour, her anxiety mounting. When a key rattled in the lock, she shot up off the bed. "Uncle!"

Conall came in the door, wearing a heavy coat and a scarf wrapped up around his face. "Ah, you're awake."

"You locked me in, Uncle! And there's no food."

"I brought you a meat pie," he said, pulling one from a brown wrapper. "Eat up. We're leaving soon."

Gemma took it eagerly. In between bites, though, she

glared at him. "Why did you lock me in?"

"Well, I want to keep you safe, Gemma girl. I've only the one key, and you were dead asleep. What choice did I have?" He gave her an odd look. "Though nothing bad ever seems to happen to you."

She gave a dark laugh. "If only that were true."

But Conall didn't ask what she meant. He only moved around the room, putting things in place and packing the last few stray items in his case. He unbuttoned the coat once he got warm, and Gemma saw a pistol belted at his waist.

"Are you expecting trouble?" she asked, nodding toward the gun.

He gave a shrug. "Must be ready for anything. Don't forget I've had people try to kill me. But I'm a hard one to kill. Must run in the family." He laughed as darkly as she did, chuckling to himself. "Are you ready, Gemma girl? It's time to go."

"I'm not going," she announced.

He went still. "What?"

"I've had plenty of time to think while I was here. It was wrong of me to leave my house last night, and I certainly can't rush off without speaking to Aunt Maura. A letter is inadequate. Besides, I…I want to stay in London. I have commitments here. I made promises to people."

"Oh you have, have you?" Conall arched his eyebrow. "Any to a man?"

"One," Gemma admitted primly.

"Well," Conall said softly. "Well, well, well."

"I'm twenty-one," she reminded him. "Or I will be in a few hours. I can make that sort of decision on my own now."

"Twenty-one," he echoed. "That reminds me. I have a

present for your birthday. Why not come with me so I can fetch it? After all, you're not coming home, so I'll have to see you get it now."

"Go with you now? Isn't it night?"

"About eight o' clock." He nodded. "And we must move. Time's running out."

Gemma finished the meat pie and stood up. She put on the heavy pelisse she'd grabbed on the way out of her house. It didn't match her gown at all, but what was to be done?

"What were you supposed to be, girl?" Conall asked suddenly.

Gemma put on the oak leaf mask. "I was a dryad." She pulled the mask off again, leaving it on the small table. "But now I'm just Gemma. Let's go, Uncle. And after you fetch the present, I must return home."

"Oh, indeed. Then let's not waste time. We can get a ride, I think," said Conall, once they reached the street. Gemma pulled the pelisse tight around her. The garment didn't even reach her knees, though, and the vivid green of the skirt was unmistakable. The streets were more crowded this time, and several people looked at her curiously as they passed by.

They got into a coach and Conall directed the driver toward the harbor in a loud voice. Gemma recalled the name. It was the same harbor where Logan kept the *Mistral*. When they got out, Gemma realized that Conall intended to actually walk to one of the ships at dock.

"Will you be sailing back to Caithny? Have you bought a new ship already?"

"Not quite." Conall hurried down the wharf. "Come, girl. It's not getting any warmer."

"Where are we going?"

"You'll recognize it when you see it!"

Gemma stopped in surprise before the ship. She did recognize it. The long, graceful lines of the hull were unmistakable, even before she read the name on the bow. "It's the *Mistral*!"

"Aye. The very ship I fell from, when my so-called partner left me for dead. That Lockridge was up to no good. And I'll see that he pays for it."

"You're not going to harm his ship!" she said.

"Of course not, girl. I'm just going to leave your body on it, so the authorities will arrest him when they find it."

She blinked. "What?"

His hand clamped down on her arm with crushing force. "Think of it as a birthday present, girl. Except the present is for me. Because once you're dead, your inheritance becomes mine."

Chapter 43

~~~

"IS THIS THE PLACE?" LOGAN asked as Jem pulled to a clattering halt.

"Aye, sir," said Jem. "One of our contacts said a woman in a green outfit covered in leaves was here last night."

Logan nodded. He tried the outer door and found it locked. That didn't trouble him too much. He pulled a set of skeleton keys he kept around for that purpose and found one that fit. The door knob turned on the third try.

"Well done, sir," Jem said quietly.

"Watch the door till I get back. We might need to leave in a hurry."

Logan stepped inside; it was quiet. He knocked at each door until someone opened and grumpily directed him to the top floor. He found that door unlocked and the room empty. But Gemma's mask blazed green on the table. He grabbed it, then stormed back down to the lower door. "Hello? Hello!"

"What?" the neighbor said irritably. "All you people running up and down at all hours! I'm not renting that room out again, just you see!"

"Where did he go? The man who rented the room? He's left. Did he say anything?"

"He told me nothing. Gave his name as Mr Smith and he paid for a month. That's all I know!" The door slammed in his face.

Logan returned to the street. "She was here," he said, holding up the mask. "But they're both gone. Trail's cold again."

Jem gave a faint shake of the head. "No, sir. We just need to ask around. Eyes everywhere." He nodded to where a hunched figure sat in a doorway. "Let's start with her."

The figure was indeed a woman, though how Jem guessed it from the layers of dirty wool swaddling the body was a mystery. She shook her head at first, but then her eyes were caught by the mask in Logan's hand. "The green girl? That's the one you want?"

"Yes," said Logan, suddenly hopeful. "Did you see her leave? Not last night, but today?"

"Aye. The green girl got in a carriage with the old man."

"Which way did the carriage go?"

Her look got sly. "How much you want to know?"

Logan held up a few coins. "Three if you answer now. None if you waste my time."

"The harbor," she burst out, giving the name of a familiar wharf.

He handed her the coins. "Good. Thank you."

"Can I have that?" she asked, pointing to the mask.

"What use is the mask to you?" he asked.

"Just to look at," she said, a faint embarrassment coming across her face. "Just a pretty thing to look at."

Wordlessly, Logan handed the mask to her.

She took it carefully. "Best hurry, sir. They left not long ago. Heard the bells ring out."

He nodded to Jem. "Harbor. And drive fast."

Jem reached the harbor in record time, then brought the carriage to a halt. Logan turned to him. "I'm going to the *Mistral*. Find Sophie and the others and bring them back here as soon as you can."

"You're sure they went to your ship, sir?"

Logan nodded. His intuition was practically screaming at him. "I'll find them. But I want all the help I can get. I want Conall Caithny alive."

Jem nodded and Logan jumped off, running toward the *Mistral*. As he ran, he saw an odd light flickering in the portholes of the cabins. He recognized the light just as a faint smell of smoke hit him. The ship was on fire.

Chapter 44

≋

ABOARD THE MISTRAL'S DECK, ICY sleet stung her face, but Gemma didn't notice. She was too entranced by the gleam of the gun barrel pointing at her.

Caithny held the gun steady. "My dear, it was really most inconvenient of you to come to London. In fact, it was most inconvenient of you to be born at all."

"Uncle…" Gemma whispered.

"I encouraged every stupid move you seemed inclined to make, from riding horses at midnight to joining smuggling runs to taking up with ruthless criminals. Yet you never got so much as a scratch! I had hoped not to resort to murder, but needs must. You have something that I want."

"You can have anything of mine! All the money."

"Gemma girl, you always were a fool. If it were that simple, I wouldn't be here now. You know too much about my activities, and I don't like loose ends. Your fortune alone will not suffice."

"You said we were family."

"I'd have said anything to get you to come along, girl. Do you have any idea how angry I was when I got word you left Caithny? I nearly had a heart attack. Damn girl almost slipped through my fingers. But I found you again." He laughed. "Fate's smiling on me once again. I can't waste it."

"Toby!" Gemma shouted, hoping the first mate would be there. "Toby!"

Conall shoved her back. "Don't scream. And no one's here. The crew doesn't sleep aboard when she's in dock during winter. They have rooms in town. No one from the crew will see you until tomorrow morning. And by then it will be too late, since I'll alert the authorities tonight. When the body of the richest heiress in the city is found, it will be the story of the Season."

"You won't get away with this. You'll be the main suspect."

He laughed. "You're forgetting that I'm already dead, dear. Everyone thinks so. Even you did. Lockridge told you what he *thought* he saw—me getting shot, then falling overboard. He underestimated me, and I'll make him pay."

"Why? I mean, why him?"

"Because he's got it in for me."

"Because you're in league with Napoleon's army!" she burst out. "Logan told me about what you did. I know about the food! Selling supplies to the enemy in a time of war is treason."

"Then why was your *Logan* so eager to help out?" He sneered at her use of Logan's name. "Think of that, girl."

Gemma opened and then closed her mouth. So Conall hadn't yet realized that Logan was a spy. And he kept calling him Lockridge. So even Logan's real identity must still be a secret. She realized something else.

"I don't think you quite understand that Logan has

some very powerful friends, Uncle. Even if you do kill me, he'll never hang for the crime."

Conall shrugged. "The murder of a lady is hard to hide. You may overestimate your lover's connections. And besides, I'll get the inheritance, and that's the main thing."

"But *how*, if you're dead?"

"Oh, I've been looking into my options. There's a year's grace before a claimant has to appear before the courts. I'll wait till things calm down, then come back to life for long enough to get the money. Then I'll leave London the moment it's done."

"You're really going to kill me?"

"I'll do what I must. Care to pray before I shoot you, girl? Your aunt would like that. She did try so hard to raise you properly."

Gemma took a deep breath. Her mind was going in a thousand directions at once, and she had only a few seconds to think of something. "Yes," she said, to gain time. "Yes, I'd like to pray."

"Do it then. This snow is starting to stick."

"Yes, it is." The wooden deck of the ship was now slippery with the icy damp. It would be easy to slip and fall. She lowered herself carefully to the deck, as if to kneel in prayer. Conall chuckled at her childish move.

But when he laughed, he lowered the gun, too distracted to keep it on her every second. Gemma lunged forward, directly at Conall's feet. The force of her weight knocked him down, and sent both of them tumbling over the slippery wooden planks of the deck. Conall cursed loudly as he hit the deck. Gemma felt the pain too, but she was younger and quicker to recover. She heard the gun clatter on the wood and she scrambled to get it. She couldn't pick it up, but she managed to send it flying down the deck away from both her and Conall.

The man scrambled as well. His body was older, but he was used to ships. He wouldn't be down for long. He made a grab for Gemma's ankle. She slipped out of his grasp, and he was left holding only her worn out green satin slipper.

"Get back here!" he bellowed.

Gemma didn't listen. She got up, snatching the gun from where it lay. But she wouldn't shoot her own family. Instead, she rushed toward the door to the below decks, ignoring Conall's scream behind her.

She shut the door. The narrow passage was pitch black and cold, but the wind no longer whipped at her.

She dashed down the passage. She would hide. Logan showed her all those secret compartments. One was big enough for a person. Where was it?

She kept moving, even as she heard the door open again. "Gemma! Where are you!"

Gemma gulped a breath and kept going, keeping as quiet as possible. Her other shoe slipped off, and she kicked it into the doorway of an open cabin. Conall would look in those rooms first.

She reached the little ladder-like stairway to the hold. The compartment was right there. She ran her hands over the wood, trying to remember how Logan opened it. All of a sudden, she felt a handhold, and popped the narrow door open. She slipped in and closed it.

The space was barely large enough for a person. It was more like a coffin than a closet. Gemma couldn't even lift her hands up in front of her, the space was so narrow. She gripped the gun hard in her right hand, the one nearest the door. She breathed once, twice, trying to calm herself down. If Conall could hear her breathing, the hiding spot would be exposed instantly.

She waited one minute, two minutes. Footsteps pounded by, once, then later again. Conall was searching for her, but he didn't know the secret.

"Gemma! Come out, girl! This is no time for hide and seek!"

She held silent, hearing the voice echo swell and fade as Conall searched for her. "Come out, girl! Or I'll smoke you out!"

Gemma didn't dare say a word. Conall wouldn't risk a fire aboard a ship, would he? People would notice that. They'd come running.

She thought she imagined the scent, summoned it up in her fear. But the smell of acrid smoke became stronger. "I'm not fooling, girl. Get out here, and I'll stop the fire. Otherwise you'll burn alive, and so will this whole ship."

Panic welled up in her chest. The smoke was real. Conall had set a fire. The *Mistral* was burning. She couldn't let Logan's lady burn.

Tightening her grip on the gun, Gemma pushed the door open.

She eased out of the tiny closet, finding the air of the passage swirling with smoke. The crackle of flames sounded in her ears. From the waft of darker smoke coming from one doorway, she guessed Conall set one of the main sleeping cabins on fire.

It was hard to breathe. She had to get to the deck. She put her arm up over her mouth and moved toward the door to the open deck. She flung it open, too intent on reaching fresh air to think of anything else. As soon as she inhaled the cold but fresh winter air, she was hit from behind. She collapsed onto her knees, the gun flying from her hand.

"Got her," a new voice said.

Gemma twisted to see who spoke, and saw the same man who attacked her and Logan the night they left the Thorne's party.

"You," she began. "You're working with Conall?"

"Course he is!" Conall said, reappearing. He bent to pick up her lost gun. "We worked it all out. I needed to die to avoid a few people who wanted money from me. My friend kindly took on the role of killer. He pretended to shoot me, and I pretended to die. It was the beginning of a new business venture."

"You planned all of this? Even coming to get me?"

"I waited by your house for days, looking for a way in. Attentive servants you got, though. I finally saw that party going on, and thought I could sneak in when Fate sent you flying right down that path." Conall reached to grab her by the hair. "Speaking of which, I shouldn't tempt Fate more. The time for praying is past."

She closed her eyes. The was nothing familiar in his voice anymore. Conall intended to kill her.

"You said you'd put the fire out," she whispered.

Both men laughed at that. Conall said, "I'd have said anything to get you out here. I need them to see your body, girl. What use is a charred corpse to me?"

He looked toward the gun, then shoved her forward. "Move. Toward the main mast."

She had no choice. She took a step, then another. She wondered if Conall intended to shoot her from behind, before she even reached the mast.

Then she heard someone ahead of her call out. "Caith-ny!"

The voice came from the darkness, but Gemma's heart

surged at the single word. She knew who it was.

"Let her go," Logan said, still unseen through the driving sleet. "If you harm her, I swear you won't live long enough to touch her inheritance."

"Who is it?" Caithny snarled.

Well you may ask, Gemma thought wryly, smiling even in the midst of this awful scene. "Show yourself!" Caithny demanded.

Logan stepped out of the gloom. He didn't look at Gemma. His eyes were fixed on the barrel of Conall's gun.

"Lockridge," Caithny sputtered. "How did you know to come here? And why are you dressed like a swell? This some new game of yours?"

"It was never a game." Logan's eyes flicked to Gemma's as he spoke. "Let me take Gemma, and you'll be detained instead of killed."

"Like hell I will," Caithny spat the words out.

"Watch out!" Gemma shouted, just as Cargo sprang at Logan from the darkness. Logan ducked just in time to avoid a knife in his chest, but then the two were tumbling away on the deck, locked in a fight that was part duel, part wrestling match.

But Gemma couldn't keep watching. Conall barreled toward Gemma, intent on grabbing her and shooting point blank. She whirled away just in time, and tried to take the gun from him. He said, "Not so fast. I'll strangle you, girl. And I'll let *him* watch."

Gemma didn't say anything. She had to get the gun in Conall's hand. She edged further away as he came for her, then shouted Logan's name.

Conall looked away, expecting to see Logan coming for him. Gemma grabbed the gun, though she lost her balance as she did so. She went rolling, evading Conall's grasp by pure luck.

He roared only a few feet away, about to catch her.

Instinctively, she swiveled back and pulled the trigger. Although the light was poor, it was a short distance, and Gemma didn't practice for nothing. Conall screamed in pain and dropped to the ground, writhing as he grabbed at his bleeding leg.

"What have you done?" Conall hissed.

"Just what you always wanted me to do," she said. "You did encourage me to practice."

Gemma stood, shaking in the middle of the deck, searching for Logan. She didn't see him, or the other man.

"Logan!" she called. "Logan!"

"Gemma." She heard the voice ahead of her, but the sleet made it hard to see anything. "Logan?" She hurried to where she'd last seen the pair struggling. Without warning, a figure stood up before her. She backed away, unsure if it was Logan or his attacker.

"Gemma," he said. He walked toward her. "Are you all right, love?"

"Am I…." Gemma rushed to him, the tears flowing freely. "Are *you* all right?" She flung her arms around him, desperate to know he was not a ghost. He felt reassuringly warm and solid, although she could sense his rapid heartbeat. "What happened?"

"Cargo's quite good with a knife," Logan said, looking behind him. Gemma peered past his shoulder and saw a body lying there, completely still, the chest of the white shirt dark with blood. "But I'm not bad either. Did you know Toby taught me?"

"Thank God. I'm going to kiss Toby when I see him next." Gemma kissed Logan first. He put one arm around her and held her fiercely. She noticed that he held the other arm tight to his body, and his hand was red. "He stabbed you!"

"I'll be all right. Where's Caithny?"

"I shot him," she said. "I never thought I'd have to.... You were in danger."

"Is he dead?"

"No." She pointed to where Conall lay on the deck, cursing and muttering to himself.

"Good," said Logan. "I have questions for him."

Gemma looked at Logan, still not believing he was alive. Then the glow of a fire distracted them both. "It's spreading," she said anxiously. "It'll destroy the ship." She moved toward the fire. "We have to put it out."

Logan stopped her. "Let it burn. We're going, and taking him with us."

"Logan, your ship!"

"I'll build another. Ships are replaceable. You are not."

Before they could even start to move, more figures appeared, rushing toward them. Gemma squinted, picking out the shapes of her servants and then Sophie, all storming up to them.

"Coming, sir!" Jem called out. "What do you need?"

Logan gave a tired nod. "Someone take charge of this man. And try to put that fire out?"

Jem took one look and yelled for the other servants to follow. Sophie remained by Conall. She pulled her own gun and pointed it at him. "I'll be delighted to deal with this man," she said, her charming French accent doing nothing to hide the threat behind her words. She looked at Gemma. "Your uncle, I believe?"

"Yes," Gemma said faintly. Lady Sophie looked extremely...confident holding a gun over a prisoner. "Please don't kill him."

"Not if he behaves," Sophie said. She turned to Logan. "Take Miss Harrington home, please. And get a doctor to attend you there immediately. Why do I feel that every other time I see you, you're covered in blood?"

"Occupational hazard," Logan said. He led Gemma to the gangplank. "Come on. Let's go home."

Chapter 45

≋

LOGAN HELD HER THE WHOLE way home, despite the fact that he could barely sit up straight. Gemma kept an eye on him, promising she'd send for a doctor as soon as possible. They returned to the house by way of the mews, taking the servants' entrance in. Gemma was sure all was lost anyway, but still, it would cause comment if everyone paraded in the front door.

Chance greeted them there, and henceforth would not be separated from Gemma. He followed her into every room and out again, his eyes locked happily onto her.

The Disreputables, as Gemma now knew them, continued to handle everything with an enviable calm. Logan was put to bed in a guest room immediately. Sally Beckett ran out with a note to fetch a doctor. Bond returned shortly after, and pried Gemma away from Logan's bedside.

"Wash, change, and a meal, miss," Bond said. "You look frightful, and that is not allowed."

Gemma submitted to everything without a fight. Aunt Maura rushed in while she was being scrubbed clean. The two women exchanged their news. Maura told Gemma that her absence was covered very well the previous night, mostly due to the actions of Lady Forester and Lord

MacLachlan.

"That lady may be a viscountess," Maura said. "But she's a decidedly odd one. I attribute it to her French upbringing."

"That's probably it," Gemma agreed easily.

Then, of course, Gemma had to tell Maura that her only living brother was a traitor and nearly a murderer, and it was unlikely Maura would ever see him again.

"Well, if that's the way he treats family, why should I see him again?" Maura sniffed. "He can rot in prison for all I care! Anyone who values money over blood has forfeit their place in society."

Gemma was impressed at her aunt's bearing, and said so.

"Well, I always knew Conall was a bad lot," Maura admitted. "I never guessed how bad.... But never mind that now. The first thing to do is to make sure your reputation is safe. You may have passed the evening with your legal guardian, but I don't suppose his word will count for much if he's in prison."

"I am not concerned about my reputation, Aunt."

"Well, you should be. Out all night with no way to prove your innocence! That's dire."

"I am engaged to a most understanding gentleman," Gemma said.

"Engaged?" Maura blinked. "To whom?"

"Mr Logan Cadwalder Horatio Hartley of St George's, Bermuda. The one upstairs waiting for a doctor."

Maura took a few seconds to process that, then her face cleared. "Ah. So Mr Hartley wasn't just a well-meaning friend of Lady Forester's."

"Not exactly. Although he is very well-meaning. And I love him."

"And based on his actions of the last night and day, he loves you." Maura nodded once. "That will do."

Later, Gemma met Sophie in the parlor. The doctor was there, explaining Logan was not critically wounded this time, but the accumulation of fatigue and old wounds would prevent him from recovering unless he rested. "I'm not joking," the doctor added. "He's young. He's not invincible."

"Thank you, Cutter," Sophie said, with a smile. "You have my word he'll not get any more wounds for at least a month."

"How reassuring, ma'am." The doctor bowed and was led out by Ivy. Chance, who clearly didn't trust the medicinal smell of Cutter, heaved a little sigh, and leaned into Gemma.

Only after he left did Gemma wonder if Cutter was his first name, his last name, or a sort of label. But before she could ask, Sophie explained that Conall Caithny was in custody, where he would remain until he was no longer a danger to anyone.

"So I didn't kill him," Gemma said in relief.

"No. Conall Caithny will survive to stand trial for smuggling and profiteering in a time of war."

Gemma looked at Sophie, a flush creeping up her cheeks. "I must apologize, Lady Forester. I spoke very cruelly to you last night. You were easy to blame in the moment. But you have been a friend, and I treated you very shabbily. I hope you can someday forgive me."

"The day is today," the other lady said warmly. "It takes a strong woman to apologize, and you certainly did have a bit of a shock. But to truly intimate friends, dear Gemma, I am always Sophie."

"Yes, Sophie." Gemma gave a little sigh.

After that, they talked about a few more things, including the Zodiac. Gemma had a wild thought. "May I ask a personal question?"

Sophie raised an eyebrow. "You may get a personal answer."

"You're married. Does your husband...know about what you do? Or is it some elaborate ruse?"

"He knows all about me," Sophie said, laughing. "Because he's also a sign."

"How do you stand it? Not each other, I mean. But the danger..."

"It can be nerve wracking," said Sophie. "But we often work together."

"Friends look out for each other?" Gemma guessed.

"Exactly. The Zodiac wasn't always that way, but things are changing. For the better."

Gemma hoped that was true, but she couldn't think about it now. "Please excuse me. With the doctor gone, I want to see how Logan is recovering."

"I'm sure the sight of you will help."

* * * *

His eyes were closed, but Logan wasn't asleep. While lying in the bed, he listened to the sounds of the house. Conversations rose and faded. He couldn't distinguish any words, but he heard the occasional laugh, and the easy cadence of the speech. People were at ease, finally. He let out a long breath, realizing that, for the first time in weeks, he could relax.

There were the footsteps of the Disreputables as they moved through their tasks, whether the usual daily chores or a few odd jobs needed because of what happened that day.

Doctor Cutter had been to see him earlier.

Cutter gave Logan a cursory examination, checking his older wound to make sure it hadn't got worse from the day's exertions. But he seemed unworried.

"Do you want anything to help you sleep tonight?"

Logan shook his head.

"Well, then I'll be off. Miss Beckett knows where to find me if anything changes." Cutter's impassive face brightened momentarily. "That's a clever girl."

"The house is filled with them," Logan said.

"Reason enough for me to leave then," Cutter replied dryly.

After he left, Logan rested, falling in and out of dreams without ever really falling asleep. A creaking sound made him think of the ropes on the *Mistral* creaking in the wind. But it was a real sound. Someone had just opened the door to the bedroom.

"Gemma, is that you?" Logan asked, sensing a presence in the darkness. She hadn't closed the door fully, and the light from the hallway made things just visible to him. Gemma's hair was pulled back with only a ribbon, creating a red glow around her head. He ached to touch her. "Come here."

"Did I wake you?" she asked.

"I wasn't sleeping. But you could wake me from the dead."

"Let's not test that," she said.

There was a slight shift of the mattress as Gemma sat down beside him.

"Well, the past few days were eventful." She put one hand on his arm, squeezing him as if to make sure he was there. "How do you feel?"

"Much better," he admitted. "Especially now that you're safe at last."

"Thanks to you."

"You were doing an excellent job of rescuing yourself," he argued.

"While your ship burned!" She sighed. "But the damage could have been much worse."

"That's true," he said, reaching his hand up to take hers. "Losing you would have been worse."

"Well, I'm here. And safe."

"Good. This marriage can't happen soon enough," he said. "I need to keep you close, and I'm sick of having to sneak around to do it."

"So am I. I want the world to know we're together." She kissed him. "We can marry as soon as banns are posted. And then perhaps sail to Bermuda. You've met my family—good and bad. I should meet yours."

"They'll love you," he said. He thought about it for a moment. "But it may have to wait. The trip, that is, not the marriage. I'm still part of the Zodiac, and I'm needed."

"To do what?"

"I'll find out only when I'm given the next assignment. The Zodiac operates on mystery."

"Yes, I noticed." Gemma leaned down to kiss him again, and the last of his pain evaporated.

The next day, Logan was up and about. He was still in Gemma's home, though now as a sanctioned sort of houseguest. The Disreputables had managed to bring his clothes from his rooms the previous night. And Maura herself was apparently the one who insisted that Logan stay.

"It will be so much easier to plan everything," she

explained over breakfast. "The wedding, your future. Be-sides, all the slipping away and sneaking into the shadows must be wearing on you both. Ah, young love!" Maura laughed at their expressions. "I'm not *that* old, you know!"

"Aunt," Gemma said, despite a pretty blush in her cheeks, "you never did tell me the story of how you met your Edward."

"Oh!" Maura's cheeks suddenly matched her niece's. "Did I not? Well, we did slip away quite early on in our courtship. You know, we married a month after we met."

Logan glanced at Gemma. "So we're being positively conventional in comparison."

"There's nothing conventional about either of you two," Maura declared. "No wonder the stars threw you together."

Epilogue

〜

GEMMA WAS NERVOUS WHEN LOGAN took her to meet the Zodiac, but she did her best to hide it. She imagined shyness was not a sought-after trait in spies.

She was surprised to meet the man Logan introduced as Aries.

"Julian Neville," he said, with a slight bow. "I've heard a lot about you, Miss Harrington."

Gemma was puzzled. He was so ordinary! And yet, he wasn't quite ordinary, she noticed after a few moments. His eyes seemed to see through everything. As they continued to talk, she got the impression that Julian was thinking of a dozen things at once, his mind able to hold a conversation with her while he was also plotting out who-knew-what in his head.

He probably owed something to his assistant for that. Miss Chattan was also fairly ordinary looking, in a plain dress with a drab linen jacket over it. The clothes fit well, but were functional, not pretty. Chattan's messy blonde hair added to the effect of a wallflower.

But what was odd about her was that she never stopped moving, and she tended to hand Julian whatever he needed at exactly the time he asked for it—sometimes before. She rarely spoke, but Gemma kept looking at her, sure that there was something familiar about the woman.

Julian was discussing the things he'd learned from Conall Caithny, who talked quite well once he realized that talking was the only way he'd see daylight again. Dobbs was detained as well. Together, they filled in the gaps of the operation Logan tracked for so long.

"Caithny used to work for John Harrington, it turns out," Julian said. "He was just one of many men who shipped cargo under contract from the firm. Evidently, Mrs Harrington hoped that such employment would offer her brother a legitimate income, and keep him from the petty crime he'd dabbled in as a youth."

"That didn't last," Gemma noted sourly.

"No," Julian agreed. "When your parents passed away, Caithny was let go. The other partners didn't trust him. But he kept in contact with one man."

"Dobbs," Logan said.

"Exactly. The two went back for years, and they trusted each other. When Caithny's smuggling operations got big enough, Dobbs was the natural choice for a contact in London. He kept an eye on things at the firm, both in terms of the smuggling and news on what the other partners were doing."

"So Conall was well informed about the firm," said Gemma. "Yet he never told me a word."

Julian nodded. "He kept looking for ways to get around the language in the will so he could take control of your inheritance, ideally without you knowing you ever *had* an inheritance of note. For what it's worth, he didn't want to hurt you. Not until he got desperate. Then he turned to the man we call Cargo."

"What was his name?" Logan asked.

"Caithny claims he didn't ever know. And with Cargo dead, it doesn't matter much. But he was a killer—we're sure of that. Caithny was reluctant to get his own niece's blood on his hands. So he told Cargo to do it. Cargo also helped Caithny fake his own death to avoid his creditors. But he wasn't able to get close enough to Miss Harrington to finish the deed. That was thanks to the Disreputables... and our own agents, of course," Julian added smugly.

"Yes," Chattan said. "We were quite fortunate that Aquarius was so devoted to his assignment." She smiled at Logan. "And that Libra was able to assist Miss Harrington in her own way."

Gemma laughed. "Sophie is Libra, is she? It's all starting to make sense." She looked over at Chattan, still wondering why the other woman seemed so familiar. Then it came to her. "Miss Chattan," she said, interrupting something Julian was saying. "We met at my party! You wore the cat mask. And Chattan means clan of the cats." She marveled at the other woman. Who would have guessed the glamorous woman in black was just this secretary?

"Well spotted," Chattan said, with a look of approval. She turned to Julian with a smile. "And you thought she wouldn't add the two together."

"I'm a little impressed," Julian said to Gemma. "Not many would recognize her like that, and not many would know what the name means."

"They would up in Scotland," Gemma said proudly. "And honestly, you're not such a wallflower. Your eyes are quite distinctive."

Julian smiled a tiny bit at that. "Miss Harrington is rather observant, isn't she?"

"Does that mean you'll make her a sign?" Logan asked, eager.

"I already decided that before the meeting." Julian nodded. "Believe me, Miss Harrington, if I had doubts about you, we would be having a very different meeting."

Gemma did not want to know what that meeting would look like. "So the Astronomer will approve of me?"

"I think so."

"Don't I have to meet him?" Gemma asked.

Chattan shook her head. "No one meets the Astronomer, apart from Aries. That's what it means to be the First Sign."

"So I need a sign as well."

"You'll receive one," Julian assured her. "After we make a final decision."

"That sounds reasonable."

"Excellent. It's good to have that all squared away before you both sail to Bermuda."

Logan looked surprised. "You don't mean to let two agents go away for months, sir. True, I want to take Gemma to St George's, but you said you can't spare anyone."

"I'm not sparing you," he said. "As it happens, I have an assignment that requires an agent to go to the Carolinas, by way of Bermuda. Some enterprising Americans are apparently shipping saltpeter from the backcountry to buyers all throughout Europe."

"Saltpeter?" Gemma asked.

"It's a key ingredient for making gunpowder," said Julian. "I'd much rather that such supplies stayed in responsible hands. Miss Chattan has all the particulars."

Chattan handed Logan a thick envelope. "And what better way to train our newest agent? She can travel with you—companion and cover all at once."

"Perfect," said Logan.

Gemma agreed.

* * * *

Several weeks later, the mostly repaired *Mistral* flew over the fog grey water of the ocean. Clouds scudded overhead, blotting out the sun. But the February wind was surprisingly warm. Logan said it was coming up from the tropics. At the bow of the ship, Gemma Hartley leaned into the wind and laughed out loud.

"This is better than Caithny!" she shouted. "Or London! Or anywhere!"

"Glad you think so, dryad." Logan said, coming up to her. "Just don't fall overboard. I've gone through too much to get you to lose you at this point."

"You can never lose me," Gemma said. "We're bound."

"So we are."

The wedding had been quiet and modest, especially considering the wealth the new Mrs Hartley controlled through the firm she recently inherited. She arranged to have Maura listed as an advisor, since she knew that her attention would be on other things.

Logan was speaking of the upcoming assignment. "If anyone asks, we've returned to St George's for family reasons, and to have a new ship built for your firm. I think she'll be called the *Dryad*."

Gemma laughed, delighted. "Can I captain her?"

"One step at a time, love," Logan warned her. "You just became a spy. What makes you think you can also become a captain?"

"Well, if you can do it, so can I! Come. Hand me the

compass."

He pulled it from his pocket and gave it to her. Gemma opened the lid and lined the needle to north. Then she pointed south west. "Go that way! Isn't that where we're headed?"

"More or less," he said, shaking his head. "No one can fault you for being too timid."

"I'm dauntless!" she said. "Besides, I *am* following directions. It says right here, fortune favors the bold."

"It does." He leaned to kiss her. "So it will favor us."

ABOUT THE AUTHOR

Elizabeth Cole is a romance writer with a penchant for history. Her stories draw upon her deep affection for the British Isles, action movies, medieval fantasies, and even science fiction. She now lives in a small house in a big city with a cat, a snake, and a rather charming gentleman. When not writing, she is usually curled in a corner reading...or watching costume dramas or things that explode. And yes, she believes in love at first sight.

Find out more at: elizabethcole.co

CPSIA information can be obtained
at www.ICGtesting.com
Printed in the USA
BVHW031135180721
612258BV00006B/431